Hounds
of Autumn

Heather Blackwood

A STEAMPUNK MYSTERY

Published by Triple Hare Press

Hounds of Autumn
Copyright © 2013 by Heather Blackwood. All rights reserved.

First Print Edition: January 2013
ISBN: 978-0-9888054-0-8
Cover and Formatting: Streetlight Graphics

CHAPTER 1

DARTMOOR, 1890

THEY SAY THE MOOR HAS eyes. The rolling hills and rock formations have a presence, not sentient, but aware. And sometimes, the moor acts.

Chloe Sullivan gazed out the airship window, her chin resting in her palm. She watched the mist form condensation on the window, tiny beads blown backward in wet streaks. The English country slid by below, gray and green, dappled by light and shadow. It was a fellow traveler who had warned her about the moor, an older gentleman she had encountered while taking in some air on the deck of the Queen Anne.

The Queen Anne was a newer airship, large and luxurious. The enormous hydrogen-filled blimp was painted crimson and gold, and the passenger quarters were richly appointed, with burgundy upholstered seats and brass-rimmed viewing ports. A wooden viewing deck formed a long oval around the enclosed passenger quarters, allowing passengers to take a stroll or look down upon the passing countryside.

She had been admiring the view and trying to ignore the sharp wind when an older gentleman sidled up to the brass railing beside her. He was returning to his native

Dartmoor and took great pleasure in telling her about the moor's supposed sentience upon discovering that this was her first visit. He had also told her ghost stories about piskies, black hounds and spirits. She had loved the ghost stories.

But after a few minutes, the cold had driven her back to her seat inside the cabin. She turned to reach for her satchel, noting that her husband, Ambrose, had nodded off. His hands were folded over his slightly rounded mid-section and his long legs were stretched out, his feet beneath the adjacent seat. Oddly, her pet mechanical cat, Giles, was not nearby. How strange. He rarely left her side.

Someone screamed.

"Get it off!" a woman shrieked. "Get it off!"

Turning to the shrill noise, Chloe spotted a well-coifed, middle-aged matron grabbing at her elaborate purple feathered hat. The mechanical cat clung to the hat, his small body ferociously clinging with all four paws, his tiny hinged jaws opening and closing on one of the feathers.

The cat's weight pushed the hat sideways on the woman's head. Chloe watched, aghast, as Ambrose leapt to the woman's aid and attempted to pry Giles off of the hat. Giles thrashed wildly, creating small explosions of feather wisps and bits of ribbon.

Chloe was at Ambrose's side in an instant, pinning the hat to the woman's head while her husband pulled one paw, then the other from the ever more shredded confection on the woman's head.

"Hold the hat down," said Ambrose. "I think I can get under his front paws."

"I have it."

"What's gotten into him?" said Ambrose.

The woman continued to scream, now trying desperately to tear the hat off, thwarting Chloe's and Ambrose's efforts. No sooner had Ambrose pulled a second clawed cat paw from the hat, than the first paw, drawn back like a magnet, reattached itself.

"I can't get him," said Ambrose.

"Then trade," Chloe said, reaching for Giles without waiting for Ambrose's answer.

As Ambrose steadied the remains of the hat atop the now crying matron, Chloe ran her fingers along Giles's velvet patchwork underside and found the tiny slit in the fabric that concealed his power switch. She flipped it. As he lost power, Giles made a tiny mechanical "Brrr?" and turned his yellow lamplike eyes to his creator in what was certainly a look of deepest betrayal.

"Sorry, sweetie," Chloe murmured. Once he was still, she folded his legs and tail in, making him into a compact brown velvet ball.

"What is that horrid thing?" the woman cried. Her hair was half down from its pins, flying around her face in mad disarray. Ambrose returned her hat, if the mass of shredded ribbon and feathers could still be called such a thing, with murmured apologies. A tiny wax pear dangled from that hat for a moment before falling off and rolling under a seat.

An airship steward, pressed to the nines in a sharp navy uniform and wearing a sour expression, appeared at Chloe's elbow and looked in horror at the tableau. The woman pointed an imperious finger at Giles.

"That, that, thing attacked me!" At the steward's hesitation, the woman's finger trembled in rage. "It jumped on me and utterly destroyed my new hat!" This last word came out as a choking sob.

"Did it injure you?" asked Ambrose, and the woman shook her head.

"He's usually quite well behaved," Chloe explained. "He must have—I don't know. He's not dangerous." She cuddled Giles to her bosom. Thank heavens the poor woman was not hurt. She felt terrible for turning Giles off. Poor thing. It wasn't his fault that his visioscopic regulators were malfunctioning. Or perhaps his synapse couplings weren't adequately transferring.

"Is that thing yours?" asked the steward.

Ambrose answered. "Ours, yes. And we're mortified, absolutely mortified by its behavior." Chloe noted that Ambrose called Giles an "it." She bristled slightly before closing her mouth and allowing him to smooth things over. He excelled at that.

"Please allow me to make recompense for the destruction of your property, madam," he said. "The malfunction of our mechanical was unexpected. Completely without precedent. I cannot understand how anyone could invent a mechanical capable of doing such a thing. "

Chloe glared at him. He continued without seeming to notice.

"We're staying in Farnbridge for a month, and if you have your hat shop send me their bill ..."

Ambrose spoke quietly with the woman, and she gradually lowered herself into her seat, patted her hair into a semblance of order and eventually gave him a weak smile. Chloe was about to return to her seat, when the steward motioned her aside.

"Are you getting off in Dartmoor?" he asked.

"Yes. In Farnbridge. Why?"

"We should be there in fifteen minutes," he said. "I expect you'll be leaving the airship without incident."

Chloe drew herself up to her full height, which, combined with her plump figure and freckles, made her about as imposing as an angry hen.

"I'll have you know that there's no possible way that Gi—this mechanical," she held up the still ball that was the cat, "could have hurt that woman. He just got overly excited. He's not dangerous."

"Be that as it may, mum. People outside of London aren't used to mechanicals other than the usual household ones. Especially not the destructive variety."

He eyed Giles. Chloe opened her satchel and slipped Giles inside, hoping that removing him from view would reduce the likelihood of confiscation. His little form slid in next to her notebook, an oil-blackened cloth, a tiny spanner and a rumpled sheaf of papers. She smiled as becomingly and demurely as she could and returned to her seat.

A few minutes later, Ambrose sank into the seat across from her and sighed heavily.

"Why did you make Giles with claws? What possible use was that?" he asked, rubbing his temples.

"He's a cat. I couldn't make a cat that couldn't climb. That's the best way to test his balancers. And what if one of the dogs tried to hurt him? I couldn't leave him defenseless."

"And it did not occur to you that he would use his claws in other ways?"

"He's designed not to harm people. I don't think his visioscopic sensors are faulty, but perhaps the regulators are malfunctioning. It's not his fault. He's a good cat."

"He's not a cat at all."

"Yes, I know. What I mean to say is, he's a good mechanical."

"And do you know what is wrong with him?"

She sighed. She had known this question was coming. "No. Not yet. But I have to allow him to run. He can stay off for now, but I've worked too hard to shut him down permanently."

"You must assure me that he will not be behaving in this manner once we reach my family's house."

They were in sensitive territory now. Chloe could make no such assurance. She knew that Ambrose's considerable tolerance for her creations had a limit. He would not force her to deactivate Giles permanently, but a mechanical that was destructive was a hazard.

"I promise to keep a close watch over him," she said.

"Please do. It is vitally important. I haven't seen the

family in years." Ambrose looked out the window.

Good. He had not told her that Giles had to remain deactivated or packed away. Per their marriage agreement, he could not forbid her from operating Giles. But he could have politely asked her to keep him confined to one room. Or he could have requested that she shut him off until they were back at their home in London. She could refuse the request, but she knew she would not have the heart. He was too good in allowing her many freedoms denied to other women. In return, when he did make a request, she tried to respect his wishes despite her instincts to do just as she pleased.

Chloe was glad that Mr. Frick, Ambrose's grim valet, was not there to witness the incident. He wouldn't have said a word, but his disapproving countenance would have conveyed plenty. Fortunately, he was traveling in another section of the airship, along with Miss Haynes, her lady's maid.

Later, as Chloe and Ambrose stood on the airship platform awaiting Mr. Frick and Miss Haynes, they watched a luggage loader roll to the base of the airship and open the luggage compartment. The loader had half a dozen wheels and its steel sides were scratched and dented. It was almost the height of a man, and like other industrial mechanicals, could only perform repetitive tasks. It hissed and clunked as it swung its hooked arms into the compartment and removed trunks and baggage.

"What's wrong with it?" asked Ambrose.

"What do you mean?"

"You're looking at it as if you want to disassemble it."

The loader released a sharp hiss of steam and backed away from the airship. It turned and rolled across the platform, another similar loader moving forward to take its place.

"Well, yes," she said. "But it's nothing serious. Two of its arms have minor problems with the joints and its directional motivator is operating unevenly."

A few people murmured and pointed discreetly as they passed. Ambrose stood more stiffly than usual, leaning heavily on his cane. He was more than twenty years older than Chloe, tall, with a hint of well-fed contentedness around his mid-section. He was not a conventionally handsome man, but she found him pleasing enough. She looked at him with concern and then regret. She slid her arm into his.

"I'm sorry," she whispered. The wind carried her words away, but Ambrose placed his hand over hers and left it there.

CHAPTER 2

THE TOWN OF FARNBRIDGE WAS on the eastern end of Dartmoor, and was large enough to boast both a railway and an airship station. Ambrose had relatives in Farnbridge, wealthy ones, as his sister Rose had married into the Aynesworth family. Unfortunately, Rose had passed away fifteen years ago and Ambrose had not seen his niece and three nephews since.

Rose's widower and the head of the Aynesworth family, William, had sent one of the family horse-drawn carriages to fetch them. The driver, a burly young man, introduced himself as Mr. James. He and Mr. Frick lifted their bags and two trunks onto the carriage. The trunks contained clothing and personal effects. But Chloe was far more concerned with Ambrose's research materials and her laboratory gear. Both would be arriving by rail the following day.

The carriage pulled out of the airship station and started through town.

"There's the mechanical shop, mum," said Miss Haynes from her seat across from Ambrose and Chloe. Mr. Frick took a glance and returned to gazing sullenly out his own window.

"Perfect," said Chloe. "I'll have to stop in."

As the airship station was on the opposite side of town from the road they needed to take, they got a good look at the town of Farnbridge. There was a dress shop, hat shop, police station, butcher, grocer, and various inns and boarding houses. Traps, carriages and hansom cabs clattered past while women with parasols and men in top hats strolled along the main avenue.

"It has changed since last I was here," said Ambrose. "More people. Money from the tin mines and manufactories, I suppose." The carriage left behind the last of the buildings, crossed a small stone bridge and continued down a road and out through the countryside.

"Why didn't one of the family come to fetch us?" asked Chloe. It seemed a tad unseemly to fail to greet visiting relatives.

"No idea," said Ambrose, distracted. "The Aynesworths were always a little odd. But they are wealthy, so no one minds it too much."

As he spoke, he studied the landscape intently. Their visit to Aynesworth House was not merely a social call, but was in large part designed to advance Ambrose's research on Dartmoor flora. A naturalist by profession, and a scientist at heart, Ambrose was mentally categorizing each plant, stream, and moss-covered rock they passed. Chloe had watched as he spent months reading up on the area, and had filled reams of paper with his notes.

His latest book, which he hoped to complete by the end of the year, was on the insect-eating plants of the moor. He theorized that the carnivorous plants like the many-spined Sundew and the harmless-looking Genlisea actually derived nutrients from the insects they lured in and consumed, contrary to the prevailing idea that trapping insects was a defensive mechanism. Ambrose pulled out a small pad of paper and a pencil from his coat pocket and made a note from time to time.

Chloe was mildly interested in such things. But for her part, the distant in-laws and insect-eating plants were distractions. She had come to call upon Mrs. Camille Granger, one of the very few other female inventors and mechanical specialists in all of the British Empire. Mrs. Granger's experimental work on cadmium and nickel batteries to store energy was a breakthrough, a revelation. Chloe's hands had trembled when she read a paper about it, and upon completing it, she had flipped to the front. The name of the author, C. Granger, was printed beneath the title. She had drafted a letter to C. Granger that very afternoon.

With the potential to store electricity in that manner, powering new types of mechanicals became possible. Without such storage devices, only the two current types of mechanicals could exist. Smaller mechanicals were clockwork, and had a winding mechanism of one kind or another. The larger mechanicals, which existed for household or industrial use, were steam powered. They burned coal or wood to create heat and thus power their mechanisms. They worked well enough, but the possibilities of electricity made the gears in Chloe's imagination spin.

After reading the paper and forming a correspondence with Camille Granger, she had spent the next three years creating Giles. To her knowledge, he was one of only two electrical mechanicals in the world. The other belonged to Camille Granger.

They approached a crossroads and the carriage slowed. Up ahead were two police horses. They were nibbling on plants while a small group of people gathered around what looked from this distance to be a bog.

Small clumps of greenery grew around its edges, and the surface of the bog, covered in a blanket of moss a few inches thick, was smooth. Four dogs of varying sizes and colors jumped and barked and a local farmer was doing his best to quiet them. Two constables in navy serge uniforms stood side by side, one talking and gesturing while the other wrote in his notebook. Near their feet was a prostrate form, muddy and still.

The carriage stopped as it reached the police horses

and their driver called out. An officer looked up and waved.

Miss Haynes craned her neck to see out the window, and even Mr. Frick looked interested. One of the officers walked toward the carriage and spoke to their driver.

"Hey there, Mr. James! Can you get past the horses all right?"

"I expect so. But what happened? Who is that?"

Three words had Chloe up from her seat and out the carriage door in a single motion: "Camille Granger" and "murder."

Ambrose leapt out after her and grabbed her hand.

"It's her. It's Camille!" cried Chloe, one hand in Ambrose's and the other gripping the skirts of her traveling dress. "I have to go."

"Come, Chloe, you don't need to see this."

"But it's her. She was my—I know we never met in person—but she was my friend."

The officer and Mr. James were still talking. Mr. Frick and Miss Haynes were now out of the carriage as well, and Miss Haynes put her hand on Chloe's arm.

Ambrose relaxed his grip and Chloe yanked free and rushed down the small rise and toward the bog. Her shoes were not designed for hiking and the ground was soft, like a wet sponge, but she did not pause. Her eyes were fixed on the form lying on the ground. She stopped short before she got too close to the body, paused for a moment and forced herself to move closer.

Camille Granger's heavy skirts were blackened with mud. The top of her body was encased in a heavy dark jacket, which was buttoned up to her throat. The white skin on her face and hands was streaked with bog slime and her hair, which looked like it had once been blonde, was a dark matted mass pressed close against her head. Her blue eyes, open and staring at the sky, were dull and flecked with mud.

She was gone, and her body was just a lifeless object,

lying on the cold earth. Her friend, her colleague, was dead. Chloe blinked involuntarily, as if her own eyes were also gritty with dirt.

The officer who had stayed by the body, a stout, short man with thick wet lips, stepped in front of her. "This is no sight for a lady," he said, looking to Ambrose, who was still approaching, to perform his husbandly duty and remove her from the scene. Chloe was sickened, and her heart was beating fast in her chest. She took a final look at Camille Granger and turned aside. Perhaps the men were right. Despite the cold, she had broken into a sweat and she felt light-headed. She did not consider herself a woman of delicate sensibilities, but in this case, she had to agree that this was no sight for a woman.

Ambrose took Chloe's elbow and gently turned her away. She did not resist. The four barking dogs had mostly quieted, and their master made eye contact with Chloe. The man was short and wiry, his skin wrinkled and toughened by a life outdoors.

"Excuse me, but did you find her?" Chloe asked.

"Ah, no. My dogs did. They got out and I found them here, barking something terrible. Then I found poor Mrs. Granger."

"You knew her?"

"Oh yes. She's Charles Granger's wife. Lives over that way." He kept hold of two of the wilder dogs and nodded his head in the direction in which the Aynesworth family lived. She had known that the Granger and Aynesworth households were in the same area, but not that they were neighbors. "I'm glad I don't have to tell her husband she's been killed."

"Why is that?" said Chloe, her stomach tightening.

The man shrugged and looked away.

"Did she fall into the bog?"

"I don't think so," he said, and whistled for one of the dogs that had wandered too far afield. "When I came by, only her arm had come out of the bog. The police pulled her the rest of the way out from under the moss. It looks like the back of her head has been bashed in by something." He stopped, becoming aware that this revelation might upset a lady of gentle birth. He wiped nervously at his face with a grubby sleeve and turned away to tend his dogs.

They took a few steps and Chloe felt Ambrose pause as he studied the ground.

"What's that then?" she asked, leaning forward with him to look at the strange prints on the ground. They looked like animal prints, but were thin and spidery with four front prongs and a center pad that was a perfect oval.

"What strange tracks," said Ambrose.

Both constables approached, eyeing the ground. Ambrose showed them the tracks and the officers exchanged a dark look. "The hound," one of them said to the other as Ambrose led Chloe back to the carriage.

From this direction, facing away from the bog, Chloe could see a small bank of rocks close to the crossroads. It was like a half-cairn, built into the side of the hill, about waist-high and twice as wide. Dark holes gaped around the stones, the perfect dwelling places for mice or snakes. Something about it drew her eye.

Miss Haynes, Mr. James and Mr. Frick were waiting. Mr. Frick held his crisp gray bowler over his chest in respect for the deceased. Miss Haynes's eyes were downcast, her arms folded loosely across her midsection.

Ambrose was frowning, and Chloe could not bear to put him out further. She followed him to the carriage. Wordlessly, Ambrose handed Chloe inside and Mr. James drove gently around the police horses and in the direction of Aynesworth House.

Ambrose tried to distract her, pointing out a tor sitting atop a hill in the distance, its giant stones eerily stacked upon one another as if an enormous child was playing with his blocks. The moor was littered with such natural formations, as well as ancient man-made stone circles and the remains of a number of equally ancient circular stone huts. They passed hills covered in bracken fern and chunks of granite, varying in size from small boulders to great stones the size of an airship engine.

"I can't imagine that Camille would have any enemies," said Chloe. "Do you think it was because of her research? Perhaps there was a competitor who wanted to patent a similar design."

Miss Haynes's head jerked up. She was not only Chloe's lady's maid, but was regularly drafted into assisting with experiments and prototypes. She was both intelligent, patient and could manage to dress Chloe's unruly copper penny hair, all of which made her an ideal employee.

When Ambrose didn't answer, Miss Haynes said softly, "Perhaps someone would have been threatened by her work and killed her to get rid of potential competition. One of the coal companies perhaps?"

"I doubt it," said Mr. Frick. "They were just early designs, right, mum?" He looked at Chloe who nodded. "No need to commit murder for that." He settled back into staring glumly out the window.

Ambrose reached into Chloe's satchel, pulling out Giles and turning him over to find his power switch.

"No, leave him for now," she said, though she did take the still form and place it in her lap. She stroked his patchwork cloth cover and thought of the sheaf of papers in her satchel. Along with various notes and diagrams were a few of the many letters she and Camille had exchanged.

After Chloe had discovered Mrs. Granger's academic paper on cadmium and nickel batteries, she had written to Cambridge University, the publisher of the paper, with a request to forward her letter to the author. She had signed the letter C. Sullivan and waited.

A few months later, the two inventors had developed a regular correspondence. After a few weeks of silence from C. Granger, Chloe had received a short letter from Mr. C. Granger stating that it was "not seemly" for a married woman to have a male correspondent. Chloe was bewildered at first, as the handwriting of this C. Granger was more stiff and angular than the soft, flowing script of her friend. In moments, her confusion turned to delight when she realized that her C. Granger was a woman.

She had immediately jotted off a note to Mr. and Mrs. Charles Granger, explaining her gender and her hope of reinstating their regular correspondence. After two weeks, another letter, this one in Mrs. Camille Granger's handwriting, arrived, including sketches for one of her prototypes.

And then, a month ago, one of Camille's letters ended with a troubling paragraph.

"Do not respond to this part of my letter, as my husband reads my correspondence. I feel, now that I will meet you in a few weeks, I can confide that our regular communications have made my existence bearable. Though confined most of the time, I feel my mind and heart could fly free, even if for a short while. I am looking forward to finally meeting you in person and collaborating with you on some new designs."

Chloe had wondered at the time if Camille's "confinement" was because she was with child. She had not mentioned it in any other letters, and surely something of that magnitude would have warranted at least a line. The only conclusion she could draw was that Mr. Charles Granger kept his wife under close watch. How then could she have ended up on the moor alone?

It was a miracle that Camille's body had been found at all in the thousands of miles of bogs and marshes. As they passed tors and hills, Chloe was grateful for Ambrose's warm shape by her side. She was not given to flights of fancy, but as the sun moved behind the gray clouds, she understood how people could imagine seeing a phantom

15

hound in this vast terrain. The shadows thrown by the boulders and tors certainly inspired thoughts of ghosts and spirits and she had heard that at night, the mist could become so thick as to make it impossible to see a person standing directly in front of you.

Ambrose muttered something and scratched with his pencil in his notebook.

"Pardon?"

"*Drosere Rotundifolia,*" he said. "A small colony. Just there." He pointed to a spot beside the road.

"Was that a featherbed?" Chloe asked.

"What are you talking about? It's a colony of Roundleaf Sundew," he said. "I'm noting the location for later."

"I meant the bog."

"Ah, yes." His voice was almost inaudible. "That type of bog was a featherbed."

"What is a featherbed?" asked Miss Haynes, eyes wide.

A bright green carpet of moss had covered the bog. It was smooth and certainly looked thick enough for someone to be trapped beneath. Ambrose flipped his pad closed and put it and the pencil in his jacket pocket.

"It's a type of bog. You can get halfway across before falling in," he said. "It's spongy, but you can walk on it. Falling through the top is like sliding under a featherbed." At Miss Haynes's squeak of horror, he paused. "It weighs you down, pushing you under. All you can do is hold your arms out from your sides and wait for someone to come and help you. Struggling is useless. To do so would simply pull you down quicker."

Miss Haynes nodded and pulled her shawl tighter around herself.

They passed a large rock that from this angle reminded Chloe of a face, and she thought again of Camille Granger's body. Her dress, which may have been a light blue or lavender for all she could tell, was now darkened by bog slime. She pictured Camille's pale face, her lips white, the teeth grayed by mud. Her blank eyes had stared at the sky.

She had been murdered.

Chloe had never seen a dead person before, and her stomach turned at the thought of this woman being hit over the head, her body discarded in a bog, like refuse. No doubt the killer had hoped the body would never be found, but the farmer's dogs had smelled her, even through the thick, wet odor of the mud.

Had she been fleeing her killer? Was that why the blow was to the back of her head? Or was it someone she knew, and she trustingly turned her back?

Ambrose placed his hand on hers and squeezed gently. She reached under Giles to locate his power switch.

CHAPTER 3

CHLOE WATCHED FROM THE WINDOW as the carriage rounded a green and russet hill and the Aynesworth house came into view. It emerged from the land as if a part of it. Heavy, ivy-covered stone walls rose three stories over the surrounding land, with wild plants growing right up to the short stone wall that served as a barrier between wild moor and civilization. Moss grew on part of the roof, from which numerous brick chimneys stood against the overcast sky. The original house must have been symmetrical, but a small, newer wing jutted sideways and back from the main house, giving it a lopsided appearance.

That was most likely where William, the patriarch and the widower of Ambrose's sister, would have his rooms, Chloe thought as they rode up the curved driveway. His four children would occupy the rest of the house. If she remembered correctly, only one, Alexander, was married. Ian, the oldest brother was not, nor was the only sister, Dora. The youngest brother, Robert, was only sixteen.

Ambrose's sister, Rose, had died of a fever when Robert was still an infant. Ambrose had adored his younger sister though he spoke of her seldom. The look that would come across his face on those occasions broke Chloe's heart.

Ambrose was of the opinion that if Rose had married and stayed in London and had not lived in what he considered the wilderness, she would have been able to receive proper medical care. He would not go so far as to say that the country doctor who had attended her in her last hours was incompetent, but he and William had exchanged sharp words after Rose's death. Taking a girl of Rose's constitution and city upbringing out to live on the moors was folly, he said. But Rose had adored William, and was so much in love with the moors, that her parents had consented to the match.

Back at their home in London, Chloe had mentioned her desire to meet Camille Granger, but had not held much hope of actually doing so. Ambrose had gotten a faraway look when she mentioned Dartmoor. She understood why her husband had not been back to visit the Aynesworth family since Rose's funeral. But she also understood when, one evening after his brandy, he had leaned back in his stuffed chair, his research books scattered on the side table at his elbow, and declared that it was time for him to pay the family a visit.

"There's just no sense in me staying away any longer," he declared. "Enough is enough."

She knew the look of determination on his face. It did not come often, but when it did, there was nothing that could deter him. And because he had asked to visit in order to study the local flora, he would save face and not appear to be asking for forgiveness.

Chloe put Giles in her satchel and they alighted from the carriage. The group crunched up the gravel path toward the house, taking care not to slip on patches of wet leaves. A heavy stone overhang protected the ancient wooden front door. Before Ambrose could knock, the door burst open and a grinning man stood in the doorway.

Ambrose took his proffered hand, shaking it heartily and then turned to introduce Chloe to his nephew, Alexander. He was a very good-looking man of about thirty years, his dark hair tidy without looking fussed over. He was tall, but well built, unlike the man behind him who was also tall but too thin.

"We were worried about you," Alexander said, escorting them into the foyer and making room so Mr. Frick and Miss Haynes could shut the door behind them. "The drive from the station normally does not take quite so long."

"There was a slight delay," said Ambrose. "We should discuss it later."

Then she understood. Ambrose would tell William, Ian and Alexander, and let them handle breaking the news to the family and servants. There was no need to create an unnecessary fuss immediately upon their arrival.

Miss Haynes and Mr. Frick, ever the proper servants, showed not even a flicker of emotion on their faces.

Alexander looked puzzled for a moment. "I apologize for not coming to meet you, but I was caught up." He smiled. "I see you've made it safely though. I trust your trip was pleasant? Which airship did you travel on?"

"The Queen Anne," said Ambrose.

The long thin man moved forward. His face was set in a frown, but Chloe saw no animosity in his deep-set brown eyes. Ambrose clasped his hand.

"Ian, so good to see you. So good."

"And you, Uncle."

Ian's face became gentle as he took Chloe's gloved hand. "A pleasure, Mrs. Sullivan."

Chloe felt a gentle squirming against her hip, and pulled Giles from her satchel. Within seconds, his visual sensors adjusted and he pointed his feet down in anticipation of being set on the floor. Chloe obliged and he circled her once, sitting obediently a few inches from the hem of her dress. He swiveled his ears and tilted his head, watching.

"I've heard of those," said Alexander. "Is that one of the companion mechanicals that I've read about?"

"It is. But not exactly like the ones they're selling in the shops," said Chloe. "He's a bit more complex."

"He can walk and follow you?"

"And more than that." She was always eager to discuss

her creation. "He's built to—"

"Oh, I really must order one for the ladies. You have to tell me where you purchased it."

"I didn't purchase him," she began. But Alexander had already turned to move past the butler.

The butler took their hats, coats and Chloe's satchel and hung them on the short coat rack bolted atop a nearby mechanical. This was a doorway mechanical, common in both city and country and one of the more popular models. Like all mechanicals, it had a very limited range of skills. A doorway mechanical was able to open and close doors, place coats, hats and umbrellas in a pre-designated location, and the newer models could sweep the entryway steps. This particular example was shining and well-maintained, Chloe noted with approval. She was of the firm opinion that a person's treatment of animals and mechanicals was an indicator of his or her character. Of course, treatment of people was important as well, but anyone could be kind to a being who could speak.

She noticed that one of the four jointed legs made a very slight squeaking sound as the mechanical hissed and stomped off, coats swinging from its hooks. Also, the tiny puff of smoke from its exhaust tube looked a tad thicker than it should have been. She would offer later to take a look at the machine. Repairing and possibly improving any household mechanicals was the least she could do for her hosts who were accommodating them for an entire month. She would just have to be careful not to make any modifications that the local mechanical shop could not maintain or replicate.

A stout, white-aproned woman appeared at the end of the hall. She briefly made eye contact with Mr. Frick and Miss Haynes, who moved off to join her. A large ring of keys jingled from her belt as she turned and held the door. This was the housekeeper, the woman who would be acquainting Mr. Frick and Miss Haynes with the rules of the household. Chloe noticed a small stone among the keys, smooth and white. It had a single hole through the center, through which a thin chain attached it to the ring of keys.

Through the door, Chloe caught a glimpse of a serving mechanical. It was the height of a side table, and its flat top was bordered by a thin brass railing around the edge to keep items from sliding off. A tea tray set on top with small triangular sandwiches arranged on a china plate. No doubt it would be making its way down the hall shortly to serve tea.

Unlike ordinary household mechanicals, Giles had little decision-making capability. He was not like the simple clockwork finches, rabbits and butterflies with which ladies in London adorned their hats. But he was often mistaken for a simple decorative item because, unlike a household or industrial mechanical, he had no practical use. The household mechanicals had a limited number of activities, stored on spools within their bodies. They were able to wind, execute and rewind these spools, enabling them to perform activities like cutting and carrying wood or moving about a house to carry items from one place to another. Industrial mechanicals were similar. They shoveled coal on steamships and railway engines, lifted and hauled freight and were able to tie and untie mooring lines for airships and sea-faring ships.

Any complex or autonomous activities were beyond them. Like them, Giles also had spools of information, but with basic electrical power, Chloe had given him a series of simple electro-neural pathways and a decision engine that provided some degree of autonomy.

Chloe paused, drawing a breath at the thought of Camille's contributions to her own creation of Giles. Her friend had proved invaluable in recommending improvements and reviewing schematics. Without Camille, Giles would never have come into being. But there were still improvements to be made. Giles still had a simple battery system that could never be recharged. Replacing his parts was expensive. If Camille's discoveries could be widely used, electrical mechanicals could become widespread.

Mistaking her pause for distraction, Ambrose took her elbow and led her down the dark-paneled hallway after Alexander. Ian followed behind. The house was expensively decorated and fully equipped with modern gaslights. Everything from the rich carpets to the carved and polished banister spoke of wealth. But Chloe noticed a few threadbare spots on the carpet and some of the picture frames showed their age as well, flecked with patches of peeling finish. Ian excused himself at the bottom of the staircase, and Alexander led them upstairs to their rooms.

"We have two adjoining guest rooms," he said, opening the door to the first. Two servants were exiting the room, having left Ambrose's trunk at the foot of the bed where Mr. Frick would later unpack it. His room was a standard guest room, complete with a large, if aging, bed, wash stand, writing desk, small sitting area and armoire. The room was decorated in browns and golds, giving it a masculine feel that she knew Ambrose would like.

She opened the door to the adjoining room to find a more feminine room decorated in shades of pale green and cream. The layout was a mirror image of her husband's. A large rosewood bed covered by a lace bedspread dominated the room, while two pale green upholstered chairs and a small marble-topped table made up the sitting area. There was also a nightstand, a washstand with a jug of water and basin, a rosewood armoire and matching dressing table. Upon the latter was an ivory mirror and comb which were not her own, most likely provided on the orders of the lady of the house, Alexander's wife, Beatrice.

Alexander was standing in Ambrose's room, shifting his weight slowly from one foot to the other and gazing out the window. Of course he would hesitate to enter or even look into a lady's bedchamber, even if she had only taken possession of it a moment ago. Ambrose was standing in the doorway and she did not want to keep them waiting. Upon her crossing the threshold from her room, Alexander turned.

"Is the room to your liking? If there's anything you need, anything at all, just ring the bell and we'll have it brought for you."

There was one thing she needed that was not present in the room: a large table or desk for her work. She did not intend to be idle for a month while Ambrose was absorbed in his research and writing. Rather, she had shipped two crates of mechanical gear, agonizing over how much she had to leave behind in her London laboratory. She fervently hoped that she could either purchase any missing items from a local mechanical shop, or perhaps borrow some of Camille Granger's supplies.

"You mentioned the use of a room for my work?" said Ambrose.

"Ah yes, it's just this way." Alexander led them to a door across the hall. "It used to be a study, but it hasn't been used in quite some time."

The room had two large windows that looked down over the front drive. Sparsely populated bookshelves lined one wall.

"Most of the books are in the library," said Alexander, following Chloe's gaze. "My brother Robert pulled some books from our library and put them in here for you. Apologies if they aren't what you will need."

Ambrose ran a finger over the spines, scanning the titles.

"Robert has read most of them," said Alexander.

"Has he now?" Ambrose's face was lit with a smile before he turned back to perusing the titles. "And he's just sixteen, eh?"

Chloe looked at her husband and determined that he was too engrossed in his own thoughts to have noticed a critical detail.

"Do you think we could get an extra desk? Perhaps over there?" She pointed to the opposite side of the room from Ambrose's desk.

Alexander was confused. "Do you not think one is enough?"

"For me," said Chloe. "I'll need some space for my work as well."

At Alexander's hesitation, Ambrose broke free of his reverie. "She makes things." He motioned at Giles, who was partially under the dust cloth that covered a chair. Giles yanked the cloth onto the floor and pawed at the fabric. Alexander glared at him.

"Oh, but there are plenty of things for a lady to do here," Alexander said. "We are not without amusements. We have a withdrawing room with a piano, you can embroider, draw, paint, or you can even get a book from the library." He smiled gently at Chloe, but she could still see the confusion, and something else, in his face. He glanced at Giles.

She knew from experience that this topic needed to be broached carefully. Females did not create complex mechanicals. Men were the ones who designed and repaired household and industrial mechanicals. This left any woman with such inclinations to design small decorative pets, like birds that made tinny chirping noises and clung with tiny metal feet to a hat or the shoulder of a dress. Chloe had created plenty of birds and other creatures, including a family of small gray mice that twitched their whiskers and ran on a small magnetic track. She had also made music boxes and a few toys. All of these were appropriately feminine pursuits, but only barely. They pushed the limits of ladylike behavior.

"I suppose I could order up a table," said Alexander, looking at Ambrose. "Is there anything else she might need?"

"Only the name of the local mechanical shop,"

said Ambrose.

Alexander brightened slightly. "It's Lydford's. On Hampton Street."

"We passed it on our way into town," said Chloe.

Giles jumped onto Ambrose's new desk and set to pawing at the blotter. Chloe grabbed him and cuddled him to her bosom.

"Let her make her baubles or she'll be impossible," she overheard Ambrose say to Alexander. Chloe shot him a furious look and then forced herself to turn away. He was doing his best to secure her not only the supplies and space she needed, but also the freedom from criticism and inquiry that her activities would produce. She was fortunate, she reminded herself sternly. He always honored their marriage agreement, allowing her to select reading material without his approval and to work on her projects without interference. In return, she went to great efforts to be discreet and not bring him shame.

She pressed a kiss between Giles's ears. Ambrose trusted her. She could do her work. It would be enough.

CHAPTER 4

CHLOE DESCENDED TO SUPPER THAT evening in a taffeta dress and light matching shawl. She splashed her face with water to freshen up, and Miss Haynes had re-pinned her wild hair so as to be presentable. The family would be evaluating her and she wanted their acceptance, if only for Ambrose's sake. She was nervous, but despite this, she had developed a healthy appetite since her small meal of bread and cheese on the airship.

The muffled whirring of Giles's gears escorted Chloe down the stairs as he padded behind her on hand-stitched felt paws. Ambrose was waiting at the dining room door, and she took his arm to enter. He held the door open an extra moment to allow Giles to enter behind his mistress.

The dining room was decorated in deep reds and browns and was dominated by a long oak table, large enough for twenty, but set for nine. Chairs upholstered in burgundy matched the curtains, which were pulled shut to keep out the chill. The fire in the marble-mantled fireplace crackled gently, leaving the room comfortably warm.

All three men at the table rose. At the head was an elderly man, gray-bearded and stout, with the build and bearing of a formerly muscular man. This must be William, the patriarch. Ambrose introduced Chloe to him first. She then curtseyed to Ian, whom she had already met, and Robert, the youngest of the Aynesworth children. Robert was a gangly youth, thin, tall and long of face like his brother Ian.

Ambrose pulled out a chair for Chloe, and Giles settled himself nearby. Four of the place settings were still unoccupied, and a minute later, Alexander came in, his wife Beatrice on his arm. She was a petite woman, finely boned with thin, mouse-brown hair that fell in frizzled curls around her face. She smiled gently as they were introduced and was seated.

"We are so glad you could come and visit us," Beatrice said. "We don't often have visitors. I know my mother and Dora will be so glad."

"I'm certain I will," said the woman in the doorway. She was tall, like her siblings, with thick dark hair. Her deep red dress was two or three years out of date, but favored her coloring and figure. She had a statuesque beauty that made her look like a young gypsy.

"It's a pleasure to meet you," said Dora as her father introduced Chloe and Ambrose. She took the seat that Ian held out for her. "I thought I'd be the last one down." She frowned. Mrs. Malone, Beatrice's mother, and a permanent houseguest, had not yet arrived.

Chloe watched her husband and their host, William, each try to keep a conversation going. The years of animosity and lack of contact had left them with little to speak of, but Ambrose was trying hard to be pleasant and agreeable. He was uneasy, but only a wife would notice. His left hand remained in his lap instead of gesturing good-naturedly. He took too many sips from his crystal water goblet, which a helpful servant refilled promptly.

"Please tell me," said Ambrose, "is my old friend John Hammond still in town?"

"He is," said William.

The two men discussed Ambrose's friend, whom he had met while visiting his sister Rose in the early days of her marriage, thirty-odd years before. A fellow natural science enthusiast, he and Ambrose had formed a friendship after meeting one day while observing a juvenile meadow pipit trying its wings. Sadly, their correspondence had dwindled and then ceased altogether.

The clock chimed once, indicating a quarter past the hour. Mrs. Malone had still not arrived and Beatrice motioned a servant over and whispered instructions. The servant girl bobbed a curtsey and left.

"Do you think your mother is unwell?" asked Chloe.

"Unlikely," said Beatrice with a weary smile.

William motioned for the first course of asparagus soup to be served. A servant placed a bowl of soup at Mrs. Malone's empty place.

"Have you decided on the trim for the dress?" Beatrice asked Dora.

Dora lifted the lid of the cut crystal butter dish and spread butter on her bread. "I think so. I do wish Father would allow me to go to London and have a proper dress made up." She shot a glare down the table at William, who was nodding over something Alexander said. "The dressmaker in town lacks the imagination for a truly fashionable dress. Too much time spent making wedding dresses for the daughters of farmers and tin miners, I think."

Beatrice smiled and turned to Chloe. "Dora is getting married in just three months. We're so excited—well, Mother and I mainly. You see, Dora wants a unique dress, but can't make up her mind on what she wants. And the dressmaker is not much help, as she doesn't know the very latest fashions. Even so, Dora will be beautiful. I just know it." She smiled fondly at her sister-in-law.

Dora's cheeks colored. She would indeed be a lovely bride with her regal carriage, raven's wing black hair and piercing dark eyes. If Chloe's calculations were correct, she was in her mid-twenties, old enough to have serious concerns about becoming a spinster. Chloe understood that feeling all too well. She had been twenty-seven when Ambrose had asked for her hand, and she had long since given up any hope of marriage.

"Who is the lucky gentleman?" asked Chloe.

"His name is Patrick Baxter. He's American," said Dora.

"And not a pauper by any means," said a new voice.

The stately older woman standing nearby was sturdily built, but not heavy. Her iron-gray hair was tastefully styled and she inclined her head politely as the men at the table rose. She set aside her elephant-headed cane and slowly lowered herself into the chair that Alexander pulled out for her. She took her time arranging her napkin before allowing her son-in-law to push in her chair. Her sharp blue eyes narrowed as she scanned the family while they ate their asparagus soup.

"He made a handsome fortune in the Yukon," said Dora. "He found gold up the river. He had an actual Indian guide. Can you imagine?"

"An outdoorsman then," said Chloe, a touch uneasy discussing a man's financial status over a meal. "Has he traveled extensively?"

"Oh yes," Dora said. "To the Continent, Northern Africa, Scotland and of course he came here. And once we're married, I'll be able to go with him all over the world." She looked pleased at the prospect, and Chloe couldn't help but feel pleasure for her.

"It's cold," said Mrs. Malone, jabbing a finger at her soup and motioning over a servant who took the bowl and brought a replacement a few moments later.

"Tell her how you met," said Beatrice, glancing uneasily at her mother who was now scowling and blowing on a steaming spoonful of soup.

Dora explained how she and Mr. Baxter had met at a party thrown by a local family who Mr. Baxter knew through some complicated series of events. Chloe was only half-listening, but she tried to look interested.

As the women continued on about wedding preparations, flowers and punch recipes, Chloe listened in on the men's conversation. Ambrose was telling his nephews about his papers on English flora and fauna, and Robert was rapt with attention. She noted that Robert's questions to Ambrose were intelligent and that he knew more than a fair amount about the local plant life.

"I would like to send a few letters in the outgoing post," said Ambrose. "I have colleagues in London as well as at Oxford. And I would like to write to a certain Mr. Brian Graves Senior. I heard that his son was working in your employ as a tutor." He smiled broadly at Robert. "And I think he's done a fine bit of work."

Robert's eyes flicked down to the tabletop.

"Mr. Graves is no longer in our employ," said William. "His mother took ill months ago and he had to leave."

"I see," said Ambrose. The soup bowls were cleared and their main meal of lamb with herbed potatoes was served.

Beatrice turned to Chloe. "Alexander mentioned that you make little mechanical animals and things."

Chloe nodded.

"And can you repair them? I have a little robin that pins to a hat, and it isn't working anymore."

"I'd love to look at it. You can have it brought to Ambrose's study and I'll examine it. My materials won't be here until tomorrow, though."

Ian leaned in toward his father and murmured something into his ear. William gave a sober nod and his mouth tightened.

"Ian has assured me that you all have been informed of Mrs. Granger's death." He swallowed. "Unfortunate. Most unfortunate. I'm certain Mr. Granger will send a notice and inform us of the date of her funeral."

"Do you think it proper for us to attend?" Beatrice asked.

When no one spoke, Robert looked back and forth between his older brothers, confused. "Why wouldn't it be?"

"She was murdered while walking on the moor," Beatrice

said gently. "Alone."

Chloe paused for a moment, not immediately understanding the implication, then drew in a breath, disgusted. Ambrose was looking down at his meal, but she saw the tension in his posture.

Robert shook his head in bewilderment. "I'm sorry. I don't understand."

"You see, we don't know what she was doing out there," said Dora.

Chloe glared at Dora, then at Beatrice, but all eyes at the table were on Robert. Understanding dawned on his face, and he nodded. He glanced at his father, who looked deeply unhappy, and then Robert took a nervous sip from his water goblet.

"I'm in complete agreement," said Mrs. Malone. "It's only prudent to decline to attend. We must be mindful of public opinion. Dora is yet unmarried, and we wouldn't want to damage Mr. Baxter's opinion of her." She put her hand maternally on Dora's. Dora started in shock before casting a wary glance at Mrs. Malone and nodding once in acknowledgement.

Chloe felt her cheeks flush hot at the thought of her brilliant and vivacious friend going unmourned because she was murdered outdoors instead of dying respectably in her own bed. She took a breath to steady herself before speaking.

"Doesn't everyone take a walk on the moor occasionally?"

"We do. But we aren't assaulted when we go out," said Mrs. Malone, fixing her with a bright blue gaze. "And we always go in daylight. She must have been involved in something dreadful to be attacked in such a way. Perhaps she was keeping company with an unsuitable person." Her last two words were spoken with too much force and venom.

"She and I have been in correspondence for three years and I can assure you that she was as upright a person as you would care to meet," Chloe straightened up and Mrs. Malone's eyes widened in shock.

"You know nothing about it. How could you? You never even met the woman."

"I know enough to understand that a good woman has been murdered. It's unthinkable to deny her a proper and fitting burial." Chloe felt Ambrose shift uncomfortably in the chair beside her.

"She will have a fitting and proper burial," said Alexander. His expression was gentle and his tone soothing. "Mrs. Granger was a great favorite in our house. She was a lovely woman and we all liked her." He looked at Mrs. Malone who leaned back in her chair, glaring. "But I implore you to understand, Mrs. Sullivan. The circumstances of her death prevent us from giving public scandal by attending. For us to be present would be to condone her behavior."

"But aside from walking, which Mrs. Malone admits that everyone does, what was this behavior?" Chloe kept her eyes on Alexander, knowing that to glance at Mrs. Malone would only anger her further.

Alexander hesitated, opened his mouth and closed it again. Beatrice spoke instead.

"She disappeared five days ago. Everyone presumed she was with another person," said Beatrice. Another person? Camille had a paramour? Unthinkable. Chloe would not believe it. "Although a few said she had returned to her family in France."

Chloe's heart sank. Poor Camille, trapped with an unkind husband. She knew from the letters that Camille was unhappy, but she had no idea that the situation was so bad. To leave her husband would create a scandal, humiliation for both her, her family and her husband. She must have been truly desperate to do such a thing. Her husband must have been a tyrant, a drunkard, or even violent. It was the only explanation that made sense. And if she had been fleeing a violent husband, then she had been forced to it.

But why hadn't Camille written to her for help? They

were friends. She would have been more than welcome to stay with them in London for an extended visit. What fun times they could have had in Chloe's laboratory. What discoveries they could have made. And perhaps an extended absence could have improved Camille's conditions at home.

"Well, I do not care," said Chloe. "I am going to the funeral if I have to attend alone." She glared at Mrs. Malone and swept the table with a defiant look.

"Chloe, please," Ambrose said so softly that he was nearly inaudible. Chloe softened and looked down at her plate of cooling lamb and potatoes. She took a bite to keep herself from saying anything further. Conversation at the table gradually resumed.

"—Can't control a wife half his age," said a female voice. Chloe looked up to see Beatrice patting her mouth with a napkin. Dora had a catlike look of satisfaction. She was the one who had spoken.

"My husband—" Chloe blazed, then felt Ambrose's hand on hers beneath the table and stopped. With supreme effort, she placed another bite in her mouth and Ambrose's hand disappeared.

Ambrose fixed Dora, then Beatrice and Mrs. Malone with a cool look. Chloe was ashamed for rising to their bait. If they found her marriage strange, so be it. The details of her marriage agreement were none of their concern. Her husband was a great deal older than she was. But Ambrose allowed her freedoms that a less mature man would have forbidden. She knew she could be impulsive, and resolved, for the hundredth time, not to shame Ambrose ever again.

At the far end of the table, William glared at Dora and Beatrice, red-faced with fury.

"We are going to the funeral," he declared, savagely cutting into his lamb. "Mrs. Granger was our friend, and we will mourn her with respect. And if we are the only reputable family in the church, then so be it!"

After a silence during which Dora scowled and Beatrice

flushed pink, the conversation returned to the safe topic of wedding preparations. Robert made eye contact with his older brother Ian, who had been mostly silent throughout the entire meal. Robert looked pleased, and a ghost of a smile passed over Ian's frowning lips.

CHAPTER 5

C HLOE REMOVED TWO TINY SCREWS, pried off the metal cover panel and squinted as she examined the innards of Beatrice's mechanical robin. It was an older model, at least three or four years old, and judging from the color and consistency of its lubricants, had never been taken in for service.

The bird's embroidered cloth plumage lay in a brown and red crumple in a corner of the worktable that had appeared in Ambrose's study while they were at supper. A gas lamp hissed softly in the other corner, its etched glass globe providing too little light. She absently reached a hand to twist one of the scroll arms and the light flared. She squinted into the bird again.

Beatrice had been vague about the bird's symptoms, but Chloe had examined it and had a good idea of what was wrong with it. She had already removed most of its casing and she flipped it over and set to work on the five screws that held on its head. Once the outer shell was completely removed, she could see the entire mechanical system. She let her eyes travel over it, easing into a relaxed concentration that allowed her to see the whole and the parts simultaneously.

Chloe held her lower lip between her teeth as she went through each potential failure point, from most likely to least. An hour later, the table was covered in tiny gears and springs.

"It's time for bed," said Ambrose in the doorway. She hadn't heard him open the door.

"Won't take too much time," she said, not looking up.

She knew if she stopped now, she would lose her train of thought. The repair was not a terribly complex one, but she was eager to finish it. She was still in a pique over Beatrice and Dora's comment at supper but, even so, she wanted to make this bird work even better than it had when it was new. She may never excel at parlor conversation, embroidery or other womanly pursuits. But she excelled at this.

Ambrose closed the door behind him and looked curiously over her table. "It looks like it will take a great deal of time. I am glad that Alexander saw to it that you could get a few tools and materials."

She murmured an acknowledgment.

"It will be better once your own things arrive, I'm sure."

She ignored him and he turned to his own desk by the window. He was never offended by either her silences or terse words when she was working. He looked over his desk, arranged a few things, selected a book from the shelf and bid her good night.

Hours later, the robin was almost finished, and she was just fitting the chest panel back on when she heard a soft, distant snort. She paused, but there was no other sound. She moved to the window, pulled the heavy curtain aside, and looked out into the slowly swirling mist that had gathered around the house.

Below, moving toward the main road was a horse and rider. If she listened closely, she could hear the muffled crunch of the horse's hooves on the gravel drive. But had she not been paying attention, she would never have noticed the sound. As the rider passed below her window, she let the curtains fall mostly shut, holding them open just enough to peek out. She was glad that her lamp was across the room so the light would not attract the rider's attention, should he look up.

She could tell neither the rider's height nor build as he rode away, presumably toward town. He was in no hurry, though she saw the indistinct shape move to a trot once it reached the main road.

She let the curtains fall shut. There was no clock in the room, so she reached into her little bag beside her work table and pulled out her fob watch. Half-past midnight.

She finished the robin and then fetched the doorway mechanical. She spent a short time lubricating its limbs and making a few minor repairs before sending it downstairs on the dumbwaiter. It was past two o'clock when she went to bed.

CHAPTER 6

THE NEXT MORNING, CHLOE SAT at her vanity as Miss Haynes pulled her hair into place. She combed the thick, frizzy tangle with a wide-tooth comb, working carefully so as not to cause her mistress undue pain. She need not have worried. Her mistress's mind was elsewhere.

"I want to ask you something," said Chloe.

"Mmm?" Miss Haynes had a mouthful of hair pins, but made brief eye contact with Chloe in the mirror.

"I'd like you to keep your ears open around the house. Last night, when I was working in Ambrose's study I heard a disturbance outside. When I looked out the window, down below there was a man on a horse. He rode slowly out to the main road, presumably to keep quiet, and then took off at a trot in the direction of town."

Miss Haynes's eyebrows bunched together. She pulled the pins from her mouth. "Who was it?"

"I haven't any idea. I couldn't tell his build from that distance. It was dreadfully foggy anyway. But it was half-past midnight and, barring the need to fetch a doctor, I can't imagine any other reason to ride to town at that hour."

"I've been up since five o'clock, and no one called for a doctor at night that I heard. And if he were fetching a doctor, he wouldn't have been trying to be quiet."

Chloe would have nodded, but moving her head at all during this stage in the process could mean disaster.

"I'll see what I can learn," said Miss Haynes. "You know it won't be so easy."

"The other lady's maids?"

"Yes, mum. Not the friendliest trio of women you ever met, if you know what I mean."

"They match their employers then," said Chloe, smiling into the mirror. Miss Haynes looked up and then sighed as tendrils of hair broke free of their confines and fell. A furrow appeared between her brows as she started over on that section of hair.

If Dora, Beatrice and Mrs. Malone's lady's maids were not on friendly terms with Miss Haynes, she would be without much in the way of social interaction. If Robert had been young enough to still need a governess, she may have had company. But as it stood, Miss Haynes was in a higher category than scullery maids, chambermaids, bootboys and coachmen. Her only peers would be the housekeeper and the other lady's maids. It would be inappropriate to keep company with the footmen and butler since they were male.

"I suppose we'll just have to make do," said Chloe as Miss Haynes patted the last of her hair into place and handed her the hand mirror to check her handiwork.

"We always do, mum."

Miss Haynes pulled a cameo necklace from her pocket and fastened it around Chloe's neck.

"The servants were all abuzz about your friend's death," said Miss Haynes. "Many of them think that Mrs. Granger had a paramour in town or a foreign lover who she was going to run off with. But the loudest arguments came from two of the maids who think her husband killed her in a jealous rage and a loud-mouthed footman who thinks it was her mechanical."

"Her mechanical? You mean her hound?" Chloe remembered seeing the early schematics and descriptions of Camille Granger's mechanical pet. They had worked on their companion animals roughly at the same time, and Chloe had dearly wanted to see the hound and learn of any possible improvements she could make to Giles.

"Yes. It seems like people around here are much more suspicious of mechanicals than back home. They just don't like them."

"But how could a mechanical like Giles kill anyone? Even a larger animal couldn't. It doesn't make any sense. Why did the footman think it was the hound?"

"I don't think he had good reason, aside from having an excuse to argue with the pretty maids. He wasn't the only one who didn't like mechanicals, though. Most of the locals seemed to think that anything beyond a household mechanical is dangerous."

"Did they say anything else? Are they afraid of Giles?"

The cat was resting on the bed and, hearing his name, raised his head and blinked.

"I don't think so, mum."

Chloe rose, smoothed the skirt of her gray and white Sunday dress and turned so Miss Haynes could inspect her. The cut of the dress was modest and simple for Sunday morning church, though a tad tight through the waist. She had put on a good half a stone over the past few months. Too many rich desserts back home.

Miss Haynes nodded her approval.

"Now, don't get in any trouble asking questions," said Chloe.

"I'll be discreet."

CHAPTER 7

AN HOUR AND A HALF later, Ambrose and Chloe walked into St. George's church for Sunday services. It stood at the edge of Farnbridge, on the older side of the town. This set it within easy walking distance of the miners and working class people who nodded and touched their hats as the Sullivans descended from the carriage. A second and third carriage rolled up smartly behind them, carrying the Aynesworth family.

The church was a long, gray stone building with a row of round-topped windows along each side. Over the two thick wooden doors, a trio of stone rabbits leaped in an endless circle, nose to tail, beneath a stone cross. An unfenced churchyard stood behind, crumbling and newer tombstones crowded together.

Inside, strange faces peered out from stone greenery on either side of a wooden cross and carved stags leapt over the tops of the windows. The stained glass windows were done in a newer style, all of them depicting saints or scenes from the life of Christ. The largest window, which stood over the altar, depicted St. George, lance outthrust, slaying a roaring dragon.

The building was barely large enough to hold the local congregation, and the Sullivans pressed snugly against the Aynesworths in the narrow family pew. At a rising murmur of voices from the back of the church, heads around them turned and a few people raised their hands in greeting. A man with a leg missing from the knee down hobbled into the church on two shabby crutches. The man's trouser leg was pinned over the stump, and many people glanced at it as he slid into his seat.

The man's rough-cheeked wife was behind him, nodding to the well-wishers and ushering their four silent children into the pew. She took a seat, and a younger woman placed her hand on the wife's shoulder and whispered something, motioning outside. The wife smiled, placed her hand over the other woman's, and Chloe could see her lips form a thank you.

Chloe gazed curiously around the church. Judging by the parishioners' clothing, the Aynesworths were one of three wealthy families. The rest of the church was filled with middle and working-class people. Unlike her upper class church in London, St. George's served the entire town of Farnbridge.

Once the service concluded, the Sullivans bid their family good-bye and two carriages carried the Aynesworths back to their house. Their own carriage waited.

"Do you mind if we spend a few minutes? Rose's grave is here," said Ambrose. She took his arm and he took her to the gravestone, now slightly colored from fifteen years of rain and wind. He did not speak, but simply looked at the stone for a minute and then turned back.

They did not head home, but instead headed toward the railway station. They passed parishioners on their way home, and she spotted the injured man, hobbling home with his wife and children. It bothered her.

"You have that look," said Ambrose.

"What look?"

"The one you get when you are concocting an idea."

"It's that man, the one with the leg. I was thinking about Camille's hound, and how she probably could have found a way to make more intelligent mechanicals, ones that could go down into the mines for the most dangerous work. Now it will never happen."

"Why couldn't you create them?"

"I can't even make a mechanical that isn't moderately dangerous." She reached under her seat and pulled her satchel, complete with small lump of mechanical cat nestled inside, onto the seat beside her.

"Giles is still new. You will figure him out and make improvements. Though I still don't know why in the name of heaven you gave him claws."

"Maybe I could work on it. Maybe in a couple of years. Or if I could get Camille's notes, I could replicate some of her work, maybe expand upon it. I'm not sure. But if I could, if mechanicals could have decision engines, if they could think, then it could change everything. No more miners caught in rockfalls and explosions. Women in the workhouses could have improved sewing machines. It could eliminate the need for people to run the most dangerous machines in factories."

"The workers may not thank you for eliminating their livelihoods."

"They could learn different things—less dangerous things." Her mind flashed back to the faces of the four children in church.

"And with what money would they do that, if they have no employment?"

"A moment ago, you were encouraging me."

He sighed and settled himself in his seat. "Your intentions are noble, but I fear it is survival of the most fit. Those who can use their talents to rise will do so, and there will always be those scrambling at the bottom, whether by reason of birth or circumstance."

Chloe looked out the window. She was not angry at her husband. He saw it as his Christian duty to help those very people who were scrambling at the bottom. His generous endowments for educating boys in the slums and providing food and necessities to widows were unknown to

Ambrose's peers. But she knew about it, and she knew his heart. He held no contempt for those lower on the social ladder. If he had, he would never have married her.

"Just because it's that way now, doesn't mean it always has to be," she said. "Things could change slowly, not all at once. Railways gradually replaced horse carriages for long distances. Airships then supplemented those. There's hope."

"That there is."

"I want to see Charles Granger. I want to see if I can get Camille's research notes. They're useless to anyone else, and if they're lost, her work will be in vain. Her work on the cadmium and nickel battery—I think it's the key to the thinking machines. I'm sure of it. A power source that small and powerful could do so much." She settled back into her seat and watched the scenery, aware that she indeed bore the look of a woman concocting an idea. They reached the street near the railway station, and asked the driver to meet them an hour later.

"I heard they have a pastry and chocolate shop near the railway station," said Ambrose, offering his arm. The mid-section of her dresses may have become a tad tight in the past month, but passing up chocolates and pastries was beyond her power.

They passed the time amicably over two steaming cups of hot chocolate and a small plate of Chelsea buns. They were fresh and warm, with plenty of sugar glaze dripping down. She set Giles on the floor, and watched as he moved around their table, looked out the window, and examined their feet and legs before settling by Chloe's chair. The little cat could make decisions, albeit simple ones. And if Camille's hound was even more complex—the possibilities were dizzying.

Ambrose glanced at his pocket watch and said, "It's time," and they walked to the railway station. Chloe scooped up Giles at the doorstep so he would not delay them. Ordinarily, they would have had a servant or two retrieve their crates from the station. But both of them were of the same mind when it came to these crates. They would check the contents of the boxes immediately upon their arrival. The crates, especially the largest, were too important to be left to a servant.

At the station, Ambrose arranged for a worker to open each of their crates for inspection. The boxes were waiting at the side of the station building, and Chloe observed with a frown that one on which she had painted "up" with a helpful arrow was upside-down. The worker lifted the lids of each straw-filled crate and Ambrose and Chloe took turns approving the contents.

Inside Ambrose's crates were books, bound stacks of papers, a microscope, slides, notebooks and a projector with small, brass-encased playback spools. Chloe's boxes were filled with mechanical parts of all descriptions, lengths of India rubber tubing, cans of lubricant and an assortment of gears, cogs, screws, fastenings and copper wire.

The largest box was last.

"The others boxes can be loaded onto our carriage," said Ambrose to the man. "But we'll need to unpack this one completely."

Inside was the steamcycle, the only one of its kind. Once the straw was brushed off, and it was rolled to a clear spot, Chloe did a quick examination. Its exterior looked undamaged. The two leather saddle seats, positioned one behind the other, were unmarred. The glass headlamp was unbroken and its empty oil reservoir intact. A covered wicker lunch basket was fastened over the rear fender and held, among other things, a few tools and a lantern. She knelt to pop open the barrel-like enclosure that covered the engine. After a few moments of probing, she nodded in approval. She filled the oil reservoir, fired up the kerosene burner, gave the mechanism a spin to start it up, and closed the barrel. It gave a low, sweet rumble.

She wiped her hand on a handkerchief and stood back,

admiring. From the grips on its handlebars to its brushed metal fenders, it was a vision in brass, leather and steel.

"Looks fine," she said. "Give it a go and see how it is."

As Ambrose mounted the steamcycle, the railway worker who opened the crates motioned over some of his loitering comrades. They jumped in shock as Ambrose gave it more steam and it roared.

"Is that one of those automobile things?" yelled one of the men. His friends laughed at him and he blushed.

"It is similar," shouted Chloe, feeling sorry for him. She moved closer so he could hear her. "It's like a bicycle, but with an engine so you can travel faster. My husband is a naturalist, and goes out into the countryside where he spends hours looking at plants and insect nests and such. This lets him travel long distances that would tire a horse, and he can spend as long as he likes."

She did not mention that she sometimes rode it when they visited the country, far from their friends in the city. Of course, even in such circumstances Chloe had to be conscious of public opinion and always wore a split riding skirt instead of men's trousers.

Ambrose motioned her over and they agreed to meet in front of the chocolate shop in three quarters of an hour after he performed a test run. As he drove away, Chloe closed her eyes to better hear the exact sound of the closed-cycle hot air engine as it sped away. There was a slight hitch, almost inaudible.

She would have to look at it later. Even with the steamcycle's need of constant maintenance, she was proud of it. Perhaps Ambrose's faith in her was not misplaced. With Camille's notes and schematics, maybe she could change the world.

CHAPTER 8

CHLOE STROLLED DOWN FARNBRIDGE'S MAIN street, allowing Giles plenty of time to take in his surroundings and follow. The more of the world he was exposed to, the more situational decision options he would develop, and the more autonomous he would become. He batted at fallen leaves and poked his nose along the base of each door as he trailed her.

The people they passed gave Giles a wide berth and a few people murmured to their companions. He never drew this sort of attention in London, but then the city was crawling with the strange and the cosmopolitan. It was probably good for the country folk to get a taste of something different than their grocer's stacking mechanical or their butcher's meat wrapper.

They were approaching the police station where a constable rested on a bench, smoking. Chloe did not recognize him as either of the two constables she had seen with Camille's body. Small blessing. He eyed Giles and, once Chloe was within speaking distance, he rose, touched the brim of his domed hat and bid her good morning.

"May I ask you about your little, er, animal?"

"It's a cat. A mechanical cat."

"Yes, mum. May we take a look at it?"

Chloe did not know who else was included in his "we," but she called to Giles. He swiveled his ears at her and trotted over. The constable squatted but pulled his hand back when Giles opened his mouth with a metallic "Brrr?"

"You can touch him if you like. It won't damage him."

The constable scowled. "This is the same one from the airship, is it not? Got at some lady's hat yesterday?"

Chloe flushed. "Yes. But he's not dangerous. It was the only time he's ever done something like that. And he's been fine ever since. I recently upgraded his electro-neural systems back at home. That's in London. Unfortunately, the data storage system in his decision engine was partially destroyed. He did not lose an excessive amount of information. But the only way for him to reintegrate information is for him to be out in the world. I try to keep him out, so he'll learn faster, you see. He can learn, in a way. He's just a baby."

The man looked doubtful, but he touched Giles' back with two fingers. "You bought him in London?"

"No, I built him."

"You mean you ordered him, from a shop? Picked out his this cloth cover and all?"

Heaven above, the man was obtuse. "No, I built him. Myself. Out of parts." Why was it so unimaginable that a female could design something like Giles? She and Camille couldn't be the only tinkering women in the world.

"I'm sure you don't know this, mum. But the sergeant is deciding whether all incoming mechanicals need to be inspected and potentially confiscated."

"Confiscated? Whatever for?"

"There have been problems. Mechanicals can be dangerous."

"It was only a hat," she said. Then she thought of the prints in the mud near Camille's body. "Is this about Mrs. Granger's hound?"

He looked at her in shock and rose. "Now how would you be knowing that?"

"Camille Granger was a friend of mine. As we were coming into town yesterday, we saw her body."

"And you know about her hound?"

She nodded. "The design of the hound is very similar to that of my cat. There's no way it could have harmed her."

"Then you know how the hound works?"

"Partially. I've seen a few drawings, but I really can't say."

"I think the inspector would like to speak with you, if that is acceptable, mum. Do you think you could give us your address? He could perhaps call on you or ..."

The poor man was at a loss. An inspector could call upon a lady, but the Aynesworth family would certainly not thank him for it.

"I can see him now," Chloe said.

The constable was relieved and led her into the dark of the police office. A thin young man was bent over a stack of folders at a paper-strewn desk. He looked up at the constable and nodded a greeting.

"Is Inspector Lockton still here?" asked the constable.

"In his office." The young man jerked his head.

The constable asked Chloe to wait by the desk as he went back. She spent the time reading the notices pinned to the bulletin board on the wall. Some were so old that the paper had yellowed and the ink had faded to a dusky blue. Most were for stolen articles, like an ivory and jet chess set or household silver. One had the name of a missing girl, aged seventeen, who was last seen in the company of a nineteen-year-old man. Not much of a mystery there, she thought.

A man emerged from the doorway. He was short and round, with a few age spots on his balding scalp. He introduced himself as Inspector Lockton and eyed Giles.

"Constable Jackson says you made this." He motioned to Giles who was nosing around the base of the desk.

"That's right."

"And you were friends with Mrs. Granger?"

"Yes. My husband and I are staying with the

Aynesworths, his family. And I had planned on calling on Mrs. Granger while we were here."

"Do you know how the hound works?"

"I have an idea, but the hound is a lot more complex than Giles."

"Giles?"

"My cat."

"I see. Please come back to my office."

He led her down a hall and opened the door to his office, holding it open for her. It was tidy nearly to the point of obsession. Books were stacked along the shelves according to size and five new pencils poked, points up, over the top of a cup on the corner of the desk. One corner of the room was filled with boxes and another corner housed multiple filing cabinets. Though the room was filled, it had an odd, impersonal feel to it.

He motioned for her to take a seat, and she took one of two slat-backed chairs facing the desk. A file lay open on the blotter, which Inspector Lockton closed and slipped into a desk drawer. He seated himself and pulled out a different file but did not open it.

"Tell me about the hound. Do you know where it might be?"

"Does this mean your men have been unable to locate it?"

"It seems to have vanished. Now please, what do you know about the creature?"

"I know it couldn't have killed Camille Granger. It's similar to Giles, and he's harmless. Even with the size difference, there's no way it could kill someone."

"I heard it can think."

"It has a decision engine. Like my cat, it can retain information and learn in a fashion. But it's not possible for it to decide to—" she paused, "crush someone's skull."

The inspector's eyes widened ever so slightly at hearing a lady speak in this manner. She held his gaze.

"So how does this decision engine work?"

"Would you like me to show you?" At his nod, she pulled Giles up onto the desk and turned him off. After the young man at the front desk was summoned to locate a suitably small screwdriver, she pulled back the velvet fur and removed a few cover panels to show the inspector the cat's innards.

"With an ordinary household mechanical, there are spools that are wound and re-wound to allow it to perform a set of tasks. Very simple. But with this," she indicated the decision engine, "he can absorb and retain information, recorded on extra sets of spools."

"So it can think."

"Only in a very rudimentary fashion."

He asked her a few questions about the mainspring barrel and strange tangles of wiring, before seeming to come to a decision. He opened the file folder and handed her a few of the sheets within.

She sucked in a breath. This was it. These were the schematics for the hound. She pored over them, though there were only two sheets. She noted with disappointment that the most complex and therefore intriguing sections were not detailed here. Even so, there was plenty to discover. Her friend's gracefully curved script covered the page, crammed into corners and creeping up the margins.

Someone had killed her, but it wasn't the hound. Chloe was sure of it.

The inspector waited, hands folded, and when she continued to study the pages, he asked her if she knew how it worked. She tore her eyes from the pages with difficulty.

"Yes, yes," she explained some of the diagrams, and though he nodded, she was fairly sure that he did not understand.

"What I am certain of," she said, "is that this creature could not have killed Camille. See? Its center of gravity is too far forward for it to get high enough to bash a human in the head. It would topple forward."

"It could have stood on its hind legs, even for a few moments, or waited until she had bent down," he said.

"Unlikely. How could it grab something, rear up and hit her with it? Even if it managed such a feat of balance and coordination, it makes no sense. What motivation could it have to kill?"

"It could have gone mad and become violent."

"Impossible."

"Like your cat attacking that woman yesterday?"

Chloe sighed in exasperation, "It has no opposable thumbs, so it couldn't grasp anything. And even if it was able to, look at the shoulder and knee joint shapes and musculature bands. There's no way it could generate the power or have the range of motion to smash a skull."

He sat back. "You helped her build it, you said?"

"No, Camille was the builder. She shared some information with me, but I had intended our visit, in part, to learn all I could about her hound. Giles is less complex, and I couldn't have built him without Camille's contributions. She's a far more gifted inventor than I am."

He was studying her, perhaps looking to detect a bit of false modesty. But she knew exactly where she stood in relation to Camille Granger's talents.

"The world has lost a great mind," she said.

"Indeed," said Inspector Lockton. "And that mind may have spawned a dangerous creature."

"I am telling you, it is completely impossible."

"Please think it over, Mrs. Sullivan. If you think of anything you would like to add, please contact me."

He rose to indicate that their interview was at an end. He thanked her and allowed her to reassemble Giles at his desk while he sorted through files in boxes. Then he escorted her out the front door. She continued down the street, spotting the carriage, steamcycle and her husband outside the chocolate shop. She raised her hand in a wave and lifted her skirts to cross the street.

CHAPTER 9

ON THE MORNING OF CAMILLE'S funeral, Chloe put on the gray dress and black shawl that Miss Haynes had selected for her. Chloe grabbed her small reticule and took Ambrose's arm at the front door. Outside, three carriages awaited, the matched pairs of horses tossing their heads. Liveried footmen held the carriage doors and the family climbed inside. Alexander, Beatrice and Mrs. Malone sat across from Chloe and Ambrose.

Mrs. Malone rested her elephant-headed cane against the side of the carriage and folded her hands in her lap. She and Beatrice spoke softly together. Beatrice's plain hat sported one spot of color—the tiny mechanical robin that Chloe had repaired. It was not moving, and Chloe hoped to heaven that Beatrice had not brought the key in her handbag. To have the little bird bobbing and twittering at a funeral would be inappropriate in the extreme.

The carriage lurched forward, the horses' hooves crunching rhythmically on the gravel drive. Once they emerged on the main road, the row of carriages turned away from the direction of town. The sun shone white through the morning mist that swirled up from the damp earth and a soft wind rustled through the moor grass.

After a twenty-minute ride, the carriages stopped in front of the Granger house, a two-story home that was respectably opulent without being ostentatious. Bright clay pots brimming with asters, pansies, irises and other flowers in reds, yellows, blues and whites lined the walkway to the front door.

"How could these plants grow in this season and climate?" said Ambrose, leaning over a lush pot of white crocus.

"Mrs. Granger had a greenhouse, a large one," said Robert. "She loved exotic plants and even ordinary ones. She let me go see them if our family came to visit. She had the servants bring some of them out in wheelbarrows each day and bring them in at night."

"One of her little eccentricities," said Dora. "She spent hours in the greenhouse, pulling off dead leaves, watering them, just looking at them. It was servant work, but she liked it. The only thing she loved more was tinkering with her little machines." She turned away to pull a handkerchief from her bag and dab her eyes. Alexander put his hand on his sister's shoulder.

"One of the servants must be keeping the flowers alive. Mr. Granger didn't much care for them," said Robert, stooping to finger a pot of blue trailing bellflower.

Chloe hadn't known about Camille's love of plants. Her friend had mentioned the greenhouse, and even mentioned some of the plants that she particularly liked. Their letters had centered on mechanics and Chloe had never realized just how much her friend had liked growing things. From the corner of her eye, she saw Ambrose studying her, gauging her emotional state. He offered his arm and she took it, biting back the tightness in the back of her throat.

They moved with the line of mourners into the house. They passed the stately portraits and the crepe-covered mirror in the hallway. The parlor clock was stopped, and the room was filled with flowers and mourners. Chloe glanced around to see if she could recognize any of the wealthier people she had seen at church. She spotted a group of them to one side, though the majority of the people were common townsfolk. They formed a slow-moving line past the walnut coffin.

As they approached the coffin, Chloe pulled back. She could not bear to see her friend again. Ambrose let her stop and then moved gently forward, his hand on hers.

Camille Granger had been transformed. The dirt had been washed from her skin and hair, which was wheat-gold and arranged in pleasing curls. Her head rested on a pale blue satin pillow, surrounded by a wreath of peonies, possibly to disguise her injury. Loosely clasped in her hands was a single white lily, perhaps from her own greenhouse. Her eyes were no longer open and encrusted with mud, but were closed as if in sleep. But she did not look asleep, not really.

Chloe's vision blurred with tears as she bent down to brush a kiss on Camille's forehead. Ambrose pressed a handkerchief into her hand. The push of the crowd moved them into an adjoining room where other mourners were sharing cucumber sandwiches, pastries and hot tea.

When Ambrose left her to fetch refreshments, Dora approached. "I was hoping to speak with you alone."

Chloe nodded, cautiously.

"I'm sorry if our words hurt your feelings the other night at supper. My father was furious with me, and said I ought to apologize."

"Think nothing of it," said Chloe. "It's forgotten. I know that the difference in ages between Ambrose and I may seem strange."

"Not so strange, no. Many widowers marry younger women." Dora sipped her tea and looked into the crowd. "Marie was a bit younger than Uncle Ambrose. I think by ten years or so."

Marie, Ambrose's first wife, had died while giving birth to their firstborn, a son. The infant had not survived. Chloe knew that after Marie's death, Ambrose had descended into a darkness so complete that his friends thought he might follow Marie and the child to the grave. It was

Chloe's father who dragged Ambrose from the opium dens and paid for his stay at a sanitarium in the country.

When Ambrose had first proposed marriage to her, Chloe was certain he only did it in repayment to her father for his past kindness. Why else would a man of fortune and intelligence make an offer to an eccentric spinster? Later, she had accepted his offer. Their marriage was not a great romance, but she thought of it as quite a pleasant partnership.

She knew that Ambrose was content as well. Even so, on occasion he would see a petite brunette or a little boy and get a faraway look. She would take his hand or ask about a bird or plant, and once she got him talking, he would be himself again.

"Marie was a good person," said Dora. "Gentle and quiet. A bit like Beatrice."

Chloe had been anything but gentle and quiet the other night. Or on the airship. His first wife had been all sweetness and propriety, painting silk screens and embroidering samplers, decorating their home in pleasant fabrics and colors. When Chloe had taken over the household, she had done nothing more than instruct the housekeeper to do things the way they had always been done.

Chloe made eye contact with Ambrose across the room and he smiled and lifted the cups of tea and large slice of Battenberg cake that he had balanced on a plate. They found a set of chairs, and Chloe picked at the cake.

People around her were chatting amiably, plates heaped with pastries. One woman wrapped a teacake in a cloth napkin and snuck it into her handbag. Another was chatting with her husband about the finery of the house. Chloe scanned the crowd for anyone who looked saddened by Camille's death. Boys dashed past the window outside. Nearby, a man laughed uproariously and his companion fanned herself with her hand, her cheeks pink. It looked like most of the mourners had come out of curiosity.

Unless they were from a few select families, it wasn't often that they would get a chance to see the interior of one of the area's finest houses. And courtesy would prevent the master of the house from throwing them out for anything less than the most egregious behavior.

It was appalling that Camille's funeral would be treated in such a way. Chloe felt a hot surge of anger, wondering if Camille's killer were here somewhere, stuffing his face with cake.

At the far end of the room stood a stocky man, with ruddy skin and thinning blond and gray hair. With his thick beard, he looked like an aging Viking, grown fat and soft with age. Make that a disagreeable, aging Viking, Chloe thought. He was scowling at the guests.

Robert seated himself beside her and, following her gaze, said, "That's Mr. Granger."

Mr. Granger seemed to be looking over the crowd with the same scrutiny as Chloe. His gaze caught on the refreshment table for a few moments, then he suddenly turned and vanished through the door.

"Would you like to see the greenhouse?" Robert asked, looking at both Chloe and Ambrose.

"I don't think we ought to," said Ambrose and looked at the door through which Mr. Granger had passed.

"I'm sure it's all right," said Robert. "There are some other guests outside, wandering the grounds. And we still have half an hour until we leave for the church."

"I'll go," said Chloe. She needed to get away from the people and the festive atmosphere. The plants may not miss Camille, but they wouldn't be celebrating her death either. Ambrose asked about the plants, and after Robert told him that the greenhouse was filled with only ordinary plants and had nothing exotic, he declined to join them. Robert and Chloe passed into the hallway, and out a pair of double French doors. The air outdoors was chilly, and a bit of wind whipped Chloe's skirts.

"Over there," said Robert, hurrying toward the large greenhouse at the edge of the grounds. He had been correct about a few souls walking through the garden, but no one appeared to be inside the greenhouse. Perhaps they shouldn't go, Chloe thought. She despised the idea of being one of the guests who acted as if this were a garden party. But Robert was so eager, and with others wandering around, she hoped no one would mind. Robert held the door and they entered the greenhouse together.

The warm humidity of the interior was a comfort after the cold outside. Moisture beaded on the windows and the air was thick with the scent of wet soil, mulch and growing things.

"I like to come here when we visit the Grangers," Robert said. "The people are pleasant enough. But it's so quiet here." She could tell he was more relaxed in this place than among people.

"The plants are indeed quiet," she said, leaning over a miniature pink rose.

"I think I'd like a greenhouse like this someday."

They spent a quarter of an hour examining the plants, noting which were sprouting and the very few in need of repotting.

"I think I'm going to go back inside," said Chloe.

"I'll be inside in ten minutes."

As Chloe rounded the greenhouse to go back inside, she discovered an aging mechanical parked under a potting bench. It looked like an older model garden mechanical. You could load it up with soil and pots and it would follow you around the garden. But it was rusted. How odd that Camille would allow such a thing. Chloe's household mechanicals were always in perfect working order, and she could not imagine someone like her allowing one to fall into such a state of disrepair. She dragged it out from its place. While Robert poked around at the plants, she pulled it open, examined and prodded inside. He noticed her looking at something and came out.

"I can have this working in two shakes of a lamb's tail. It only needs oil and a good cleaning, but mechanically, the regulator is the only faulty part," she said.

Robert nodded, but looked uncomfortable at her poking around in a mechanical.

"Here," she pried out the regulator box. "A few minutes, and it will be all fixed."

Robert's eyebrows rose at the sight of her filthy hands and the grease-covered box. She sighed.

"Wouldn't you like to go back inside?" he said.

"Just give me a minute." She rotated a piece until she heard a satisfying click.

"Are you certain you don't want to go in?" Robert asked.

"You can go on without me."

Robert didn't move. Of course, he didn't want to return to the festivities any more than she did. He returned to the greenhouse.

She was careful to keep the oil and grease off her dress as she worked. She needed a small spanner and one of the gears was stripped. She had the parts at home, but then, Camille had a laboratory. She looked up at the house's windows, wondering which one might be the right room. Maybe it was not even on this side of the house. It would be the height of rudeness to be discovered wandering around a house uninvited, during a memorial gathering. But the laboratory—it was here. All of Camille's work was here.

It was too much to resist. She wrapped the regulator in an oily cloth from the bench and held it out carefully. If anyone asked her, she could explain her presence with it and she would still be clean enough to go to the funeral. She took a quick glance around the lawn, judged that no one aside from Robert was close enough to see her, and rushed inside and up the servants' staircase in back. Thankfully, it was empty, as was the long upstairs hallway. She hurried along, past empty rooms and then into what she knew must be the main house. She glanced into doorways as she went, but had to skip a few when she heard voices within.

One of the doors was almost completely closed, and she eased it open a crack. It was a woman's bedroom, all decorated in shades of apricot and cream. Books filled a small bookshelf and she longed to take a look. The paintings on the walls were all of idyllic pastoral landscapes that reminded her of the French countryside. Camille's bedroom. A door at the side of the room was ajar, and she slipped inside the bedroom to investigate just as a maid turned the corner. She sped through the side door and into the next room.

This was the laboratory. She set the regulator on a workbench and waited. The maid had, of course, followed her.

"Mum, are you in need of anything?" The maid was young and doe-eyed, but her look was keen and sharp.

"The garden mechanical had a problem, and I was going to fix it."

The maid looked doubtful.

"I'm Mrs. Sullivan. Mrs. Granger and I were correspondents. I build things too." She motioned around the laboratory. "I'm sure I can find what I need, thank you." She turned away, and felt a guilt-pang at her unladylike dismissal.

The maid left, but Chloe knew that her time was limited. She took a look around the laboratory, which was much messier than her own, with unfinished projects covering most of the work surfaces.

There were two large tables in the shape of an L, one along a side wall with the other leg running under the window. The other two walls were covered in shelves, some filled with books stacked willy-nilly, and others with boxes, most of them unlabeled. A desk stood in one corner, covered in parts and papers.

She started with the desk, rifling through papers,

keeping a few in a stack to the side. She found a number of note pages, a few diagrams, but nothing on the hound. There were, however, a few notes on advanced data spool recording and retrieval, and one on battery design. She kept those.

She pulled open the drawers, but the jumbles of papers and parts made it difficult to sort through them quickly. Well, at least no one would notice more mess, she thought, removing a few pages and jamming things back into the drawers. She tapped her stack of papers on the desk and folded them as tightly as she could, cramming them into her reticule which bulged from the pressure. She wished she had her satchel with her, but she would have to make do.

Next she moved to the two long tables. She guessed that this would be where Camille's current projects were. Near a roll of tubing, a box of ph test strips and a spare mechanical limb of some sort, she found a prototype of Camille's battery. She knew that Camille had been working on a cadmium and nickel battery that could be used over and over again. But to see it was extraordinary.

According to the notes, the cadmium and nickel electrodes were placed in a potassium hydroxide solution. An aqueous electrolyte that was alkaline? She had never heard of such a thing.

She took these notes also and crammed them in with the rest, immediately regretting it, as the reticule became impossible to close. She pulled a few pages out, folded them and slipped them into the top of her stocking. She mashed the reticule under her palm until it was small enough to pull the drawstring closed. She would have to remember not to open it until she was in her own room.

She looked back at the battery. Potassium hydroxide was expensive to obtain, though not prohibitively so, for someone of Camille's or her own station. She glanced around the room and found a shelf containing a few bottles. Rummaging through, she saw that the small potassium hydroxide bottle was almost empty, though nearby was a bottle of murky fluid marked "13.5." Curious.

She grabbed the box of ph strips from the work table. She opened the 13.5 bottle and was greeted by a murky, watery smell. She dipped one strip into the 13.5 liquid and set the strip aside. Then she tipped the potassium hydroxide bottle until she could wet the other strip, which she set beside the first. She looked over Camille's books and through other shelves and boxes while she waited. Finding nothing but assorted wiring and gears, she came back to the strips. The strips were nearly identical shades of deep blue. Interesting.

Returning to the workbench, she noted with interest that many of the parts used in the projects were unevenly worn. Old parts were mixed with new, indicating that some were re-used from elsewhere. She could even spot rust on some, especially a spool playback machine similar to the one Ambrose owned and a household mechanical that stood in one corner. The Grangers were wealthy. Why would Camille need to re-purpose old parts? Perhaps Mr. Granger kept her on a restricted allowance. And if he was as controlling as Chloe imagined, Camille was fortunate to have a room to build in at all.

Footsteps came down the hall, but passed by. Time was short. She tore through boxes, finally finding one with a notebook. It was too large for her to take with her and she cursed under her breath. She paged through it and tore out a few pages, which she folded and crammed into the bodice of her dress. Her eye caught a small black wooden box which had been hidden beneath the notebook and assorted parts. Opening it, she found a stack of bills resting in the red velvet interior. She thumbed through it. It was a handsome sum. And all of the bills faced the same direction. Odd to have such care taken when the rest of the room was a disaster.

She heard footsteps, and threw the box back and tossed

the notebook on top.

"Pardon me," said a voice. Chloe spun around to see the housekeeper in the doorway, scowling. "Guests are not allowed in Mrs. Granger's rooms."

"I was merely trying to help. You have a broken garden mechanical, and I can fix it easily enough. Save you a trip to Lydford's to repair it."

"That is not necessary, thank you. I must ask you to rejoin the guests downstairs."

"Thank you. I will do that shortly. I only need a minute or two more." She grabbed a handful of wiring and moved back to the workbench.

"Please, mum." Something in the housekeeper's voice was plaintive. Chloe looked up. "You really mustn't be here. The master will be furious. He doesn't want anyone in this room."

Chloe hesitated.

"Please."

She couldn't afford to anger Mr. Granger, not when there was so much she wanted here. She put down the wiring, cleaned her hands on a nearby rag and followed the housekeeper downstairs.

CHAPTER 10

DOWNSTAIRS, AMBROSE WAS WAITING FOR her. "Robert returned twenty minutes ago. Where were you?"

"I'll tell you later," she said, and took his arm.

They proceeded with the group to the waiting carriages. The gleaming black hearse was four carriages ahead of theirs. Matched horses pulled the hearse, their sleek black sides shining in the sunlight. Their harnesses were festooned with black ribbons and feathers. The driver was finely dressed and the hearse itself was beautifully decorated in black and silver. If Mr. Granger had suspected his wife of having a lover, he had not retaliated by scrimping on funeral expenses.

The group that assembled at the church was smaller than the one that had been at the Granger home. For the second time in as many days, Chloe found herself in the Aynesworth pew. At the front of the church, Mr. Granger sat in the first pew. He did not look to the right or the left, but kept his eyes fixed on the vicar, his hymn book or on the floor.

Chloe was torn. She half pitied him. Aside from herself, he had been the only person who appeared saddened by Camille's death. He had allowed her to have a whole room of the house as a laboratory and had thrown her a lavish funeral. She remembered the books on Camille's laboratory shelves, and how completely unsuitable they were for a woman. Aside from Ambrose, she had never thought a man could allow such freedoms for his wife. It was his sacred duty to guard her, physically, mentally and spiritually. But Mr. Granger had allowed it.

Someone had murdered his wife, and now everyone in the church occasionally glanced at him, wondering if he had killed her. The rumors must have been painful for him. If the Aynesworth servants were any gauge of public opinion, the scandalous idea that Camille was going to run away with her paramour was all over town. She thought of the box of carefully kept money in the laboratory.

But then, Mr. Granger had been unkind to Camille, monitoring her letters and driving her to whatever caused her to be out on the moor at night. Maybe she had been fleeing him. But if she had, why would she have left the money back in her laboratory?

Chloe tried to focus on the service, but her mind was not on the hereafter. Her concern was for the living. At the end of the service, six men at the front rose and carried Camille's coffin down the aisle. The vicar followed them, with Mr. Granger last. He grasped his brass-knobbed walking stick and moved down the aisle with a limp that proved the stick was not merely decorative. She had not noticed the limp at the house earlier.

The people filed out of the church, forming a crowd around the door. As the Aynesworth pew was near the front, they were pressed in the midst of the crowd for a few minutes. Chloe listened for strains of French, hoping that Camille had family present, but she heard none.

"A puff of sulfurous yellow smoke, I tell you," said a young man. "Every time they disappear."

"That's poppycock. Don't repeat things like that, especially in church," said a young woman who had the same black hair and freckles as the young man.

"No, it's true. The pair of them go from Okehampton to Tavistock, and back again. Have to pick a single blade of grass each time. When the hill is bare, then their penance will be done," he said.

"There's nothing out there and you know it. I'm not a little girl anymore and you can't scare me with ghost stories."

"You wouldn't say that if you lived out there like I do," said a tiny woman with wild gray hair and large square teeth. "You've seen things. I've known you since you were small and you told me. You know it. You don't have to act like you don't."

"Oh, come now. You still leave out saucers of milk for the piskies," said the girl.

They passed out of earshot, and Chloe and Ambrose were able to move into the churchyard where the group assembled around the gravesite. As the vicar spoke of ashes and dust, Ambrose touched Chloe's arm and pointed discreetly behind them.

She gasped. There were prints in the mud with four marks in front and a perfectly oval pad at the base. They were identical to the ones at the bog. They ran along the edge of the churchyard, and then vanished into the gorse behind it. So the hound was still functional and apparently still wandering the area.

Men with ropes lowered the coffin into the grave, and a few women sniffed and dabbed their eyes with lacy handkerchiefs. Mr. Granger was dry-eyed as he stared at the lid of the coffin, deep in the dark earth. The crowd started to disperse to return to the Granger house for the obligatory funeral meal, which would undoubtedly be more lavish than the lighter fare served earlier. Mr. Granger remained, his hands clasped in front of him on the knob of his walking stick. Chloe thought that the tip of his nose looked pinker than it had been before.

She wanted to follow the hound tracks to see if it was perhaps nearby, but there were too many people about. The black-haired brother and sister were arguing nearby.

"Look there," said the man. "Those tracks. See? It's the churchgrims. They should have buried her at a crossroads."

"That's for suicides, you dolt," said his sister.

"Then what are those?"

"How should I know? But I'm hungry. Let's be going before the entire roast is taken." She pulled his arm.

Ambrose walked Chloe across the churchyard and to the road, where a row of carriages awaited.

"Would you mind if we went straight home and missed the luncheon?" She would have said that she didn't feel well, but it would be a lie. Physically, she was well.

Ambrose instructed the driver to take them to the Aynesworth house. Once they were ensconced side by side within the privacy of the carriage, Ambrose raised an eyebrow.

"Would you like to share with me what you have in your handbag?"

She blushed and hesitated for a moment before opening it. She hoped he would not be upset with her. Ambrose whistled low as she handed the stack of papers. Then she reached into her stocking to draw out another paper, which made him chuckle. And finally, she pulled pages out of her bodice, and he gave a wicked laugh.

"Pussycat, pussycat, where have you been?" he said with a small, mischievous smile.

"Not to visit the queen, I assure you. I wanted to see Camille's rooms. I found her laboratory and discovered these."

After perusing the pages, he put half of the papers into his coat pockets.

"I'll carry these to the house for you," he said, handing the rest back to her. She fitted them back into her reticule.

"Unfortunately, there are so many more notebooks and things in Camille's laboratory. I could only grab these. I need to see more. There was just so much."

"Were you discovered?"

"Yes, but only by a maid and the housekeeper. And she seemed so frightened of Mr. Granger that I doubt she'll tell him I was up there."

"Then why don't you want to go for the luncheon?"

She wouldn't usually pass up such luxurious fair as would surely be on offer at the Granger home. And she was dreadfully hungry.

"It's the people. They're all, well ... too happy. Enjoying themselves too much."

His smile faded and he looked out the window. "Yes, I think it was more a party for many of them."

"I just want to go home," she said. He took her hand and she leaned her head on his shoulder.

CHAPTER 11

C HLOE CLOSED HER BEDROOM DOOR behind her and pulled out the note pages from her reticule. She unfolded them and laid them between the pages of a large hardbound art book on a side table before ringing for her lady's maid.

Miss Haynes entered and helped Chloe out of the dress she had worn to the funeral and into a more relaxed blue dress for the afternoon.

"I'm glad you thought to pack that one," Chloe said as Miss Haynes shook out the gray dress, examined it for rips or stains and hung it up.

"Well, I certainly didn't think you'd need it for a funeral. But it's one of your more versatile dresses. A white ribbon and a cameo around your neck, and it's cheered up. A black shawl and your onyx cross pendant with it, like today, and it's fit ... well, for mourning." She glanced at her mistress's face. "Are you all right, mum?"

"I'm all right. It was awful seeing Camille laid out like that. But what I just couldn't abide was being with all those mourners. They were having too grand a time, feasting and all."

Miss Haynes nodded. "The other servants were talking. Mr. Granger's household put together quite a spread under such short notice. Must have bought up half the bakery and butcher shops while they were at it."

"Likely they did. And whoever they hired to dress up

Camille made her look beautiful."

"I heard she was quite a beauty, even if she was French."

Chloe smiled and stroked Giles who was resting on the windowsill. He swiveled his head and watched a tree branch wave in the breeze.

"Down," she said, and he paused before jumping off the windowsill. "I'll be in Ambrose's temporary study."

"Just a moment, mum," said Miss Haynes, shutting the door. "It's about the rider you saw the other night."

"You heard something?"

"I wasn't sure who to ask, or even if I could ask," she said. "It's not as if the other servants are fond enough of me to tell me secrets. I was going to ask Mr. Frick to try to find out, but decided against it."

"Why?" Mr. Frick had been Ambrose's valet for decades. He was the soul of propriety and discretion.

"Well, he might mention it to Mr. Sullivan, and I wasn't sure if you wanted him to know that you had been in the laboratory so late that night."

"Ah. Thank you for thinking of that. But he already knew. He came in to tell me it was bed time, but I wanted to keep working. He didn't seem to mind. I think he worries about me if I work too much and neglect myself."

"Yes, I know how you can be when you get on a project."

"Back to the rider, if you please."

"Right. I couldn't just go around and ask the other servants without them thinking I was a gossip or a busybody. So I had the idea that I could say that the rider frightened me, and I thought he might be an intruder. I thought that if any of them knew who he was, they might tell me to keep me from going to the butler or causing a commotion about it."

"Very clever."

"Thank you. I asked a maid who has a room near mine. My room faces the front of the house, so I told her that I had heard something, looked out my window and saw the rider. Told her I was terrified it was a bandit, maybe the one who murdered that poor woman. I said I wanted to ask the master or call the police. The more hysterical I got, the more she tried to quiet me." Miss Haynes crossed her arms with a smile.

Chloe was willing to let her relish her story, but was growing impatient. "So who is it?"

"Ian. He goes out a few times a week. Though for the last few weeks, he has been going out every night. Goes into Farnbridge and sees someone there. No one knows who. At least, the chambermaid didn't. He's been doing it for years. The servants were instructed that if anyone spoke of it, they'd be dismissed. The chambermaid was terrified that I was going to cause trouble. She told me, but made me take a vow of secrecy."

"Which you then promptly broke by telling me," said Chloe and smiled.

"I had my fingers crossed! And I'm not going to talk to anyone else, that's for certain."

"Did you learn anything else?"

"That was all. But I'll tell if you if I learn anything more." She tidied a few things on the vanity, straightened some of the books that Chloe had left lying about and closed the door behind her as she left.

Chloe grabbed the art book, and called to Giles who had vanished under the bed. He poked his head out and bounded toward her. Something was in his mouth. She commanded him to "drop," "open up" and "give the blasted thing to me!" but he would not relent. With difficulty, she managed to pry the thing out of his mouth, only to discover it was an old brass button with some threads attached.

"Irritating creature," she said, tossing the button onto the table. He sat on his hind legs with his paws up to his chest, like a rabbit.

"Brrr?"

"Well, that's new. And yes, you are adorable. Come."

She opened the door that connected her rooms with her husband's room to find him reading a book. He glanced up and motioned to a second chair.

"I won't be very long," she said, sitting across from him with the art book in her lap.

He kept his eyes on his book as he reached into his jacket and handed her the stack of notes he had kept for her. She slid them into the book with their brethren.

"I have a favor to ask," she said.

"You want me to ask Mr. Granger if we could visit."

"Yes. How did you know?"

"Because you want the rest of her notes." He looked like the cat that ate the codfish.

Exasperating man. "I do. Do you think you could manage it?"

"I already have."

She waited until she was sure he wasn't going to say anything more.

"And?"

"As soon as we got back, I sent a note requesting that we pay Mr. Granger a brief visit. I said that I was eager to make the acquaintance of the husband of my wife's friend, wanted to pay our condolences, etcetera." He waved a hand, but kept his eyes on his book. "When we are there, we can delicately broach the subject of you having access to Mrs. Granger's work. That's assuming, of course, that he didn't hear about your private expedition to get the items yourself."

She jumped up and kissed his forehead. "You are wonderful."

"I know."

"I'm off to your study. I'll see you at supper."

"Enjoy your study of fine art."

She closed the door to the sound of his laughter.

CHAPTER 12

THE NEXT MORNING, CHLOE HAD spent a few hours working on the steamcycle in the carriage house. When Ambrose had gotten it back from town, she found that one of the steam valves was not making a proper seal. A shadow passed over her and she looked up to find her husband in the doorway. She flipped her notebook to the front cover, turned a few pages, then flipped back to a spot held by her finger and wrote a few lines. Ambrose lowered himself beside her. She held up one finger while she finished, and then closed her notebook.

"I received this after breakfast."

After she cleaned her hands, he handed her an envelope. Inside, was a card with pinched script.

Mr. Sullivan,

Thank you for your kind letter and your condolences. If you are available, you and your wife may call upon me at my residence for a brief visit today from one thirty until two o'clock in the afternoon. At this most difficult time, I would request your indulgence in limiting the duration of your call. Unless I hear otherwise, I will expect you both at the time indicated above.

"Not the most gracious invitation we've ever received," she said. "And at that time of day, he wouldn't even have to serve us tea or biscuits."

"It is the very model of efficiency. I thought you, of all people, would appreciate it."

"Don't tease."

"Very well." He folded the card and inserted it back into its envelope. "You can find me in my temporary study after lunch, and we can proceed. I will arrange the carriage."

"Do you think he knows?" she said. "About my visit to the laboratory?"

"This may be his typical way of addressing people. I only know the man by reputation, and even the ever-amiable Alexander has hesitated to say much about the man. I gather he's a taciturn sort."

"So you have no idea."

"None."

"Ah, well. Faint heart never won fair lady's schematics."

"Indeed."

They stepped out of the carriage in front of the Granger house. Giles bounded out behind them and followed them up the walk. It was a calculated risk to bring him. Ambrose had thought it a good idea, saying that if Mr. Granger was grieving, making Chloe seem as similar to his wife as possible may work to their advantage. Also Giles would show Mr. Granger that Chloe was not a mere dilettante, but a serious inventor, capable of understanding and utilizing all of Camille's designs.

The Granger house seemed larger this time, with no people filing in through the door and loitering on the front walk. There were no pots of colorful plants this time, only the clean-swept front yard. A burning smell floated in the air, most likely from a groundskeeper burning piles of leaves out back. Ambrose rapped the doorknocker. Chloe looked down to see that Giles had a wet piece of leaf in his mouth. He was chewing it, his head tipped sideways.

"Drop it," she said.

Giles blinked and stared. She heard footsteps and quickly pried the leaf loose and tossed it aside just as the door opened.

The butler admitted them, placed their coats on a doorway mechanical and led them through the house. The hall was still adorned in black crepe, though it smelled pleasantly of the flowers that still filled the front parlor. It was so much quieter without hoards of neighbors crowding and chatting. It was a large house, and now with only Mr. Granger living there, Chloe thought that it must feel so empty.

The butler opened the door to a sitting room, announced them and allowed them to enter. Mr. Granger was seated in a large armchair, his back to the window. The room was small but pleasant, with patterned blue wallpaper and a bird cage in one corner. The bright-plumed bird inside was silent and completely still. Chloe had to glance at it a second time before realizing that it was mechanical. Camille had covered the little creature in real feathers. It even had small seed and water dishes attached to the bars.

Ambrose and Mr. Granger made their introductions and Mr. Granger took his seat. The chairs near him were a bit lower than his, Chloe found, after seating herself beside Ambrose. The table before them was bare, and no fire burned in the grate. Even the curtains were closed. Well, there was no danger of them becoming overly comfortable.

Giles settled near her feet, and she moved her toe to touch him. If he moved, she would know it before he caused any trouble. Mr. Granger glanced at the cat before turning to Ambrose.

"We want to convey our deepest condolences on the loss of your wife," said Ambrose. "Mrs. Sullivan was quite fond of her. Very fond. And I am greatly saddened that her life was cut short in the bud of youth."

Camille was over forty, and thus a few years past the bud of youth, Chloe thought. But it was a kind thought and well expressed. Ambrose paused, giving Mr. Granger the appropriate time to reply. Mr. Granger nodded his acknowledgement but did not speak.

"I'm sure you are wondering about the purpose of our call, so I will be brief."

"That would be a kindness," said Mr. Granger. "I am weary and grieved, and I am not in the habit of receiving visitors with whom I am not personally acquainted. I made an exception in your case because of the police."

"The police?" Ambrose said.

"Your wife spoke with them, I trust you know?" Mr. Granger's face held the first sign of pleasure Chloe had seen.

"When we went to retrieve our crates," said Chloe and Ambrose nodded and relaxed.

"Yes, she spoke to them about the design of Mrs. Granger's mechanical hound. She explained as much to them as she was able."

"Much of Mrs. Granger's designs were beyond what I understood," said Chloe. "Part of my hope of calling on her was to have her explain them to me."

Mr. Granger ignored her and spoke to Ambrose. "As much as she was able? I thought she was my wife's equal. Inspector Lockton said that she understood the schematics down to every detail. How disappointing." He eyed Chloe with what looked like faint disgust.

The audacity! Hot anger bubbled up and then she had a tiny flash of understanding. Mr. Granger was not merely a deeply rude and unpleasant man. This was calculated to throw both Ambrose and her off their guard. But why? Her anger surged at discovering the manipulation, but she tamped it down. She needed a cool head if she wanted to obtain her goal. She relaxed her face into a look of pleasant feminine obedience, or what she imagined to be such a look, and folded her hands in her lap.

Ambrose hesitated. "She is well able to understand the

schematics if she had all of them. The police did not have the complete set. If they had, I'm certain she would have been able to comprehend and explain them."

"Perhaps. But it is now moot. The hound is being hunted as we speak, and will be destroyed. The police have concluded the obvious: that the creature murdered my Camille." The last words were uttered with unexpected tenderness.

It gave Chloe pause for only a moment. "There is no possible way the hound could have harmed her. That was the whole point of my conversation with Inspector Lockton. The center of gravity, the impossibility of it generating enough velocity—"

"But you had never seen the creature," said Mr. Granger. "I have. And it was no pleasant little plaything like your animal there," he pointed at Giles. "The hound could be given behavior spools to become a guard dog. And we all know that guard dogs can turn on their masters."

A glint of satisfaction was in his eye as he turned back to Ambrose. "The thing is a monster."

"Even if the hound was dangerous," said Ambrose, "there are other things that Mrs. Granger created that could be of benefit to society, if they were developed. For example, my wife has mentioned some battery designs."

Mr. Granger leaned back in his chair. "I'm afraid not."

"I'm sorry?" said Ambrose, uncomprehending.

"You may not have them. Not now, not ever."

"But, but why? What possible use do you have for such things? They are only useful in the hands of someone who can understand them."

Comprehension dawned for Chloe. "Do you plan on sending them to a university?"

"No. They won't be going anywhere."

Chloe glanced at Ambrose, but he was equally dumbfounded. Mr. Granger sat back and steepled his fingers, watching them both.

"I had them burned this morning. All of them. Everything."

Chloe gasped and the room swam for an instant.

"Every notebook. Every blueprint. Every scrap of paper. And the gears and wires and strange mechanical limbs and anything else that wouldn't burn has been smashed and thrown in the rubbish heap, to be hauled away."

Chloe stared at the empty table. All of it, gone. All that information, all that genius. The work, the years of labor and imagination. Her friend had been murdered twice.

"Why did you do this?" Ambrose's voice was so soft that it broke Chloe out of her shock. His expression was so sad. It took her a moment before she understood. He imagined that Mr. Granger had destroyed everything in the depths of his grief. She wondered if Ambrose would do the same to her things if the situation were reversed.

"No other monstrosities will ever be created from her designs. That infernal creation out there is the only thing left, and the police will destroy it. Good riddance, I say." He sat forward and slapped his knees. "And if any other things from my wife's laboratory were still in existence, I would demand that they be destroyed as well." He looked straight at Chloe and stood, towering over them.

Immediately, Ambrose rose to face him, and she thought for an instant that the men were going to fight.

"Thank you for your time. You have been most hospitable." Ambrose's voice held no sarcasm, though his meaning was clear.

"Good afternoon," said Chloe. Ambrose placed his hand on the small of her back and they left the room, Giles trotting behind.

Once in the carriage, Chloe bit back her fury and disappointment. She stroked Giles, which helped calm her. She needed tea, hot tea. And a pillow to slam her fists into.

"He knew," she said. "He knew exactly why we were there. And he was playing with us."

"He is grieving. There's no telling what a man will do when in that state."

"Yes, like playing cat and mouse with us. It was hateful."

"Perhaps he wasn't himself."

"You are too generous, my love. He knew all along why we were there, and he was toying with us."

"But judging from his countenance, he derived little pleasure in the exercise."

"Just because he's a miserable old blighter doesn't make him pitiable. Though he was pitiable, I suppose. A little. Even so." She looked out the window. Somewhere out there was Camille's hound. "I think we need to take a little stroll this afternoon."

CHAPTER 13

AFTER A BRIEF STOP BY the house, they set out. The walk to the crossroads was almost two miles. Chloe wished they could have taken the steamcycle, but it was sitting partially disassembled in the carriage house.

They walked together down the road toward the crossroads, pausing only twice for Ambrose to examine a plant or bit of bluish moss. At last, they reached the crossroads.

"Why don't you go around in that direction," Ambrose pointed. "And I'll circle around the other way."

"A sound plan."

"Oh, and do be careful."

Chloe plunged into the green and purple moor grass, lifting her skirts and looking for the signs of dangerous ground, just as Ambrose had taught her. Bogs could be disguised, and even the sure-footed native ponies slipped into them on occasion.

The bog in which Camille Granger's body had been found was covered in smooth moss and edged with waving reeds. Its scent was not unpleasant, a combination of rich mud and composting plant life. She had not noticed when she had seen Camille's body, but it did not stink of death or stagnation. At the far side of the bog, nearest the crossroads, was the bank of stones that looked like a half-cairn.

She picked her way around the bog, eyes on the ground,

scanning. The grasses hissed in the wind, and her skin prickled in the chilly breeze. She decided to circle the bog and end her circuit near the crossroads. She would have to step over a small stream that trickled out of the bog, but she thought she could manage it.

She arrived at the base of the bog, but there was nothing but grass, scrubby plants and rocks. She lifted her skirts to hop across the trickling stream, where a few rocks shone slick and moss-green in the water. Her shoes were muddy, but they would dry on the walk home and she could scrape them clean before going into the house.

Ambrose was taking the opposite direction around the bog from the one she had taken. He would arrive at a point near the topmost edge of the bog when she did. They could then go on to the bank of rocks together. She waved to him, but his eyes were intent upon the ground.

"Ah! There we are!" cried Ambrose. "Footprints from the hound again. And fresh!"

She hurried over and examined them. They were in the same place as the ones they had noticed when they saw Camille's body. Only now, there were more of them. Both of them tried to discern a pattern to the hound's movements, but the prints circled back over themselves repeatedly. They got fainter, and then vanished altogether in the bracken and grass.

"Why would it be circling? Perhaps its directional controls are damaged?" She squinted at the prints, willing them to provide her information.

"I don't see a discernible pattern," said Ambrose.

Chloe headed for the stone bank. She was feeling more sure-footed now that she was farther from the bog. The ground felt more steady here, and dryer. Ambrose was behind her.

The rock bank rose before them. It seemed larger now that they were closer. It had seemed waist-high from a distance, but now proved to be as high as her neck. It was twice as wide as it was high, and the stones were large and moss-covered on one side. She passed in front of it slowly, looking into the little black crevices, but only saw the shadows of more rocks inside. She turned away from it, put her hand up to shade her eyes and scanned the landscape.

"Where could it be?"

"If those tracks are any indication, it's probably malfunctioning and wandering around without direction or purpose," said Ambrose.

"No. It circled, but it's not aimless. It visited the churchyard, you recall. I think it is still functional."

"Grim thing to do," he frowned. "It's as if it wanted to see her buried."

"What do you mean?"

"If it visited the churchyard, you have to wonder why. It acted in anticipation of her burial. The thing can think, Chloe."

Perhaps its visit to the churchyard was by chance. But no, there were hundreds of square miles of moor, and the likelihood of it arriving in the town was small.

"Hold on a moment," she said. "If the hound were attracted to light or buildings, it may have ended up there of its own volition. It wouldn't need to anticipate a burial for that."

"Perhaps not. But still ..." He pulled his coat tighter around him and studied the bog.

"What are you thinking?"

"First, I am thinking that this isn't a bog." He brightened. "It's a fen. See the stream going out? And note those sedges and rushes there? Bogs are acidic, but these plants couldn't survive in such an environment."

He was ever the naturalist. But she was in no mood for him to change the subject. "And second?"

"And second, I am thinking that it is possible that the hound killed her. Possible, I say. Not definite. That will be up to that inspector and the police to discover."

"Yes, and if they are twice as competent as the imbeciles at Scotland Yard, they could have the Ripper himself murder ten women, and the townsfolk would be speculating about angry spirits or churchyard grims—"

"Or murderous mechanicals."

"Precisely. Everyone is more concerned with this fearful mechanical than with a real killer. Whoever he is, be he Mr. Granger or someone else, he must be as pleased as Mr. Punch with all this ridiculous speculation."

"You have to admit, it is a possibility that the hound killed her."

She threw up her hands and spun around to face him, but before she could reply, her eye fell on a rock that was different than the others. What was it? She tried to focus, to calm her mind as she did when examining the innards of a mechanical. Then she saw. It had no thin covering of moss on its side as did its brothers.

"What do you see?" asked Ambrose.

She bent over the place at the edge of the cairn where there were only a few stones and the furthest ones lay buried in the grass. Two feet from the end of the bank sat this odd stone, resting on its edge against the others. It was shaped like a very jagged octagon, flatter than the others, and the diameter of a serving platter. She tried to pull it, but its base was deep in a groove in the dirt. The groove was a foot long, and the dirt was disturbed. Her blood ran chill. This stone had been moved recently.

She squatted and pulled up her skirts so as not to dirty them. She shoved the stone again, and it moved to the side, half-rolling and half grinding into the earth. Another push, and a hole behind it was revealed.

Chloe heard Ambrose grunt as he lowered himself to see, but she was already reaching inside. Within the hole was a wooden box lid about a foot and a half long. It was shoved back like a drawer, and she pulled it out.

Inside the lid were bits and oddments, three pieces of metal, some coins, colored glass, feathers, and some newspaper scraps. The scraps were not whole articles, but rather random samplings of pictures, text and edges. There was no order to them. It was as if a small child had torn them out.

"They're new," said Ambrose after picking up a scrap. "But they're badly crumpled."

"Do you see a date?"

"No, but they aren't yellowed. The paper fiber is not even warped by the moisture. These are fresh."

She rifled through cloth scraps, some smooth pebbles and turned over a coin. It was old and weathered and she could barely make out the face on it.

"Do you still think it cannot think?" said Ambrose.

"I don't know. But if it can, then it's all the more vital that I find it before the police do. They'll only destroy it."

"If it harmed her, then it should be destroyed." His voice behind her was soft.

"But even if it harmed her, it cannot be held responsible. It doesn't know right from wrong. It possesses no moral compass. And it isn't like a vicious dog that must be destroyed because it will hurt someone again. It can be turned off, like Giles. And perhaps examined. That's if the idiot police don't smash it to bits first."

She pushed the box lid back into its place and Ambrose helped her reposition the stone in front.

"The police may not destroy it," he said. "Mr. Granger can demand what he likes, but they may not be a pack of destructive brutes, as you fear."

"Then they would summon whoever runs the local mechanical shop. Then, when he cannot make heads or tails of the creature, they might send it to someone in Bristol or Exeter or maybe London. And then, it would rot in a box in the police evidence warehouse, or in some attic of a mechanical shop where no one understands it. Our only hope is that it might be sent to a university somewhere, where someone could work out how it operates."

"Even then ..."

"Yes," she sighed. "It could take years. We would never hear of it."

"You are the only person in all of Britain that could decipher the thing, aren't you?"

She glanced at him, but his eyes were far of in the distance, where the shadows were lengthening and the wind was blowing the grass into undulating waves.

"I suppose that is why I must find it first."

CHAPTER 14

CHLOE BALANCED ON THE LIBRARY ladder, her arm outstretched and fingers straining to reach the book. Just a few more inches, and it would be hers. She climbed up a step and held on with one hand, repositioning herself for another try. She balanced on one foot, the other dangling in air and stretched.

She would rather not ask a servant to fetch the book. Something told her that she was already the topic of enough household disapproval without showing undue curiosity about the area. As a family guest, she would be expected to take a few walks through the garden, daily ones if she liked. If accompanied, she could take walks around the nearby countryside. But going further out into the wilderness, especially with a killer on the loose, crossed the line from merely eccentric into the bizarre.

The library was well-stocked, though it appeared largely unused. She had noted that the tops of most of the books were dusty, especially the higher ones, where she was dangling now. The blasted ladder only rolled so far on its track, and the far end of the bookshelf was reachable only by the tall. Chloe was built like a teapot, which, under other circumstances was not so inconvenient.

Her fingers brushed the top of the atlas, but she could not pull it out. She found if she pulled closer volumes out, her desired book, *A Dartmoor Companion*, leaned closer. She did so, and at last, she had it in her hands. She arranged the other books back on their shelf and climbed down the ladder.

She turned to leave when footsteps sounded in the hallway and the library door swung open. She was still in the corner of the room, so the door blocked her view of the new arrivals.

"—for Harvest Home?" asked a young female voice.

"In three days at sundown. Same circle as the last time," said a woman's voice.

"Will Granger be there?"

"No reason for him not to be."

They moved into the room and one of them pushed the door shut behind them. Mrs. Block, the housekeeper, froze for an instant upon spotting Chloe, but then nodded and moved aside as Chloe passed. The girl beside her looked horrified, but a moment later, her face became expressionless. Both of them had the same straight, dainty nose and red hair, although Mrs. Block's was mostly gray. Chloe guessed they were aunt and niece.

Chloe went to her room and seated herself by the window where Giles sat on the windowsill. She flipped through map after map of the cities of Dartmoor: Princetown, Two Bridges, and the nearest, Farnbridge. The book was twenty years old, and the few streets she had seen had in town boasted far more shops than were shown here. Also, there was no airship station on these maps. But that was less important than finding likely hiding places for the hound.

There was a knock at the door. Chloe sighed, set aside her book and answered. Beatrice stood outside.

"Would you care to join me and the other ladies in the withdrawing room? We were chatting before supper, and all were in agreement that we had not had the pleasure of your company very often in the past few days. I hope you are settling in nicely?"

She glanced at the room behind Chloe. Thankfully, Miss Haynes and the maids kept the room tidy. Aside from a few books and papers, it looked presentable.

"I am quite comfortable." She thought of the book of maps with longing. She dearly wanted to go out on the moors as soon as it was light in the morning and look for the hound. The police had more manpower and knew the moors far better than she did. But she would have time after supper to go through the maps. And she could hardly refuse Beatrice's invitation without being unpardonably rude.

"I would love to join you. Allow me to bring something to read while there." She grabbed the first book from her nightstand and followed Beatrice through the hall and down the main staircase, Giles trailing behind.

"Thank you very much for repairing my little robin," said Beatrice. "It's a silly little thing, but I enjoy it. I wear it sometimes, but I mainly like to keep it in my room, near the window, and pretend that it's alive. I have a little perch for it on the windowsill."

"Why don't you get a real bird?"

She shrugged. "A cage by the window just seems ... I don't know. Cruel somehow. Now, a little pet like your Giles, that might be a pleasant companion."

"I would gladly make you one, but he is a prototype."

"Pardon?"

"He's an experiment. He's not entirely—well, not perfectly functional. He still makes mistakes and has some difficulty with verbal commands. But, in time, once I get all the imperfections worked out, I would be pleased to send you a little cat of your own. It would probably be a good year or two, however."

They entered the withdrawing room. It was tastefully decorated, showcasing the wealth and status of the family without being showy. The room was feminine, with lacy curtains and floral-printed upholstery on the deep-buttoned sofa and matching chairs. A collection of ceramic milkmaids, various candlesticks, a clock and a potted fern crowded for position on the mantle.

Dora played softly at a piano in the corner of the room. She looked up and nodded to Beatrice and Chloe. Mrs. Malone was reading in one of the chairs with her back to the window to catch the best light. Beatrice picked up an embroidery sampler that was sitting on the sofa and indicated that Chloe should sit beside her. Giles jumped up and settled himself on Chloe's other side.

"Mr. Baxter, Dora's fiancé, will be coming to supper tonight," said Beatrice. "We are all hoping he will regale us with more stories of his exploits in South America or India or wherever else he has been of late."

Dora put away her sheet music and joined them.

"Please tell me about Mr. Baxter and the wedding," said Chloe. With luck, the other women would carry the conversation, with her inserting polite encouragements. Once the topics of Dora's fiancé and their impending nuptials were exhausted, she knew to ask about fashion. Let it not be said that she could not be feminine and social if she chose.

"Well, the flowers are going to be imported from a florist in Bristol," Dora said, leaning forward. "In a refrigerated railway car. Can you imagine?"

"I thought the cold cars were only used for some medical supplies or for—for other things," said Chloe, stopping herself before she said that she had heard of dead bodies being transported for burial. She wondered briefly if Dora's flowers might be sharing a car with the deceased.

"Oh no," said Dora. "And though Papa is paying for most of it, as is proper, Mr. Baxter has allowed me to pick some things that he will pay for."

She went on about bridal jewelry and reception tarts while Chloe nodded and smiled. Mrs. Malone and Beatrice added enough further details and exclamations of their excitement over the festivities to keep them talking for some time. They discussed the autumn air, fashionable hat trends and one of the neighbors before Mrs. Malone pointed at Giles, who had crawled into Chloe's lap. She had been petting him absently.

"Tell me about this creature," Mrs. Malone said. "I have never seen one like it. My son-in-law says you built the thing."

"Yes. I built him. What would you like to know?"

"Mrs. Granger built things also. Now, you ought to be careful, young woman. You may be comfortable, with a husband and all you may wish, but you ought to be thinking of the future."

"What do you mean, the future? What harm could come from building things?"

She wagged a finger. "That little thing is pleasant enough. And I estimate it is harmless enough. But with time, who knows what you could make. Things don't always go according to plan. It's best to leave creation of things to the Lord."

"I hardly think I'm in competition with the Lord. In fact, I believe that he blesses creative actions, be they through art, music, or building things. After all, if He is the Great Creator, then to create is to imitate Him, and is that not the highest goal of our existence?"

"That is bordering on the blasphemous, young lady."

"If you say so."

"You listen to me. I say this for your own good. Look at what happened to Mrs. Granger. Lies. Secrets. Intrigues. A disturbing sort of independence. All because she liked to build and tinker in that room of hers. It warped her mind thinking about those things. No good can come from such masculine behaviors. It's a matter of the natural order of things. Oh yes, I have heard of those bluestockings who wish themselves to be the same as men. A woman violates the precepts of nature at her own peril. And if you ask me, Mrs. Granger was not without fault in her untimely end. One way or another, she brought it upon herself."

Chloe gaped, too shocked to speak.

Mrs. Malone nodded smugly. "But then, maybe she was no better than she should be." She sat back, her lips pressed together in satisfaction.

"Mother, stop," said Beatrice. Her face was white with shock. "Mrs. Sullivan is our guest."

"I disagree with Mrs. Malone," said Dora gently. "Though I respect her opinion highly, I was close with Mrs. Granger. We visited each other often and were good friends. If that creature did accost her, then I know it was none of her own doing." She turned to Mrs. Malone, who was growing pinker by the moment. "I do not think we possess sufficient information to conclude that Camille was in any way at fault for her own death."

Mrs. Malone opened her mouth, but Beatrice interrupted. "What book are you reading, Mrs. Sullivan?"

"Oh this?" Chloe flipped the book over. Oh dear. She had grabbed the first book she had seen in her room and had not checked to make sure it was appropriate reading. "It's just a little thing that Ambrose lent me."

"Well, what is it?" said Mrs. Malone.

"It's by a Mr. Darwin. Have you read any enjoyable books of late? I would love to hear of any recommendations you may have."

"Mr. Darwin? I know of him," said Mrs. Malone. "It is disgusting rubbish. My late husband, God rest him, would never have allowed such a thing in the house. Your Mr. Sullivan ought to be more discriminating in what he allows you to read, especially as young and easily influenced as you seem to be."

"Now Mother," said Beatrice. "Everyone has their own tastes. What book are you reading there?" She motioned to the volume in her mother's lap.

"Never mind that. And stop trying to change the subject. Do you know what Mr. Darwin says in that abhorrent book? That we are nothing more than apes, swinging by our tails in the trees! I am appalled that your husband allows such a thing. I will ask Mr. Aynesworth to have a word with him later. Or I will have a word with him myself."

"You shall do no such thing," said Chloe, picking up Giles and the offending book. "First of all, how my husband runs his home and how he treats his wife are none of your concern. I have not asked you to read this book nor agree with its contents. And secondly," she straightened up, wishing for a moment that she had Dora's height, "only New World monkeys have tails with which to swing in trees. You, as a hairless ape, would not."

Only silence followed her as she swept from the room.

CHAPTER 15

"AND THE ASS'S HEAD. THE ass's head!" roared Mr. Baxter. "It must have had some mechanical device inside that allowed the ears and the eyes to move while the actor's head was inside and his arms were free. It was ingenious." He took a healthy swig of wine. "The play wasn't bad either. And the fairies moved on ropes hung from the rafters or some such thing. Graceful and lovely they were. Like, well, like fairies. And all played by Scots too. But they weren't nearly as pretty as my pretty little English pixie."

Dora tipped her chin down and smiled. She was seated next to her fiancé at the supper table, with the rest of the family arranged around their guest of honor. "What else did you see in Scotland?" Dora asked.

"Not anything else worth mentioning, my dove."

Thankfully, Chloe was seated near Robert, Alexander and Beatrice. Mrs. Malone was at the far end of the table. Chloe wondered if the sudden seating change for this meal was Beatrice's way of separating her from her mother. Well, if the old woman was content to be far from her, then she was glad of it.

Mr. Baxter was of average height and build, with sandy hair and fierce blue eyes that were always moving from one person to another. He was highly animated, and though he wasn't larger than the other people at the table, he somehow seemed to be so.

"Mr. Baxter," said Robert, "how is your mining operation

in the Yukon?"

"Well enough. Well enough. A little trouble with the mechanicals, but nothing my engineers won't be able to handle in time."

Ambrose raised his attention from his sole in lemon sauce. "What are the mechanicals doing? Or not doing, as the case may be?"

"Ah," Mr. Baxter waved his hand dismissively. "The diggers are only operating at partial power and the haulers keep breaking down. I have my best men on it."

"If your best men are unable to find an adequate solution, I know of a superior mechanical specialist who could look over any machine, provided you were able to ship the mechanical to London. This individual could make it work better than ever."

"Is that so? My Americans are good, but I am losing patience with the continuous interruptions in production due to mechanical failures. I may ask you for this man's name after all."

Chloe was not sure if Mr. Baxter was being polite to Ambrose or sincere. Shipping a mechanical across the Atlantic was impractical. She hazarded a glance at Mrs. Malone. The woman's lips were pressed together hard and she thumped her wineglass down with unnecessary force. Mr. Baxter caught Chloe's eye and gave her a wink. She averted her eyes, unsure how to respond. She had heard that Americans were bold and flirtatious, and it made her uncomfortable.

"I would be happy to provide the address of the person." Ambrose seemed pleased with his little joke.

"I may take you up on that offer," said Mr. Baxter.

"My uncle and aunt haven't heard the story of when you discovered gold," said Robert.

"Oh, I don't know," said Mr. Baxter. "Would you like to hear the story?" he asked Chloe. Ambrose was buttering his bread, and did not notice the wolfish smile that crossed

Mr. Baxter's face for a moment.

"I would love to hear it," she said.

"Then far be it from me to refuse a lady."

Mr. Baxter kept his eyes on hers too long, and she was shocked when he let his gaze slowly take in her bosom and then return to her face. She grabbed her water and took a gulp. She thought she heard a snort of disgust from Mrs. Malone's vicinity.

Mr. Baxter allowed a servant to remove his plate, and he sat back in his chair.

"I had taken a train from Kansas City to Dawson City, that's in the Yukon. I was only up there at all because my brother had need of my help, so I stayed with him and his wife for a season. That country, that land, it captivated me. I couldn't get my fill of it.

"I considered staying, getting Canadian citizenship perhaps, finding a wife. I'm glad I didn't rush into that too quickly." He winked at Dora.

"Anyway, I was outside Dawson City, and I had hired a Tagish man and a few of his tribesmen as guides and workers for a trip up the Klondike River. I had some men with me, and I was thinking of seeing what was up there. Maybe claim some land. So we went up the Klondike, and eventually up Rabbit Creek. And, well, by Providence, we found gold in the creek."

"That was it? You looked down and saw gold?" asked Ambrose.

"It wasn't me who found the first piece. It was one of the guides. I can't remember which one. But then I spent the rest of the afternoon in that creek, and we found more and more. I came back with a little pouch of gold nuggets."

"Are the Tagish tribe wealthy now too?" asked Robert.

"Nah. They don't need the money. They like sitting around smoking and talking all night. Singing songs and such. Wouldn't appreciate the money anyway. I mean, they got some gold. I saw to that. I'm not going to keep a fair wage from my men, mind you."

"So you walked back to town a rich man then?" said Robert.

"Yes and no. On the way back to Dawson City, our packs held a bit of gold, true. But we got hold of some bad food. I would have thought the Tagish knew their land front to back, knew what to eat and what not to. But I suppose someone made a mistake. Everyone was terrible sick. I'll spare you a description. But we were laid up two entire days before we could go further."

"What exactly did they eat?" asked Ambrose.

"I haven't any idea. They were very ill though."

"What were their symptoms? I'm something of an expert on plant life, if I may say so."

Robert stopped chewing and sat forward. Mrs. Malone exchanged a look with her daughter.

"Well, it's not the best suppertime conversation. But we were tired. Real tired. The men slept a lot. And none of them could hold any food down. Their stomachs were in bad shape, if you know what I mean." He grimaced in memory. "Two of the Tagish even thought they saw some vision or other. Something about a bear. They all chattered together in their own language over that."

"Hmm. Delirium," Ambrose scratched his chin. "I can think of a few things around here like that. Black hyssop, pennyroyal or maybe wodinsroot, if you consume enough. But I don't know if they are indigenous to Canada. I would have to check my books."

"I couldn't say. But the fever was particularly nasty."

"It sounds like the fever that Dora had last winter," said Mrs. Malone. "She was in bed sick, just as you describe. Even sick and in pain though, she was such a sweet gentle lamb."

Mrs. Malone was trying to draw Mr. Baxter's attention back to his fiancé. Dora sat with a horrified look before composing her face and offering Mrs. Malone the bread basket. Ambrose gave Dora a curious look and she blushed crimson. Moments later, servants cleared the table and placed crystal glasses of custard in front of each of them.

"Mr. Baxter," said Beatrice, a desperate edge in her voice. "You mentioned that you had a picture to share with us over supper. We are all anticipation. Could you indulge our curiosity?"

"Oh, sure. Here. I brought this for you." He gave Dora a sepia photograph which she gasped over, wide-eyed. "La Tour Eiffel," he said.

Dora handed the photo around the table. Ambrose held it for both he and Chloe to view. The tower soared to the sky, glittering with a thousand lights. Chloe wondered what kind of wiring they used and what type of filament was inside the bulbs.

"I missed the International Exhibition of Paris," said Mr. Baxter. "But I did get to see the world's tallest building. It's too bad America doesn't have a building of that magnitude."

The photograph had returned to Dora and she placed it beside her custard glass. "It would be lovely to go and see it. Do you think we might be able to go next spring or summer?"

"I don't see why not. We could even go there for our honeymoon if you wish."

Dora gasped in delight. She and Beatrice chatted over the photograph while everyone finished their custard.

They proceeded into the withdrawing room, where Chloe made sure to sit far enough away from Mr. Baxter that he could not wink at her or examine her bosom.

"Mrs. Malone," said Mr. Baxter. "I must say that you look a vision tonight. That dress suits your coloring."

Chloe thought that the brown dress made her look like nothing so much as a rotted apple, but Mrs. Malone relaxed and smiled at the compliment. Chloe checked the clock on the mantle. With luck, she could excuse herself soon and have time to examine the maps of Dartmoor. She also needed to spend some time in her laboratory.

Giles's auditory processing unit was definitely in need of examination. But more intriguing was Camille's battery design and how she could apply it to Giles. While Dora played, she went through the intricacies of his power system in her mind. By the time she and Ambrose excused themselves, she had a mental list of items she wanted to explore.

"You seemed to enjoy the music," said Ambrose in the hallway.

"Hmm? Oh, yes. It was fine."

"I'm going to have brandy and cigars with the gentlemen. You don't want to stay and visit with the ladies?"

She gave him a look. "I have an engagement to visit with Giles."

"Well, enjoy your time together."

"Always."

CHAPTER 16

CHLOE PAUSED UPON ENTERING THE work room she shared with Ambrose. She ought to take a look at the maps of the moor, but she also wanted time to go over Camille's notes. If she worked efficiently, she would have time for both.

Mr. Frick, who was familiar with the way his master liked his things, had set up Ambrose's end of the room in perfect order. The shelves on one wall were now populated with books. Ambrose's black leather camera case lay closed next to the desk. The spool playing machine rested on a box behind the desk with two boxes of brass spools on either side of it. One set had handwritten labels while the other set was blank. The microscope case sat on a shelf with three cases of fungi, plant and insect specimens stacked nearby. Chloe knew without looking that the contents would be in alphabetical order by kingdom, phylum, class, order, family, genus and species.

Her own work table was undisturbed, and just as disordered as she had left it. Ambrose must have instructed Mr. Frick to leave her crates open on her end of the room. The straw had been removed and the contents waited for her. Perfect.

She found her three-tiered wood and brass toolbox as well as the pocketed toolkit roll she used when traveling. She found the case for her magnification spectacles and opened it. The fitted pair of eyeglasses had a series of magnification lenses that flipped down with the turn of a tiny knob at the corner. She laid her heavy work corset on a shelf. She would not be doing anything dirty or dangerous enough today to need the protection of its heavy brown leather. Nor would she need her heavy laboratory coat. She stacked her books, much fewer in number than Ambrose's, on a shelf behind her desk.

She selected one book, pulled Camille's notes out from under a spool of heavy wire, found her notebook at the top of a teetering stack and settled into her chair. She spent the better part of an hour going through Camille's notes, her book on electrical design open beside her.

After wandering around the room, Giles jumped onto the desk, knocking over a pencil cup. Pencils rolled everywhere. She gathered them up and put them back in the cup.

"Stay," she said. Giles swiveled his ears and blinked. Then he settled down, tucked his front paws under his chest and curled his tail around his legs. He looked like a loaf of bread.

"Good boy." She smiled and stroked his back and he made a soft grinding noise that approximated a purr.

"At least that function works. What do you say we see if we can upgrade your battery?" The grinding sound continued.

"It won't happen today, puss. You'll have to wait until we get back home. It'll take some work. See, your battery has a manganese dioxide cathode dipped in a paste I made from ammonium chloride and plaster of Paris. Then I had the idea to add zinc chloride to extend the life. Wasn't that a brilliant idea? Yes it was."

She stopped petting him and the grinding sound gradually ceased. She dug through her notes.

"Then I put an array of these little cells into zinc shells. See, Giles, you are fearfully and wonderfully made. You don't know this, but the zinc acts as an anode. Isn't your mummy clever? Hmm? Clever mummy."

"Are you two willing to admit a third party to your conversation or shall I come back at another time?" said Ambrose from the doorway.

"Do come in. Giles and I were discussing his adorable innards."

Ambrose smelled pleasantly of pipe smoke. The pink flush of his cheeks and the end of his nose told her he had consumed a fair quantity of brandy or some other spirits with the other men.

"Mr. Baxter is quite the storyteller," he said. "I have serious doubts about a few of his tales though. Still," he pulled a chair in front of her table and sat back, "I suppose an overactive imagination is not too much harm. And Alexander, Ian and William all seem to like him well enough to let him marry their sister and daughter. Well, who wouldn't, with all that money, waiting to be spent?"

"Dora genuinely seems fond of him. Even though he's American, and doesn't have any family connections, it's a fair match. I think she really likes him, loves him even. You saw her at supper."

"She may not be so fond of him if they have any attractive female servants," Ambrose said. "He didn't say anything improper, but I got the feeling that he is over fond of female company."

Chloe made a noncommittal sound and flipped a page. She felt him watching her and glanced up. The look on his face was serious.

"You saw him at supper?" she asked.

"Yes."

"I'm all right. It was rude. And shocking. And boorish. But I am not upset. I didn't think you had noticed."

"I noticed," he said.

"The man has wandering eyes."

"I don't like it. And I don't want his hands to follow where his eyes lead. I would hate for either you, Dora or

Beatrice to be placed in an uncomfortable situation."

"I will instruct Giles to attack him if he acts in an ungentlemanly manner," she said with a grin. "And, as I will have no occasion to be alone with the man, I foresee no difficulties. So tell me, did you and the men discuss anything interesting over your drinks and smoking?"

"Nothing worth repeating. William is as intractable and taciturn as ever. Mr. Baxter and Alexander did most of the talking and Ian did most of the silent frowning. But I know he's a kind fellow. He's simply not the lively sort. No harm in that."

"Speaking of Ian, Miss Haynes told me something that you ought to know. The other night, while I was here working, I saw Ian riding out toward town. No one knows where he goes, or why. But it was past midnight, and he was obviously trying to keep the sound of his departure quiet, as he rode the horse at a walk to the main road before trotting off."

"Strange."

"Indeed. Miss Haynes says that he goes out a couple of times a week. He has been doing it for years. I wonder if the police have questioned him."

"The police, why?"

"A woman is murdered on the moors, and he takes mysterious rides at night. It seems like an obvious line of questioning."

"But if he's still doing it, then the rides are continuing after her death. That would suggest that the two are not related."

"Not necessarily." She tapped her pencil on her lower lip. "If he's doing something nefarious, then the police ought to know about it."

"There's no evidence that he's doing anything of the sort."

"Then why is he doing it under cover of night? What is there to hide?" She stroked Giles. "Are you trying to defend

103

him? You're defending the family name, aren't you?"

"There's nothing wrong with that."

"There is if a woman's life ended because of it."

"That is an extraordinary leap, my dear," he said.

"Perhaps so. But don't you think the police ought to decide?"

"I thought you said the police were incompetent fools and brutish idiots."

"I did. But now you're just being difficult."

"Simply stating facts," he sat back.

She shut her notebook, jabbed the pencil into its cup and crossed her arms. "Tell me why we shouldn't tell the police about the night rides. Tell me what you really are thinking."

He adjusted himself in his chair and his gaze drifted to the wall behind her. "I don't know where Ian goes, or what he is doing. But I can't see any way he is connected with this. You said that Mrs. Granger had a box of money and though wealthy, used old parts for her mechanicals rather than buying new. She was saving up money, perhaps to flee her husband. Ian's rides have been going on for years, and they continue still, even after her death. He goes in the direction of town, which is in the opposite direction of the Granger house. I don't think he was ever going to meet her in town, certainly not a few times a week for years on end. And not after she's gone, either. Therefore, I see no connection."

Chloe considered. "All the same, I am curious where he goes."

"Curiosity killed the cat, you know."

"I know. I think I would like to go into town tomorrow. I'll take the steamcycle, unless you will be using it." She knew he would not.

"I think you should take the carriage."

"Well, I'd also like to take a look at a few likely places that the hound may be hiding."

"And you want the steamcycle so you won't need a carriage driver."

"Precisely."

"I will go with you. The steamcycle can carry us both."

They had ridden it together before at their house in the country, though it was uncomfortable. But for short rides, they could manage. She had at least five places she wished to see though. And she worried that Ambrose might tire. But she would never hurt his pride by saying so.

"You don't have to come," she said. "The hound isn't dangerous. I keep telling you. And it will be broad daylight."

"The moor isn't like anywhere else. The fairy stories about people vanishing are told for a reason. People get lost and are never found."

"Now you sound like the old man on the airship that told me that the moor is alive and watches people."

He sighed. "It can be dangerous. You saw that bog, and there are hundreds just like it. Tomorrow, we will go out together." He stretched. "I am a little tired. I think I will turn in." He rose, gave a half-bow and left.

She leaned her pocket watch against a book so it faced her. Giles batted a paw at it.

"No. Leave it be."

"Brrr." He knocked the watch over and poked it with his nose.

She picked him up and set him on the floor, where he wandered from one end of the room to the other. He circled Ambrose's desk and jumped onto his chair. He leaped onto the windowsill and banged into the window. Chloe jumped.

"You are lucky that was closed, or the fall might have killed you."

Giles ignored her and settled on the windowsill, watching the dark.

CHAPTER 17

CHLOE ROSE FROM HER VANITY and set down her comb. She took the page that she had copied from *A Dartmoor Companion* and set it on her dressing table, ready for the next morning. She pulled back the bed covers and turned down the gaslight.

"Giles, come."

The cat was on the bedroom windowsill. He had developed a fondness for windowsills and seemed to be remembering their locations in the rooms she frequented. He liked watching birds and plants moving in the wind. He also enjoyed sitting on shelves or anywhere he could look down upon the room's proceedings. But unlike a living cat, his eyes were always open, taking in as much as his visual receptors could process. He also took no pleasure laying in sunbeams or curling up on soft beds or cushions.

"Giles, come."

His ear flicked, but he did not move. He was captivated by something happening at the back of the house.

"What do you see out there?" she whispered and came up behind him.

The gleam of a lantern swayed and flickered as a figure hung it on the doorframe of the stable in the distance. A horse stood nearby, its head up, snuffling the air. A second figure, tall and lean approached. It must be Ian. He spoke to the first man, who had to be the groom. The groom took the lantern from its hook and seemed to be trying to get

Ian to take it. After the light bobbed and dipped while they talked, the groom replaced it on the doorframe and Ian mounted the horse.

She could understand why Ian had refused the lantern. The night was clear and there was plenty of moonlight. If one's eyes were to become accustomed to the dark, she supposed there was enough light by which to ride. She looked up. The moon was almost full. It would be only a few more days—maybe three or so until it was completely full.

Three. Just as the little maid in the library had let slip. Three days from now at the circle.

Chloe stepped back from the window. She turned to search for *A Dartmoor Companion.* Would it show where the local stone circles were? She did not recall any circles depicted on the maps.

She heard a door in the hallway open and close. It must be close to midnight. Who would be up at this hour? She heard footsteps pass her door, the soft thudding rhythm of someone without shoes. It couldn't be one of the servants, as their rooms were not on this floor. The footsteps hesitated, and then moved on.

She pulled a dressing gown from the armoire, wrapped it over her cotton nightgown and stepped into the hall. She padded down the hall in the direction of the footsteps, passing closed doors and staring portraits. She paused just before she reached the top of the stairs, straining her ears in case the person was still on the stairs or the landing. She heard what she thought might be the soft turn of a doorknob in the downstairs hallway, but she did not hear the door shut.

She hazarded a glance down the stairs. Moonlight poured through a window onto the landing, leaving a rectangle of silver light on the patterned carpet. She hurried past it, holding up the hem of her nightgown and moving down the stairs as silently as she could. She poked her head around the edge of the wall and looked down the hallway. The library doorway looked darker than the others. It must be ajar.

She heard the sound of curtain rings sliding along a curtain rod. By now, Ian would be down to the main road, so the person must be closing the curtains, not opening them. She spun around and darted into the closest room, the front parlor. She could wait here until the person retraced his or her steps and climbed the stairs. Then she could risk a look and see who it was while the person's back was turned.

The parlor doorway was large enough that anyone at the base of the stairs could see most of the room. A door at the back of the room was closed. If she wanted to pass through, she would surely be seen or heard. She'd have to stay here. Though the room was packed with chairs, plants and a few tables, there were no decent places to hide. And in the dark room, her pale blue robe and white nightgown would be a beacon.

There was barely enough room for her between the door opening and the hutch, but she squeezed in and pressed her back to the wall. She gathered the edge of her robe so it wouldn't poke out around the doorframe.

She strained her ears, but did not hear footsteps or breathing. She stood unmoving, holding her breath. Listening.

The parlor's lacy curtains were ghostly and still. Moonlight poured in through the window, illuminating the shelves of silent curios. A picture caught her eye. Something about shape of the woman's nose and chin looked familiar. In the darkness, the woman's face was only half-lit, but as Chloe studied it, she recognized the resemblance to her husband. This must be Rose, his late sister.

There was still no sound from the hallway. Had the person taken another route back to his or her room?

"Come out, little rabbit," sung a man's voice from the front hallway. He was so close. And he had an American accent.

She froze. She could run for the door at the back of the room, then go through the kitchen, up the servants' staircase, or even double back to the main staircase. Or she could race outside, go around the back—

"Now, don't run or I'll have to catch you," he chided. His voice was low and soft. He was closer now, only a few feet away. But she had not heard him move. She half felt and half heard him lean up against the wall behind her. They were back to back.

"Shouldn't you be in the servants' quarters, little one? I know you should. Very naughty little bunny to be snooping about."

So he thought she was a maid. Well enough.

"Please, sir. I couldn't sleep and I thought I'd get some water." She hoped his American ear would accept her imitation of a lower-class accent as genuine.

"Now, no fibbing little rabbit. I heard you follow me. I saw you for a moment too. I didn't survive the wild animals and savages in the wilderness by being oblivious. In fact, I rather liked you following me. Watching me in the dark. Waiting for me."

"I—I wasn't waiting, sir. I thought I heard a sound. I came to look. It's Master Ian, isn't it? The rider." Maybe she could distract him. He must have wondered who the rider was.

"So you saw him too, then. Where is he going to, so late at night?"

"I don't know. I have no idea. I have to get to bed. I have to go." She pulled away from the wall. But a huge hand darted in the dark and grabbed her wrist hard, pulling her back. Her shoulder clunked against the wall. He was still on the other side of the wall, but holding her arm around the doorframe.

"Is the little rabbit frightened? Scared I might hurt her? I won't hurt her. We can have a little bit of fun together, you and me. Now don't make a sound, or you'll be sorry."

He spun around the doorframe, clapped a hand over her mouth and pressed her into the wall in one swift movement. He was huge, larger than she remembered, and her face was crushed against his chest. She struggled, tearing at the hand over her mouth as his other hand grabbed a handful of her bosom.

"Hush, hush, little bunny." He leveraged his weight to hold her against the wall. She tried to push him away, but his bulk held her fast against the wall. She twisted her head hard. His hand loosened just enough for her to open her mouth a tiny bit. As his hand smashed against her mouth again, she bit down with all her might. He pulled back for an instant, and then slammed her backwards. Her head cracked against the wall. He crushed his hand back over her mouth, but he was now staring into her face.

"You!" he said in horror. He pulled his hand away and backed up a step.

She wanted to scream, but she had no breath. She grasped the hutch. Mr. Baxter shook his head as the full impact of what he had done hit him. She was a lady, and his actions were inexcusable under any circumstances.

Her mind spun as she tried to breathe. She thought of screaming for help, but drawing attention to herself would bring questions. She thought of Ambrose, and how it would hurt him if she was discovered following someone in the dark of night.

Chloe drew a shaky breath and pulled her robe closed, painfully aware that she was in front of a strange man, a violent man, wearing very little. She glared at him, spine straight, chin up, as her mother had taught her. She was a lady, even in her nightclothes.

"How dare you accost me in such a fashion," she hissed and stabbed her finger at his chest. He backed up a step. "You shameless, disgusting animal! You get away from me and never so much as come within ten feet of me again. Do you understand?"

He nodded, and backed up until his legs bumped a coffee table. He gave her a final glance and hurried from the room. She sank into a chair. Her heart was still pounding and her lip throbbed hot. She thought she tasted blood. She'd have to check it back in her room. The back of her head would have a nice goose egg, she thought as she touched it gingerly.

She waited until she was certain Mr. Baxter would be in his room and then climbed the stairs to her own. She found the door key on the bureau and locked the door. She would have to open the door for Miss Haynes in the morning, but no matter.

She leaned over and examined her lip in the mirror. The inside had a small cut where it had been smashed against her teeth. She took a sip of water to get the taste of blood out of her mouth. Thankfully, the outside of her mouth was only swollen a little. With her hair down and tangled she looked like a wild woman.

Bloody hell. The poor family servants. She would have to tell Miss Haynes to be careful or to avoid Mr. Baxter completely. And poor Dora was about to be married to a man of such character. She considered. Would telling William or even Alexander or Ian about the incident stop the marriage? Ambrose had said that Mr. Baxter had told some wild tales that evening, so surely the Aynesworth men had at least hints of his character. Would Dora wish to call off the wedding? Or, like so many other women, would she simply overlook her husband's dalliances and keep on, content with fortune and material comfort?

She looked at her wrist where finger-shaped pink marks were starting to show. Fortunately her long sleeves would cover them. Her heart still pounded. She needed to calm herself down or she would never get to sleep. Her mother had done two things for her when she was upset as a child. She would make tea, and she would brush her hair. Chloe picked up her hairbrush.

She didn't want to tell Ambrose about what had happened. He would immediately know that she was indulging her curiosity about Ian's rides by wandering at night. The thought of his disapproval stung. She could tell him that she had left her room to get some water. But she had a jug of water in her room, as well as anything else that she might need during the night.

Even if she emptied the jug, she did not think she could lie to him. No, if she told him, she would tell him the complete truth. It was probably best to wait until they were back in London. Then, if he felt it necessary, he could write to William and inform him of his potential son-in-law's character. It would be up to the Aynesworths to handle their own affairs.

A soft snore came through the door of Ambrose's room. Her heart surged in gratitude that her husband was not a drunkard, a womanizer or a gambler. She was one of the fortunate ones, though she had not always thought herself so.

They had been married for three years, but it felt like longer. She had known him for more than ten years before that, since she was a young girl. He had gone from being an uninteresting friend of her father, to an occasional conversation partner, to someone with whom she enjoyed long walks and animated discussions. He had always loaned her interesting books, many of which her father would have forbidden, had he known. But he had never known. It had become a delicious little secret. But even as she reached marriage age, she had thought of Ambrose as her father's friend, and not as a romantic partner.

No, she had thought of another man in that way. Her older brother's classmate, Phillip, caught her eye. He was intelligent, laughed often and looked at her in a way that made her stomach jump. They courted.

One day, her brother took her for a walk in Kensington Gardens and asked about her feelings for Phillip. He asked if she thought she might accept Phillip's offer of marriage, were he to make one. That evening, she heard the muffled sounds of her father and brother talking in the study. She could not make out a word through the heavy door. She walked outside and leaned back against the garden wall. How beautiful the sky was that evening.

Then there were whispers from acquaintances about bad investments, gambling debts, a ship that had not come into port and many others that had lost money. While her father's income was good, he had been able to keep creditors at bay. But when the payments stopped, the creditors threatened legal action.

The family released the servants, sold the house, the silver, most of the furniture and even the antique pearl pendant that had been her grandmother's and great-grandmother's. Her spools of wire, unopened bottles of lubricants, boxes of gears and everything else she had kept on her bedroom desk were sold, as were all the household mechanicals. The family moved to a small home in a neighborhood that was not only unfashionable, but low enough that their friends ceased to call. All except Ambrose Sullivan, that is.

Phillip came to visit her once in that place. His manner, which was usually so jovial, was reserved. He stayed for twenty minutes, enough time to have tea and inquire about her well-being. He looked at her in a new way—with pity. She thought she felt his hand tremble when he took her hand to say good-bye. He did not call again.

In the five years that followed, her mother had taken in sewing work, and her brother dropped out of college. He worked long hours and ate little. Her father drank too much. One afternoon, he and Ambrose had a row. She and her mother sat shoulder-to-shoulder on the second-hand sofa in the front room while the two men shouted in the next. The walls were so thin.

She had never known that Ambrose had lost a wife and

son. Nor that he had nearly died when he was snared by the lure too much drink and of opiate-induced forgetfulness. Her father had helped him, saved his life, Ambrose said. And Ambrose roared that he would fight the devil himself before he allowed his friend to follow that dark and evil path.

Her name was mentioned, and her mother's, though in quieter tones. Ambrose offered to give her father money, or to loan it if her father insisted. Her father shattered a brandy snifter and told Ambrose never to set foot in his house again.

Ambrose had arrived the next morning with two more books for her. She gave him the three she had borrowed, and he asked her to take a walk.

As a lower-class woman on the verge of spinsterhood, as well as one whose reputation was of little consequence, she did not need a chaperone. Their walks became longer and their conversations more interesting. His fascination with the natural world and its classification intrigued her. He listened to her complicated descriptions of her mechanical experiments. And she loved the way he laughed—with his whole body, head thrown back, and hands holding his stomach.

When he had asked for her hand, at first she had refused. They both knew that she was a woman of practicality, and that fanciful notions of romantic love had not been a part of her inner makeup for years. Ambrose had known about Phillip.

"Why not marry?" Ambrose asked, stopping mid-stride on the riverfront. He planted his walking stick and turned to her.

She shook her head. "You are asking for my father's sake. And I am grateful, for his sake as well as my own. I know you want to help him, and my mother and brother. But I cannot indebt myself to you in that way. I would be like one of those women. Trading myself for the sake of money."

"Is that what you think? Truly?"

"I would not say it otherwise. We are beyond polite falsehoods, you and I."

"Then think on this," he took her hand, and his skin was much warmer than she expected. "I wish to marry you for myself. There is no charity in my offer. It is pure and complete selfishness." He watched her face, his eyes steady. "You are everything I want in a companion. You are kind, unselfish and fiercely intelligent, though a tad stubborn."

At her cry of protest, weak though it was, he gave her a knowing look. His expression softened, and he looked down at her hands. "Besides which, you are my dearest friend."

She bit her lip. "I will think on it."

A week later, she had accepted his offer, but only after a long walk and a conversation about the terms of their marriage. He had laughed one of his belly-holding laughs, when she insisted upon having his word. He was to allow her to read whatever she pleased, be it shilling shockers, the violent stories in the newspaper or scientific papers. Especially scientific papers. She was to be allowed to create what she pleased, and she wanted a laboratory. Not a fancy one, simply a room in the house where she could do what she liked without interruption.

She was twenty-seven when they married. Her father still did not accept money from her, but her mother did, and she paid for groceries, household items, a housekeeper and one female servant out of her "pocket money." Her brother went back to school, and her father did not ask who had loaned him the money. Her brother swore he would pay back every cent if he had to work for twenty years. Chloe knew he would.

Giles leaped onto the vanity, and she picked him up. She glanced at Ambrose's door, hating herself for what she planned to do. But what other option did she have? Camille was dead, and her killer was free. Tomorrow night, she thought, would be the night. After she and Ambrose spent the day looking for the hound, he would sleep soundly. He would never notice her absence.

She resolved to tell Ambrose everything when they were back in London. It was not strictly a lie, but rather a brief delay in the full disclosure of the truth.

After all, someone had killed Camille and the police were of no use. They would chase the hound, destroy it, and congratulate themselves on a job well done. The killer would be snug in his bed, just as he was at this moment, wherever that was.

CHAPTER 18

C HLOE GRIPPED AMBROSE AROUND THE waist as they bumped down a narrow dirt road on the steamcycle. Her teeth clacked together for the hundredth time, and she thought with irritation how she would have to check the steamcycle's shock springs before either of them took it out driving again. At least the valves were giving no trouble. She wanted as much time as possible for their task, so she had gotten up early to repair the leaky valve before breakfast.

Dust coated her driving goggles, and she tried to wipe them on a sleeve. But no sooner had her hands unclasped from around her husband's mid-section than they hit a hard bump, jarring her backwards on her small leather seat. She gripped him harder. That was another thing that needed improvement on the steamcycle. The passenger seat was entirely too small. She squinted through the grime-covered goggles, looking for any sign of the hound or a place where it might hide.

Ambrose stopped in the middle of the remote, narrow road. There was no need to pull to the side, as it was doubtful anyone would come along during their short visit. Chloe dismounted and shook out her split skirt. It was made of heavy brown wool with so many folds of fabric that the bifurcation was almost invisible when she stood. She had designed it herself after the sight of her riding through the countryside wearing a pair of Ambrose's belted trousers had given one of their neighbors in the country a shock.

Chloe pushed her riding goggles onto the top of her head. There was nothing to be seen in any direction but scrub and grass. A small patch of pale heath violet drew Ambrose's attention, and he went to investigate while Chloe opened the basket behind the seats. Inside her satchel was the map she had copied from *A Dartmoor Companion*. She rubbed her nose. Blasted dust.

"It should be a bit of a walk in that direction," she pointed and Ambrose looked up. A hundred yards away, over a rise that hid it from view from the road, they found the remains of a stone hut. It was small, barely large enough for two people to have slept inside. Only two thirds of the original round wall remained, and it was crumbling. Stones were scattered around the base of the wall, and it looked like some had been restacked at the top. The roof, which had once been made of branches, was long gone. A small circle of rocks was in the center of the floor.

"There are ashes here," said Chloe. "This place has been in use."

"Sometimes people camp on the moor. There are wanderers, as in any place. It must have provided a little shelter for them."

Chloe walked the perimeter of the hut and did a second examination inside, but found no prints or any other evidence of the hound. She found Ambrose with his hand shading his eyes, looking at a skylark which took off in a flutter of wings at her approach.

"Nothing," she sighed. "I was so certain that the hound would seek out shelter. If it had a decision engine as simple as Giles's, it would have. And its engine is more complex, I'm sure."

"The moor is a big place."

"I know. But we've already seen two rock caves, that place at the base of that tor with the small sheltered place and so many hills and valleys I cannot count. I am going to check the map again."

He followed her to the steamcycle, found their canteen in the basket and drank while she glared at the map.

"I don't suppose we brought any victuals," he said.

"I'm hungry also." She pulled out her pocket watch. "It's after two o'clock."

He grunted and stretched.

"Do you want to go home for lunch?" she asked. She desperately wanted to keep looking for the hound, but they were both hungry and she knew that Ambrose was tired. They had been out for hours, and she had anticipated him wanting to return home by lunchtime. He had already agreed to visit two extra places that were not originally planned.

"I could stay out. But I am hungry, yes."

"By the time we go home, have something to eat and come back, it will be late."

He took the map. "We're not too far from town. Let's grab a pork pie or a sandwich there. Then we can look a while longer before dark."

Chloe returned everything to the satchel, cleaned her goggles, fastened the basket lid and got on the seat behind Ambrose. She knew that Ambrose would park the steamcycle outside of town. He would not give the townsfolk any reason to breathe a word of scandal about the Aynesworth family.

Ambrose parked beside a stone bridge about a quarter of a mile outside town. They removed their goggles and placed them in the basket. Both of them had clean circles around their eyes standing in contrast to the rest of their dust-covered skin. Chloe found a clean cloth and poured water from their canteen on it to wash her face and neck, then folded the rag, wet it again and handed it to Ambrose. Chloe shook her skirts and Ambrose slapped his trousers. They then took turns brushing off each other's backs until most of the dust was gone.

"For such a damp place, there is an awful lot of dust," said Chloe.

"Only on a few of the roads."

"We seem to have driven them all."

They turned off the main street and eventually found the Taper and Spoon. They were in the middle of their meal of battered fish and fried potatoes when Ambrose pointed out the window.

"By Jove, I think that is John Hammond. Would you mind, my dear?"

"By all means, go and say hello."

The bell over the door tinkled pleasantly as he rushed outside. John Hammond was with a younger woman with features similar to his own. Chloe watched as Ambrose hailed them and John Hammond's face went from uncomprehending to shocked surprise. He pumped Ambrose's hand and clapped him on the shoulder. Ambrose was motioning toward the Taper and Spoon when the serving boy came to see if Chloe needed more to drink.

"I think we're nearly done," said Chloe. Then, glancing out the window, and verifying that John Hammond and her husband were still in animated conversation, she turned back. "Could you tell me something? Are there any stone circles about? The ancient kind."

"Yeah, I know what you meant. You're not from here then? Sure, there are all sorts of circles within a few miles of town. Maybe six or seven."

Six or seven. That was five or six too many.

"Are there any ones that people still go to? For instance, on the solstice? Times like that?"

The boy's eyes widened for an instant and he shrugged. "Wouldn't know about that, mum."

"Of course you wouldn't. But if you did, which one would you guess?"

She reached into her satchel and felt around at the bottom. Finding what she was looking for, she slid two coins onto the table.

"If I had to guess?"

"That's right."

"I would guess the one southwest of town. About three quarters of an hour's walk, maybe less."

Chloe turned to see Ambrose listening as the young woman spoke to him. She turned back and the boy and coins were gone. She pulled out the map. If a person walked at two miles an hour over the rough country, then three quarters of an hour was one and a half miles. She used the pencil as a ruler against the crude legend to measure the distance and marked a faint O in the place where the circle should be. She had just put away the pencil and map when the bell over the door jangled.

Ambrose fell into his seat. "That was a pleasant surprise. Most pleasant. That woman with him is his daughter. He has a younger son also. We will be joining them for supper tomorrow night."

On the way out of town, they passed a bakery where Ambrose purchased four sweet buns and had them wrapped in paper. "For later," he said and tucked the package under his arm.

They left the shop and were walking down the main street when they saw three familiar faces. Robert was carrying two small parcels and a thin stack of envelopes. Beatrice and Dora were on either side of him, pink and lavender parasols open.

"What a pleasure to see you!" said Dora. "Are you enjoying your time in town?"

"We are. I had the pleasure to see my old friend Mr. Hammond not twenty minutes ago," said Ambrose.

"Speaking of friends, you received a correspondence." Dora reached into her bundle and pulled out an envelope.

"From Graves," said Ambrose with a smile. "I didn't think he would be so prompt."

"And this," said Robert, handing him a book-sized

parcel. It was large, and Chloe wondered if there would be enough room for it in the basket with their canteen, the sweet buns, a few things Ambrose had brought and her satchel. It was a good thing she had not brought Giles.

"Would you be so kind as to take it home for me?" said Ambrose. "Our mode of transportation requires us to travel lightly."

"You could join us in the carriage. It's waiting for us just there," Robert pointed down the street.

"No thank you," said Ambrose. "We have a few other places to explore before the evening comes."

"Do be careful, Uncle," said Dora. "And don't stay out after dark."

They assured them they would be home before supper and left town. The steamcycle was where they had left it. The engine was cool enough now that Chloe could open the hatch and refill the water reservoir. They rode in the opposite direction from the area they had covered that morning, but, aside from a fascinating array of butterwort that Ambrose insisted on taking the time to sketch, they found nothing.

"Well, if we are having this much difficulty, then I imagine the police are doing no better," said Chloe.

Ambrose was silent as his pencil scratched on the drawing pad. The sun was getting low, and when Ambrose closed his pad, he said that they had to get home.

"There is only one more place. And it is on the way," Chloe said.

They stopped at the crossroads, and Chloe's stomach sank at seeing the bog where Camille had lay. She hurried to the cairn, not wanting to risk anyone seeing her and asking questions, or worse, finding the place where the lid full of oddments was hidden.

Ambrose had just come up behind her as she got the rock to the side. She slid out the box top.

The newspaper scraps, bits of metal, feathers and the

odds and ends were all gone. All that was left were the coins, though it seemed there were more of them than there had been last time.

"It appears that our wanderings today have not been a complete loss," murmured Ambrose.

CHAPTER 19

CHLOE HUNKERED DOWN IN THE dark. She had been sitting on a slope halfway beneath the stone bridge for nearly an hour. The small creek behind her trickled and gurgled as the water poured over the slick, black rocks. The water glimmered in the moonlight, that is, when the moon wasn't hidden behind clouds. She had checked under the bridge a few times, having gotten the sharp feeling of being watched. Of course, no person or animal had been there.

Now that she was no longer walking along the road from Aynesworth House to the town, the chill of the night air made her pull her long fitted brown coat around her. For warmth, she had also worn her leather work corset. It was heavy and snug, but she still wished she had worn an extra layer. She sported heavy stockings beneath her split skirt and had wrapped her hair in a large coffee brown scarf. Her bright hair would be a dead giveaway. If someone were to catch a glimpse of her and inquire, she had no possible excuse for being where she was, or what she was doing.

A new sound mixed with the trickle of the creek. It was rhythmic, and Chloe pulled herself tight against the side of the bridge. She was low and facing toward the town. Any rider coming in from the moor would be twenty paces past her and would have to turn backwards to see her. And she hoped that anyone riding out of town at this hour would be too inebriated or in too much of a hurry to even glance at the darkness beneath the bridge.

The faint rumbling resolved into the steady trot of a rider, and then the sharp clatter of hooves on the stone bridge above. The rider passed onto the road. He was thin and tall, and his back was poker straight. She waited until he had gone on ahead, and hurried over the last bit of road toward town. Ian slowed his mount to a walk at what had once been the town gate, and passed inside.

She followed. Ian turned off the main street immediately. His horse was walking now, and it would be easy enough to keep up. Her main concern was being seen.

She scanned her path for shadowy spots in case he turned back, but aside from doorways, there were few. She scurried to a gap between two buildings which was partially blocked by a few decaying crates. She peeked around the edge of the building to see Ian still riding straight ahead.

Hearing a sharp cry to her right, Chloe looked past the crates to see a man and woman entangled in a writhing embrace. The woman's skirts were pushed up around her waist, and her legs were wrapped around a man's bare bucking hips. The woman turned toward her, and the instant their eyes met, Chloe flew out of the alley, heart pounding.

She found herself in front of a tavern, standing in the glow of lamplight falling through the window. She looked up just in time to see the rear of the horse disappear down a side street. She ran the rest of the way.

Maybe she should not have come. Ian was still riding, and the town was dangerous at night, especially this section of town. It had no chocolate and pastry shops or pleasant inns for eating battered fish. The stench of rotted garbage rose from an alleyway and a couple shouted an argument from a window overhead.

She wanted to turn back, but knew she could not. She thought of Camille, with her laboratory and her greenhouse, her silky blonde hair and delicate hands folded over the lily on her chest. It was enough. Her anger drove her forward.

Ian was halfway down the street when he dismounted and tied up his horse. She moved as close as she dared without risking him seeing her. A slice of yellow light illuminated the street as the door in front of Ian opened. She moved closer, until she could clearly make out the building and the woman who was talking with Ian. It was a boarding house.

She was straining to hear when two men turned the corner and swayed toward her. They bellowed a tuneless ditty, shoving one another and then joining arms. They paused to stomp their feet to what she presumed to be the chorus of their song and hooted with laughter.

She watched with a sinking feeling as the door closed behind Ian, leaving her in the dark. She had not thought of it before, but if something had happened, she could have called out to him. The two men would be upon her soon, and though she had never seen anything like the couple in the alleyway before, she knew enough of the world to know what drunken men could do to women, willing or no. She pulled herself into a doorway. Maybe they would turn down one of the side streets between them.

"I think I see someone," said one of the men.

"It is the moon! She is my lady love!" cried the second and howled, raising his arms to the sky.

"You're drunk, you madman. I see someone. She's just there."

"Yer drunk too, Mr. Kettle."

"What?"

"I am Mr. Pot, and my bride is in the yonder sky!" The last word became a shriek of laughter.

She darted down the street in the opposite direction from the men and Ian's boarding house. She turned the corner and headed for the only lit building.

"What are you doing out here, girl?" said a woman

leaning against the wall. Despite the cold, her arms were bare, as were the tops of her breasts.

A shout came behind Chloe. "It's the moon lady!"

The woman looked past her. "Looks like you have yourself a couple of gentlemen admirers."

"I would hardly call them that."

The woman took in Chloe with a glance. "I see." She shoved the door open with her heel and Chloe hurried inside. As the door closed behind her, she heard the woman shout a greeting to the two men.

The tavern was packed with rickety tables and chairs, though most were unoccupied. The bar was at the back, and a stooped old man was bending over something on the floor. The walls were without paintings or decorations of any kind, save two stuffed stag heads on opposite walls. Both looked so mangy that they must have been old when the bartender was a boy.

A man looked up from his mug and then, sticking a finger in his ear to scratch, went back to his drink. A few other people looked up in languid curiosity and then looked away.

"Oi! Over here," said a voice. She turned to see a doe-eyed young woman seated with a young man at a table in the far corner. They were both seated on the same bench, side by side. There was one mug between them, but two empty mugs sat at the edge of the table.

"It's you, isn't it? I knew it was you," said the girl.

"You're the Granger maid, aren't you?" said Chloe, recognizing the girl from Camille's laboratory. "I saw you at the funeral."

"Used to be," said the young man. "Before that evil man threw her out."

"You mean Mr. Granger?" said Chloe, taking the seat across from the pair without an invitation. She supposed her best parlor manners were of little use here.

"That's right," said the young man.

"Your name was Sullivan, wasn't it?" asked the girl.

"You have a good memory."

"I'm Nettie Cobb, and this here is Tommy, my fiancé. How did you know Mrs. Granger?"

"I am also an inventor and she and I were correspondents. I'm visiting with the Aynesworths. They're family of my husband."

"Yeah, you did say you were the inventor friend when you were in the laboratory," Nettie said. "I've seen your letters then. I was the only one Mrs. Granger would let in her laboratory, and she had stacks of envelopes from you. She even had one of your drawings tacked up over her desk for a bit. Something that looked like an animal."

"I'm flattered."

"Well, it's all gone now. Mr. Granger burned everything up, or had it smashed to bits. Wicked old screw."

Tommy turned to Nettie. "I'll go beat 'im to a bloody pulp if you asked, my poppet. Just say the word."

"Tommy!" She bumped her shoulder into his and shook her head, smiling.

"He doesn't mean it," she said. "He's just angry for me."

"What happened?"

"She's out on the streets now, is what happened," said Tommy.

"What he means is that I'm currently seeking employment."

"Fat lot of good that'll do without a character."

The girl shook her head. "Maybe things will be better once we're married." She turned to Chloe. "We'll be going up to Gretna Green to be married in two days. That's when the next train will be. The airships are so expensive, you know. But the train will get us there just the same. And I'm certain our circumstances will improve in time."

The young man did not look so convinced, but he slipped his arm around her.

"Congratulations. I wish you both the best of luck," Chloe said, and meant it. "Why did Mr. Granger release you without a character?"

"He says I stole some of Mrs. Granger's jewelry. Said some of it turned up missing when he went through her things."

"Do you know who took it?"

She gave a wry smile. "No one took it. She sold it. Though God only knows how she got as much as she did for it. Mr. Granger said he didn't believe I was innocent, so it was out on the street I went without a character. If it wasn't for Tommy, I'd have had nowhere to go."

"Wasn't it possible that someone else took it?" Chloe asked. "How can you be accused when you had neither the jewelry nor the money that would have been earned from it?"

"I hadn't been working for them very long, only two years. Aside from her lady's maid, who had been working for them for something like eight or nine years, I was the only one who went into Mrs. Granger's rooms. I was the one who cleaned her chambers, and I was the only person who was allowed in that laboratory. Not her maid or anyone else could go in."

"Why were you the only one allowed in?" Chloe thought she knew the answer already. She didn't like people in her laboratory either.

Nettie took a sip of beer. "Mrs. Granger was a queer sort of woman. Liked to tinker with things. Build strange machines. She liked that laboratory just so—just the way she had left it. So whenever a maid came in there, she'd tidy up. Put papers with papers, things into boxes, dust off the tables. Things like that. Mrs. Granger hated it and would shout at them when she couldn't find her things. So she banned all maids from going in. But then the floors got dirty, as did the windows. Dust collected and the carpet and curtains needed beating. So she had me promise not to disturb anything, and I was allowed to clean up in there. I never disturbed a thing. I wouldn't dust often, but when I did, I would move one item at a time, and put it back just as it was."

"Why do you think she was selling her jewelry?"

"Well, that's the question, isn't it? But I can add two and two. And more letters were stored in that laboratory than just yours."

"Whose?"

Nettie shrugged. "Why are you so interested in town gossip? You aren't even from here."

"Mrs. Granger was my friend. And I would like to understand why she was killed."

"Wouldn't we all," said Tommy.

Nettie shifted in her seat. "I mentioned that we were getting married soon. And we're real tight on money right now." She scanned Chloe's neck, fingers and then looked where a handbag would hang. Chloe had worn no jewelry and had brought no handbag.

She reached into her greatcoat pocket, only to find a few slips of paper and a small spool of wire.

"I don't have anything with me. When I get back to the Aynesworth house, I could send a bit of money, perhaps?"

Tommy snorted.

"Look, it's late," said Nettie. "We've been down here too long anyway and need to get to sleep."

"Wait a moment." Chloe pulled out her pocket watch. She unclasped the chain and handed it to Nettie, slipping the watch back into her pocket. Nettie looked at the chain and handed it to Tommy.

"Thank you. I suppose I can spare a few minutes, seeing as she was your friend and all. It's a bit of a long story, but you asked. Mrs. Granger was born in France. Ran off with Mr. Granger when she was seventeen. He must have been dashing and swept her off her feet. But she wasn't happy for long. She saved up her allowance and went back to her family in France once, trying to escape him. But he brought her back. He kept better watch over her after that.

"Didn't give her money any more for things, only let her buy things on credit and then he paid the shops directly. I heard all this from the rest of the staff, as most of it happened before my time. But anyhow, Mrs. Granger got clever, and managed to sell some small pieces of jewelry, hair combs, pins, things like that. Little things they were, things a man wouldn't notice were gone. Although as time passed, she sold some larger pieces, though they weren't worth too much. How she managed to save up as much as she did, I'll never know. When you went up there, you saw her little box, yeah?"

Chloe nodded.

"Well, when he went through her laboratory, he found the box. Kept the money, naturally, but burned everything else."

"But if he knew about the money, surely he knew that Mrs. Granger had sold her jewelry and kept the money. Why release you?"

"Because he found the letters when he went through the laboratory." Nettie scooted forward and Tommy sipped their beer. "Mrs. Granger kept all sorts of letters. Some were in her desk, but others were hidden in hard-to-reach places. Two of them were from years and years ago. From an old beau in France, I think. But there were other letters, newer ones. I slipped a few out of their envelopes and took quick looks here and there. Always put them back exactly so. She never knew I saw them.

"They were love letters. Praising her beauty and all that. The gentleman who wrote them wanted to run off with her. He said he'd learn French and they could live near her family vineyards, walk in the sunshine, things like that. He even said that if Mr. Granger tried to stop him, he'd kill him right on the spot. A week later, Mrs. Granger was gone."

"I'm sorry. I am not following. What did that have to do with you?"

She sighed. "See, if word of those letters and the money box got to the police, then they'd know Mr. Granger was guilty. The fact that she ran off to France once is known, but wouldn't be any reason for him to kill her now. But, you put the past and present together and get a picture. His wife has letters from a lover, has tried to leave before and he brought her back, now she's saving up money, selling jewelry, and the letters say she's planning to leave again.

"By getting rid of me, he helps himself. See, if I go to the police and say how there were letters, money and all that, then he can say I made it up because I was angry about being released for stealing. They wouldn't believe a servant girl over a wealthy man of position, now would they?"

"I suppose not."

"Canny, that one. Canny." Nettie tapped her temple.

"But why would he kill her rather than just let her run off? Or if he really wanted her to stay, why not just take the money, or take away her jewelry and keep all of it locked up where she couldn't get to it?"

"Because of his pride. He wanted to keep her under lock and key and not bring scandal. It would shame him terribly if she left. And he's a man with a temper. You don't know it, Mrs. Sullivan. In public he's as silent as a tomb. In his own home, it's different."

"Who do you think her admirer was?"

"If I had to guess? You would know him, as he's part of that family that you're here visiting."

"Ian?"

"Oh, heavens no. The other one. His brother."

"Alexander? Why do you think that?"

"The way Mrs. Granger sometimes talked to him. The way they looked at each other when no one was around. We servants are invisible, but we see things. Also, once I saw something he wrote when he and his family were visiting. A note to Mr. Granger for something. But the writing looked familiar, and then when I was in the laboratory the next day, I thought the writing in the letters looked the same."

"But you didn't hold them side by side?"

Nettie shook her head.

"Then it's just your memory. A lot of men have similar handwriting."

"Could be. But you asked."

"So you think Mr. Granger killed her?"

Tommy set down his beer. "That's what most people think. Either him or that hound."

"It wasn't the hound," said Chloe. "I can assure you of that. Is there anything else you can remember?"

"What more could there be?" said Tommy. "Mr. Granger is as guilty as sin, but the police will tear apart that hound and Granger will go free. If it had been a servant who killed her, he'd be hanged by now."

The pair took turns sipping their beer. It was late, or early depending on how she looked at it, and Chloe needed to head home. She thanked them and stood to leave.

"I wish you both every happiness in your marriage. And I hope you have a pleasant trip. Thank you for everything." She pulled the spool of wire from her pocket and set it on the table. "It's copper. It's not much, just a little something to get you started."

Nettie blinked in surprise and looked up at her. "Thank you, mum. Thank you kindly."

Chloe turned toward the door.

"Just one other thing, because you've been so kind," said Nettie. "I have one letter. Just the last one. It's hidden, and I may still not give it to the police. I took it when Mrs. Granger's body was found. I thought it wasn't safe where it was. I can add two and two, as I said. But once we're on our way out of town, Mr. Granger can't do nothing to us. Then the police can see if Mr. Aynesworth's handwriting matches up with what's in the letter. That is, if Mr. Granger can't convince them that I had it written by someone else. No telling what they'll believe."

"Yes, no telling. If you gave me the letter, I could take it to the police."

"And say what? That you'd gotten it from me?" Nettie said.

"I could say I found it in the laboratory when I went up during the funeral."

Nettie looked to the side as she considered it. "No, if I do give it to the police, and I'm not sure I will, I want to do it myself. I want them to know everything about that monster, whether they believe me or not. It's either that, or I don't give it to them at all. I'm worried about what Granger could do to us. Tommy and I will decide on it together. Thanks for the copper and the good wishes though."

Chloe entered the black night, wondering what exactly Mr. Granger could do to a girl like Nettie. He could tell the police she was a thief and have her arrested. And if Nettie and Tommy thought that Mr. Granger had killed his wife, why wouldn't they think he would do the same to them?

The couple in the alleyway was gone, and Chloe hurried out of town. When she reached the stone bridge, she slowed, conserving her energy for the long walk back. All the while, she listened for hoofbeats behind her. None came. She arrived at Aynesworth House, slipped up the back servant's staircase, through the silent halls and into her own room.

CHAPTER 20

CHLOE AWOKE TO ACHING MUSCLES. The fire was burning brightly in the grate, indicating that Miss Haynes was in her room, though Chloe had not awakened. She pulled herself upright and listened for signs of life from Ambrose's room. There were none. The clock showed eleven o'clock.

"Blast," she muttered. She had missed breakfast by hours. Why hadn't Ambrose woken her?

She stood and painfully discovered a blister on one heel. Somehow, she had not felt any pain on the way back from town. Well, there was nothing to be done about it. She would just put a little square of cloth in her shoe and hope for the best. All in all, she had gotten off easy for all her illicit travels.

After dressing, she felt presentable enough. She found Ambrose at a wrought iron table on the back lawn, an empty chair opposite him. A silver coffee pot and a cloth-covered basket sat in front of him, along with a folded newspaper and a book which he was reading.

At her approach, he looked up and raised his cup. He pulled a pastry from the basket.

"I asked the cook to warm up the sweet buns I bought in town. They're cold now, but still good, I assume."

He buttered one and offered it to her. Something about his manner was off, though she couldn't say what. She sat and he poured her coffee, but his eyes stayed on her face.

"Where's Giles?" he asked.

"I haven't the slightest. I haven't seen him since last night. Why didn't you wake me this morning? Or have Miss Haynes do it?" She took the cup with gratitude and sipped.

"I thought you could use the sleep. And it looks like I was right."

"Do I look that terrible?" she said in alarm and reached up to touch her hair.

"Not at all. But, you rarely sleep late, so something must be amiss. Are you well?" The corner of his mouth twitched, and she felt a pang inside.

"I'm well enough."

She sipped her coffee, and he returned to *A Handbook of Plant Dissection*. His eyes snapped over the lines and he frowned.

"I was hoping to go out today and examine a few of the places where I had seen some interesting plant life. You are welcome to join me," he said.

She thought about it. It would give her more opportunities to locate the hound, even if she had to endure the unpleasant ride.

"I would be just as happy alone, if you are otherwise engaged," he said.

"I would love to come."

"Very well. I will be leaving in about twenty minutes."

A breeze rustled the trees. The weather was pleasant this morning, which was probably why Ambrose was dining al fresco.

"Do you remember the friend I saw in town, the Hammonds?" said Ambrose. "Tonight we will be joining his family for supper." He paused. "Unless you have more pressing matters to attend to."

She scowled into the garden and chewed her pastry.

"Enough. Just stop this," she said.

"Stop what?"

She waved in the general direction of his person. "This!"

He shrugged, slipped a bookmark between the pages and set the book down. He waited for her to speak.

"I'm sorry, but I had to go and see where Ian went. I was so sure that it had something to do with Camille. How could it not? And so I followed him."

"That was dangerous," his face darkened.

"I know. But I didn't know at the time. But I do now. At any rate, he visits a boarding house."

"Just that? A boarding house?"

"That's all. But I wonder with whom he is visiting."

"Well, it isn't Camille Granger, so I think you had best leave him alone."

"Maybe. But I also saw someone else in town—one of the Granger maids. She has been released from her position without a character."

She related the conversation with Nettie.

"An interesting twist," he said. "But inconclusive."

"It's much more conclusive than the police chasing the hound around the moors."

"And you think you are more knowledgeable about these things than the police?"

"Well, yes."

"Chloe, you may be intelligent. Upon occasion, frighteningly so. I know that. But your expertise in mechanicals is not enough here. You go beyond yourself. I have to forbid you from going out again alone, especially at night."

"Forbid me? You can't do that. You promised."

"I promised to let you read what you liked and create whatever mechanical monstrosities you chose. I did not ever, nor would I ever, promise to let you put yourself in harm's way. It will not stand."

She stood up and glared. "My friend is dead. Do you understand that? She was killed in cold blood, and I cannot stand idly by, embroidering or plinking away on a piano, while her murderer walks free." She turned to leave, but

Ambrose shot up and grabbed her arm.

"And would you follow her? How does sacrificing yourself help her? She is gone. She is cold in her grave, while you, my love, are very much alive."

She pulled, but he held fast.

"You will end this fool's errand and leave the police to do their work," he said. "If a madman killed her, he is just as likely to kill you. And if it was the hound, then the same holds. If it is someone sane, God help us, then he will wonder why you are asking questions and poking around where you should not be."

He glanced over her shoulder, and released her arm. She turned to see the butler coming toward them, a silver tray in hand. Ambrose took an envelope from the tray and thanked the butler, who remained where he stood. Ambrose read the envelope in puzzlement. It was addressed to Mrs. Sullivan.

He hesitated for just enough time that Chloe wondered if he was going to keep the letter to himself. He handed it to her.

"Thank you," he said to the butler pointedly, and the man turned and left, walking more slowly than was necessary.

Chloe glanced at the butler's back and opened the envelope.

> *Mrs. Sullivan,*
> *The Farnbridge Police Department finds your expertise in mechanical fabrication necessary in a matter which has recently arisen. Please come to the police office between ten o'clock and noon.*
> *Sincerely,*
> *Inspector Lockton*

"That's the inspector with whom I spoke," she said.

"They must be in quite a pickle to be asking a woman for help."

"My thoughts exactly. Call the carriage."

CHAPTER 21

THE POLICE STATION WAS UNCHANGED from her previous visit. The notices on the board were the same, as was the thin young man at the desk. He looked up at Chloe and Ambrose as they entered and waved them toward the back offices.

"He's expecting you."

The young man pulled his coat and hat from a hat stand beside the door and rushed out, the door banging shut behind him.

"I wonder where he's got off to in such a hurry," said Ambrose.

Chloe pointed out Inspector Lockton's door, as it had no name on it. Ambrose knocked and the door opened. Lockton studied Ambrose as they shook hands. It took only a moment, but Chloe saw the subtle change in his manner. He relaxed a fraction, and she thought perhaps Inspector Lockton was anxious about summoning a gentleman's wife and feared her husband's reaction.

"Please have a seat," said Lockton. "I hope you do not mind me asking your wife to come to the station."

"Not a bit. I am certain she is eager to help in any way she can, as am I. I merely accompanied her out of curiosity."

It was not strictly true. A lady should not have been summoned to a police station at all. If they had wanted to speak with her, they could have discreetly dispatched a constable, or the inspector himself could have called upon her.

This visit, Ambrose had asked the driver to leave them a block from the police station. Anyone in town might have recognized the carriage, and to have it sitting in front of the police station would have been an invitation to town gossip. She was fortunate that her previous visit to the station had passed unnoticed by anyone with a wagging tongue.

"We have three other people for whom we will need to wait," said Inspector Lockton. "I apologize for the delay. Would you like to take a look around the station to pass the time? Perhaps some coffee?"

They declined. A few minutes later, Lockton's office door opened. Accompanying the young man from the front desk were three men, all of them in working men's clothing.

"Mr. and Mrs. Sullivan, may I introduce Mr. Van der Smoot, the railway chief engineer, Mr. Tucker, the airship deck chief and Mr. Lydford, the proprietor of our local mechanical shop."

Each bowed in turn and when Chloe turned back to Lockton's desk, she felt their eyes on her back.

"Mrs. Sullivan." It was the first time the inspector had addressed her directly this visit. "These men are the foremost experts in mechanics in town. We have an item in question, and they have examined it, but they haven't been able—It is a common item, I am to understand."

"We couldn't tell where it came from," said Mr. Lydford. "I think the inspector was hoping that you could help him with it."

"A damned waste of time," muttered Mr. Van der Smoot to Mr. Tucker, who crossed his arms. "It's a common item. No telling where it came from. I don't see how this woman could know any more about it than we could."

Inspector Lockton did not answer, but Chloe had a guess. If he had shown the hound schematics to these men and they had known less than she had, then Inspector Lockton had every reason to ask her. Lockton pulled a cloth-covered item about the size of a man's fist from his desk drawer and set it down. He opened it carefully, using the cloth to hold the few pieces which had fallen off. He set these in a row to the side.

It was part of a mechanical object, though with a glance, she knew the men were correct. There was nothing to indicate what it was. To the untrained eye, it was a mass of gears, wheels and springs.

"May I?"

"Of course," Inspector Lockton pushed the cloth toward her.

The three men circled around the desk. She picked up the main piece and turned it over. Two of the pinions were broken, but that was nothing. It was mostly clean on the outside, as if it had been rinsed off. But the inner parts were crusted with a layer of dirt.

"What happened to this? This isn't the residue of old lubricants or normal dust, it looks like—Oh God."

"What's wrong?" said Ambrose.

"It's from the bog, isn't it? Camille's bog?" She looked at Inspector Lockton. His expression was pitying. He nodded. Mr. Van der Smoot and Mr. Tucker exchanged a glance. She steadied herself. No time for emotions.

"As I'm certain the men present have already noted, this is from a wind-up mechanical. Not a clock, as there is no mechanism for a pendulum. It wasn't too large either. It's self-contained. So it is either something small enough to be on its own or a mostly independent part of a larger mechanical."

"We saw that," said Mr. Tucker. "We agreed it was probably part of an industrial mechanical. The main machine would be steam-powered. But one or two auxiliary systems could be wind-up."

"I say it's part of a regulator for a hauler," said Mr. Van der Smoot. "Something that got lost out on the moor. Or broke down and got scavenged for parts."

"It's not from a hauler," said Chloe. "Look at this gear

train. It would change the rotation to a different axis."

"I know what a gear train does."

"Of course, but if this were from a hauler, there would be no need, as the regulator mechanism parts would all be in a straight line."

Mr. Lydford had an odd little smile.

"Not all haulers are the same," said Mr. Van der Smoot.

"True, and correct me if I am in error, but a manufactory outside of Leeds has a monopoly on hauler construction, at least in Britain. Their only competitor went out of business, what, six years ago?"

"Seven," said Mr. Lydford.

"Seven then. And these parts have not been exposed to the elements that long. See this piece? Iron. It isn't even rusted."

Inspector Lockton leaned forward and pressed his folded hands to his mouth.

"But this piece isn't from a newer mechanical. It's old," said Mr. Lydford. "See the number of spokes on the escape wheel?"

"What do you mean?"

"The newer ones have four spokes. Newer alloys allowed the manufactories to use less metal. So anything with six or more spokes is twenty years old at least."

"I didn't know that," she said.

Out of the corner of her eye, she saw Mr. Tucker made eye contact with Inspector Lockton and jerk his head in her direction. He didn't look pleased.

"You knew Mrs. Granger, then?" asked Mr. Van der Smoot.

Chloe blinked and lost her train of thought. "Yes. I knew her. I had come to visit her. We were colleagues. Friends."

"And you have some mechanical animal like that hound out there? That's what Lockton said."

"Yes." She wondered again where Giles had got to. She would have to look for him when she got home.

"So you're friends with the dead woman, and have a liking for mechanicals that can act on their own? Right?"

"Couldn't we do this without them present?" said Ambrose to Inspector Lockton. "They've already seen it and have provided their information."

"They have to stay because he wants to ensure that what I say can be validated," said Chloe in the lowest voice she could. Lockton was silent.

"I think it's independent," said Lydford. "See, the two corners? Here? They both have openings for a screw to fasten them into a larger piece, a cover. No need for that if they're inside a larger mechanical."

"Oh, that's brilliant," said Chloe and Mr. Lydford gave a little shrug.

"But indoors or outdoors?" he said. "It could be a piece of a ticket dispenser, a stamper, even a decorative object, like a large parlor mechanical. I saw a koala mechanical once, in a shop window. This was in Hamburg. It had this tree branch on a stand. It was on order for a local—"

"I need to be getting back to work, if there's nothing more you need me for?" said Mr. Tucker. Mr. Van der Smoot grunted agreement.

"If you would wait a few more minutes. Mrs. Sullivan, are you finished?"

She picked up the flat metal ribbon that sat to the side of the cloth and coiled it. She inserted it into the corresponding barrel and held it with her thumb. There was no longer a cover to hold it in place, but if she didn't tip it, it would stay.

"I think it's an indoor mechanical. See the diameter and depth of the hole for the winding key?"

Lydford leaned over. Mr. Van der Smoot and Mr. Tucker didn't move.

"The key would be a short, fat brass key, not a long and thin one," she said.

The three men nodded.

"I don't understand," said Lockton.

"Almost all mechanicals for in-home use would have the short brass keys. You usually keep the key near the mechanical itself. As with a clock. And it is made for household people to use, so it's thick enough not to break off inside. Maids and such have to be able to use it. For industrial mechanicals, the keys are longer and thinner, so you can wind a mechanical part that is deeper within the machine. And they are typically used by people who are careful with their mechanicals."

Mr. Lydford was smiling now.

"That doesn't prove anything," said Mr. Tucker. "Anyone can make something with a short key like that. And if this is part of something Mrs. Granger made, there's no knowing what this thing was a part of."

"I agree," said Mr. Lydford. "From looking at it, it appears to be manufactured, not homemade. But there is no way to be certain. It is too bad we don't have the rest of it."

Chloe set it down and glanced at Mr. Lydford. He added nothing more.

"Is that all?" asked Inspector Lockton.

"It's a good bit more than you had before," said Mr. Lydford.

Mr. Van der Smoot looked at the door.

"Thank you, gentlemen," said Inspector Lockton. "I appreciate your assistance. You are free to go."

Chloe and Ambrose rose as well and Inspector Lockton showed them out. Mr. Lydford was waiting outside. Mr. Van der Smoot and Mr. Tucker were halfway down the street, presumably on their way back to the railway and airship stations.

"Mr. and Mrs. Sullivan, it was a pleasure talking with you," said Mr. Lydford. "I'm sorry about the death of your friend."

Ambrose took her arm and she followed. It would not do

for townsfolk to see them coming out of the police station. Mr. Lydford joined them.

"I hope the police are able to discover something," said Chloe. "That mechanical part was a dead end. They are no closer now than before."

"Perhaps and perhaps not," Mr. Lydford said. "You never know what else they might be able to get out of that bog. Assuming they're still looking. Well, if you are ever in the neighborhood, my shop is on Hampton Street, down this street and right on the next," he pointed. "Next to the dress shop."

"I saw it on the way through town when we arrived," said Chloe.

He made his good-byes, tipped his hat and crossed the street.

"Penny for your thoughts," said Chloe once she and Ambrose were seated across from each other in the carriage and he was looking out the window.

"My thoughts?"

"I know you have them."

"Saucy woman. I was thinking about the *Labridae* family of fishes. There are ordinary males, and then there are males who were born female. The latter live among the females their entire lives, even after they became male. The ordinary males don't usually bother to challenge them."

"I think Mr. Tucker and Mr. Van der Smoot did a fair amount of challenging. Besides, I'm all female."

"Don't think for a moment that I am unaware of the fact."

CHAPTER 22

"**M**RS. SULLIVAN, PLEASE. YOU HAVE got to make it stop!" panted Robert. He was standing in the laboratory doorway, pink-cheeked and frantic. His shoes were covered in dirt, as were his knees and hands. "It's destroying everything!"

Chloe leaped up and removed her magnification spectacles. Robert rushed through the house and out the back, Chloe close behind him.

"I tried to stop it. But it clawed me. I kept trying to chase it, but it's faster and stronger than it looks." His hand had four equidistant bleeding scratches amid the grime.

They passed the back lawn and the rose garden, turning sharply toward a vegetable garden. The plot of land was fenced and well-tended. Near the back was a scarecrow, or what was left of it. The post upon which the scarecrow had hung was barely upright. It had worn an old skirt, which was now in a heap in the dirt to one side. Its coat was halfway off, and a sleeve was torn. Half of the brown yarn that served as the scarecrow's hair was torn off and lay scattered. The rest hung from one corner of a men's hat, which had blown up against the fence.

Giles was in the corner, digging madly at the dirt. A spray of earth flew out behind him, and as Chloe ran for him, he darted off. He found a carrot and began to dig.

Chloe grabbed around his midsection, falling on her knees in the dirt. He squirmed, bucking until he caught his front paws in the earth and gave a mighty push. He fled to the far corner, turning to look at her as she crept toward him.

"Giles, come."

He did not respond. His head turned to one side, and she knew he was evaluating distance and how quickly he could cover it. She threw herself at him, dragging him toward her as he flailed. He attacked with claws and teeth, and he gave her thumb a hard bite. She ignored the moment of pain and held him steady, bracing him against the earth. She reached around his belly and his back feet rabbit kicked. He caught her in the stomach once, but she managed to flip his switch. He did not make a sound as he lost energy, but struggled to the last.

Robert was beside her. "Are you all right?" He offered her a hand up, which she accepted.

"I'll be fine. It is only a bit of dirt." She wiped at the dirt on her front, but it made no difference.

"What did you do to it?"

"I just turned him off. He has a switch, here." She showed him.

Robert nodded, but his eyes were already scanning the garden. He headed for the far corner and knelt down. It was the most damaged part of the garden, with more than half of the plants shredded or uprooted.

"I'm so sorry," said Chloe. "I didn't think he was capable of this."

Robert was silent, and he gathered some of the shredded plants in his arms, cradling them against his body with one arm. None of them had roots left or any hope of survival. He rose and made a pile of them off to one side.

"I thought this was the kitchen garden," said Chloe. "Is it yours?"

"Only this corner. I grow some things out here, and the kitchen staff doesn't mind. I weed and water their section sometimes, and keep an eye on it."

"I'm sorry, Robert. I'll help you replant it."

"I know it was an accident."

"Still, I'll help."

He knelt and pushed dirt back around a leaning plant.

"You grow herbs, not vegetables," she said.

"Yes. I like them. I would like to learn about medicine some day. I want to be a doctor." He sighed.

"But?"

"But my father wants to purchase a commission for me in the navy."

"The navy's not such a bad life. And being a doctor is difficult work."

He looked up at her, and the disappointment on his face startled her. It was not disappointment over his future, but in her. She set Giles down near the gate and joined him amid the plants. She pushed dirt back around plants that were still in the earth and collected leaves and other non-salvageable parts. She left most of the replanting to Robert who worked gently and slowly.

"Why won't he let you be a doctor?"

He gave a mirthless laugh. "Doesn't think we should be doctoring the masses. Thinks we should do something respectable."

As the third son, Robert would inherit no property and little money. The military or clergy were the traditional paths for young men in his position. And a doctor was little more than a high-level tradesman.

"I understand a bit about not doing respectable things," she said. Robert glanced at Giles and smiled for the first time. She said, "You know a lot about herbs already, don't you?"

"Mostly from books. But Mr. Graves was teaching me more before he left."

"Was that your tutor?"

He nodded.

"And he left?"

He nodded again and turned aside to gently lower a mugwort plant into its hole. He moved off to get a spade.

Chloe stood and stretched, and the wind caught tendrils of her hair and brushed them against her cheeks. She could understand Robert's attraction to the garden. It was a good way to get out of the house and occupy his time. She wondered if he was lonely or if he knew any other boys his age.

She surveyed the drunken scarecrow. That would be easy enough to repair. She pushed the main post upright and shoved dirt around it. Then she pulled the coat the rest of the way onto its horizontal post and fastened the one remaining button. She gathered up the skirt from the ground, and had moved behind the scarecrow to fetch a shoe when she saw a series of dirt mounds about two yards from the fence. It was as if something large had leapt the fence and skidded to a halt inside.

"Robert, come here!" she called. "Look."

He squatted and examined the earth. "Those are bigger than your cat's feet."

"They're not from my cat. They're from the hound."

"Mrs. Granger's hound? What would it be doing here?"

She scanned the garden now with new eyes. She walked up and down the rows, examining every disturbed piece of earth.

"When did you find Giles?"

"Right before I came for you. I came out here to water, and he was digging up plants."

"So you didn't see him destroy the scarecrow?"

"No."

"I had thought maybe he climbed the scarecrow, like he could climb curtains. That is why it was torn up. But maybe it was the hound."

"If it was the hound, why would Giles then go and tear things up even more? Why dig up my plants?"

"I don't know."

Giles was small enough to walk beneath the fence rail, but the hound was not. If the hound had leaped the height of the fence, it was stronger than she had thought.

CHAPTER 23

AFTER HELPING ROBERT IN THE garden for another hour, she apologized again and excused herself. She needed to ready herself for supper with Ambrose's old friend, John Hammond, and his family.

Miss Haynes sighed at the sight of the mud-covered dress. "I'm not sure about it, mum, but I'll do my best."

By five o'clock, she was bathed, her hair was pinned in a simple style and she was laced into a green dress that was fitting for her station, but not so fine as to draw attention to the difference in class between the Hammond family and herself.

According to Ambrose, the Hammonds lived in a respectable section of town, but he had the impression that they were not as well-off as they had been years ago. Of course, that would not prevent Ambrose from sharing a meal with his old friend.

Ambrose knocked on the front door and they were introduced. The family consisted of Mr. John Hammond, a thin man with stooped shoulders, his wife, who was too ill to join them at the table, and his two children. The oldest was Rebecca, who had been walking with Mr. Hammond when Ambrose had hailed them in the street. The younger was Stephen, who was fifteen.

"How are you enjoying your stay with the Aynesworths?" asked Rebecca. "They are a pleasant family, aren't they?"

"You know the Aynesworths?" asked Ambrose.

"Oh, yes," said Mr. Hammond. "Our Rebecca worked for them for almost a year. My acquaintance with you and your sister helped her to obtain the position."

"I had to leave when Mama took ill three months ago," said Rebecca. "But I liked working for them very much."

"What sort of work did you do?" asked Chloe.

"I assisted their lady's maids. They have three, and I would do any work they did not have time for. Or work they didn't like to do themselves. I would fetch and serve tea or do a little mending. Maybe some shopping that didn't require any knowledge of fashion." She smiled at the memory. "I could go into town and pick up anything the ladies had need of, thread or ribbon or sheet music. Although Miss Aynesworth almost always liked to pick her music herself. She's very accomplished on piano."

"We have had the pleasure of hearing her play," said Ambrose.

"It was good work, while I had it. When Mama is better, I hope I can go back."

Chloe sipped her tea. There was nothing for her to say. Rebecca had been required to keep the house when her mother fell ill, and if her mother did not recover, there Rebecca would stay. She could take in washing or mending, as Chloe's mother had done. But there was little else she could do without hiring herself out. She thought of Nettie, waiting for her train to Gretna Green. Rebecca could hope for a husband who made a decent living, perhaps a tradesman. But then, who would care for her family?

"Our Stephen has found some work," said Mr. Hammond. "He's working afternoons at the newspaper."

"Oh, that's wonderful. What do you do?" asked Ambrose.

The boy blushed. "Not much to tell about. I help the newspapermen. I lay type and they're teaching me how to maintain the presses. It is dirty work, but I like it well enough."

A chittering came at the window, and Stephen jumped

up. "It's Gus! He's back!"

Rebecca and her father both rose and hurried to the window, which Robert threw open. A little gray squirrel ran up the boy's arm, across his shoulders and poked its nose around the other side of Stephen's neck.

"I thought he was lost or killed!" he said, returning to the table and stroking the animal. Mr. Hammond and Rebecca did not seem to mind an animal at the table, though Chloe was glad that all but the coffee was finished.

"Something got into our yard last night," said Mr. Hammond. "It got into the shed. That's where Stephen keeps Gus. We thought Gus was killed. A few of our neighbors have had something come into their yards also."

Chloe exchanged a look with Ambrose. "Can we take a look?" Ambrose said. "Something similar happened at the Aynesworth house."

"Certainly." Mr. Hammond found a lantern and lit it. He led them out the back door into a small yard that was mostly a vegetable garden with a shed to one side.

"What happened at the Aynesworth house?" asked Rebecca.

"Something tore up the garden," said Chloe. "It went at the scarecrow also."

"That's odd," said Rebecca. "The window of the dress shop was smashed the other night and a mannequin was torn up. From what I heard, nothing was stolen from the shop though."

The garden was undisturbed, but the shed door was ajar.

"It looks like it broke the door latch." Ambrose lifted it. It had been twisted and the wood was splintered around it.

"Do you know what did this?" asked Stephen. "I thought it was—I don't know—an animal trying to eat Gus. We thought it might be a burglar, but nothing was taken."

Ambrose pushed open the door and took the lantern from Mr. Hammond. Chloe stood behind him and looked around the shed. It was filled with the usual items:

gardening tools, boxes and a small work table. There was also a large cage with a dish of food and water. The wire door was bent, leaving a hole. A wire-framed dressmaking dummy stood in one corner.

"I am going to look at something outside," said Chloe.

"Wait a moment and we can take the lantern," said Ambrose.

"No, keep it inside."

She walked around the outside of the shed. A small window was set into the wall farthest from the house, and though the glass was dirty and warped, with the light inside, she could make out the dummy. It looked nothing like a person. She thought of the way Giles saw the world. Though he might mistake a scarecrow or mannequin for a person, he would be highly unlikely to make the same mistake with a headless wire torso. And without a light inside, the hound could not have seen inside anyway.

Chloe returned to the shed to find Ambrose on one knee, looking at something on the floor. Two cans were on their sides, their black and brown contents mixing in a pool under the work table.

"I must have missed that when I cleaned up in here," said Stephen, bending down to set the cans upright. "Those are from the newspaper. That one is cleaner for getting the dirt out of the machines and the other is lubricant. My supervisor let me bring home part of an old broken printer engine to work on. He wanted me to see how they worked inside."

Ambrose looked up at Chloe and motioned to a smear of dark red on the side of one of the cans. The color did not match the contents of either can.

"Is that blood?" she breathed.

He touched it with his handkerchief and examined it. "No. Too dark." He sniffed. "Definitely not."

"What is it?" asked Mr. Hammond. Ambrose handed him the handkerchief.

"What do you think that is?"

Mr. Hammond held it up to the lantern. "Let's get it inside."

Under the kitchen gaslight, the liquid appeared a dark reddish brown. It had a bitter scent.

"It looks like one of the solvents the miners use to clean the machines in the reverberatory furnaces. Though it could be from anywhere. That's not the only place they use it, but they use a great quantity of it because of the machinery," said Mr. Hammond.

"What is a reverberatory furnace?" asked Chloe.

"Furnaces used for smelting tin. They built them out near the mines."

"How close are the mines?"

"The closest one still in use is about three miles out of town. Seems like the person who broke into our shed might have had this on his hands, do you think? But he didn't take anything."

"Are you going to tell the police, Papa?" asked Rebecca.

"I suppose I should. But if nothing was taken, then it's simply a broken door latch. What can the police do? I don't want to waste their time."

Rebecca went to check on her mother, while Mr. Hammond and Stephen moved into the front room. Chloe took Ambrose's arm and they followed at a distance.

"I should tell him. It could hurt someone," he whispered.

"It hasn't hurt anyone."

"It tried to. The scarecrow and shop mannequin."

"But it's not going after people," she said.

"That may be its next step."

She sighed and looked down at the carpet runner.

"I will just advise him to report the break in to the police," Ambrose said. "It's up to them to figure it out."

It was the right thing to do, though she disliked it. "Fine, then. Are you going to be researching outdoors tomorrow? And might I join you?"

"I had thought of spending some time out of doors, yes." He patted her hand. "Don't fret, my dear. If the police haven't found the hound yet, they probably won't any time soon. It seems to be canny enough to avoid detection."

CHAPTER 24

O NCE THEY WERE HOME, CHLOE unfolded her copy of the map. Her eye caught on the place where she had marked the stone circle. Two days had already elapsed, and she dreaded defying Ambrose and going out without him. But this task was different. She opened up *A Dartmoor Companion* and double-checked her locations. The hound had visited the Aynesworth house and the bog where Camille had been found. It had also visited the dress shop, which, according to Mr. Lydford, was next to his shop. That was on the opposite end of town from the churchyard and far from the Hammond residence. Even so, crossing town was not too difficult on foot if you had the time.

There were no abandoned mines in or near the triangle created by drawing lines between the bog, town and the Aynesworth house. But if she added the Granger home as a fourth location, one mine came close.

The next morning, she and Ambrose drove out to the mine. A quarter of a mile away, they had to stop the steamcycle and leave it. The road to the mine was long overgrown and would have to be traveled on foot. Chloe pulled a lantern from the back basket and unwound the protective cloth that she had wrapped around it to keep it from rattling or breaking. She threw her satchel over one shoulder.

They passed scattered mortar stones in the grass and

the ruins of an ancient blowing house, where tin was smelted in centuries past. The entrance to the mine was clear of rocks or debris and the interior was cool and shady, if a bit musty.

Ambrose motioned for the lantern and lit it. "I'll go in first."

Many of the mine's overhead support beams were splintered or broken and in some cases, missing completely. The lantern threw lurching shadows on the walls and floor. They stepped around rocks, large pieces of rusted metal and other rubble. They ducked beneath a low-hanging beam and Ambrose stopped.

"It forks up ahead." His voice sounded startlingly loud in the silence.

He lifted the lantern, and the outlines of two equally black caverns emerged from the darkness. She did not want to go into either of them. They were already far underground, and the dark and the silence unnerved her. Besides, sometimes people disappeared in mines.

"Let's take a look around before we go any further," said Ambrose.

He examined the ground for tracks, and Chloe wished she had brought a second lantern. She glanced back the way they had come, and thought she saw something. But the light danced and waved in her husband's hand, and she couldn't be sure.

"Bring the lantern here. I think I see something. There appears to be a spot where the wall breaks off," she said.

She took the lantern. They retraced their steps until they came to a spot where a wide, flat board the size of a small table leaned close against the wall. It was as dark as the surrounding area, and with all the other debris, was easy to miss. Underneath it was a newspaper, partially torn, an empty can and some rocks.

She handed Ambrose the lantern and unfolded the paper. It was torn in various places.

"Do you think this is the paper that the hound used when it left those scraps at the bog?" asked Ambrose.

"I can't tell. I don't recall any dates on the scraps. Here's the date. This paper is a week old. But without the scraps, I can't compare."

"Do you remember any of the pictures or text from the scraps?" he asked.

"No."

"Neither do I," he sighed.

She wished she had taken the scraps when she had seen them. But it was too late now.

"The pages are torn, seemingly at random," he said.

"True. It could be the hound. Or rats could have torn it to make nests."

"No, rats would have nibbled at the outer parts. This was opened and then torn."

"It still leaves the question of who brought it here," she said. She folded it and put it in her satchel. "Let's just go down one of the forks a little bit. We'll turn back in a minute or two."

He paused, and she knew he was weighing his own desire to keep her safe, his own dislike of the mine and a burning curiosity. Curiosity won.

"Left or right?" he asked.

"You pick."

They moved to stand between the two forks and Ambrose smelled the air at each side.

"What are you doing?"

"Seeing if one is fresher. It means there would be an air hole somewhere. A second way out. If I were a creature hiding, that's what I would want. A rabbit warren always has a secondary egress in case the animal is trapped."

Chloe sniffed with him, but only detected the dusty, dank scent of old earth. They tried the right tunnel, but after the first turn, it was blocked by a cave-in. They turned back and went down the left tunnel.

An old rail track appeared a few yards down the tunnel, and they walked down the center, careful not to trip over the rail ties. Up ahead, a ceiling beam had fallen and blocked the path.

"We should go back," said Ambrose. "If the beams have broken, it could cave in."

"One moment," said Chloe. "May I have the lamp?"

Up against the wall and hidden by the fallen beam was a crate. Ambrose pulled open the lid. Chloe held the lantern up and smiled.

"There we are. More coins, paper scraps," she pushed things aside. "Is this a can of that solvent?"

Ambrose took the can and opened it. Inside was a dark powder, though she could not tell the color.

"It needs liquid to reconstitute it," he said. "Do you want to take it with us?"

"No. Let me take a sample though." She pulled an oily rag from her satchel and tapped a small pile of powder into it. She knotted the cloth and put it in the satchel. "If the hound comes back, I don't want him to get frightened off if his hiding place is disturbed."

"Do you think it would behave like that?"

"I don't know. I see that it is applying a repetitive behavioral pattern to new situations as it encounters them. And it is choosing to place objects in consistent hiding places."

"You are saying that the hound is thinking."

"No, this is different."

"How?"

"I don't know yet. It just is."

She was about to pull an old cloth out of the crate when she realized that something was wrapped inside. She unwound it and gave a low whistle.

"What is it?"

"Do you recall the object that Inspector Lockton showed us? I can't be certain, but I think this is the other part of it."

They exited the mine and rode home. Once in her temporary laboratory, Chloe pulled the curtains wide open, flooding the room with afternoon light. She set aside the handkerchief with the powdered solvent and set her tool kit on Ambrose's desk.

She put on her magnification spectacles and turned the knob at the corner. Lenses dropped down, one by one, until she had the correct level of magnification. She turned over the mechanical piece.

Ambrose appeared and set a cup of tea at her elbow.

"I hope you don't mind me using your desk. The light is better," she said.

"Not at all. Have you learned anything?"

"It's definitely the other part of Inspector Lockton's piece. The components and workmanship match up perfectly. But this one wasn't in the bog. No dirt inside."

"The hound could have washed it. Submerged it in a stream perhaps."

"Maybe, if it could hold it in its mouth. But more likely, it never fell into the bog."

She turned it over, and thought she caught a flash of green from within. None of the parts were that color. She turned it slowly, and heard the softest sound, as of a broken piece sliding. She unfastened a few screws and pulled the piece in half, then turned the bottom piece back and forth.

"Here we are," she said. She grabbed a pair of tiny pincers from her tool kit and pulled the green object out from where it had been nestled.

"A piece of glass?" Ambrose leaned in.

She set down the glass shard and searched through the mechanical piece but found nothing more. She flipped a few lenses on her spectacles back up and held the object at arm's length. She imagined Inspector Lockton's piece with it, and the whole joined together in her mind.

"Zoetrope," she said.

"Pardon?"

"I think this was a zoetrope. A wind-up rotating glass cylinder that has a gaslight inside. People have them as novelties, as decorations."

"I've seen them. My sister had one when she was a girl. Our mother would light it and wind it and Rose would watch the colored light dance on the walls when her room was dark."

"And did she take it with her when she married?"

"My God. Do you think it could be?" He reached to touch the piece, but then withdrew his hand.

"There's no way to know for sure. It's an older piece and it's definitely a zoetrope. But those are common enough household objects. And many families have older ones."

"You're sure of what it is?"

"Completely sure. If I had both parts, I could put it together myself. All we're missing is the mechanism casing, the gaslight and the glass cylinder." She reassembled the piece and wrapped it back in its cloth.

"No, just the mechanism casing and the gaslight," said Ambrose. "The glass cylinder was broken. There were glass bits in the hiding place by the bog, remember?"

"You're right." She picked up the wrapped piece of the zoetrope and put it in one of her open crates.

"You said in the mine that the hound hiding pieces of things or attacking human replicas wasn't thinking. What did you mean?"

"Hmm? Oh, I don't know." She took out Giles and pulled off his cover. She needed to see why he had chosen to destroy the garden. "I think there's a difference between thinking in the sense that we do and a creature applying repeating behaviors to situations that have similar characteristics. The hound seems to be finding patterns in unstructured environmental information and then deciding on behaviors. That's low-level data usage and organization. It's not really thinking."

"I fail to see the difference."

"It's like this. Imagine if I think of a word. The first part is a grass-eating bovine, and the second part is a young male human."

"A cowboy."

"Right. The hound, given enough information on its data spools could puzzle that out. It has a two-part puzzle that is easy to organize and solve in a linear fashion. Now, if I give the hound a pencil and ask it to draw something beautiful and something ugly, it cannot. The only way it could understand such concepts is through examples of each, which it would then apply in a repeating pattern."

"Then why do you treat Giles as if he is alive? You call him 'he' instead of 'it.'"

She shrugged. "Because he has the form of an animal with a sex? Because he behaves as if he is alive? You know, he likes windowsills and high places and dislikes the dark. He has memory and movement, which makes him different than a simple assembly of components. He doesn't seem like an 'it' to me."

"So he occupies an interstitial space between living thing and a non-living thing? Do you say he is a living thing or not?"

"That's your area of expertise, dear." She gave him a little smile. "Besides, what I call something has no effect on what it is. You can call the hound a murderer or a monster, but it is simply a mechanical. A wonderful, beautiful, clever mechanical. But a mechanical, all the same."

After a minute of Chloe working silently on Giles, Ambrose headed toward the door. He paused and turned back. "Is there any way we can know if the zoetrope was Rose's?"

She glanced at the crate that held the bundle. "I believe so, but you should probably do it. It involves talking with William."

He stuck his hands in his jacket pockets and sighed.

"My sister is a difficult topic between us. We've avoided it so far on this visit, and thus have remained cordial."

"If family peace is at stake, I can do it myself."

"As long as you don't stir up any ill feelings."

"I'll do my best."

CHAPTER 25

CHLOE PROMISED HERSELF THAT THIS would be the last time she kept something from Ambrose. But she would be home before it got too dark and with luck, he wouldn't notice.

She regretted that she had needed to cut short her visit to Lydford's Mechanical Shop. Mr. Lydford ran a clean shop, with decorative and household mechanicals filling the shelves at the front of the store. He was more than willing to chat about the machines and had even invited her to visit the back of the shop where he was repairing a few mechanicals and also had some projects of his own. Mr. Lydford had been disappointed that she had not brought Giles along for him to examine. Their time had passed too quickly and Chloe had needed to excuse herself.

Greater needs called her forth and she had to attend to one last, but vital, thing. She drove down a bumpy road, and then another until she was certain she was close to her destination.

She stopped the steamcycle and pushed its bulk down a little slope, just enough so that it would not be visible from a distance. Anyone close up would not miss it. She hoped that anyone else who was coming to the stone circle would be travelling on foot, and coming either from the side of the Aynesworth and Granger houses to the south, from town to the northeast or from the L-shaped road linking them. She put away her goggles and driving gloves and straightened her head scarf over her hair. She made sure the lantern and the flint lighter were in her satchel. She would need them later.

It was close to sunset and she hurried. She did not need to check her copied map as she covered the distance between herself and the stone circle.

She looked behind her often as she went, memorizing the exact path from the steamcycle. She would need to retrace her steps in low light. This area of the moors had more rock and grass than marsh and there were no bogs or fens that she could detect. She was grateful.

She hurried, becoming winded but pushing on. Time was short. As she crested a hill, the stone circle came into view. It was not as large or impressive as she had expected. The entire circle couldn't be more than a mere twelve yards across. Nine standing stones circled the perimeter, but there was no flat center stone, as she had anticipated. The stones were lumpy and irregular, like contorted dancers. They had no cross-stones resting between their tops, like the ones she had seen in pictures of Stonehenge. Aside from being ancient, the circle was neither particularly impressive nor intimidating. Nevertheless, she did not approach it.

She circled a little way around it until she found a hill to one side, a bit farther away than she liked, but high enough that she could see the circle. She lowered herself to her stomach, poking her head over the top of the hill and adjusting her position until she could see every part of the circle.

She had a moment of alarm when she heard snatches of voices and could not determine their direction. She turned behind her, but the area below her was empty. Spinning back around, she relaxed when she saw two men and a woman come from the direction of town. The woman cradled a white bundle against her body that appeared to be a baby. The group looked to be in conversation and just then, another snatch of sound carried to her. It was strange how the air currents worked here.

Chloe squinted and tried to estimate how long it would be until dark. There was no almanac in the library, so she had just done her best to estimate the time. She experienced another twinge of conscience, remembering that she had told Ambrose that she would visit Lydford's and return home before dark. With luck, the time between sunset and full dark would be enough for her to see what Mr. Granger and Mrs. Block, the Aynesworth housekeeper, were up to and then ride home before Ambrose was cross with her for traveling alone at night.

Four figures were approaching from the south. Of the group, one woman was plump and another smaller, lithe and thin. Both wore hats that blocked their faces, but she knew them by their shape alone to be Mrs. Block and her niece. The other two figures were not familiar, though they could easily have been two of the Aynesworth servants. There were other homes in the area, and since they were not in servant's uniforms, she could not be sure. The woman carried a large picnic hamper. The man carried a large cloth pack over his shoulder, like Father Christmas. It did not appear heavy and he moved easily.

The two groups converged and chatted just outside the stone circle. The sun was nearing the horizon when she saw a final figure, stout and male, appear from the south. He used a walking stick and his movements were slow and stiff. He did not raise his hand in greeting when the group hailed him, but gradually met up with them.

The man with the large pack moved to the center of the circle, and Chloe came to attention. He opened the pack and pulled out wood and kindling and set to making a fire at the center of the circle. The others gathered around and the woman with the picnic hamper set it down. Mrs. Block opened the hamper and pulled out a green wine bottle. She uncorked it and poured liquid into a wooden cup, but did not drink. She did not pour any for the others, but stood to the side with the cup, chatting with the woman who held the white bundle. The woman pulled back the covering a few inches and Mrs. Block nodded approval.

Chloe studied the bundle. It was the right size for an infant, though it appeared to be fast asleep and still. The woman held it cradled like a baby and never set it down or handed it to anyone else. But something about the way she held it was not maternal. And who carried a baby with a fold of cloth over its face?

The fire was crackling now and the sun had touched the horizon. At a word from Mr. Granger, the people fanned out in a circle around the fire. The woman handed the bundle to Mr. Granger, and he took it gently. He and Mrs. Block were at opposite sides of the circle, one to the east and one to the west. Once everyone was in place, Chloe saw the pattern. The fire was at the center surrounded by a circle of people who were themselves surrounded by the circle of stones. The symmetry might have pleased her, if her heart were not in her mouth. Why did Mr. Granger have that baby, or whatever it was in that bundle?

Mr. Granger spoke a few words which were lost in the wind. Then Mrs. Block spoke, and then Mr. Granger. They alternated like this for some time, with the other people occasionally responding with a word or phrase in unison.

Chloe thought she heard a scuffling behind her, but it was small and faint, like a mouse or vole in the underbrush. She ignored it.

Mrs. Block poured the cup of wine on the ground and said a few words. Mr. Granger then knelt and placed the bundle on the ground. Chloe raised her head a little more. Mr. Granger said a sharp word and one of the men broke out of the circle and rummaged through the picnic hamper. In his hand, Chloe caught the glint of steel in the firelight. The blade was larger than a kitchen knife, but not by much. Or did it only seem larger? The man handed the knife to Mr. Granger, who held it aloft with one hand. Chloe did not hear him say anything, but the other members of the circle spoke a word in unison.

The little white bundle remained still on the ground.

No, this could not be. She had read of such things in sensational novels and magazine articles, but she had enough sense to not believe them. Most of them anyway. She knew there were primitive tribes that performed cannibalism, and that her own Norman and Saxon ancestors had engaged in brutality of the worst sorts. But this was modern Britain.

The voices below rose in a rhythmic chant, one phrase over and over again. Bodies swayed, and the chant became a song, slow and rhythmic. It would have been pleasing to her ears if not for the knife and the poor creature inside the bundle. Mr. Granger opened the cloth, and in the light of the failing sun and the dancing flames, she saw what looked like a rounded head.

She leaped to her feet, staggered forward and drew breath to shout when something jumped into her field of vision. It passed her by a few feet and then turned to face her.

It was a wolf, no, a wild dog, standing tall and ferocious before her. Its black body was lit from behind, and she could only make out its silhouette and the glint of its eyes which were fixed upon her. It did not growl, but took a step toward her, and then stood, watching. Its complete lack of motion as it stared at her was unnerving. Then, its ears swiveled in a way all too familiar to her.

"My God," she whispered. "It's you."

CHAPTER 26

THE HOUND STOOD FROZEN, THEN bolted to the side and tore off around the edge of the hill. She could not call to it without risking being heard by the people in the circle. The people in the circle!

She leaped up the last few feet to the top of the hill. Mr. Granger was sawing into the thing lying on the cloth, blocking her view with his body. Oh God, please let it be a young pig or some other animal. Mr. Granger handed a piece to the person beside him, but there was no blood. The man took it, tore off a hunk and handed it to the next person. Mr. Granger then handed another large piece to the person on his other side, took a piece for himself and sat back. He took a bite.

In front of him, lying on the white cloth, was a bread man. It was now headless but it had arms and legs and was clearly a large loaf in the shape of a man. Oh, thank heavens. Her heart still beat hard in her chest and her hand was at her throat. She crouched down now, hoping no one had seen her.

Mrs. Block pulled cups from the hamper and filled them with wine, handing them around. When everyone had a cup and a hunk of bread, they all sat down. The ritual must be over, and they were chatting now, eating, drinking and laughing. In the flickering firelight, the shapes of their bodies, some wide and some narrow, resembled the stones.

Chloe walked the rest of the way down the hill. She

would have to think about Mr. Granger and Mrs. Block later. She circled around the hill, looking. How sensitive was the hound's hearing? She moved as softly as she could, and wished Camille had chosen a color other than black for the creature's covering. It could be anywhere in the gathering dark.

Perhaps the creature was shy, trying to avoid the people and would move away from the circle. But then why had it come so close to her? Unless it had not seen her. She had been holding very still, and though the hound seemed to be able to perceive patterns, she had been neither upright nor in a place that it would anticipate a human to be. Then she had jumped up.

She had been searching for a long while when she heard voices close by. She dropped behind some thick brush and held motionless. Twenty paces away, Mr. Granger, Mrs. Block, her niece and the two others were passing.

She had to get home soon. She could not risk being on the moors in full dark, not even for the hound. Once she was sure the people were gone, she went back in the direction of her original hiding place. The hound must have come from behind her, where the abandoned mine was. But where was it now?

When she reached the spot she had last seen the hound, she checked the circle. Everyone was gone, and the fire was extinguished. No sign of the hound. This was her chance to get a closer look at the circle. Had the hound only accidentally come upon the people, or had it been going on purpose?

As she walked toward the circle, she felt the air become suddenly colder. It was moist and touched her skin like soft, icy fingers. The scent of the earth and the moor grass was stronger here, and something was watching her, she could feel it. She kept moving, and the air warmed, but the feeling of being watched remained. This was ridiculous. The moor didn't watch.

The stones stood in pools of darkness, though the shadows were not sharply defined in this low light. There were only darker and lighter areas. It looked like the worshipers, for she was now sure that this was what they were, had left nothing behind. There would be no reason for them to return tonight, she hoped.

She was still outside the circle when she pulled out her lantern, lit it and held it aloft. Something was off about the stones, but what? She was one step inside the circle when she realized what it was. One of the dark areas at the base of a stone was too large. Something just the size of the hound was in its shadow, crouching.

Her thoughts raced to the store mannequin, then the scarecrow and to Camille's muddy corpse. She was suddenly not so sure of her safety. How certain was she, really, that the hound would not harm her? Had it been imitating the murder?

The hound rose and walked toward her. There were no squeaks or sounds. Its movements were as graceful and fluid as a real animal. Beautiful. It turned its head toward her, and in the lantern light, she saw the apertures in its eyes constrict and then dilate.

"Hello, beautiful. Come here." She put out her hand, as if toward a dog.

Its ears swiveled, and it turned away, toward the fire pit. It poked its paw in and started to scoop ashes into a pile. Smoke rose from the ashes and the hound stopped and sat back. She knew the ashes had to be scorching hot, but the hound had no ability to sense pain. Perhaps it had seen the smoke and stopped? If so, it was able to understand things that could harm it. How had it learned that?

"What are you doing?" she said. It lifted its head and watched her approach. She found a stick and squatted at the far edge of the fire pit. She stirred the ashes, studying the hound's reaction. Its visual apertures dilated and constricted, focusing as it studied the ashes, then her face.

"Now, what do you want with these?" she asked. The

hound stood again and pawed at the ashes. She scooted a few inches around the fire pit to be closer to it. She wracked her brains about the power switch on the creature, and thought she remembered it being underneath its body. Or was she mixing it up with Giles? If it was as strong as Giles, she could not overpower it, but maybe she could get a hand under it without it knowing.

The hound looked at her as she stirred the ashes again with the stick. She scooted closer when the hound pawed at them again.

"Are you cooling them? Is that what you're doing?"

They took turns stirring and pawing the ashes until Chloe had scooted up next to the hound. The creature was huge, as large as an Irish Wolfhound. His head was large but not blocky. Camille must have gone to great care to create the skull. Its ears were elegantly pointed, as was its tail. Its cloth covering was close-fitting, giving it a sleek and powerful appearance.

She placed her hand on its shoulder and it leaped up, backing away from the fire, crab-like until it got its footing.

"It's all right. I won't hurt you."

She stirred the ashes again. It watched the ashes, and if she hadn't known better, she would have said it desired them. But of course, a machine could feel neither desire nor repulsion. She kept stirring until it moved closer and was at the edge of the pit. It put its front paws into the pit, digging and digging until it had a new pile in front of itself.

Chloe pulled back in horror at what it did next. It opened its jaws. The action was unnatural and abnormally slow and its mouth opened far wider than it should have. Inside was a row of pointed wooden teeth set into its jaw with screws. The hound lowered his head and scooped a huge mouthful of ashes and then tipped its head back, closing its jaws slowly.

What in blazes was it doing? It couldn't eat. And even if it had been trying to imitate the action of another animal or a person, nothing ate ashes.

"Ashes. Ashes," she muttered. "Why ashes? You apply patterns, so have you done this before? Have you seen someone else do it?"

It had spent the most of its life with Camille. Why would she need ashes? Ashes were used in what? She thought. Gardening? She had heard of potash fertilizer, but was that really made of ashes? What else used ashes? Soap making. But Camille wouldn't have needed to make soap. But wait. Soap dissolved things because it was a base, an alkaline.

She thought of the bottle of potassium hydroxide and the murky liquid in the bottle in Camille's laboratory. Ashes could be used to create an alkaline fluid. They had been used in just such a way for centuries in soap making. And the solvents used in cleaning mechanicals, like the dark red powder she and Ambrose had found in the mine, were also alkaline.

The hound was eating, in a fashion. It was gathering items to make an alkaline solution, just like the one in Camille's battery, the battery that was inside the hound.

How sad. It could not possibly succeed. It must be imitating what it had seen Camille do but it was in vain. It could not actually open its own battery casing and work on itself.

The hound turned and started up the hill.

"Wait!" she called. It turned its head for a moment, and then was gone.

CHAPTER 27

CHLOE RACED THE STEAMCYCLE HOME, going too fast and hitting ruts and bumps much too hard. It was full dark, and though the headlamp illuminated the road, she knew Ambrose would not be pleased that she was out so late. It started to rain as she arrived home. She parked in the carriage house and hurried inside, pulling off her head scarf and coat as she came through the back kitchen door. Ambrose was not in the sitting room or in his temporary office. She opened the door to his rooms to find him reading in bed, Giles sitting on his nightstand.

"Isn't it a little early for you to turn in?" Chloe said.

"Yes, and I wish I didn't have to be here." He shivered and coughed into a handkerchief.

"You're sick." She sat down on the edge of the bed.

"Yes, and I hope by resting well tonight, I can be up and about tomorrow. How was your visit to town?"

"Fine, just fine. Is there anything I can get you?" She took in the cup of tea and glass of water on the bedside table. "Have you eaten?"

"Yes, I had a little supper. But I'm not very hungry."

He assured her twice more that he was in need of nothing before insisting on being left alone.

After breakfast, she made sure Ambrose was comfortable and then found William in his study. He sat in a brown leather chair with his ankle resting on his knee. A book was open in his lap.

"Excuse me," said Chloe from the doorway.

He looked up and registered a moment of surprise before rising and offering her a chair.

"I would like to ask you a question," said Chloe, seating herself. "I am in need of a certain set of parts that can be found in a zoetrope. They are one of the few household mechanicals with a rotational axis joint that I require. I was informed that you might have an old broken one about."

He assessed her and rubbed his beard. Her heart leapt to her throat when she thought he might see through her false request or think she was offensive to ask to destroy his belongings.

"No, I don't," he said.

"You don't have one, or you don't have one I may use?"

"Both. I used to have one, but even if it were still in my possession, I would not part with it. It belonged to my late wife."

"But you no longer have it?"

"As I said," he gave her a sharp look.

She had to be cautious.

"Could you tell me more about Rose? Ambrose says she was an extraordinary woman."

"She was extraordinary. She was as kind and good-natured a woman as ever a husband could wish. Although she had an independent streak that could cause tension."

"A trait she shares with her brother."

He smiled at that, and shook his head. "Her brother and I have not always gotten along, as I'm sure you know. Our natures seem to be incompatible. But Rose was devoted to him."

She knew better than to broach the subject of Rose's death and the circumstances surrounding her medical care, or lack thereof. How could she get William back onto the topic of the zoetrope? She could hardly mention that

Ambrose had told her that Rose had one without appearing monstrous to want to disassemble it.

"Did Rose enjoy plants as Ambrose does?"

"Yes, though she loved them for their own sake. She had no interest in classification and study. She merely saw and enjoyed. She painted them also. That's one of her paintings there." He motioned to a painting of a flower-carpeted hillside.

"Not unlike her brother. He draws, but does not paint. It looks like she had a love of beauty, light and color."

"Yes."

"And she had a zoetrope?"

He nodded. Now she was getting somewhere.

"Did it break?" She tried to look appropriately concerned without betraying her keenness to know exactly what happened to it.

"I suppose a servant broke it and threw away the parts. I noticed it was missing a fortnight ago. I asked Mrs. Block who then questioned the maids, but none of them admitted to it. Of course, they wouldn't be willing to get in trouble for breaking an item like that. It could be taken out of their wages."

"Of course." Chloe's heart was pounding. Camille had vanished from her house five days before Chloe had arrived. And she and Ambrose had been staying with the Aynesworths for eight days now, for a total of thirteen days. If the zoetrope had gone missing two weeks ago, then it would have disappeared around the same time Camille had vanished.

William spoke a little more of his wife, but Chloe was only half-listening. Someone had taken the zoetrope. It could possibly have been Camille or Mr. Granger who could have taken it during one of their visits to the Aynesworths. But that seemed unlikely. Was Camille desperate enough to steal to obtain money for her escape?

It was either that or a member of the Aynesworth family

had taken it outside. There was no innocent reason for that. Part of it had been found in the bog. Could it have been the object used to bash Camille's head? Her blood ran cold. If that was the case, then the killer was under this very roof.

Chloe checked on Ambrose and found him asleep. She touched his forehead with the back of her hand. He had a low fever. Well then, rest was best for him. It was better that he was asleep anyway. He would not approve of her planned activities. She placed a light kiss on his forehead and gently closed the door.

She got the zoetrope part out of her laboratory, dressed for a ride and took the steamcycle into town. She parked it outside of town with a stab of frustration. It was a longer walk this way, and she had too much to accomplish. But she felt bad enough without scandalizing the family by riding through town astride a roaring machine.

No one was smoking or sitting outside the police station this time, and she hurried inside and closed the door quickly behind her. The young man at the front desk was surprised to see her, but regained his composure when she asked to see the inspector. He went to fetch him.

"I did not think I would again have the pleasure," said Inspector Lockton. "Is Mr. Sullivan with you?"

"No, he is ill at home. I came alone. May we talk in your office?"

"Certainly."

He closed the door behind him and remained standing. Chloe lost no time, but set the bundle on the desk and opened it.

"This is the other half of the object you showed me the other day. It's a zoetrope. Do you know what that is?"

"No."

"It's a cylinder of colored glass set over a gas flame.

You light the flame, wind it and the mechanism turns the cylinder, creating a light display. Some of them have attached music boxes that play simultaneously."

"Oh yes, I have seen those. But how can you be sure? If we showed this to Lydford, Van der Smoot and Tucker, would they agree?"

"Yes, they would. There was also a piece of glass." She indicated the green shard that lay on the cloth with the piece. "It was trapped inside the mechanism. And, there were multi-colored glass pieces in a little hiding spot near the bog where they found Camille. It was definitely a zoetrope."

"What hiding spot?" His expression was sharp now.

"There's a rock formation between the bog and crossroads. Like a cairn. One of the stones moves, and there was a box lid inside with paper scraps, broken glass and other oddments. But the glass was gone when I checked a second time."

"Describe for me exactly where this place is. I will go out myself later to see."

She told him and he scribbled down a few notes. "It's odd that my men didn't find it. How did you?"

"I saw the footprints from the hound near the bog. It looked like it had been there repeatedly, circling and moving back and forth. So I took a look. That was all."

"You wanted to find the hound."

"Yes." There was no point in lying.

"Why?"

"I was afraid you would have it destroyed. Mr. Granger already destroyed Camille's notebooks and from her laboratory, and he said that he had instructed the police to destroy the hound. That creature is the only hope we have of understanding Camille's design."

"If the creature harmed a woman, then it ought to be destroyed."

"But it didn't! There's something else. The zoetrope

is from the Aynesworth house. It used to belong to my husband's late sister, Rose. She was William Aynesworth's late wife. The zoetrope went missing two weeks ago, and now it is found on the moor in pieces."

"So you don't think that the hound killed her because this thing was from the Aynesworth house?"

"I don't think it killed her because ..." she shook her head. She wasn't so certain any more that the hound was harmless. She remembered its strength and size, and the fluid motions of its body. She thought of its teeth and gaping jaws. "I think that you and your men should turn your attention to Mr. Granger or someone in the Aynesworth house. This zoetrope changes everything." She took a seat. "I see two possibilities."

He seated himself across from her. Nothing in his manner indicated condescension or scorn, but neither did he seem eager to hear her conclusions.

"Mr. and Mrs. Granger both came to the Aynesworth house as regular visitors. One of them could have taken the zoetrope. There would be no reason for Mr. Granger to do so, but Camille did have cause."

She told him about the box of money in the laboratory and her conversation with Nettie in the tavern.

"Camille could have stolen it to sell it," she said.

"And your second possibility?"

"Someone in the Aynesworth house. A zoetrope is heavy and mostly metal. It could conceivably be used to hit someone over the head."

"Why not just use a rock? Far less conspicuous. Far easier to hide afterward. And it wouldn't leave glass or metal fragments lodged in the skull."

"You're right." Of course. There would be no reason to use the zoetrope for such an act. She did not possess the understanding of the criminal mind that Inspector Lockton had.

After a silence, he went to his window and rested his

hand on the frame. "So a zoetrope from the Aynesworth house ends up in pieces in the bog, in a hiding spot nearby and—where did you find this piece?"

"The abandoned mine. Southwest of town. North of the Granger House. It's beyond this stone circle—"

"I know the one. Does your husband know that you have been somewhere so dangerous?"

"He was with me."

The corner of his mouth twitched. "You were looking for the hound in the mine?"

"Yes. I thought it might like sheltered places."

"But you did not find it."

"I would tell you if I had."

"Would you?" He turned to her. "Would you truly?"

She held his gaze. "Give me your word that you will not destroy it, and I will do my best to help you find it. Just find Camille's killer."

"I intend to. I presume you would want the creature for yourself after we examine it?"

She nodded. He looked back out the window and seemed to be debating something.

"I can make this agreement with you," he said. "If we determine that the hound killed Mrs. Granger, we must disassemble it. There could be no chance of it harming anyone else. Then, I am under the authority of my superior, and he might want to send the parts elsewhere for examination. But as much as it is within my power, I could try to see that you receive the pieces."

"And if you determine that a human was the killer?"

"Then the hound is yours. Just take it back to London."

"Agreed."

"Now, tell me why you think the zoetrope was from the Aynesworth house instead of somewhere else? They are fairly common, are they not?" he said.

"William Aynesworth told me that a zoetrope went missing two weeks ago. This one is an older model, as was the one that his wife would have had. The timing and age of the thing are too much to be coincidence."

"It's still circumstantial."

"So is the idea that the hound killed her with a rock or branch or its own foot?"

"True."

"There is something you are not telling me," she said.

"Naturally. This case is still under investigation and information is not available to the public."

"But I'm not the public."

"Of course you are." He had a tight smile. "I appreciate the information you have provided, but I cannot share the information of my own investigation. What I need the most from you is the location of the hound."

"I told you, the old mine. I think that's where it has been hiding. Also, it's trying to repair its battery. It appears to be trying to obtain substances that are alkaline, though there's no imaginable way that it could have the understanding to make changes to its battery array. It must be imitating what it saw Camille do when she created it."

"Extraordinary."

"You can see why I want to examine the creature so much. With the information on battery design, as well as how to create a complex decision engine, better mechanicals could be made. No people would ever have to go down into a dangerous mine again. And other manufacturing jobs that are dangerous or difficult could be performed by mechanicals. We could see this advance within our own lifetime. You see the people of this town. The injuries and the deaths."

For the first time, he looked at her with genuine surprise. There was admiration in it, and caution.

"Why does a woman of your station care about miners and workmen?"

"I was not always a woman of this station. And I would ask you to keep that to yourself, if you please. And even if I had always been in possession of wealth, I still have a keen interest in the well-being of my fellow man."

"That we share."

Of course, she thought. He solved crimes and protected the public. This grim and fastidious man had more in common with her than she had imagined. She felt like they had an understanding now, and though their stations would never permit them to have any other than the most fleeting acquaintance, under other circumstances, they might have been friends.

CHAPTER 28

CHLOE RODE AWAY FROM TOWN as fast as she dared and down the bumpy road to the mine. The previous night's heavy rain and the day's intermittent drizzle had soaked the dusty road and left puddles and slick, mud-filled ruts. She had to slow down repeatedly to avoid them, lest she risk an accident. If she was seriously injured, she could lie there forever before someone happened by.

But she could not turn back. Inspector Lockton's assurance that he would do his best to get her the pieces of the hound was not sufficient. Why hadn't she thought of it before? Lockton was a street officer in a small out-of-the-way town in the middle of nowhere. He didn't even have a name on his office door. Of course he would have superiors, and of course he would have to obey them. Since when would those in authority allow something like the hound to fall into hands like hers? If they didn't destroy the hound, it would be sent to a laboratory, most likely a military one. It would be lost to her forever.

She parked the steamcycle when the road became impassable, grabbed the lantern and flint lighter and hurried to the mine. Once inside, she lit the lantern and held it aloft. The air was colder than when she had come with Ambrose, and it seemed darker, though that must be her imagination. There was something else about the smell that seemed different. The air was heavier somehow.

"Hello!" she called. "Are you in there?" She tried to

keep her voice light and pleasant, hoping that it was how Camille had spoken to the hound. There was no sound.

The entrance shaft of the mine was just as she and Ambrose had seen it. There was no sign of the hound. As she went deeper, the play of light and shadow on the walls became disorienting. The crevices and rock formations bounced as she walked, though she tried to hold the lantern steady. She stopped frequently, listening and scanning the shadows for any sign of movement. She remembered how quietly the hound had come up behind her at the stone circle. It could move silently, and it did not want to be found.

At the fork in the tunnel, she stopped and smelled the air, just as Ambrose had. A sound came from the left fork, the far-off drip of water. Now she knew what the heavy smell in the air was. It was moisture. Of course, the rain had soaked the ground, so it would be dripping down, down until it reached groundwater.

Should she go left or right? If the hound was here and she picked the wrong tunnel, it could escape out the mine entrance. She had to think. If the hound was a creature of habit, and its crate of items was down the left tunnel, then that would be the most likely spot. But if it anticipated her move, it would have hidden down the right fork when it heard her. No, it was not capable of such complex reasoning. She descended down the left tunnel.

The sound of dripping grew louder, and now and then a drop splashed into her hair, down her collar or onto her outstretched arm. How many tons of water-soaked earth were over her head, held up only by splintered wooden beams and an age-old tunnel?

She traced the dripping sound to a broad puddle that stretched from wall to wall and far enough ahead that she would have to step in it to make it across. She crouched down. If she had to step through the puddle, so would the hound, and the surrounding earth was wet and a perfect place for tracks to be captured. Yes, there were prints, going both in and out.

She splashed through the shallow water until she reached the broken support beam. The crate was still there. She crawled over the beam and checked further down the mine, in case the hound was in the shadows, watching. A huge pile of debris blocked most of the path ahead. If she wanted to pass, she would have to climb over it, passing through an opening near the ceiling. She held up her lantern and a black rat dashed into a crevice. How agile was the hound? Would it be able to climb over an obstacle like this?

She did not want to go further. There was no telling if she could get back up the pile from the other side. If she was too heavy, the rocks could slide. And if her lantern broke, she could become lost. She knew she could eventually find her way out by keeping one hand on a wall and walking until she reached the entrance, but the thought of being trapped in the blackness frightened her.

The sound of water dripping had increased in pace and the air here was so wet and thick that she felt as if it could seep from her lungs into her very bones. No, she would turn back and then check the other tunnel. Besides, the crate was still waiting for her inspection near the fallen support beam. She turned back, climbed back over the beam and opened the crate.

"So much," she whispered as she sorted through paper scraps, whole newspapers, and pieces of glass, both clear and colored. There were wires, bottles, brass spools, a corked bottle of muddy water, coins and a few pieces of paper money. A large can held six inches of ashes. How many mouthfuls had it taken to get this much?

A chunk of mud plopped into the box, splattering her. She held up her lantern. The entire roof was heavy and shiny with water. The dripping of the puddle sounded faster now, almost a running trickle. By the time she passed it, it was running non-stop.

She rushed back to the fork, then down the right tunnel as quickly as she dared. She had to be thorough, or her trip would be in vain. She went all the way to the cave-in. Nothing. She hurried back out of the mine, sighing in gratitude at the first scent of fresh air and the gleam of daylight.

Emerging from the mine, she extinguished the lantern and moved into the daylight. The moor grass swayed in the wind and the clouds had parted just enough for sunlight to shine warm on the rocks of a distant tor. So why did she feel like something was wrong? She turned to look toward the top of the mine. Everything was still until two warblers tore into the air in a flutter of wings. She thought she heard the crunch of footsteps.

She climbed the hill, and as she rounded the top, she found herself looking into the eyes of a blackface sheep. It was alone, and raised its head to look at her.

"Where is the rest of your flock?" She knew next to nothing about livestock, but she knew that a lone animal had little chance of survival. She checked it for a brand mark on its rump. Did people brand sheep? She watched it take a few steps and she checked its legs for injuries. It appeared healthy.

She should head home, but she couldn't leave the creature out here alone for wolves or wild dogs. But what was she going to do, load it onto the steamcycle and give it a ride to the nearest farm?

"You wouldn't thank me for that," she said and pulled up a handful of grass. It sniffed it and lowered its head to graze. She patted its back.

"Hello there!" cried a woman's voice, and Chloe spun around to see a tiny old woman striding toward her, her arm raised in greeting. The woman's gray hair was loose and flying wild in the wind. Her wide-spaced dark eyes stayed fixed on Chloe as she walked. She neither hesitated nor looked at the ground as she closed the distance between them.

"You seem to have found my sheep," she said, smiling with a mouth full of yellowed, square teeth.

"I thought it was lost."

"She was. Got separated from my flock." She placed her hand on the back of the sheep's neck and leaned down until they were almost forehead to forehead. She made a little noise in the back of her throat, and straightened up. The sheep butted its head against her hip.

"Why are you here?" she asked, still looking at the sheep. Then she turned her eyes to Chloe.

"Er, I was looking for something. Looking for the mechanical hound. Have you seen it?"

"Are you hungry?"

"Pardon?"

"Do you want something to eat?" the woman said. "You're out here alone, your face has a little bit of mud splattered on it, your feet are filthy and I know you're not from here. So do you want some tea or a bite to eat?"

"Do you live nearby?"

"My cottage is a bit that way," she pointed. "Least I can do for taking care of my sheep."

"Oh, I didn't do anything for it."

"You tried to feed it, and you looked it over for injuries."

How good was this woman's eyesight? She had to be at least eighty, but she moved like a younger woman.

"I have fresh honey too," the woman said.

"That would be lovely. Thank you." Chloe followed the woman down the hill. If anyone had seen the hound, it would be this woman. And she had never seen one of the local farmhouses before. She wouldn't stay long.

"I know where I've seen you before," said Chloe. "Were you at Mrs. Granger's funeral?"

"That I was. You were there?" Something about the way she said it was too casual. Chloe suspected that the woman had remembered her on sight.

"Yes. I'm a friend of hers. I'm Chloe Sullivan."

"Maggie."

"A pleasure to meet you."

Maggie moved on, the sheep trailing at her heels without any encouragement. They walked in silence until they reached a small thatched-roof cottage. Who still used thatch for roofing in this day and age? Maggie opened the front gate for the sheep, and it trotted around the back of the house, presumably to its pen.

The ancient house was squat and sturdy. Moss grew on one side in a few crevices between the wall stones. Wind chimes jingled from the eaves in between hanging pots of plants, their tendrils swinging in the breeze. Cats of all colors lounged in shadows and sunlight, on windowsills and on the doorstep. At Maggie's approach, a few rushed forward and circled her legs. Gangly shrubs lined the cracked rock path to the front door, which Maggie opened for her.

"Make yourself at home, I'll make some tea." Maggie went to put on the kettle.

The interior of the house was cramped, but clean. The front room held a few chairs, a table and a large rug. At the back of the room, a patterned cloth hung over a doorway to what she presumed was the bedroom. A cat slept in the center of the kitchen table. Maggie pushed it aside, and it stretched and moved a few inches before settling back and closing its eyes.

"You live here alone?" asked Chloe.

"I'm the only person, but I'm not alone, no." She moved her hand to encompass the dog at the kitchen hearth and the cat on the kitchen table. "So you were a friend of Mrs. Granger?" said Maggie.

"Yes. I had hoped to spend some time with her while I was visiting. We both make mechanicals."

"Oh, do you now? Like that dog she made?"

"You've seen the hound?"

"Hound? Like the old ghost story?" She laughed and shook her head. "You like biscuits?"

Chloe said she did. Maggie opened the kitchen cabinet and revealed row upon row of mismatched herb jars, some filled all the way to the top. It was far more than any person would need for personal cooking. She had heard of people using old plant remedies instead of modern medicine, but she could not fathom why anyone would do so. Why not avail one's self of the best and most modern cures? Perhaps the poorer people in town could not afford a decent doctor.

Maggie arranged biscuits on a plate, poured hot water into the teapot and set it on the table with two cups and a pot of fresh honey. "Now, tell me about your friend Mrs. Granger."

"What do you want to know?"

"That invention of hers. They say it killed her."

"And you believe them?"

"No, but I want to know if you do," said Maggie.

"I think it was a person."

"And who do you think it was?"

"I don't know. I'm hoping the police can figure it out." Chloe nibbled on a biscuit.

"And that's why you have come out on the moor a number of times, alone or with someone, poking about?"

"I'm trying to find the hound."

"You want to know how she built it? Is that why?"

"Have you been talking to the people in town? To the police?" Chloe was distinctly uncomfortable. Maggie knew more than she was letting on, and something about her questioning was too intense. There was something else also, but she couldn't put her finger on it.

Maggie poured the tea and placed a cup in front of her. For an instant, Chloe wondered what sort of herbs were mixed with the tea leaves.

"I talk to everyone," said Maggie. "But not to the police. Not recently anyway. There are people all over the moor, watching. They like you." She stroked the cat on the table.

"The townspeople have not shown any great love of me. The police even considered confiscating my mechanical cat." She did not mention the fallen women or drunken men she had encountered that night in town.

"Oh, it wasn't them I was talking about. Now, tell me about the Aynesworths."

"You don't know them? They've lived here for years."

"Oh I know them. Our families have been neighbors for generations. I wanted to know what you thought of them."

Chloe was getting weary of this. "I like them well enough. Why don't you stop asking me questions and tell me something?" She set her teacup down. "What happened to Camille Granger?"

"Hoo, hoo! You're very blunt for a lady." She chuckled and sipped her tea."If I knew, I'd be telling the police."

"But what about these people who live on the moor? Have any of them seen anything? Have any of them reported anything unusual to the police?"

Maggie giggled. "No, they don't talk to the police. No." She continued chuckling for awhile longer, as if Chloe had said something quite humorous.

The woman was clearly a lunatic. Chloe looked out the kitchen window. Outside, she could see a row of beehives up the hill and a small shed closer by. On the windowsill was a round stone with a single hole through the center. It was the same size and shape as the one Mrs. Block wore on her key ring.

"What is that stone?" she pointed to it.

"Oh that? It's my hag stone. Keeps away evil spirits."

Ah, country folk superstition. She thought back to the stone circle, but Maggie had not been among the worshipers.

"There's a stone circle nearby. Do people still go to it?"

Maggie's gaze fixed on her with such intensity that she

was afraid for an instant. The old woman knew she already had the answer.

"You want to know why, in this day and age, anyone would have old meetings and things like hag stones? You grew up in the city, yes?"

Chloe nodded.

"Well, that place changes with the times. This place doesn't. Simple as that. Different places have different rules, if you understand my meaning."

Chloe didn't, but wasn't about to ask and listen to Maggie go on about piskies or sidhe or whatever superstitious nonsense she believed.

"I need to find the hound," said Chloe. "Have you seen it? Or do you know where it might be?"

"I've seen it a few times, and some of the bees were telling me about it going far south of here, all the way to the Granger house."

Talking bees. Delightful.

"I think I should be getting back home," said Chloe, rising. She couldn't waste time with a mad old woman, even a relatively benign one. She needed to keep looking for the hound.

"Wait a moment, I have something for you." Maggie opened the cabinet, took a jar and tapped some of the dusty green contents into a paper. She folded it into a packet and handed it to Chloe. "I heard your husband is sick. Make a tea of that. It's nothing much, just something to help him rest."

Chloe thanked her and Maggie followed her out the front door.

"Your motorcar thing is that way," Maggie pointed. "It's very shiny. I like it. You made that too, didn't you?"

"I did."

"I can see why they like you, even if that thing is too loud. You're a strange one, you are. Anyone tell you that?"

"I could say the same about you."

Maggie's eyes were round, and for an instant Chloe thought she had angered the woman. Then Maggie roared with laughter, one hand on her heart.

Chloe let herself out the front gate and turned to see Maggie scoop up a cat and go inside, still chuckling.

CHAPTER 29

C HLOE CHECKED A FEW OTHER places, but saw no sign
of the hound. She was about to turn down another
side road, when the engine began to make a terrible
grinding sound. Her heart sank. She had been driving the
poor machine too hard. No wonder it was having trouble.
She hoped there would come a day when her machines
did not require so many repairs. But the steamcycle was
a prototype, and with each malfunction she improved
upon it.

She drove it home and parked it on the side of the
house. Before she went into her laboratory for her tool
box, she checked on Ambrose. He was in his room, sitting
in his dressing gown near the window, a book and a note
pad balanced on his lap. Chloe waited until he looked up.

"Feeling better?" she asked.

"Some. I cannot abide being confined like this. I had to
get out of that bed or go mad."

She felt his forehead, and he waved her hand
away impatiently.

"You still have a fever," she said.

"I know. I know. Leave me be. More importantly, I had
an idea about Giles. Correct me if you believe I am in
error, but could he have been imitating the hound when
he tore up the garden?"

"You believe that he saw the hound do it, and then
copied it?"

"Exactly."

She thought about it. "That would mean that Giles is intentionally copying the behavior of a similar creature. Yes. It could be. So he's not malfunctioning. He's trying to learn. That's wonderful!"

Ambrose gave a weak smile at her delight. "He has been a good companion for me today." At the top of the armoire, Giles sat as prim and straight as an Egyptian statuette.

"You aren't a naughty boy, are you?" said Chloe.

"Brrr."

"This is fantastic," she said. "Do you mind if I take him outside? I have to work on the steamcycle this afternoon. Giles can sit and watch the birds."

"Be my guest."

Chloe ordered up a pot of tea, made the bed and opened the window a crack to get him some fresh air. She felt his forehead again.

"Enough! I'm well enough to be downstairs for supper. Now go work on your machine and stop moving around like a worried hen. It's making me dizzy."

She kissed his cheek and went outside to pull the steamcycle to the back corner of the house. She spent the afternoon in her work corset and rough skirt, the engine in pieces on the ground and her tool box open beside her.

At the table on the back lawn, Ian and Beatrice were chatting while he read a newspaper and she embroidered. Beatrice waved when she saw Chloe watching and Chloe smiled, her hands engaged in inserting a loose piece of tubing into a coupling. Giles was sitting on the brick garden border, and he alternated watching his mistress and Ian and Beatrice.

The back door opened and the butler appeared. "You have a visitor, sir," he said to Ian. He had no silver tray or card.

"A visitor? Who is it?"

The butler paused. "He is waiting inside."

Beatrice was looking at the butler with a cold expression. Chloe knew that it was not typical for a servant to avoid a direct question and withhold the identity of a caller. Once the butler and Ian were gone, Beatrice rose in a swirl of pink and cream and approached Chloe.

"Would you care to take a stroll to the front of the house?" she asked, with a look of mock innocence.

"Who do you think is here?"

"I don't know, but the butler obviously thought it might be indelicate to say. So naturally, I have to know."

"Naturally," said Chloe and wiped her hands on a spare rag.

They strolled around the side of the house and took a look at the front drive. A sturdy bay mare was tied up, placidly munching at the plants.

"Do you know whose horse that is?" asked Chloe.

"No. But let's take a walk down the drive. I'm in need of a bit of fresh air. It benefits the lungs, you know."

They strolled down the drive, taking time to pause and watch Giles bat at bobbing flowers or scamper around their feet.

"Does Ian get visitors often?" asked Chloe.

"No. Hardly ever, unless it is household business. I'll tell you what I am thinking. I think the visitor might be for Alexander, but he is in town today. So they would have to talk to Ian. But since it may involve Alexander, I'm curious."

Poor Beatrice. Had she heard about the rumors of Alexander and Camille Granger being paramours? Chloe hoped not.

"Why not speak with William?" Chloe asked.

"Oh, Ian handles everything in the household now. He has for years."

At the sound of the door opening, both women turned to see a small, lean man in a brown suit. He placed his hat over his balding head, adjusted it and untied the mare.

"That's Doctor Fleming," said Beatrice.

As he rode toward them, Beatrice smiled broadly, the perfect hostess.

"It is a pleasure to see you, Doctor."

He stopped and touched his hat. "My apologies, Mrs. Aynesworth, but I cannot stay. I have an urgent errand. Good afternoon."

"Good afternoon," Beatrice said and he rode down the drive. She stared after him for a while and murmured, "Strange."

"Who do you think is sick?"

Beatrice shook her head, and there was something in her look that took Chloe by surprise. It was a look of determination and ferocity. But there was apprehension also. "Let's find out."

Ian was sitting in the front parlor, his head in his hands. He looked up at them as they entered, and started to rise.

"No, no. Please sit," said Beatrice. She lowered herself beside him, and at his look of anguish, she drew back. "What is it?"

"Nothing." He looked at the carpet, trying to regain himself.

"Ian, please."

He shook his head. "My brother is fine, as is everyone in the household. It's nothing."

"Has someone died?"

"No."

"Then why—"

"I'm sorry, Bea. You will have to trust me," he said.

She studied his face, and something passed between them. After a few moments, Beatrice nodded. There was some kind of understanding between them, perhaps born of their years under the same roof or their shared relationship with Alexander.

"I will be upstairs," Ian said and rose. "Excuse me," he whispered as he swept past Chloe.

Beatrice was motionless, lost in her own thoughts. Chloe thought of asking her about the exchange, but knew she would get no answer. She left Beatrice to her silence and her thoughts.

She got back to work on the steamcycle. After replacing the defective gears and tightening the fastenings, she had only to put everything back together. This part of the work was simple and required only a small amount of concentration.

Chloe was fairly sure that Beatrice knew about Ian's rides. Beatrice had not been happy to let Ian leave the parlor without saying why the doctor had come, but she had accepted it. There was a trust between them, though it had been difficult for Beatrice to allow him his silence. Chloe did not think she could have done it. She would have demanded an answer. But then, Beatrice was a woman of discretion, prudence and self-control. Chloe wished she had more of those qualities.

Chloe fit the final piece into the engine with a sharp click and fastened on the cover. Daylight was fading, and she was stiff and tired from being bent over half the day. She would have to test the machine tomorrow. She rolled it to the carriage house and checked her pocket watch. She had an hour until supper to clean up.

She was on her knees, packing up her tool box when she heard the back door bang closed. She froze when she saw Alexander following Ian out across the back lawn. Ian turned to face his brother. She saw Ian's mouth move, but could not hear what he said. Alexander stepped forward and jabbed a finger into his brother's chest.

"She's no better than she should be. I don't see why you have to upset everyone with this."

She heard the low rumble of Ian's voice, and was taken aback at the fierce coldness in the way he looked at his brother. Alexander's face was red, and he was shaking with rage.

"How in hell should I know?" Alexander threw up his hands. "You are the one who brought this to our doorstep! You are the one who created this." He turned away and headed for the house.

Ian shouted after him, and this time, his words were clear. "There is no family. And she is a little girl."

Alexander spun around and came at Ian. Chloe thought for a moment that the brothers would come to blows. Ian was a few inches taller than his brother, though Alexander was broader across the shoulders. Ian said something that she could not catch. The men glared at each other for a moment more and Ian spun on his heel and strode toward the stables.

"Come back here and say that! You come right back here!" shouted Alexander, but Ian was gone.

Alexander slammed the door, and she was left alone. Giles turned his head and swiveled his ears.

"Best forget you saw that," she whispered.

She took her time packing the rest of her tools, not eager to encounter Alexander if he was in the hallway. She opened the door to find that he was gone.

Before she pulled the door shut behind her, Chloe caught a glimpse of Ian on horseback, galloping at full speed past the house, earth flying from his horse's hooves.

CHAPTER 30

THE SUPPER TABLE WAS ONLY set for five: William, Dora, Robert, Ambrose and Chloe. Beatrice was not feeling well and Mrs. Malone was taking her supper upstairs. Alexander was holed up in his study and no one knew where Ian might be. Chloe thought it prudent to keep silent on the matter.

Dora picked at her steak and greens and glanced at her father a number of times. He eventually acknowledged her and gave her a nod.

"I don't know if you have heard," she said to Chloe, "but Mr. Granger has been brought in for questioning for Camille's murder and I heard that they might formally accuse him."

"You're joking," said Chloe, though she knew Dora was not.

"No. It happened this afternoon. There was something about a letter proving that Camille had a paramour." She muttered the last words and her father gave her a sharp look.

It was Saturday, the day that Nettie said she would be leaving with Tommy for Gretna Green. So she had decided to talk to the police after all.

"But what proof do the police have?" asked Ambrose. Though he was able to sit at the table, it was clear that he was ill. Chloe noted that he had only eaten a few bites.

William cleared his throat. "The police believe that

Mr. Granger killed her in a jealous rage when she was about to run off with another man. He must have lured her outdoors, where he killed her and hoped to dispose of her where she would not be found. Very upsetting. Most upsetting." He shook his head.

Chloe chewed thoughtfully. If Mr. Granger had hoped to keep the body concealed, why had he chosen a bog that was so near the road and so close to the hiding hole in the rock cairn? Something about it wasn't right.

"Will he hang?" asked Robert, his expression was full of dismay and compassion.

"Most likely," said William gently. "If he took the life of an innocent woman, then justice must be done."

"I would hardly call her innocent," said Dora. "If she had a paramour."

The look her father gave her was unexpected. William was not angry at such a crude remark during supper. Nor was he saddened or indignant at Camille's indiscretion. Rather, his expression was confused and surprised. He looked at Dora as if she had said that the moon was made of cheese. Dora raised her chin a fraction and met his gaze.

Again, Chloe had the distinct feeling that there was something passing between two people to which she would never be privy. Robert was watching them, and for an instant before he looked away, Chloe saw pure fury in his face.

A moment later, the penny dropped, and Chloe understood why Beatrice and Mrs. Malone were not at the table, and why Robert might be so angry. If the town gossips knew about the letter, surely they also were speculating on the gentleman who wrote it. Nettie's opinion, whether right or wrong, would be picked up and repeated. It was too delicious a piece of gossip. And Nettie had said she thought the author was Alexander.

Poor Beatrice.

Ill though he was, Ambrose had not missed the

exchange. Chloe wondered if he had come to the same conclusion about Beatrice, but could not ask. He cleared his throat. "I will be absent for supper tomorrow night," he said. "I'm meeting with your fiancé, Dora, to discuss a few things."

Dora registered a look of alarm. "Why? What do you have to discuss?"

She must have been afraid that Ambrose would say something unflattering about her or her family. A man with Mr. Baxter's wealth could break off an engagement without too much damage to his own reputation. The scandal would be minimal. But for Dora, the stakes were much higher. Her years of marriage eligibility were shrinking and wealthy men were in short supply.

"Only business matters," said Ambrose. "Otherwise, of course, he would be calling on you as well. In a few months, he and I will be family, after all. And during his visit a few days ago, we found that we both have connections that may be mutually beneficial. He knows a few people of high standing in Boston, and I am hoping that people at the university there may be interested in some of my books and papers. It would be a singular opportunity to be published in America.

"As for Mr. Baxter, I know a few gentlemen from my club in London who may be interested in investing in some of his mining projects. Also, I am interested in this sickness his workers encountered. I can't resist a botanical puzzle, I suppose."

"Would you tell me anything you figure out?" said Robert.

His father's fork stopped on the way to his mouth. "I don't think that will be necessary. You ought to be keeping up on your regular studies while we find you a new tutor."

"Yes, father," said Robert, and again, Chloe saw the flash of anger as he looked down at his plate.

For the rest of supper, Chloe's thoughts churned. She had brought evidence to Inspector Lockton that the zoetrope found with Camille and in the hound's mine came from the Aynesworth house. That would have little or no connection to Mr. Granger, unless he had stolen the thing on one of his visits. And what cause would he have for that? Mr. Granger may have had the motive, means and opportunity, as the police said in the shilling shockers. But, as Inspector Lockton had noted, the evidence was still circumstantial. Had his superiors pressured him for an arrest, or did he have information that she did not?

"I suppose you are pleased that the hound has been found innocent?" asked Ambrose as they climbed the stairs after supper. He paused on the landing to catch his breath.

"Yes and no. I don't think that Mr. Granger killed her."

"Because of the zoetrope?"

"Yes. I don't know. I suppose it could be nothing. A servant could have stolen it and sold it and it ended up out on the moor. It could be unconnected."

He took her arm and climbed the rest of the stairs. "It seems like too much of a coincidence to be nothing," said Ambrose. She helped him to his rooms and into bed. The effort of going down to supper had taken a toll on him. She pulled the blankets up over him. His eyes were already half closed.

"I'll let you sleep," she said. She refilled his water glass and left him to rest.

She was about to go to her laboratory, when she paused. She was fond of Beatrice. Though she had smiled at Dora's cruel comment over supper on the first night of her visit, otherwise she had been pleasant company. She must be suffering terribly.

Chloe knocked on Beatrice's door. No sound came from inside, but then the door flew open. Mrs. Malone scowled at her.

"I came to see Beatrice," said Chloe.

"She is not feeling well."

"Let her in, Mother," called Beatrice from behind her. "I'm sure she has figured it out."

Mrs. Malone stepped aside and Chloe passed into Beatrice's room. It was larger and more opulent than Chloe's room but then, this was no guest room. It was half of the grand master suite. Alexander's rooms would be through the side door. Beatrice caught her looking at the door and buried her face in her hands. She slumped on a settee under the window, the light behind her making a frizzy halo of her disheveled hair.

Chloe realized that she had not thought of a single thing to say. She seated herself beside Beatrice and put an arm around her shoulders. Mrs. Malone took the chair across from them.

"Mrs. Sullivan, you've been married a while, haven't you?" asked Mrs. Malone.

"Three years."

She pressed her lips together lightly and nodded. "Now Bea, when I had been married three years, there were rumors."

"About Father?"

"Yes, but I paid them no mind."

"Because they were untrue!"

"No, because I am a lady. And so are you."

Beatrice shook her head and Mrs. Malone reached her hand to pat her daughter's knee. "It's a hard truth, Bea. But one you will grow accustomed to."

"I don't want to be accustomed to it! It's shameful."

Mrs. Malone glanced at Chloe for help. Chloe was taken aback. She had never seen the old woman be anything but in complete control.

"It's no shame on you," said Chloe. "Everyone knows that you are a good wife. It's just the way some men are."

"Not your husband, surely," Beatrice snapped and glared at her. "I would bet he doesn't have dalliances with other women."

How to respond to that? Beatrice's anger was not directed at her personally, but the woman's fierce stare was unsettling. Then Beatrice's shoulders fell and she shook her head.

"Not all men are the same," Mrs. Malone said. "And Mr. Sullivan is also a lot older than Alexander."

Chloe doubted that Ambrose had betrayed his first wife, even when he was young. And age would not stop an unfaithful man until he became too decrepit to do any more damage. It was a sad fact of life that many women had to accept.

"But Alexander says he loves me."

"And no doubt he does," said Mrs. Malone. "You don't know for certain that the letters were from him. It's just gossip."

"But everyone else thinks they're from him."

"And what if they do? Your best recourse is to hold your head up and act with grace. Then if they are correct, you can keep everyone's respect. And if they are wrong and the letters are from someone else, it will seem as if you knew all along that it wasn't your husband."

Beatrice sniffed and blew her nose delicately into a handkerchief and then wadded the damp thing in her fist. "I think they are from him," she said, barely audible. "I ... suspected. I saw them together, laughing. She came over often, sometimes a few times a week, to see Dora or me, but she would eventually find him, or he would find her, and they'd talk and laugh over things."

Mrs. Malone's face darkened. "Well, that's not real proof. Alexander laughs with many people, men and women."

"Oh Mother. How can I keep from it happening again?"

"If I knew the answer to that, my poppet, I'd tell you in a heartbeat. But sometimes the only way a man can find to reinvent himself is to see a new man reflected in a different woman's eyes."

"You said that before."

"Because it is true. Just watch. Once Dora is married, I would bet you'll hear a rumor or two. And she'll ignore the rumors, just as I did and just as you will do."

"But I married for love. Dora has entrapped Mr. Baxter with her wiles and by saying cruel things about other women. Neither of them are entering into the arrangement with an expectation of his fidelity."

Ah, so the Aynesworth family was aware of Mr. Baxter's character. Chloe was relieved that she was not tasked with revealing it to them.

"We really are fortunate, the three of us," Mrs. Malone said, looking to Chloe and then to her daughter. "We are secure and both of your husbands are kind to you. If you hope for perfection, you will be miserable all of your days. Many women have cruel husbands. Vicious husbands. Gamblers who leave them in cruel financial straits. And those men spend time with other women on top of that." Mrs. Malone was warming to the topic. "The best you can realistically hope for is security and respect. Alexander respects you, and you are taken care of. A true gentleman won't flaunt his indiscretions and he would never be deliberately cruel."

Beatrice wiped her eyes and fixed a steely gaze on a painting on the wall. A flicker of something passed in her face, just for a moment, and then it was gone. Then her face was again a mask of pain and she dabbed the corners of her eyes. She rose and smoothed her dress.

"I'm going to freshen up," she said.

"You do that," said her mother. "It will make you feel better."

Beatrice passed through a side door, the one on the opposite side from Alexander's room. Chloe saw her approach a mirrored vanity and heard the splash of water in the basin. How fortunate she was that Ambrose was nothing like those other men. He never would have caused her so much pain. And even if he could have been certain that she would have remained ignorant, it was simply not in his internal makeup to do such things.

Mrs. Malone heaved a heavy sigh. "I knew the day was coming. I knew before they were married that Alexander might do this. And though Beatrice isn't a young girl, she still holds some girlish notions. I suppose it was time for her to grow up and learn the way things are."

"She said she suspected something before. Do you think she knew?" Chloe recalled with a chill the look on Beatrice's face.

"I do not know. If she knew, she didn't speak to me about it. But sometimes we suspect things, deep in the back of our minds and we don't recognize them until they come true." Mrs. Malone's hands clenched in her lap. "As a Christian woman, I should not say this, but perhaps Mrs. Granger's death wasn't all bad. She is no longer around to disrupt the household any longer. She was so charming and lovely, even if she was a little older. Men can't help themselves around a woman like that. And for her to come over, accept Bea's hospitality, and then lure her husband away. It's terrible. Simply revolting."

Chloe was not tempted to defend her friend. If Camille had tempted Alexander, then she was not the person Chloe had thought her to be. But then, so much of Camille's life had been a shock to her. Days ago, Mrs. Malone had been correct in her assessment that Chloe had not known Camille Granger at all.

CHAPTER 31

THE NEXT MORNING, THE FAMILY gathered for breakfast before going to church. Only Ambrose and Mrs. Malone were absent, the latter taking her time in descending from her room. Beatrice looked fresh as she nibbled at her toast. Her husband sat beside her, his manner cautious even as he leaned toward her and spoke in low tones. Though her cheeks were pink, her small smile reminded Chloe of a marble statue, whole of form, but without life.

Fascinated with the pattern on the rug, Giles walked the perimeter, pawed at a corner and walked the perimeter again.

Upstairs, Ambrose was in bed, his eyes dull and his skin ashen. Chloe had not needed to persuade him to stay home from church. She hesitated to leave him, but aside from ensuring that he ate and drank a little, there was nothing more for her to do. She set a few interesting-looking books on his nightstand and asked his valet, Mr. Frick, to check on him.

Mrs. Malone strode into the dining room and nearly tripped over Giles, who leapt sideways with a metallic yowl. Mrs. Malone cried out in alarm and bumped into a chair, losing her balance. Chloe darted forward, grabbing Mrs. Malone's elbow and held her firmly until Mrs. Malone managed to steady herself. No sooner was the crisis averted, then a crash sounded from behind Mrs. Malone.

A serving mechanical swayed drunkenly in the doorway.

Giles scrambled for purchase on the mechanical's flat top, finding his balance amid the teacups, saucers and a steaming teapot. The mechanical teetered sideways as Giles shifted his weight, his legs splayed and his tail pointing straight up.

"No!" Chloe cried and ran to grab the cat. Thankfully, Giles did not struggle as she lifted his stiff and straining body, but as she lifted his weight from the still-wobbling tray, the serving mechanical overcompensated for the sudden imbalance and tipped sideways. She lunged for the tea set, throwing her arm around the mass of dishes to try to catch them all. The teapot was the heaviest, and as it hit the thin brass railing at the edge of the mechanical's flat top, it flipped over, pouring boiling water over her arm.

Her burning sleeve clung to her skin. She sucked air in through her teeth, only just managing not to scream. Pulling desperately at the cloth, she managed to peel her sleeve up to her elbow. The delicate skin of her inner arm was a furious red, and hurt like the devil.

Alexander was at her side in an instant. "Are you all right? Let me see." He took her arm with gentle fingers and shook his head. "Mrs. Block can help with it. I think it's bad."

Chloe knew that already. "Thank you. I'll find her."

Alexander insisted on walking her to the kitchen. Pots and pans hung from rows of hooks and all of the dishes were dried and neatly stacked in preparation for luncheon after church. Mrs. Block was chatting with the cook. She turned, and her smile faded as she saw Chloe clutching her arm. She wiped her hands on her apron and hurried forward to get a better look.

"Ah, that's a good one. How'd it happen?"

"I knocked over the teapot. It was stupid of me."

"Now, now. I can't count on both hands the number of times I've been distracted and burned myself. See?" She pointed out two old rubbery scars on her own forearm. "No shame in it. Now let me get something before it blisters."

Alexander saw her to a chair and left her to Mrs. Block's tender ministrations. Her bulk disappeared into the pantry and Chloe heard her searching through the bottles and boxes that lined the shelves.

"We've got onions that I can put on it, but they're not chopped yet. I do have some treacle though."

She saturated a clean cloth with treacle and pressed it over the burn. Chloe flinched as the scratchy cloth made contact, but then relaxed as a cooling sensation spread over her skin.

"Now that's just for now, to take the heat out," Mrs. Block said. "I'll make you a poultice, but it takes a little while to prepare." She disappeared back into the pantry and alternated between rummaging through the clinking bottles inside and pulling bottles from a shelf below the kitchen window. She didn't appear to read the labels, grabbing instinctively, sometimes opening a bottle to sniff, and then either setting it back or placing it on the table. By the time she finished, six bottles sat in a row on the table.

Robert appeared in the doorway. "Are you going to be coming to church?"

"I don't think she'll make it," Mrs. Block said for her. She was in her domain and Chloe thought of how many scrapes and burns she must have tended in this kitchen over the years. The boy disappeared and Mrs. Block continued to drop pinches of herbs into a ceramic mortar.

"Do you do a lot of doctoring these days?" Chloe asked.

"Ah, not much. Not since the children were grown. Robert hasn't hurt himself badly in a long time. Broke his arm when he was eleven. I suppose that was the last time he was hurt badly." Her full face curved into a fond smile. "I do miss those days in a way, though. Alexander always laughing and bringing me bouquets of flowers he picked from our garden, and Ian sitting right where you are now

210

and chatting with me as if he were already grown. That boy was born old."

She poured a splash of hot water into a bowl, added more herbs and mashed them with a pestle.

"Tell me more about when the children were young."

"Well, as I said, Alexander was a trickster. Always laughing and making jokes. He ran through a period when he liked to drop little frogs and things in his sister's shoes and pockets. Poor Dora. He tormented her so. But then one day, like that," she snapped her fingers for emphasis, "he started acting like a gentleman. He matured a bit, no doubt." She chuckled to herself. "Either that or she gave him something to think about. Whatever happened, he never troubled her afterwards."

"Now Ian and Robert, they were both good boys. No playing pranks or tormenting their sister. Robert was such a sweet little boy, always eager to please, but Ian could be a tad prickly. Still can be, in fact. Always telling Alexander what to do, and going on about how he should behave better. Of course, the more he went on, the worse Alexander got. Alexander was stubborn, in his way. That's why I was surprised when Alexander turned one day from wicked older brother to being kind to Dora. I don't think Ian had anything to do with it, though. I think Dora put a stop to it herself."

She shrugged and turned back towards to the pantry. She returned momentarily, carrying a long piece of cheesecloth, which she laid flat on the table then coated thickly with the mass of herbs. She peeled off Chloe's makeshift treacle-soaked bandage, which was now warm from the heat of Chloe's skin, and placed the poultice on the pink area. Drawing a piece of lavender ribbon from her apron pocket, Mrs. Block and tied it loosely, making a small, neat bow on top.

"There you go, pretty as you please. But you'll have to hold it on. The little ribbon won't be much good for that," she said, smiling faintly. "I used to do up Dora's little scrapes like that, with a bow. A pretty little thing like a cheerful bow and she'd forget all about the hurt." She stopped for a moment, lost in a memory, and then brightened. "Would you like some tea? This time for drinking, not for bathing?"

Chloe laughed and agreed. "Could you tell me about Rose?"

"Ah. Curious about your husband's sister? She was a lovely lady. Kind. And a fine mother as well. She had dark hair, just the shade of Dora's. In fact, the older Dora gets, the more she looks like a younger version of her mother."

Chloe accepted a cup of tea and Mrs. Block settled into the chair across the table from her.

"I do miss her," Mrs. Block sighed. "Mr. Aynesworth hasn't been the same since her death. Not that I'd expect him to be, but you'd think he would heal in time."

There was a scratching at the door, and then a muffled, "Brrr?"

"That's my cat." Chloe opened the door and Giles came in, tail high. He strolled around the room, completely unaware of the chaos he had caused.

Mrs. Block watched him. "Now that's a strange little thing. I've never seen its like."

"And probably never will again. Although I hope that someday engines like his can be improved upon to allow mechanicals to perform more dangerous tasks."

"Like serving hot tea?"

"Precisely." Chloe thought of Ambrose upstairs. "Do you think I could bring some tea up to my husband? He's not doing well today."

"Certainly. I'll send some up. And I'll make him some of my special soup. Takes a few hours to simmer, so I'll get it started and he can have some this afternoon."

Chloe thanked her and set down her cup. Giles was reluctant to leave, as he had developed a fascination with the copper pots and pans. Chloe picked him up.

"You had better be careful, my friend," she murmured to him as she climbed the stairs. "Or I might start keeping you on a leash."

He looked into her face, and she paused. It was almost as if he understood her.

CHAPTER 32

AFTER CHURCH, THE FAMILY RETURNED for lunch. Chloe examined the faces of Alexander, Dora and Ian. She tried to imagine the solemn little boy Mrs. Block had described who would sit and talk with her in the kitchen. She tried to picture Dora in braids, admiring a purple ribbon tied around her bandaged finger. Chloe pondered for a moment the mischievous Alexander, who had gone from a mischievous miscreant to what? But those children were gone, and in their places were these people. Ian, sitting grim-faced in the corner, avoiding looking at his brother. Alexander was a solid presence beside Beatrice, but even Chloe could feel the distance between them. Dora chatted with Robert, who listened with a weary patience as she went on about the places she wanted to visit once she was married.

"You could come visit us," she said. "Maybe stay with us for a few months."

Robert nodded, though at a glance from his father, the hopeful look on his face faded.

"Mrs. Sullivan. I am sorry that your husband is doing poorly today," said Beatrice.

"Yes. He has been in bed most of the day. Mrs. Block said she has a special soup that she makes that will make him feel better."

"Her soup has medicinal herbs in it," said Robert. "Though it won't cure him, it will ease his symptoms a little. Settle his stomach too."

Chloe thought of the envelope of herbs that Maggie had given her. She probably should toss them out. She trusted Mrs. Block more than the madwoman who spoke to bees.

The butler came into the room then bent toward Ian and whispered a message in his ear. In an instant, Ian leaped up, tossed his napkin across his full plate and rushed from the room. The door banged shut behind him.

"What was that about?" William demanded of the butler.

"If you would, sir?" The butler motioned to the hallway, his expression neutral. William followed him out of sight, but returned a minute later, his expression dark. No one dared to speak to him the rest of the meal.

At supper, a servant ladled onion soup from a white porcelain tureen and placed the steaming bowl in front of Chloe. No sooner had she blown on the first spoonful than a second servant ran past the open dining room door. The pounding of his feet ceased abruptly as another servant barked out an order, sending him running back from whence he came.

A door slammed in the front of the house, and muffled voices exchanged pitched tones. Suddenly, a high-pitched wail sounded loud and shrill, drowning out everything else. It stopped and started again like a bugle call, this time louder than before.

Chloe turned back to the table to see her surprise mirrored in the expressions of the rest of the family, save Alexander's. He was bent over his soup. He lifted his spoon and then returned it to the bowl. Beatrice stared blankly, a look on her face that vaguely repelled Chloe.

Chloe identified Mrs. Block's voice amidst the cacophony. The woman barked out an order and the chatter eventually faded out. Blessedly, the shrill crying tapered off too, and Chloe let her fists uncurl in relief.

For a heartbeat, no one at the table moved or took a bite. Then William rose, breaking the spell, and with a muttered apology, headed for the door. He stopped short as Ian appeared in the doorway, his hair a rumpled mess and his face haggard. Aside from seeing him argue with his brother, Chloe had never seen the man in such a state. Robert and Dora gasped, confirming that they too were shocked at his appearance.

Ian gripped the doorframe. He looked at the people around the table before addressing his father.

"I have an introduction to make," he said. "I have put it off for too long."

"Enough of this!" Alexander slammed his palm on the table and shot up from his seat. "This cannot stand. It is unconscionable."

"What is unconscionable?" said his father, but Chloe saw a grim satisfaction in his expression as he looked at Alexander. William's position afforded him a view into the hallway, past Ian, but if he was shocked or surprised, he did not show it.

Alexander rubbed his neck, agitated. "Father, this is madness. We cannot do this," he said.

"It is already done," said Ian. He stepped into the room and a little girl in a worn brown dress followed him in, reaching to thread her small hand into his. "This is my daughter."

The girl was about five or six years old. Her hair was long and dark and she had the same straight, long nose as her father. Her eyes, a vibrant grass green, must be a gift from her mother. Though the color shown unnaturally bright, set off by the tear-stained, swollen red skin around them. Her right hand clenched about the worn handle of a yellow flowered carpet bag, though it appeared nearly empty, its sides curving inward. Her simple dress looked as if it had been taken in and let out too many times.

After a shocked pause, the room erupted; the high-pitched tones of Mrs. Malone and Dora vying for most shocked. Robert watched the little girl with an expression of concern, as the other adults gesticulated and shouted. Amid the chaos, he slowly got up from his chair, knelt before the girl and said something quietly. She pulled back shyly and pressed her face into Ian's hip.

Only Beatrice was still. She watched Ian with an expression of awe and confusion. Her expression changed to one of careful evaluation when she looked at the girl. Surely she must see the family resemblance, Chloe thought. She probably was trying to ascertain who the girl's mother might be.

In the midst of the melee, Alexander grabbed Ian's shoulder and spun him around, but Dora pushed between her brothers, facing Alexander. He shouted at her, and she pointed a finger into his face, not backing down an inch. Chloe could not hear what she said, but Alexander took a step back from her.

"Enough!" bellowed William. He gradually drew the family back to the table, and everyone took their seats except for Ian and the girl. A servant set two bowls of soup down at two empty places.

"You can sit here," said Robert to the girl, patting the chair beside him. But the girl looked up at her father, uncertainly, her lower lip trembling. Her head dropped, her hair falling in a dark cascade to obscure her face, and her shoulder began to shake. Ian bent down and picked her up, adjusting her weight expertly, as if by old habit. The girl buried her face in his neck, her body limp and exhausted.

"I will take her to bed and see that she eats," said Mrs. Block from the doorway.

The girl clutched Ian all the harder. He murmured something into her ear and she raised her head and looked him straight in the face. She released her grip on his neck long enough for him to transfer her to Mrs. Block's arms.

The pair disappeared down the hall.

"Outside," hissed Alexander. "Now."

"No, brother. I haven't eaten a bite since midday and I'm famished. I'd like to join you all for supper if you will allow me." Ian seated himself and scooted in his chair. He took up his spoon.

Alexander, face red, looked as if he might drag Ian outside by force.

"Her name is Josephine," said Ian evenly. "Not that any of you asked or showed any sort of civilized welcome to her. She is six years old and her mother died this afternoon."

Voices rose in protest and shock once more, and William slammed his fist on the table so hard that the dishes clinked and the wine in his crystal glass sloshed dangerously.

"I will speak with both of you after we eat," said William to Alexander and Ian in a tone that brooked no argument. Ian was almost too calm and even seemed pleased as he nodded his assent.

The rest of the meal was eaten in silence. Beatrice pushed the food around her plate and sipped her water. She glanced at her husband and Ian now and then, but Chloe could not tell what she was thinking.

CHAPTER 33

"**Y**OU'RE COOLER. THE FEVER BROKE," said Chloe, laying her hand on Ambrose's forehead.

"Indeed. I was thinking of taking the perilous journey to that chair."

She offered her arm, but he waved it away. He got up and seated himself in the chair that had become his favorite.

"I dare say you will not be meeting with Mr. Baxter tonight?" she asked.

"No. I already had Mr. Frick send word that I would have to meet him in another day or two."

"Good. You shouldn't be outside anyway. The cold air is not good for you."

"I seem to recall saying that you shouldn't go out at night either," he said with a wicked look.

"Only that I couldn't go out alone. And as you can see, the cold air and evil vapors of the moor had no effect upon my health."

"I am glad to hear it."

Once she was sure he was well enough to take a shock, she told him about Josephine's appearance at supper.

"That was most likely why Dora was anxious about you talking with Mr. Baxter alone," she said. "He probably doesn't know about the girl and she was afraid he might break off the engagement after such a scandal emerged."

Ambrose nodded. "Something tells me that Mr. Baxter would not blame Dora if her brother behaved in an undignified manner."

"I wouldn't have thought it of Ian," she shook her head. "Alexander seemed like the one who would do that."

"You only say that because you heard it from others. A few days ago, you would not have thought it of Alexander."

"I suppose not." She got up and rang for a servant. When a maid appeared, she asked if Mrs. Block had supper for Ambrose.

A few minutes later, the young maid who had accompanied Mrs. Block to the stone circle appeared with a covered bowl, bread, a teapot and cup. Chloe lifted the cover off the soup bowl.

"There's all sorts of healthful things in there," said the maid. "Carrots, mushrooms and leeks, beef broth for strength, spinach and garlic for the blood and potatoes for energy. Also beets, but I forget what they're for."

Chloe thought about the medicinal herbs that Robert said would be included, but did not ask.

"It sounds wonderful. I believe I actually have an appetite now," said Ambrose.

"My aunt says to make sure he eats the whole bowl," said the maid to Chloe. "The bread too, if he can manage it. And he should try to drink a cup of tea every hour until bedtime."

The girl turned to leave, but Chloe called her back. "How is the little girl, Josephine?"

"Oh, she's eating down in the kitchen. She'll be all right. She's had such a rough time of it with her mother and all. Very sad. We're all seeing to her though. And Ian came after supper to sit with her."

"Do you think she'll be staying?"

The girl blinked in surprise. For a family member to ask her opinion was unusual. "I suppose so. We made up a room for her just down the hall." She bobbed a curtsey and left.

As Giles curled up on the windowsill, Chloe sat with

Ambrose the rest of the evening, ensuring he finished his soup and drank his tea as instructed.

That night, as she pulled on her nightgown, she thought she heard a sound in the hallway. She listened, and it came again, a soft sniffling sound. She pulled open the doorway slowly, so as not to startle the person she thought was there. Josephine was in the hallway, but she jumped back and turned to run when she saw Chloe.

"No, wait. It's me."

Of course the child wouldn't know who she was. She was just another face amid a sea of arguing strangers in this house. But the girl turned back and looked at her, evaluating. She looked tiny and too thin in her cotton nightgown. She smelled of soap and her hair hung in damp coils over her shoulders. Her feet were bare on the cold floorboards and her arms were wrapped around her middle.

"Are you cold?" Chloe said. Josephine paused and then nodded. "Did they make a fire up in your room?"

The girl shook her head.

"I have a fire in my room. Do you want to come in and warm up?"

Josephine glanced at the door behind her and took a step toward her. Chloe stepped aside and dragged two chairs near the fire. Josephine knelt down on the rug and put her hands out to absorb the heat. Chloe pulled a wool blanket off the bed and put it around the girl. Josephine's eyes did not leave the fire.

"Who are you?" said Josephine. She sat back, pulled her knees up and wrapped the blanket around her body.

"I'm Chloe, I am married to your father's uncle."

Josephine drew her brows together in consideration and opened her mouth to say something, but then shut it and nodded. "And you live here too?"

"No, my husband and I are just visiting for a month. He's in the next room but he's not feeling well."

"I hope God doesn't take him. He takes people sometimes when they're sick."

"Oh no, I'm sure he'll be fine." She wanted to offer some comfort, but was not sure if she should bring up Josephine's mother. But then, how could the girl not be thinking of her? The firelight played across her small face and she looked far away.

"Are you hungry?" Chloe asked.

"No, Mrs. Block gave me supper before my bath. Hot soup with carrots and potatoes and lots of things. Also bread with lots of butter and sugar sprinkled on top." She turned to look around the room, taking in the furniture, the objects on the dressing table, the bed. She did not notice Giles on the windowsill, hidden by the curtain with darkness behind him. Maybe she should bring Giles over. Children liked animals.

"What did Ian say about me?" the girl asked.

"Not much. Your father told us that you were going to stay here, but that's all."

"My mum died. God took her this afternoon. So now I'm to live with my uncle. And my father. And that's all there is to it." She set her mouth in a manner that was far too old for her years.

She lowered her forehead to rest on her knees and took a long and shaky breath. Chloe knelt beside her and pushed her damp hair over one shoulder. She rubbed the girl's back in slow circles. A minute later, Josephine launched herself into Chloe's arms. She caught her balance in time to keep from falling over.

"I want my mummy back," she whispered, her face hot and wet against Chloe's neck.

"I'm sorry," Chloe whispered into her damp hair. The child's arms tightened around her neck as she took one sobbing breath after another.

"I hate God," she whispered.

"I know." Chloe held her, not knowing what to say. She

rocked her and rubbed her back until her breathing slowed.

"I want to go to her," she whispered, so faintly that Chloe wasn't sure she had heard her.

"No, no you don't."

"I do!" she said, pulling her head back. Her eyes were wide and burned like green flames. "Then I wouldn't be here with these dreadful people."

"They're not dreadful." But that was a half-truth and they both knew it.

Josephine sighed heavily and laid her head back against Chloe's shoulder. "If they're so good, why weren't they glad to see me?"

"They were just surprised, that's all. They weren't expecting you."

"Ian never told them about me."

"No, he didn't."

"They don't want me."

"They do, they just don't know you yet. I bet in the morning they'll be all smiles at breakfast. And if not, you come have breakfast with me. I'll be glad to see you."

"You will?"

"Without a doubt."

She heaved a great sigh. "I'm tired. Can I sleep here with you?"

"I don't know." Chloe thought for a moment. What if someone came to check on the girl in the night and wondered where she went?

"I'm scared in my room all alone. And it's cold."

Well, if anyone raised an alarm, she would hear it and bring the child out.

"Fine then, you can have the side of the bed nearest the fire."

Josephine got up. Her mouth quirked into an exhausted half smile. As she pulled the back the blankets and crawled under them, Chloe realized where she had seen a smile like that before. It was Alexander's.

CHAPTER 34

JOSEPHINE WHIMPERED IN HER SLEEP and kicked Chloe with an icy foot. Chloe jolted awake. The fire had died, and the room was bitter cold. Chloe made sure that the blankets were tucked snugly around the sleeping girl. Her hair was dry now and lay across the pillow in dark wisps. It slid across the pillow as the child rolled over, pulling the blankets with her.

An odor, sharp and foul came from the girl. Vomit. Chloe lit the table lamp and looked at Josephine's sleeping face. A small amount of vomit was crusted on the side of her mouth, but her breathing was regular and she seemed fine otherwise. Chloe touched her cheek with the back of her fingers. Her temperature was normal. She hated to wake her and bring her back to the world of a dead mother and chaotic family. She wiped off the girl's mouth and watched her for awhile.

Josephine whimpered again and pulled her body into a ball. Poor girl. She must be having terrible dreams about her mother.

"Hurts," she whimpered.

"I know. But your mother is with God now, and she will always be looking after you from heaven."

"No, my stomach." Her stomach gurgled and she moaned louder and then after awhile, she grew still. Chloe waited, listening in the dark. Josephine was breathing deep and slow. She must have fallen asleep.

When Chloe awoke, she found Josephine's side of the bed empty. A cough from near her dressing table told her where the girl was. One of the gaslights was on very low. Josephine was crouched like a toad in front of the dresser, the washing basin in front of her as she coughed and spat into it. The sharp, sickly smell of stomach acid filled the room and Chloe's stomach lurched in response. She flew to the door, yanking it open for fresh air and then turned up the gaslight. The washbasin was filled with vomit and Josephine was dry heaving and coughing, her small body shaking with the effort. She was crying silently as she heaved, her arms clutched around her middle. Her eyes were large and hollow.

"I'll get Mrs. Block," Chloe said and ran upstairs to the servants' floor. The doors were all closed. Which one was it? She didn't even know if she was in the men's or women's side. She knocked on a door and a woman with puffy eyes blinked at her.

"Where is Mrs. Block's room?"

The maid pointed Chloe down the hall. She pounded on the door a few times until it cracked open. Mrs. Block got one look at her and was immediately alert.

"What is it?"

"It's Josephine. She's very sick."

Mrs. Block disappeared behind the door and reappeared in a heavy robe and slippers.

"She spent the night in my room," Chloe said as they headed up the hall. "She was missing her mother and wanted to stay with me. And then she woke up, vomiting, and complaining of stomach pains."

"Fever?"

"I don't think so. She was healthy earlier this evening. She's in a lot of pain. She's holding her stomach and crying."

Mrs. Block sped up and they descended the stairs and turned toward Chloe's room. Josephine was now lying on her side beside the basin, breathing, but either asleep or unconscious. Mrs. Block rushed to her side and lifted her upper body. The back of Josephine's nightgown was smeared with something dark and wet and a puddle spread out beneath her. The smell was unmistakable. The girl had lost control of her bowels.

"It looks like she vomited up her whole supper," said Mrs. Block. "I want you to rouse Alexander or Ian and get them to go fetch the doctor. It should be Ian." She looked up. "Now. Don't just stand there!" she barked. She looked at Josephine with undisguised fear.

Chloe ran to Ian's door and pounded. She was about to open it and shake Ian awake when the door flew open.

"What is it?"

"Josephine. She's sick. We need to get the doctor."

She followed him to her room, and by the time she had come up behind him, he had already taken in the scene.

"Get the doctor," said Mrs. Block, cradling the small body against her own. "Something is very wrong."

"Chloe!" cried Ian, his face full of anger and terror. "Go to the stable and get Mr. James to get the carriage ready. Tell him we're taking her to Doctor Fleming."

He swept Josephine into his arms and strode into the hallway.

"Why don't you bring Alexander along for help?" Mrs. Block asked him.

"He was no help to her mother when she was alive. Why would he help her daughter?"

Chloe rushed past them, down the stairs and into the kitchen. She grabbed a lantern and hurried out the back of the house toward the stables. The back lawn was cold on her feet, and as she ran past the brick border into the rougher area of the yard, twigs and gravel stabbed her feet with every step. She did not slow. She knew nothing about medicine, but if Mrs. Block was frightened, then Josephine was in grave danger.

The stable was dark and the horses stirred and snorted

at her approach. At the back of the stable was a closed door. She pounded on it until Mr. James pulled it open, allowing a crack of light to pierce the stable from his room. He was wearing nothing but flannel pajama bottoms and his chest was dark with hair. Flustered, Chloe looked away.

"What is it?" He reached for his shirt, which seemed to be flung over some piece of furniture next to the door.

"Get the carriage right away. The little girl is sick. No time for the doctor to come so we need the carriage."

He grunted and pulled a horse from its stall.

"Do you need any help?" Chloe asked. She knew little about horses, but she could follow instructions.

"Nah. Just get back to the house. Take that," he said and pointed to an oversized black coat that hung on a hook next to his bedroom door. It smelled of animals and hay. She gratefully pulled it on and ran back to the house.

In the kitchen, Ian was holding Josephine in his lap near the fire and Mrs. Block was removing a large bowl from the table and replacing it with a smaller one. She placed the large bowl in the sink and Chloe saw the thin, watery vomit collected in the bottom of it. Whatever the girl had eaten, it was out of her system now. She couldn't possibly have anything left in her stomach. They had wrapped Josephine in a woolen blanket and she was conscious again, though her lips were white. Her breathing was more labored now but her crying had stopped. Except for her breathing, she sat as still as a statue, her face blank and her eyes glassy and hollow-looking.

"He'll be here soon," Chloe said.

"I want Mummy."

"There, there," Ian soothed. He carried Josephine to the window and Chloe leaned over to see Mr. James's progress. The carriage was nearly ready and two lanterns glowed from the front of it.

"It's time," Ian said.

"Mummy!" Josephine moaned and reached her arms

toward Chloe.

"I'm not your mummy, darling," she said as gently as she could.

"Mummy! I want Mummy!" she yelled, her face reddening with effort. She squirmed in Ian's arms and tried to pull herself free.

"Mummy's coming," said Ian, looking at Chloe pointedly and jerking his head toward the back door. The lanterns were moving toward them now and the horses' hooves crunched the gravel. Mr. James leaped from the driver's seat and opened the carriage door. Chloe climbed in first, followed by Ian with his charge.

Mrs. Block said something into Ian's ear as Mr. James climbed back into the driver's seat and then she slammed the door shut and stepped back from the carriage. The horses started at the sharp sound, jolting the carriage forward and throwing Chloe against the seat back. Josephine's face was white in the darkness, her eyes wide and alert.

"Uncle Ian, I want to sit with Mummy," she said.

Chloe nodded to Ian and he transferred the girl to her lap. Josephine's body reeked of vomit and excrement, but she cradled her close. A few minute later, the girl felt too still. Chloe put her hand against her side to check her respiration. She was breathing, but asleep or unconscious again.

"She's out," Chloe said quietly and Ian's face relaxed. He sighed heavily and ran a hand through his hair.

"What do you think it is?" Chloe asked.

"I have no idea," he said. "But Doctor Fleming will. He's good."

The carriage jolted sickeningly over the rough road and threw her back again. Mr. James was driving too fast. Good.

"Here," Ian said, holding out his arms.

Chloe passed Josephine over. "Do I look like her mother?"

"A bit."

Something stirred in the back of Chloe's mind.

"Was she a housemaid? Yours?"

"Ours, yes."

Chloe tried to hold her face expressionless as she glanced out the window. The moor was covered in mist and scarcely lit by white moonlight. So Ian had a child with a maid. And now he had the product of that encounter lying near dead in his arms. Something didn't seem right about it though. There was Alexander's reaction to the girl and Ian's almost smug behavior at supper. Ian was watching her. She met his eyes and pulled her mouth all the way closed, setting her jaw.

"Alexander's?" she asked.

"Pardon?"

"She's your brother's child?"

He did not answer, but checked on Josephine and gazed out the window.

"But why ..." The carriage turned. They were getting closer to town now.

Ian was the more responsible brother. So she understood why he would support the girl's mother, even though he was in no way responsible for the situation. But why would he claim the child as his own?

Beatrice. Ian would want to protect Beatrice from the pain of having her husband's illegitimate child acknowledged, and eventually living with her. He had decided to bear the whispers and shame to protect her.

"Have you been supporting her mother all these years?"

"Yes, but it hasn't been that much really. It was the least I could do to try to set things right."

"Is this the first time this has happened?" It was a dangerous question, but something about the darkness and the closeness of death made her bold.

"To Alexander, yes." He paused. "Well, as far as I know. If Robert ever does anything like it—" He shook his head.

"And you did it for Beatrice."

He did not answer. The carriage was nearing the town and Ian watched anxiously out the window as they passed through. When they reached their destination, he flung the door open and strode up the narrow walkway to a small but neatly kept house. After pounding on the door, a light came on inside and the door cracked open revealing a thin woman with a narrow face.

"I'll fetch the doctor," she stated, opening the door wide without waiting for Ian to explain. Josephine mumbled in her sleep and then was still. Chloe carried her into the house.

"Any idea what it is?" A voice came from the dark stairway as Doctor Fleming thumped down the steps.

"No, she just started having stomach pains in the night," answered Ian.

The doctor muttered something as he examined the girl.

"Vomiting and soiling herself, I see," he said. "Has she been insensible the entire time?"

"No, she wakes and sleeps on and off. What is it?" said Ian.

"Can't say yet." He took her pulse, felt her forehead and listened to her breathing. "Let's get her upstairs into a bed. My wife will help you bathe her and give her some fresh garments."

Ian carried Josephine upstairs and the doctor's wife told them she would be back shortly. As Chloe was about to pull off the soiled nightgown, Josephine opened her eyes.

"It's time for Ian to be here," she mumbled. "Time for Mummy to leave."

"We're here, sweetheart," Ian said.

"That's better," she said, grimacing. "I'm cold but I need to—"

She cried out and clutched her stomach. Her torso stiffened and relaxed as she dry heaved.

"No, Mummy." She flashed her eyes on Chloe and reached out her hands.

She gathered Josephine into her arms as the girl heaved and lost bowel control again. She was whimpering weakly, a small sound, like a pup. Her head fell back and she lost consciousness again. Chloe looked helplessly to Ian. He was leaning against the window frame, holding the heavy curtain with one hand and looking out into the blackness.

The doctor's wife opened the door and brought fresh nightclothes for Josephine and a cup with a spoon sticking out. She unfolded a tiny paper square, poured powder into the cup and stirred. The clinking of the spoon on the cup and the wind at the window were the only sounds.

"When she wakes again, see if she will drink this," she said. "We think perhaps she ate something rotten and her body is trying to rid itself of the toxin. Do you know what she ate today?"

Ian took a deep breath. "Well, for lunch, she had bread with cheese, and for supper, the housekeeper gave her—"

"Soup. Oh God. Soup," Chloe said. "Ambrose and Josephine had the same soup tonight for supper. I need to get home. Now."

Josephine was so small and pale. She was breathing, but shallowly. It was hard to tell in the low light, but her lips and hands appeared to have a dark tinge.

"Go," said Ian. "I have her."

He took Josephine into his arms and Chloe rose. Her nightgown and borrowed coat were covered in foul things, but it didn't matter. The doctor's wife rushed down the stairs calling to Mr. James. Ian held Josephine tenderly, and his eyes met Chloe's. There was nothing to say.

"I'll tell the doctor to send someone to the house," called Ian as Chloe raced down the stairs. By the time she reached the front door, Mr. James was already holding the carriage door open for her. She threw herself inside and sent up a desperate prayer as the driver climbed up and the carriage jerked forward.

CHAPTER 35

A S THE CARRIAGE PULLED UP to the house, the door burst open and Mrs. Block flew out to meet them. She was wringing her nightcap. The light from the swinging lanterns on the front of the carriage made her look as if she had aged a decade. She said a few words to the driver and took Chloe's arm the moment she opened the carriage door.

"We found Mr. Sullivan on the floor after you left. He had the basin, just as Josephine did. And he was in the same horrible condition. We got him into the bed and he's asleep now."

They rushed inside. The gaslights in the house were on, but dimly. A few servants were up, and there were noises from the kitchen.

"How is Josephine?" asked Mrs. Block.

"She's fading in and out of consciousness, just as before," Chloe said as they climbed the stairs. "She is still in terrible pain. But she had some medicine just before I left. The doctor suspects she ate something bad."

Chloe couldn't tell for certain in the low light of the upper hall, but the pink in Mrs. Block's cheeks seemed to vanish and her hand flew to her mouth.

"They both had my soup and bread."

Chloe moved past her and entered Ambrose's room. The covers were pulled up to his chest and his body was relaxed in sleep. He looked peaceful, but the stench of vomit and excrement told a darker story.

"He was lying over by the window," Mrs. Block said from behind her. "I had some of the girls clean up a bit in here, but we didn't change him. We didn't want to disturb him further and the doctor was sent for and we didn't know if we ought to and—"

"We can change him in a little while."

"We sent for the doctor as soon as we saw him. If Doctor Fleming is treating Josephine, he'll send his assistant, young Doctor Michaels."

If Doctor Fleming had sent for his assistant as she left, Chloe reflected, help could not be too far behind. She willed the man to ride fast.

She sat at the edge of the bed and took Ambrose's hand. It was cool and limp, but after a minute, his fingers curled weakly around hers. His eyelids fluttered and he muttered something.

"What is it, love?" she said and leaned closer.

His lips moved, but she couldn't make anything out. She wondered how much he could understand. Perhaps his mind was still alert.

"It looks like you ate something rotten and your body is expelling the toxin. A doctor is on his way."

His eyes fluttered open and his face contorted in agony. He wrapped his arms around his middle and rolled onto his side, toward her. Chloe dropped to her knees beside the bed and pressed her cheek to his, putting her arm around his shoulder.

"I know it hurts," she whispered. "The doctor will bring something. He'll be here soon."

"What was it?" Ambrose groaned. "What toxin?"

Even in such distress, he was a scientist.

"We don't know. It was something in the soup."

She felt his head nod against her cheek and he seemed to relax. She stayed there for a minute until his breathing slowed, and then she rose and pulled the blanket up over his shoulders.

Mrs. Block dragged a chair to the side of the bed. "I can stay with him if you want to get cleaned up."

Chloe hesitated. Ambrose needed her and she did not want to leave him.

"There's nothing you can do right now," said Mrs. Block in a tone that she probably used with underlings. "And you are more use to him if you are out of those filthy clothes. I promise to yell for you if anything changes. And the doctor will be here any moment."

Mrs. Block was right, of course. Chloe went into her room and threw the filthy clothing into a pile on the floor. One of the maids would collect it eventually, either for the laundry or, more likely, the refuse bin. Armed with a bar of soap, a basin and a jug of water, she cleaned herself up as best she could. Donning a simple dress that she could get on without Miss Haynes's assistance, she pulled her hair into a messy knot and returned to her place by Ambrose's side. He was still unconscious.

She heard the sturdy oak of the front door bang shut below, followed by hurried talking on the stairs. She rose and opened the bedroom door. A young man with a black physician's bag nodded to her and went to Ambrose's side. He introduced himself as Doctor Michaels and pulled back the covers to begin his examination.

"Would you mind opening the window a crack?" he said, absently.

She obliged. The night air was chilly and moist, but fresh. The doctor examined Ambrose's throat and ears, took his pulse and temperature and listened to his breathing. Chloe tried not to hover. She always found such interruptions distracting when trying to diagnose a mechanical problem.

The doctor pulled the covers back over Ambrose and stepped back. "Please ring for a servant to bring some warm water, fresh sheets and fresh nightclothes. We need to get him cleaned up."

"Of course." Chloe rang for a servant. "Do you think he is likely to soil himself again?"

"Yes. But it will be less and less as time goes on, as his body rids itself of the toxin. That's if my guess is right."

"And what is your guess?"

"Something rotten in the soup. Not in the bread, as the whole family ate that. But only Mr. Sullivan and the little girl ate the soup, correct?"

"As far as I know. But what in the soup would cause this?"

"I don't know. I asked Mrs. Block to tell me everything that was in it. She's in the kitchen right now, gathering everything so I can have a look. After we get your husband tended to, I will speak to her and learn what I can."

While Chloe gave instructions to a housemaid, the doctor checked Ambrose again. She caught a look at the side of Doctor Michaels' face, and saw his deep concern as well as a flash of something darker. It was gone when he turned to her and gave a reassuring nod. Her insides twisted. He was trying not to worry her, to give her comfort and hope. Though she appreciated the gesture, it terrified her.

"What is it? Is he going to be all right?"

"I expect so," he said and pulled three bottles from his black bag, two with white tablets and one with a liquid. "I'm going to wake him and see that he gets some medicine. Then we will get him cleaned and he can sleep."

Chloe nodded and woke her husband. When the doctor tried to open Ambrose's mouth, he moaned and turned his head away, but with Chloe's encouragement, he eventually took the tablets and liquid. He muttered some more.

"The doctor gave you medicine to help," said Chloe. "We're going to clean you up and then you can rest." She turned to Doctor Michaels. "Do you think he can understand me?"

"Perhaps. It can't hurt to talk to him. It might help him be less frightened."

She hadn't thought of Ambrose being frightened, only

in pain. But if the situation were reversed, she knew she would be afraid. She wanted to crawl under the blankets with him and reassure him. She wanted to be reassured herself. She took a deep breath. Ambrose needed her to keep her head.

"What next?" she asked.

"He needs to be cleaned. Do you want to assist, or call someone to do it?"

She pushed back the sleeves on her dress and helped move, wash and dress her husband. Servants came and stripped the bed and removed all the soiled items. A maid placed folded blankets over the sheet as a makeshift absorbent pad and once Ambrose was back in bed, Chloe spread fresh blankets over him.

"That's all we can do for now. I need to speak with Mrs. Block," said the doctor.

Chloe examined the bottles. One of the tablets was laudanum, for pain, and the other was a strong sleeping drug. The liquid tonic was to settle the stomach.

"Doctor, wait. What about something to cure him? To absorb the toxin or get it out of him somehow?"

"His body has already expelled the toxin, or most of it. Now we need him to keep down broth or tea and to rest."

"But, there has to be something you can do. He's in pain."

The doctor sighed. "I know. The medicines will help the pain and help him sleep. While he's unconscious, he isn't suffering and it's the best we can do for him at this time. After I speak with Mrs. Block, I hope to know more. I will come back to check on him."

He took his bag and left. Maybe he planned to collect samples of the soup or the ingredients into little vials in his bag. Did he have some medical laboratory in which he could study them under a microscope? She imagined the doctor testing samples and isolating the toxic agent, then devising a cure. But she knew that was a fantasy.

She dropped into the bedside chair and studied Ambrose. The lines of his face were relaxed in sleep, but his skin was yellowish. His lips had a slightly bluish cast, as did his fingers.

A mechanical brought a tea tray. There were two cups, and she filled one for Ambrose, setting it aside to let it cool. When in doubt, drink tea, she thought ruefully as she raised her cup to her lips.

An hour later, the doctor returned and gave her written instructions on how often Ambrose was to take each drug. Then he checked on Ambrose again. Ambrose stirred as the doctor opened his nightshirt to listen to his heart.

"Baxter," Ambrose muttered. "Met with him."

"No darling," said Chloe. "You had Mr. Frick send word that you were going to meet him another day. Don't fret about it. When you are well you can see him."

"Doctor," he whispered.

"I'm here," Doctor Michaels said.

Ambrose looked at him as if confirming something and nodded. He sighed and his eyes closed.

The doctor left, telling her that he would be back in the morning and to send word if Ambrose showed any change. He was going to consult with Doctor Fleming.

"We can't do anything unless we know the nature of the toxin," he said.

Chloe could not have agreed more. If they knew the cause, they could look up a cure or purgative. As Ambrose slept, she went into his temporary study and browsed through his books. She pulled out any and all that could relate to botanical poisons. She brought a stack of books to his room and went through them.

As the dawn sun lightened the sky, a mechanical brought coffee, buttered bread and two poached eggs. But she was too anxious and sick to her stomach to have any appetite. And she was no closer to an answer. As mid-morning daylight flooded through the window, she turned off the gaslight beside the bed and moved her seat under the window so Ambrose could be in as much darkness as possible. He had not regained consciousness, and she considered that a blessing.

Mrs. Block came to check on Ambrose and stood at the foot of the bed, wringing her hands. "I don't know what it could have been. I've made that soup a hundred times."

She glanced at the books scattered around the room before leaving. Robert knocked on the door a few minutes later.

"Mrs. Block said you were looking up things on herbs and toxins?"

"I am, not that it will do any good. But I can't just sit here doing nothing. The thing is, I don't understand half of what is in these books."

"Mrs. Block thought I could maybe help. There is so much I don't understand either, but maybe ..." he shrugged.

"I could use all the help I can get."

Robert squatted down and collected the books, placing them in a few organized piles.

"What was in the soup?" he asked.

"Carrots, potatoes, leeks, spinach, garlic, beets and beef broth," she said, consulting a list Mrs. Block had written for her. "Also these herbs and salt." She handed him the list.

"Good."

"Pardon?"

"There was no meat in the soup, correct?"

"That's right."

"And the beef broth would have to be simmered for hours, killing any bacteria. That means it's a botanical poison for certain."

She was not certain, and it was little comfort. She imagined a cloaked villain emptying a vial of poison into the soup pot as it cooked on the stove. But she said nothing. She did not want to dampen Robert's optimism. She needed his sharp mind, as hers was dulled by exhaustion, and only getting worse by the minute. She had read the same paragraph in Koch's *Postulates on Bacillus Anthracis* three times, absorbing nothing. She slapped the cover closed and tossed the book onto the nearest pile.

Robert frowned. "The thing is, most toxins are killed with the heat of cooking. I wonder if there are heat resistant bacteria." He dug through the stacks of books until he found the one he wanted.

"I wish Ambrose could help us. He would know what to look for. He would figure it out in a minute." Chloe rubbed her eyes.

Robert glanced at his uncle, then at her. "You should sleep. I can keep looking. I'll have your maid fetch you if he wakes up."

"No, I couldn't sleep if I wanted to."

He did not try to convince her but started to page through a book. She tore out a few blank pages from her notebook and gave them to him along with a pencil.

In the late morning, Doctor Michaels returned. He examined Ambrose with a careful eye and administered another dose of drugs. Then he glanced at the stack of books between Chloe and Robert. He scanned the titles.

"Where did you get those?"

"They belong to my husband. He's a naturalist."

He took in the sheets of notes and he gave a little nod. Chloe suspected that he thought she was just keeping herself busy so she did not feel helpless and hysterical. Perhaps she was.

"I will be downstairs if you need me. I will check on Mr. Sullivan every hour, but call me immediately if he shows any change."

"How is Josephine?" asked Robert.

The young doctor took off his glasses and rubbed the bridge of his nose. He looked miserable. "I'm sorry, but she passed about two hours ago. There was nothing we could do."

"Child ..." moaned Ambrose.

"It's all right, sweetheart." Chloe shot a look at the doctor. He should have known not to say such a thing at a man's sickbed.

"Graves. The girl," he murmured.

"You aren't going to die. You're going to recover and be just fine." She got him to take a few sips of tea before he fell back into merciful oblivion.

Chloe took her husband's purplish hand and sat watching him. The sweet little girl was dead. God had taken her, and she was with her mother, just as she wished.

Robert got up and stood alone in Ambrose's sitting area for a long while. Chloe knew he had liked the little girl. He returned without a word and picked up his book with a new sternness in the set of his shoulders and jaw.

At midday, Mrs. Block brought up a tray with mutton sandwiches and pickles. Robert tore into his, but Chloe had to force herself to eat a few bites.

Mrs. Block looked at the sheets of scribbled notes and the books lying open around them.

"Are you having any luck?"

"No," said Chloe. "None."

Mrs. Block picked up some papers and flipped through. Chloe wanted to snatch them from her hands, but stopped herself. Mrs. Block knew herbs and plants. Perhaps she could see some kind of pattern, some hint. The housekeeper came to the list of soup ingredients and stopped.

"You've added something to my list. There were no mushrooms in my soup."

"Yes there were. Chopped fine."

"No, I'm certain there weren't."

Robert and Mrs. Block locked eyes in horror.

"What is it? Do you think it was bad mushrooms?" asked Chloe. "But how can that be? The people at the market in town would never sell poisonous ones. It makes no sense."

"It wouldn't be something someone bought at the market," said Mrs. Block. "Oh God, no. No." She shook her head in horror. "There's a mushroom that grows on the moor ..." her eyes filled with tears.

Chloe dug through the stacks until she found Harrod's *Mycologia* and flipped to the table of contents.

"What is the damned thing called?"

"The Destroying Angel."

CHAPTER 36

C HLOE STOPPED SHORT AS SHE opened the book. "Where's the doctor?"

"In the kitchen," said Mrs. Block.

Chloe raced down the stairs and burst into the kitchen. Doctor Michaels looked up in shock. He had a half-eaten sandwich in front of him and a book open on the table. So he had been investigating, as well.

"It's Destroying Angels," she said.

"What?" She saw his confusion, and then he grew thoughtful, weighing the symptoms.

Chloe heard Mrs. Block yell for someone named Sarah, but she did not look away from the doctor.

"There were mushrooms in the soup," said Chloe. "And Mrs. Block said she didn't put any in. Do the symptoms match?"

Doctor Michaels shook his head and blinked in confusion. "Well, I would have to check, but I believe so. But everyone who lives around here knows what the poisonous mushrooms look like. Everyone knows not to bring it in the house or even touch it."

"But people have eaten it before?"

"By accident. I've heard that sometimes some fool eats one, but it's always someone out on the moor who makes a mistake. It wouldn't be someone like Mrs. Block—"

"Never mind that. What is the cure? How do you treat it?"

"I—There is nothing. Some people die and some

survive. It depends on their age and constitution as well as random chance."

She was not going to entrust Ambrose to random chance.

"What about Doctor Fleming? Would he know? Have you ever personally treated someone who ate them?"

"No, I haven't been in practice that long. But yes, Doctor Fleming would know. But who would be fool enough—"

"For God's sake, man, fetch Doctor Fleming!"

The doctor rose from his seat, furious at being addressed in such a fashion. Chloe glared at him, but then muttered an apology. She was clearly overwrought and could not afford to be.

Mrs. Block yelled again, this time for someone named Billy. A boy appeared in the door and she told him to have Doctor Fleming summoned.

"Destroying Angels," she said. "Don't forget it. Destroying Angels. Now repeat it back."

He did, and she sent the boy running out the back door toward the stables. Chloe turned back to the doctor.

"That book there," she pointed at the doctor's book which lay open beside his plate. "Would it have information on how to treat him?"

The doctor shook his head. Chloe turned to Robert. "Get the mycology book, the red one."

The boy ran out the door. A maid came in as he left, the young woman who was Mrs. Block's niece.

"Sarah, you are the one who brought up the soup to Mr. Sullivan, yes?" said Mrs. Block. Her voice was shaking.

Sarah nodded. Her eyes were wide.

"And were there mushrooms in it?"

"Yes. They were in the pot when I dished it out, just like you told me to. You told me to give it to him."

"I know. And you're sure there were mushrooms?"

"I'm sure. I remember thinking you put them in for extra flavor. I thought nothing of it." The girl's hands were clasped at her chest and she looked terrified. "And I served the soup for that poor little girl. She ate it right up."

"And the soup was simmering for hours," said Mrs. Block. "Any time from when I put it on the stove to when it was served, someone could have put the mushrooms in."

"Just a moment," said the doctor. "You are saying that someone intentionally put Destroying Angels in the pot? That's madness."

But Chloe knew it was beyond madness. Someone in the household knew that Ambrose was sick and would be the recipient of the soup. It was no accidental oversight.

"We need to find out who did this," said Mrs. Block.

"More importantly, we need to make sure the patient survives," said Doctor Michaels, turning toward the door.

Robert appeared with Harrod's *Mycologia.* He already had it open to the page on *Amanita virosa.* His expression was grim. Chloe grabbed the book.

"Cap is white in color." She skipped ahead. "Symptoms include violent vomiting, diarrhea, intense stomach pain and cyanosis of the extremities."

"What is cyanosis?" asked Robert.

"His hands and feet have a bluish tinge," said the doctor.

Chloe ran her finger down the page. "Poisoning causes complete disruption of metabolic system, and symptoms mimic that of Asiatic Cholera. Patient experiences periods of consciousness mixed with insensibility. Jaundice and degeneration of cardiac muscles, organ failure in kidneys and liver. Some victims survive, depending on age and previous state of health. In most cases, the victim lapses into a coma and dies." She stopped. "There are no known antidotes."

No known antidotes. She felt Robert's steadying hand on her arm and someone took the book from her hands. The victim lapses into a coma and dies.

"Are you going to be all right, mum?" asked Mrs. Block.

Chloe blinked. No known antidotes. But some people survived, depending on age and previous state of health.

Ambrose was not elderly. He was still active, and he was much larger than little Josephine. So his dose of the poison would have been relatively smaller in proportion to his mass. Perhaps he would survive. Perhaps.

"Of course I'll be all right. I just needed a moment."

Doctor Michaels headed out the kitchen door to tend to his patient.

"We should go with him," Robert suggested. He was the one who had taken the book from her and now held it with his finger holding their place. He offered his arm, but she shook her head and strode up the stairs beside him.

The doctor was examining Ambrose. He was conscious, though the whites of his eyes were now more yellow, as was his skin, except for his purplish hands. The doctor got him to take more of the tonic and tablets. He forced Ambrose to drink half a glass of water.

"If he can pass fluids, there's a greater chance that he can expel the poisons," he said.

Later, Doctor Fleming arrived and talked with Doctor Michaels in the hallway. She could hear their voices, but could not make out anything they were saying.

Doctor Fleming entered. "So he was vomiting and had the diarrhea at the same time as the girl?" he asked Chloe.

"Yes. Mrs. Block said they found him right after Ian and I brought Josephine to you."

He nodded and rubbed his beard. "Good. That's good." At the look on Chloe's face, he explained. "He vomited a few hours after consuming the mushrooms. That means the poison was in his system for a shorter period of time than if it had been a full day. Sometimes patients do not exhibit symptoms for a day or two. By that time, the damage is worse."

"So there is hope that he'll survive?"

"It depends on how much of it he ate and other factors. We need to encourage him to drink, as Doctor Michaels has told you, to get the poison to pass out of him. After that, we just hope that his body is strong enough to overcome the damage done to it."

The doctors came and went through the day. Robert rarely left her side. He helped the doctors administer more of the drugs and checked Ambrose's breathing and pulse occasionally. He also made Chloe eat a little.

Chloe tried to get Ambrose to drink more, and managed to get him to take some broth. Giles sat on the bedside table, barely moving as people came in and out and tea trays were brought and replaced.

Members of the family came through to check on Ambrose throughout the afternoon. Beatrice came with her mother, who stood silently gripping the end of her elephant-headed cane. Dora came with Alexander and their father. William asked the doctors twice if they were doing everything they could. They said they were.

Mr. Frick and Miss Haynes came also, and sat with her until supper, when they left to attend to their evening duties. Doctor Michaels visited again after supper, and from his expression, she knew Ambrose was not progressing as he had hoped. By that night, they could not wake him.

She held Ambrose's discolored hand and laid her head on his pillow, murmuring comfort to him. She told him how they would take a walk on the windy moor when he was better. He had papers to write and books to publish. There were still so many plants and animals to study and books to read and things to learn.

After everyone else had gone and when dawn approached, she told him all the stories of heroes and enchanted animals and adventure that she could remember. Then she sang him songs that her mother had sung to her when she was a little girl.

CHAPTER 37

AMBROSE WAITED BESIDE THE RAILING at the edge of the Thames. It was the precise spot where he had proposed to her, and she liked the familiar feeling of the place. A large black dog sat beside him, its ears alert and its eyes watchful and appraising as she approached. It was not threatening and she was not afraid. A foghorn boomed in the distance where a barge toiled upriver, its hulking form indistinct in the mist. Though it was foggy, she did not feel any chill.

Ambrose took her hand and she looked into his eyes, brown flecked with amber. He looked younger somehow, the picture of health and vitality. An overwhelming feeling of well-being emanated from him and somehow transferred into her, and she felt pleasure and warmth. She did not ever want the feeling to end. She could stand here with him forever.

The dog nudged its head up under Ambrose's hand, and when he looked down, the animal made a short chuffing sound in its throat.

Ambrose took her hand, and she felt all of him, his thoughts, his feelings and his soul through the touch of his fingers. She was aware of every part of his being, every cell of him thrumming with life. She felt his contentment and his sorrow, his love for her, both fierce and gentle. And there was something else, a pulling feeling. He bent to kiss her hand, and afterwards he did not release it, but held it in both of his.

Then, without a word, he let her hand fall. He touched the brim of his black top hat, turned and walked away. The dog trotted beside him and Ambrose's long coat flapped around his legs as he vanished into the swirling London fog.

"Wake up, dear."

Someone was shaking her shoulder.

"You have to wake up now, love. He's gone." It was a woman's voice.

Chloe raised her head. Someone had pulled a sheet over Ambrose. No, he wouldn't be able to breathe like that. She reached over and tore it off. He was asleep but something was wrong. She climbed up next to him and put her arm behind his head and shoulders to raise him. She tried to wake him and pressed her cheek against his forehead, and then froze. He wasn't there. His body was lifeless.

Her Ambrose had gone. She had seen him by the river. She cradled him there on the bed, holding him to her body. His head lolled back and his mouth was slack, the lips pale. His eyes were closed, but he did not look asleep. Not at all.

He was still limp. He would stiffen in time, she knew. There was a word for that, but she could not think of it. Oh God, her Ambrose, dead and stiff and cold. His arms had been folded over his chest, but now fell to the sides. His discolored hand lay palm-up on the covers, a hand that would never wrap hers with warmth and reassurance. A hand that would never hold his stomach as he laughed his easy rolling laugh.

She crushed him against her, wrapping herself around him. People came into the room. There was a terrible sound, high and keening, but she did not know if she made it or if it came from somewhere else. She wanted it to stop, but it was the sound of her heart, crying out. It would always be crying out.

Someone pulled her backwards and off the bed. She was being held against someone. It was someone large, a man. She was being held against his chest, and she clung to him. It was not Ambrose. No, this man smelled different. He felt wrong. His voice was not the right voice, though it spoke reassuring words.

She turned to see Alexander pulling the sheet over Ambrose again. The cloth poked up where his nose was and she could see the line of his chin. Mrs. Block was nearby. She had been the one to shake Chloe awake.

The air would not come into her lungs properly. She couldn't breathe. She gasped and pulled air into her lungs with heaving effort. She recognized the man's voice as he made soothing sounds. He shushed her, like one would do with a young child. A small sensible part of her told her to breathe deeply and slowly. She tried.

"Brrr?"

She looked at Giles, sitting on the side table. He turned to the bed and leapt up beside Ambrose. He let out a long, high yowl, a sound like the one she had heard a few moments before.

Alexander snatched up the cat and tossed him out the door, slamming it closed. Chloe almost called out not to break him, but the words did not come. Giles could be repaired over and over. His parts were interchangeable with other parts. He could be fixed.

The arms around her loosened and she relaxed against the man who held her. The terrible sound in the room was gone, and she stepped back from William, who kept his hand on her shoulder. Faces peered into the doorway, and a few people entered.

Mr. Frick and Miss Haynes were there, and the valet stood close to the younger woman as she wept, but did not touch her. He was speaking quietly into her ear. They had lost their master, Chloe thought. Mr. Frick had known Ambrose for decades, Miss Haynes less time. But she knew they both considered Ambrose a good employer and a good man. There were others who would mourn.

People came and left, one by one, until only she and Mr. Frick remained, along with Doctor Michaels. Mr. Frick closed himself in Ambrose's dressing room. Perhaps he was packing his master's belongings.

She felt as if she were not entirely in her body, but was operating it from a distance, like a remote mechanical. She saw and heard and could respond, but she was somewhere else. It was not with Ambrose.

It was full daylight outside. She did not know what time or even what day it was. Robert was there. Then Beatrice was beside her, leading her down the hall to a quiet sitting room. She wanted to stay with Ambrose, but Robert had said something. She couldn't remember what, but it had been sensible and she had let him lead her away. Beatrice, Dora and Robert sat with her, but she did not know why. They could not help her. All they could do was to offer her a handkerchief, which she took, and cup of tea, which she refused over and over. Finally, she relented and drank.

"How long has it been since you ate or slept?" asked Robert.

She shrugged and shook her head. The clock on the wall read eight thirty. She thought she had fallen asleep just at dawn, but she couldn't be sure. Ambrose had taken that time to slip away quietly and without fanfare. A gentleman to the last.

She allowed Beatrice and Dora to take turns reading to her, but she did not hear the words, only the drone of their voices. Robert brought Giles to sit in her lap. She stroked him. He was unbroken and whole. There were parts in his legs that allowed him to absorb an impact. There were names for all of the mechanical pieces. Beautiful, scientific names.

They stayed with her for lunch, which she ate. They stayed with her through the afternoon. Robert had tablets from one of the doctors, which he wanted her to take. She obeyed.

Evening came. Miss Haynes, red-eyed and teary, drew a bath for her and she bathed. She dressed in her nightclothes and Miss Haynes combed her hair.

As her maid spoke to her and combed, each stroke gave her the gradual sensation of coming back into herself, back into her body after an absence. It was both better and worse than the previous feeling.

It was time for bed. Miss Haynes wanted her to take a sleeping tonic that the doctor had left for her, but she refused. There was a reason she needed to be awake and alert.

Miss Haynes left the tonic for her if she changed her mind. Then she poked the fire and bid her good night. Chloe turned off the gaslight so the only light in the room was from the fire. She knelt on the rug and watched the flames for a long time. She sat until her hair was completely dry and the skin of her face was overly warm. Fire was hot, and it consumed. It destroyed. She watched it. A log popped.

A flicker of something came into her mind. And slowly, something dark and mighty rose within her, like a leviathan rising from the black depths. The thing was powerful and it was large. Larger than her pain, and larger than her grief. Her agony fed it, and it blossomed, immense and powerful. It was a dragon awaking from a thousand year slumber, its dark wings unfurling, stretching until they blocked out the entire world. Its fury was searing and good. It engulfed her until she felt like she was buried in its heat. It fed her.

Death. There was too much death. She was surrounded by death. Camille had mud in her eyes, her skull bashed until she was dead. Josephine was crying, tortured and helpless in her arms, wishing for death. And Ambrose. Her Ambrose.

A person had done this. Death was not an impersonal force. It was not a ghostly hound at the riverside. It was a person. A person had murdered her husband and a little girl and Camille. And the person who did this would pay, yes. They would suffer as their victims had suffered. It was right.

The law said that the punishment for murder was hanging. But hanging would be an undeserved mercy for a demon like that. It was cheating justice, even if the murder would spend his or her last days contemplating death and the fiery hell that waited after that last dance on the gallows.

The heat of her fury poured down her spine and out her limbs. Her hands felt larger and stronger. Her eyes were keen.

She needed rest. The voice in her mind told her this. To rest. She could not do anything tonight. Her body and soul were exhausted. She needed to replenish them. Even a mechanical required periodic maintenance or it would fail. She needed her wits about her. She needed to be able to think logically, to see.

Deadly bogs and mine cave-ins and drunken men in alleyways no longer frightened her. The dark thing within her did not know fear.

CHAPTER 38

THE NEXT MORNING, MISS HAYNES set out the clothing that Chloe had worn to Camille Granger's funeral. It was the only mourning clothing she owned.

"How are you feeling, mum?"

Chloe rubbed her eyes which felt pinched and tight. She pulled on the underclothes that Miss Haynes had laid on the bed.

"I'll be all right," She had to be. She needed to discover why Ambrose was killed. There was something tickling the back of her mind from the night before, but she could not identify it. "I am as well as can be expected when one's husband has been murdered."

Miss Haynes paused in her activities and shook her head. "Everyone is saying that, but it's hard to believe it wasn't simply an accident."

"It would only be an accident if everyone didn't know what the Destroying Angels look like." Chloe pulled her dress over her head.

"I don't know what they look like," said Miss Haynes, pulling the dress down and arranging the skirts.

"Neither do I. But from what everyone says, it seems to be common knowledge for those who live here, especially anyone who would pick edible mushrooms."

"Funny that the master wouldn't have recognized them. Doesn't that seem strange to you?"

"They were chopped up fine. I don't think anyone would

recognize them in that state."

Miss Haynes laced up her dress and worked on her hair. She kept glancing at Chloe in the mirror, as if assessing her.

"What is it?"

"I'm just worried about you, mum. I think you should stay and rest for a day or two. Not strain yourself. You've been through too much."

"No. There will be time for resting when we return home. But for now, I have things to do."

"And when we get back home, we will have to go to your dress shop and order some mourning dresses and things."

Chloe paused. Of course, she would be dressing in black mourning for at least a year. The thought pleased her, in a dark way. Let the dark veils and black bombazine show the state of her soul. It was fitting.

"Yes, but while I am here, there are things I need to do," Chloe said.

"The elder Mr. Aynesworth is arranging for everything. He has already sent word to Mr. Sullivan's solicitor and arranged a cold car to take him to London."

It took a moment for the thought to register. Ambrose would be shipped in cold storage to London to be buried. She wanted him there, in London with her. Not out in this desolate place. Not near his killer.

"Mr. Aynesworth asked me to tell you that he has arranged an airship to take you back to London the day after tomorrow. The funeral is set to be the next Monday." She caught Chloe's eye in the mirror. "I think you should take a day to rest. Please. Just stay in your rooms for the day. I can tell everyone downstairs that you need to have rest and quiet for your nerves."

"Absolutely not. In fact, I need to be out of these rooms or I truly will fear for the state of my nerves."

"I think I should insist, mum."

This was unusual. Miss Haynes had never pressed her

mistress into doing much of anything she did not wish to. She knew that Chloe was an active sort of person who hated being confined with nothing to do.

She studied her own reflection. Her appearance was not lovely by any means, but was acceptable. Her hair was in order. She could use a little color in her cheeks, but perhaps she only looked pale because of the dark color of her dress. Her eyes were puffy, but with good cause.

"Why do you want me to rest today? Tell me truly. You know I would be better off with a brisk walk outdoors or time in my laboratory. Lying about in bed will only make my mind twist and turn."

Miss Haynes sighed and gave her the hand mirror for her to inspect her hair. "The inspector from town is here with a constable. They're asking questions."

"That's good. They should be asking questions. I have a few questions of my own. I expect they are talking to everyone in the house?"

"Yes. But today they said that they wanted to see you."

"I would expect so," said Chloe.

"You don't understand. Once everyone knew that the little girl and Mr. Sullivan were poisoned with the soup, the police wanted to talk to you. They wanted to question you yesterday, but Mr. Aynesworth chased them off. They just arrived a bit ago and asked for you."

This was a new development. She had not thought that she might be a suspect. But the pieces were falling into place.

"They think I killed my husband."

"Yes, mum."

"I will inherit his fortune." She had not considered this. Ambrose had no other heirs.

"I expect so."

Chloe stood. "Well, if they want to ask me questions, they are welcome to do so. I have not harmed a soul, and they can ask me anything they like. I have nothing to conceal."

"I can tell them to come back tomorrow. I could ask Mr. Aynesworth to do it."

"I appreciate your concern and protection, but I do not require it. Where are they?"

"In the front parlor."

"Please tell them I will be down in a few minutes."

"One more thing. I heard that Mr. Granger is no longer a serious suspect. Word is that he threatened to bring down the entire police force. They didn't have enough evidence to do anything."

"I didn't think they would."

Miss Haynes left and Chloe took another look at herself in the mirror. She straightened her carriage and lifted her chin. Her eyes were too puffy to be imperious and commanding. But yes, she could still cut an imposing figure. Well, as imposing as she was capable of being. If only she were taller. She sailed down the stairs and heard voices from the front parlor.

"You know what they say about mushroom hunters?" The man's voice was unfamiliar to her.

"I don't believe this is appropriate." That was Inspector Lockton.

"There are old mushroom hunters, and there are bold mushroom hunters," said the unfamiliar voice. "But there are no old, bold mushroom hunters." He laughed, but stopped when he saw her in the doorway. The constable, a heavy man in his twenties with close-set eyes, sat beside Inspector Lockton. They both rose as she entered. She saw a hint of pleasure in the inspector's expression, but it was gone immediately. He needed to question her about murder, and Chloe knew that he could not allow his past acquaintance with her to interfere.

"Mrs. Sullivan," said Inspector Lockton. "May I introduce Constable Bell."

She inclined her head as the constable gave a small bow. She took the seat opposite the two men which placed her with the sunlight in her face. She wondered if the servants and family had been questioned in the same uncomfortable position. Giles jumped up onto the windowsill and sat so he could see both the outdoors and the parlor.

"You would like to question me about my husband's murder?"

"I would," said Inspector Lockton. "We understand if you would like us to come back at a later time, after you have had some time to grieve."

She got the impression that he was saying it as a courtesy and treated it as such. His note pad was already open on his knee.

"No, I am able to talk to you today."

"Thank you, Mrs. Sullivan." Inspector Lockton licked the tip of his pencil.

"How long had you and your late husband been married?"

His use of the past tense made her pause. She was a widow now.

"Three years."

"And you will stand to inherit a considerable fortune, will you not?"

"He has no other heirs. No children."

The thought stabbed her. After three years of marriage, she had suspected that she might be barren. Now there was the certainty that she would have no children. It had not mattered so much before, but now the thought gave her pain.

"And what was the age difference between you and your late husband?"

"Twenty-four years."

"That's a large age difference."

It was not terribly unusual, she thought, especially among the upper classes where young women were routinely married off to older men to acquire titles, fortunes or to solidify social connections. The inspector knew this.

"It is not unheard of. He was a friend of my father's. He

257

and I have known each other for many years."

"And you knew he was wealthy when you married?"

"Naturally."

"And from what I understand, you came from a lower class family. Some sort of financial ruin?"

For an instant, she remembered revealing to him that she had not always been wealthy, but she had said nothing of financial ruin. But then she understood. Of course the police had spoken with Mr. Frick and Miss Haynes. And had either of them lied or said that she came to the union with money, the police would have discovered the falsehood with little trouble. All of the Aynesworths most likely knew of her origins also.

Constable Bell leaned forward. "A younger woman marries a wealthy older man. He dies under mysterious circumstances, leaving her with a handsome inheritance. It just seems strange is all." He was watching her with too much intensity, his lips parted in anticipation. She would not give him what he sought.

"And what question are you asking me?" she kept her voice low.

"Doesn't that sound strange to you?" The constable tilted his head slightly. The gesture infuriated her but she kept her face composed.

He was at least five years her junior. He couldn't have been on the police force very long, and with three recent murders, it would be quite the feather in his cap to aid in the capture of a killer. But he was over-eager and jumping to conclusions.

"Do you think you will marry again, Mrs. Sullivan?" he asked.

She turned her body to face to the inspector, where before she had been facing both men. It was a slight not lost on the constable, who scowled.

"Are you asking me questions to gather information or are the local police now in the habit of making baseless accusations about bereaved women?"

"My apologies, Mrs. Sullivan," said Inspector Lockton. He gave the constable a long silent look that made him sit back.

"Inspector, my husband was murdered. Josephine was murdered. Someone gave them Destroying Angels and they died horribly. I did not add the mushrooms, but someone did and you need to find this person, not waste time with me."

"We are doing our best to do exactly that. Now, tell me about the soup."

She did. She described Ambrose's sickness, the soup, her search through Ambrose's books, and her discussion with Doctor Michaels.

"That soup sat there all Sunday afternoon, simmering on the stove. At least, that's what Mrs. Block told me," she said.

"Yes," said the inspector. "Everyone agrees on that point. Please tell me where you were Saturday. You came to visit me, but the household says that you were out of the house most of the day."

She felt her face grow warm. "I went to look for the hound in the tin mine that I told you about. He wasn't there. And when I left, I saw the woman named Maggie who lives nearby. I spent some time at her house, and then returned home."

"Mad Maggie?" said Constable Bell. "You went to visit her? She sells a few things that could kill a man if he took too much."

"But not Destroying Angels," said Inspector Lockton. "Now, you say that you went to search for the hound? Why?"

"I'm sorry, but I had to go straight there after I saw you. Your assurances that I could get the hound after the police examined it were not enough. I know that you cannot guarantee that I would have the opportunity to examine it before it was destroyed, so I hoped to find it on my own. I'm sorry."

The inspector nodded and made a note. "Did you do anything else when you were out on the moor?"

"What do you mean?"

"Did you collect poisonous mushrooms while you were out? I have to ask."

"Of course not. I don't even know what they look like. But apparently everyone else who lives around here does. My maid and I may be the only ones who are unable to identify a Destroying Angel." She gave them a pointed look.

"But your husband was a naturalist. He would have known. He could have told you."

"But he didn't. He had no cause to."

"The doctor said that you and the youngest son were looking through your husband's books when he was ill. That there was a book on mushrooms."

"Yes, there was a mycology book. But I looked at it after Ambrose was already sick."

But there was no way she could prove it. The book had been sitting in Ambrose's temporary study since they arrived. She had access to it at any time. And she had the time to collect mushrooms on the moor, save them until she could give them to her husband, watch him die and inherit his fortune.

"Just a moment," she said. "What happened to the rest of the pot of soup after Ambrose and Josephine ate from it? Surely they did not finish all of it."

"Mrs. Block said it vanished. The killer must have come back to empty it out."

CHAPTER 39

CHLOE LOOKED PAST THE MEN and out the window at the sound of approaching hooves. Giles, who was still sitting on the windowsill, tipped his head, watching. Ian dismounted his horse and handed the reins to the waiting groom. He was unshaven with dark shadows under his eyes and he looked exhausted and a little wild. She thought back and realized that she had not seen him at all since they had taken Josephine to Doctor Fleming's house.

"That's the oldest son?" Inspector Lockton asked the constable.

"Yes."

"You don't know the family?" Chloe asked.

"I was called in from Exeter for the Granger murder."

Of course. A town like Farnbridge would not require its own inspector. She thought of his office, with no name on the door. So Lockton was a stranger here too.

The front door banged and Alexander took off outside toward his brother. Ian turned to him with a dark look, full of hatred, anticipation and a kind of pleasure. Alexander shoved his reddened face into his brother's and said words Chloe could not make out.

"Someone should stop them," she said. She looked from the constable to the inspector. "They're going to hurt one another." Neither of them made any move.

Alexander was shouting something at his brother while

Ian stood tall and still, his fingers slowly flexing and unflexing. Chloe got the impression of a sleek black jungle cat, waiting for the right moment to spring. The inspector and constable had moved closer to the window and showed no indication of intervening. She rushed out the front door but froze on the bottom step.

"You say another word, and I swear, I'll kill you," said Alexander.

"More killing, brother? I thought you might have had enough of that by now."

"I haven't hurt anyone."

"No? Deborah Walker is dead as is her daughter. Both of them erased, just as you wished."

"That wasn't my fault. I never did a thing to either of them."

"And there it is," said Ian. "Perhaps you should have done something for them."

"For that tart? I wasn't the first to soil her. What, did you expect me to marry her?"

"No, but you left her to make her living on the street and raise her daughter—your daughter—in a boarding house."

Alexander raised his hands in a gesture of indifference and took a step back. "What's it to me where she went? And who knows if the child was even mine? It's only the word of a loose woman."

"Don't call her that," Ian's voice was very soft, almost gentle.

"Why not? Did you love her? Were you jealous that I got there first, brother?"

"Don't be an imbecile. I felt sorry for her."

"But that's not why you helped her. Oh, but I know why." A mocking smile curved Alexander's mouth.

Ian did not answer.

"I've seen how it is with you two, don't think I haven't. I'm not the idiot playboy you take me for."

Alexander turned as if to go and then spun around to

punch his brother. In one fluid movement, Ian grabbed his wrist, twisted it and with his other hand, struck his brother in the jaw. Ian released him and Alexander reeled backwards. Ian had a look of pure pleasure.

"Father isn't here to help you, you worthless animal," Ian said in a smooth voice. "You never should have been born. You have brought nothing but pain and suffering your entire life. I would be doing the world a favor to remove you from existence."

"You're mad."

"Am I? But you are the one who killed Uncle, are you not? He knew about your irresponsibility and your gross indiscretions."

"What reason would I have for that? The girl was already here, the letters were already in the hands of the police. My life was already ruined because of you."

"Because of me? I did my best to clean up your messes. And you were right. It was never for your sake, you feckless arse."

Alexander charged him and got in one good punch to Ian's mouth. Ian touched his lip, looked at his fingers and smiled.

"There we go, now. First blood."

Ian leapt forward and punched Alexander in the face so hard that Chloe heard a dense, muffled crunching sound. Alexander shouted. Ian did not even pause, but kept punching and hitting until he was straddling his brother on the ground. The whole thing had only taken moments.

"Stop it now!" yelled Chloe and ran toward them.

Ian was methodically pounding his brother's face and had gotten in a few good hits, but Alexander twisted and threw him off. The men scuffled in the dirt, grunting and thrashing.

In a moment, Constable Bell was there and he pulled Alexander in one direction while Inspector Lockton pulled Ian in the other. Alexander was shouting curses, but

Ian wore a satisfied smirk as he watched his brother. Alexander's nose and mouth were bleeding. Even his teeth were covered in blood. As for Ian, the area around his eye was turning red.

Dora and William were yelling nearby while Robert stood watching from the doorstep.

"I swear to God, I will kill you," said Alexander as he looked up from the blood on his handkerchief.

"Please. Do try."

"Stop this!" cried Dora. "Just stop it! You leave him alone," she said to Ian who gave her a cold look.

After awhile, Dora and Robert escorted Alexander into the house to tend his nose. Someone would most likely be sent to fetch a carriage. Doctor Fleming would certainly be getting his fill of the Aynesworth family.

The constable and inspector were speaking with William in the doorway. Ian had walked a little way down the drive, and he glanced toward the side of the house. Beatrice was half hidden in the building's shadow. Her hands were at her sides and though tears streaked down her cheeks, she did not seem aware of them. She was watching her brother-in-law.

He took a look at the front of the house and then walked toward Beatrice. He stood before her for a moment in the shadows before she crumpled into his chest. He slowly, very slowly, placed his hand on her back.

"The girl was Alexander's?" Inspector Lockton appeared beside Chloe.

She blinked and turned to him. "Oh, I believe so. Ian pretended that she was his child to spare Beatrice from shame. At least, I think that's what happened."

"Who else knows this?"

"Everyone now, I suppose."

"Did Mrs. Aynesworth know that the child was her husband's when the girl came?"

Her stomach turned cold. It was impossible. Beatrice

would never harm anyone. Besides, she could not have anticipated that the girl would eat the soup. "I believe she had an idea, but you would have to ask her yourself."

"I don't believe Mrs. Aynesworth set out to harm the girl, if that is what you are thinking. From what I understand, your husband was the target and the girl's death was an unfortunate coincidence."

"Sadly, the killer can only hang once for both of them."

They walked together back into the house. Constable Bell held the door and followed them into the front parlor where they took their seats. Well, that was a bit of excitement. The inspector flipped through his notebook.

"Is there any reason why someone would want your husband dead?" asked Inspector Lockton. "Ian said that your husband knew about Alexander's illegitimate daughter. Is that true?"

She didn't know what Ambrose knew, not really. It gave her a pang to know that he had kept secrets, even if she had kept some herself. "I don't think he knew. Or if he did, he did not share it with me."

There was a silence. Inspector Lockton turned to Constable Bell. "Would you please check on the family? I want to make sure the brothers do not do more violence to each other. And if everything is calmed down, please ask the elder Mr. Aynesworth to come speak with me."

The constable left and Inspector Lockton shut his notebook and tossed it onto the table between them. He rubbed the bridge of his nose.

"Tell me, who do you think killed your husband?"

"What did he know that would cause someone to murder him, you mean? If I knew that, the killer would be in your custody already." She adjusted herself in her seat and sighed. "Ambrose was about to talk to Mr. Baxter about some business arrangements and everyone knew it. Something about investments and publishing my husband's work in Boston. But there was no danger of him telling Mr. Baxter anything damaging to the family or endangering Dora's impending nuptials. Others already knew about Josephine, so there was no cause to silence Ambrose. It doesn't make any sense."

"No, it doesn't," said the inspector.

There was only one thing that did make sense, she thought bitterly. A young woman marrying an older man, poisoning him and inheriting his fortune.

The constable returned, along with William.

"Mr. Aynesworth," said Inspector Lockton, rising. "I am going to post a guard at your house. Constable Bell and another officer will be remaining here for the rest of the day. Other officers will come tonight to relieve them. No one, not even a servant, may leave the premises without notifying Constable Bell or his replacement. They will be keeping a log."

"What are you on about? We are not prisoners in our own home," said William.

"No, you are not prisoners, but someone in this house killed Ambrose Sullivan and Josephine Walker. Until we know who it is, we cannot risk the perpetrator escaping." He stepped through the parlor door and pulled his coat from the doorway mechanical. William followed him.

"Everyone down to the bootboy or scullery maid who needs to leave for any reason will notify Constable Bell," the inspector said. "And anyone who has necessary business in town must be accompanied by a constable."

"We are being held under guard? You must be joking. Are you saying that if we want to go anywhere at all, we have to ask permission from your people?"

"That is precisely what I am saying. And please, Mr. Aynesworth, think of it as a security guard."

CHAPTER 40

A T LAST, CHLOE WAS ALONE. After holding the door open for Giles, she sat down in Ambrose's old room. She had considered going to her own rooms, but that made locating her too easy. After Alexander had left for the doctor, the chaos had died down and she found herself able to slip away unnoticed.

All of Ambrose's personal belongings were gone except for a few books and pages of notes which had all been collected together into one lonely pile. The bed had been stripped and remade and the room had been aired out. It was an empty guest room once more.

The door to Ambrose's dressing room had been left ajar and Giles darted inside. Chloe opened the door to find that Mr. Frick had already packed up all of her husband's clothing. A moment later, she was startled by the familiar scent of Ambrose's shaving soap. She stood without moving, wanting both to stay and to leave.

Miss Haynes opened the door that connected her room to her husband's and stopped short just as she was about to gather the books and notes from the table.

"There you are. Were you looking for something?" Miss Haynes said.

"I just came here for some quiet. It's mad downstairs."

"All the servants are talking about it. How are you feeling?"

"I'm all right." She turned to the cat. "Come, Giles." The

cat obeyed and she closed the dressing room door.

"When you have some time, Mr. Frick needs to see you," said Miss Haynes. "He has been in the study most of the morning. I'm helping him pack up a few things." She picked up the items on the table.

So much for solitude. Chloe crossed the hall and found Mr. Frick setting sample slides into their cases. From the way he turned and squinted at them, it appeared that he was arranging them in alphabetical order. The accompanying microscope case was closed and set on top of other boxes. He took one slide to the window and held it at arm's length, then adjusted the distance, trying to read it.

"I can take care of those," said Chloe.

Mr. Frick nodded and she finished up the slides. She had to make sure that Mr. Frick had a comfortable per annum amount to support himself once they returned home. He had been an experienced older valet when Ambrose had hired him decades ago. It would not be fair to ask someone of his years to find new employment. She would have to check with Ambrose's solicitor to see if Ambrose had made any arrangement for him, and if not, she would see to it herself.

"I would like to leave the slides for Robert," said Chloe. "And the microscope as well. It's not as if I will be needing them."

"As you wish, mum."

The room felt wrong. Her laboratory items were untouched and still scattered in the disarray into which her work space always seemed to descend. Her tools and materials were like artifacts from a different life. Most of Ambrose's things were packed into crates stacked one upon the other. His side of the room felt nothing like him anymore.

Mr. Frick stacked the last of the slide boxes and set the stack on top of the microscope box before turning to face her.

"There is the matter of the steamcycle that I wished to discuss with you," he said. "We need to arrange its transport to the railway station, but it is too large to have it crated and hauled."

"I hadn't thought of that. Of course, someone needs to drive it. I can take it into town tomorrow."

Mr. Frick nodded, relieved. She wondered if he had somehow thought that he or one of the other servants would be required to drive it into town. She imagined Mr. Frick, goggled and leaning over the handlebars as he rode.

"Also, there are some items of the master's that you may wish to go through." He gestured toward the desk where a stack of papers and envelopes sat in a neat pile. "I've gone through them myself, and you could take them all to his solicitor if you wish. Some require a response and others are related to financial matters."

Yes, she was heir to a fortune. The thought was a lead weight inside her. She should be pleased, if not with the money itself, then with the lifelong independence it would purchase for her. But it felt like ill-gotten gains. The fortune of a dead man.

"I will go through them myself," she said.

Mr. Frick busied himself with other things and she sorted through the various papers. Two letters were in reference to printing some of Ambrose's papers in a scientific journal. She set those aside. She could contact one of her husband's colleagues in London and ask them to see to the posthumous publication. It would honor Ambrose to let his life's work educate a few more people after his death.

There were letters from friends in London, and one made her pause. It was from a Mr. Brian Graves. Something about it stopped her. A thought was close, but she could not grasp it. It was like a rubber balloon, hovering just out of reach.

She had to think. It had something to do with sitting

at Ambrose's bedside. He was delirious and he had said something. *Graves.* At the time, she had thought that he feared for his life, considering the doctor's indiscrete reference to Josephine's death.

This was one of the letters that she and Ambrose had received when they met Beatrice, Dora and Robert in town. She pulled the letter from the envelope.

Dear Mr. Sullivan,

I am pleased to hear from you once more. It is good news that you are enjoying your stay with your family in Dartmoor, although the appeal of the place has always eluded me personally. However, I am sure that the plant life is distinctive and I hope you will find many fascinating specimens to add to your collection. May your trip be intellectually profitable, my friend.

The questions in your letter left me surprised, but I will answer them. First, my wife has been in good health and has not had any serious illnesses in recent memory. She is sitting near the fire at this moment, and sends her greetings to you.

And secondly, as you know, my son did indeed work for the Aynesworth family in the position of tutor for the youngest son. He enjoyed his time there and found the boy to be a quick study, if a bit serious for his years.

Now to the difficult part. Brian Junior was released from his position without warning. He keeps his own counsel and has not indulged my requests to know why he was forced to leave. He is a grown man and owes no obedience to me, though it bothers me that he was visibly distressed after his return home and was out of sorts for weeks.

I am glad to report that he is much recovered and has secured a position with a good family in the city. His mother is pleased to have him living so close by.

There was more, but Chloe set down the letter. She needed to speak with Robert.

She located him in his garden, hoeing an empty row at the far end. The garden seemed recovered from its former destruction. The plants were all upright and the one closest to her even had some new shoots. Robert was wearing gardening clothes and his knees were damp and dirty. He leaned on the hoe.

"Come back again?" he said. "I don't see Giles with you."

"I left him in the house. I was unsure what he would do if faced with the sight of all these fresh plants."

"I've gotten everything back to the way it was, more or less. But I would appreciate you not bringing him anywhere near here, if you can help it."

She crossed the distance between them. "Do you have a moment?"

"Certainly." He leaned the hoe on the fence.

"I want to thank you for helping Ambrose. I know you worked long and hard to find out what was making him sick, and then you tried to find out what we could do about it. I just want you to know that I am grateful."

All of a sudden, he found his shoes fascinating. "It was nothing. And anyway, I couldn't save him."

"No one could. But it was certainly not nothing. You helped check his vitals, watched over him and you gave him medicine. More importantly, you maintained calm and reason in the face of death. I think you have the makings of a fine physician one day."

The boy became a deep shade of pink and fidgeted with a button on his coat. Chloe would not press him further.

"But I wanted to ask you something else too. About your tutor, Mr. Graves."

"Oh, what about him?" His expression was wary. "My father is still trying to find another tutor for me."

"Did Mr. Graves get along with your family?"

"Well enough. Ian didn't like him, but then Ian doesn't like much of anyone. Alexander and my father thought he was adequate. Father did not like him teaching me any medical things, because he worried about my interest. He thought I should be content to learn about naval battles and military campaigns."

"And Dora? Did she like him?"

"I suppose."

"Did she like him a great deal?"

"How should I know?" He grabbed his hoe. "It was no concern of mine."

"It would be if it caused Mr. Graves to have to leave."

"He left because his mother had taken ill." He gave her a look that dared her to contradict him. "He had to tend to her."

"Is that what your father told you?"

"He had no reason to lie. No reason." He grabbed the hoe, strode off and threw himself into hoeing the empty row, breaking up the earth clods with vicious efficiency.

"Robert, wait." She followed him.

"What?" He did not pause or look up.

"I'm sorry. I am. For everything."

He raised his head and looked long and hard at the back of the house. "If you will excuse me," he said.

She felt terrible as she walked back to the house. She hated having to question Robert like that. No boy should have to live in a house riddled with intrigue, lies and death under its roof.

The mechanical creature on the moor was not the only hound in this place. The house was filled with hounds, vying and conniving for power, dominating and indulging in seductions. There was violence between the brothers and there were secrets, betrayals and forbidden things. And somewhere in the pack was a murderer.

Poor Robert, living among these creatures. She should not have pained him with difficult questions. But then a new thought came, a dark feeling of ruthlessness and sharp intensity. If the questions hurt him, there was no helping it. The truth had to come out, even if it caused pain.

The dark thought faded and she thought about turning back, but still there was nothing she could say to him. Nothing could help or ease the next years he had to spend here. She hoped he was able to study medicine some day, but if he was dependent upon his father, he had no choice in the matter. He was the youngest of three sons. He had neither title, property nor money.

She had money now. How much, she did not know. But perhaps it was enough to pay for university. She tucked the thought away for later, after she discussed things with Ambrose's solicitor in London. She went to look for Miss Haynes in the house and found her mending a set of stockings.

"Tomorrow, we need to go to the dress shop in town," Chloe said.

"I thought you wanted to wait until we were back in London," said Miss Haynes. "We leave the day after tomorrow and there won't be time for the seamstress to make up the dress in time."

"Maybe I will just pick out a hat, veil and maybe some gloves." She narrowed her eyes in thought. "No. I think I need a complete fitting in the back of the shop. I can always have the dress shipped to our address. Yes. That's what you will tell the constable at any rate, if he asks."

"What do you mean?"

"After you are finished with your mending, please tell the constable on duty that we need to go to the dress shop tomorrow afternoon to get suitable mourning clothes for the new widow. Make it sound like it will take all afternoon. We just need to have as much time as possible in the shop. The police will send someone with us, but I think I have accounted for that."

"Accounted for it? What are you planning?"

"Don't look at me like that. It is nothing sinister. First off, I need to drive the steamcycle to the railway station tomorrow so it can be shipped back home. A constable can't ride on the back of it, so have them make whatever arrangements they like to keep an eye on me in town. Then, you can take the carriage into town and we can meet at the dress shop."

"I don't want to do anything that would get us in trouble with the police."

"I wouldn't put you in that position. No, you will be accompanying me as my maid, and nothing more."

"I don't think I like this. Why do we need to do this?"

The dark thing moved inside her. One of the hounds in this house had killed her Ambrose.

"Another piece of the puzzle has fallen into place."

CHAPTER 41

AS SOON AS CHLOE DROVE into town, she had a strange feeling. Ambrose could not request that she be discreet so there was no reason she could not be seen riding through town on the steamcycle. After the family's own activities, nothing she could do would bring further scandal. Heads turned as she drove down the street, past the police station and toward the railway station.

As she turned into the wide alleyway behind the railway station, she saw Constable Bell waiting for her on the street corner. She parked in the cargo area at the back of the station and Constable Bell came around the corner.

"Good afternoon! You must be here to accompany me," she said in her brightest tone. She wished she had been assigned a different constable, but she supposed there were only so many officers to go around. Constable Bell did not like her and he probably did not trust her. Her plan was dependent upon her having enough time in the dress shop without interference.

"I need to handle a few things here at the station, and then we can meet my lady's maid at the dress shop."

She went to the station window and filled out the paperwork to have the steamcycle shipped to London. She checked her pocket watch. There was just enough time to walk to the dress shop before Miss Haynes arrived.

They walked to Hampton Street, and just as Mr. Lydford had said, the dress shop was next door, on the far side. She had not paid any attention to the shop on her previous visit to Lydford's and it was more fine and fancy than she had anticipated. Perhaps, she wondered, she had grown too snobbish, assuming that a country shop would not have the fashionable items that her Bond Street shop offered.

She looked at the shop front. This was the display that the hound had broken into when he mauled a window dummy. The glass looked new and was squeaky clean. The window display was immaculate with three perfectly dressed shop dummies in a row. All had been repaired.

This moment was critical. She needed Contestable Bell to wait outside for her plan to work. If he waited indoors, things would be much more difficult. She was weighing what she should say when he cleared his throat.

"I'll wait here," he said and took a spot leaning against the wall between Lydford's and the dress shop.

"I may be a while, but I'll be as quick as I can."

"Never known a woman to be quick about anything, but I'll manage."

The carriage pulled up with Miss Haynes.

"Please return for us in two hours," said Chloe to the driver, making sure she said it loudly enough for Constable Bell to overhear. He sighed and looked with longing at the club and the bakery across the street, and then to the pub next door. She would not have minded if he nipped in for a bit, but she doubted he would.

She found the interior of the dress shop light and airy, with feathered hats on faceless display heads and beautiful flounced dresses displayed on headless dummies. Tables of gloves, ribbons, sashes, slippers, scarves and handkerchiefs filled the small central area of the shop.

The proprietor appeared, a stout, ruddy-faced woman in yellow and pale green. Chloe explained that she was in need of mourning clothing.

"I will need a few things shipped to London."

The woman nodded a greeting to Miss Haynes and showed them bolts of their most expensive fabric. Chloe pointed to the first few that didn't look too terrible. Time was short.

"Miss Haynes will pick out a few more," she said and Miss Haynes nodded. A thin shop girl worked with Miss Haynes while the owner took Chloe to the back of the shop to get her measurements.

Chloe stood on a small platform in a curtained area and couldn't see the back of the shop. If the shopkeeper thought her split riding skirt was strange, she did not say anything. Chloe felt the seconds tick by as she stood in her corset and bloomers, the shop woman's tape measure wrapping around her here, then there.

Miss Haynes and the shop girl came in with an assortment of handkerchiefs and gloves. Chloe picked out a matching set of black with gray lace trim and chose a black hat with a veil that was ready to be boxed up and taken home that day. Once she was back in her clothing and the shop women were gone, she called Miss Haynes back.

"I need you to keep them up at the front of the shop as long as you can. Tell them I'm having trouble with my shoes or some such. Come back alone to check on me, whatever you need to do. Just give me a time. And keep them from notifying the constable for as long as possible."

Miss Haynes looked terrified. "I don't like this, mum."

"I know. And I wouldn't ask if I didn't have to."

Miss Haynes nodded.

"And Regina. Thank you."

Miss Haynes gave her a pained look over her shoulder as she left.

Chloe passed through the rest of the shop and went behind a three-paneled screen where the back door ought to be, only to pull up short. There was no door that led to the alleyway, just a blank wall. There was a door to one side, but it led to Lydford's. If her guess was right, it would open into his back workshop.

She tried the knob, but as she expected, it was locked. She knocked on the door gently, but loud enough for someone inside the workshop to hear. He must be up front. She gave the door five hard raps, hurting her knuckles in the process. She heard another door open inside the workshop and she knocked again. She heard something slide and the door opened.

"Mrs. Sullivan! What are you doing here?" Mr. Lydford glanced behind her at the interior of the dress shop. "You are shopping?"

"I need to come in. It's urgent. Please."

"Certainly." He got out of the way and she closed the door behind her and bolted it.

"Why in the world doesn't the dress shop have a back door?" she demanded.

"It used to be one shop with mine, but then the landlord split it in two and rents out both sides. The dress shop uses my back door for shipments."

The back workshop was as she had seen it before, filled with parts, gears and tubing. It still smelled of oil, lubricants, and this time, something else. Something was burning.

"What's that burning smell?" Chloe asked.

"I don't smell anything."

"I'm sure of it. It smells like rubber."

He shook his head and then gasped as something dawned on him. "Wait here. Will you be all right? Of course you will," he said as he bolted out the door to the front of the shop.

Whatever he was working on, she hoped it did not burn the place down. Not that it wouldn't be a convenient distraction, she thought as she slipped into the back alley. She ran down to the street, hailed a hansom cab and told the driver the address.

After a brief ride, she exited and paid the driver,

using a small part of the money she had brought in her reticule. She gave the driver a large tip and turned toward the Hammond residence. She wondered if the constable had noticed her absence yet and how Miss Haynes was handling things. She had purposely withheld information on where she was going from her maid. Miss Haynes was an honest soul, and if there was a penalty to be paid for her actions, she would pay it alone.

She knocked on the front door of the Hammond house and Rebecca answered. The young girl's mother was in a chair in the room behind her, a blanket tucked around her legs.

"Mrs. Sullivan, I didn't expect to see you. What brings you?" Rebecca said.

"In fact, I am here to see you."

After a moment of surprise, Rebecca admitted her.

"Are your father and brother home?" asked Chloe.

"No, they are both working."

Chloe wished she could be alone with Rebecca, but if she was correct, then her mother listening in to their conversation was the least of her problems. She took a seat next to the ill woman and Rebecca sat opposite her.

"My condolences on the death of your husband," said Rebecca's mother in a weak voice.

"Thank you." Chloe was tempted to correct her and use the word "murder" instead of "death" but restrained herself.

Rebecca nodded, her expression concerned. "I am also very sorry to hear about Mr. Sullivan. He was so kind and my father was overcome when he heard the news."

"Thank you. I want to ask you something about the Aynesworth family. I'm sorry to be so direct, but I am in a terrible rush."

"Is everything all right?" Rebecca looked worried and her mother pulled herself up straighter in her chair.

"Everyone is fine. I just have some things I need to know. It's very important. I once heard Mrs. Malone say that

Dora was ill last December. Do you remember her illness?"

"Yes, she was sick for a few days."

"And did she have a fever, vomiting, fatigue, perhaps cramping or delirium?"

"I believe so. I'm not sure about the cramping and delirium, but I know about the rest. Her lady's maid was sick also, but milder. The symptoms must have built up slowly though, as the mistress asked for medicine before they were very sick."

"What do you mean, they asked for medicine?"

"I really cannot say any more, I'm sorry."

Of course she couldn't. She hoped to work in the Aynesworth household again, and any violation of the family's trust would place her out of reach of that goal forever.

"It's important that you tell me what you know. Do you know Inspector Lockton?"

Both mother and daughter shook their heads.

"He was brought here to investigate Mrs. Granger's murder. Now he is questioning people about the death of my husband and the little girl. More people could potentially be hurt by the killer. I know you are hoping to work for the Aynesworth family again, but please reconsider. They are not all the respectable people you thought they were."

"That's not true!"

"We've heard of the scandal with the little girl," Rebecca's mother took a raspy breath. "Terrible business."

"And it's not the worst of the business that has gone on in that house."

Rebecca shook her head. "I'm sorry. I can't help you."

"If you will not speak to me, they may send the police to question you. They will not be as delicate."

It was a lie, but a lie in service of a bigger truth. Chloe felt the deep anger spark within her. The reputation of the Aynesworth family was as dust to her. She did not wish to force Rebecca to violate her sense of duty, but her loyalties were misplaced. She had to figure out how to make her understand.

"I'm sorry," Rebecca said. "If the police come and ask me, then I am forced to obey and answer every question. But I can't be repeating gossip to just anyone. You seem like a nice woman, Mrs. Sullivan, and I'm sorry about your husband. But I cannot help you."

Rebecca stood, moved to the front door and opened it. Chloe rose and stood before her.

"Please reconsider. This could be a matter of life and death."

"I'm sorry Mrs. Sullivan, good-bye."

"Rebecca, Mr. Sullivan was murdered. He and the little girl died in terrible pain. They were vomiting and writhing in agony for hours."

Rebecca blanched and covered her mouth with her hand. "That's horrible."

"They died covered in their own filth, their stomachs eaten away, their skin yellowed and their hands purple. They cried out for mercy. They screamed in their delirium."

"Oh my God, please stop."

"They begged for the pain to stop, but no drug could help them. Death was a mercy for them, the only end to their agonizing pain. And they died because someone murdered them."

Rebecca shook her head, looking past Chloe at some insubstantial thing in the distance. She still held the doorknob, waiting for Chloe to leave.

The girl shook her head. "There is nothing I can do. I'm sorry."

Chloe felt the rage leap up. She no longer cared about Rebecca's feelings or her honest desire to do her duty. All of it was rubbish. She wanted to shake the girl until she spoke, to force the words from her mouth. Her hands itched to grab the girl's shoulders and slam her against a wall.

"Tell her," said the sick woman.

Rebecca glanced at her mother, oblivious to the struggle for control going on in the woman before her.

"Tell her, darling."

"I'm not sure I should say. It's not proper to discuss these things, even among women, you understand." She closed the door and returned to her seat. Her mother was speaking to her now, and the girl was listening. That was better. Chloe moved to take a seat again, trying to recover an air of serenity and grace.

With another look at her mother, Rebecca took a breath. "Miss Aynesworth's maid asked me to fetch a special tea. It was medicinal, to help with a health problem that Miss Aynesworth had. They gave me a note, sealed, and I brought it, got the tea and brought it back."

"You brought the note to the doctor?"

Rebecca stared at her folded hands.

"To Mad Maggie?" Chloe's voice was low, but there was no chance of her being misunderstood. She wished she knew Maggie's last name, but since Constable Bell had called her Mad Maggie, the name had stuck in her mind. Rebecca colored a deep pink and after a while, she nodded.

"And why didn't Miss Aynesworth summon Doctor Fleming or Doctor Michaels?"

"I know what you're thinking, and it's not like that. Miss Aynesworth is a lady, a proper lady. You shouldn't say things like that."

"I didn't say anything about Miss Aynesworth. I simply asked a question."

"I don't know."

It was probably a lie, but one Chloe could live with. She had gotten the answer to her question.

"One last thing. Did Camille Granger know about any of this?"

"Well, yes now that you mention it. But how would you know that? She came when Dora was sick and had a visit with her. They were close enough for visits like that. Good friends, very close."

"Thank you, Rebecca. You have helped immensely."

Chloe's hands were shaking when she rose and said her good-byes. She felt wobbly on her feet as she passed through the door that Rebecca held for her. But once the door closed behind her and she started walking, the feeling gradually faded and she felt a steely determination take hold. There was no time for emotion, only action.

She hurried away, moving on to a busier street and hailing a hansom cab. She told the driver to let her out a block away from the dress shop. If Miss Haynes had been able to keep the ladies in the dress shop busy, then she could slip in the back. She stepped out of the cab, paid the driver and checked her watch. It had been over an hour.

She sped around a corner, and stopped in her tracks. Two police officers were shouting and struggling with something in the back of a cart. The cart driver gave anxious looks behind him, as if ready to leap from the seat at any moment. She moved closer to see what thing was in the cart, though she was sure she already knew.

CHAPTER 42

CHLOE RECOGNIZED THE TWO OFFICERS in the cart as the ones who were at the bog with Camille's body. Each officer held a rope that had been looped around the hound's neck. Both were pulling in opposite directions, trying to keep the ropes taut as the hound reared and struggled. A third man moved around the cart, pulling first one rope and then another and fastening them to metal ties at the edges of the cart.

The hound was not making any of it easy on them. It bolted and pulled, yanked and thrashed in an attempt to escape. Its jaws snapped whenever a man got too close and there were shouts from the officers as well as the townsfolk who watched the struggle. The cart was moving slowly, but judging from the whites visible around the horse's terrified eyes, it was better than the alternative.

A small crowd had gathered and was growing by the moment. Whenever the hound lunged, someone would scream. Two other officers came through the crowd and called out to their colleagues in the cart. The largest of the men had a cricket bat and he muscled through the crowd, which parted easily for him.

No. They couldn't be allowed to destroy the creature. Chloe pushed closer. The crowd was thick now, everyone craning their necks and pushing. Someone stepped hard on her foot.

"Come see the monster!" screamed one boy to another

and they jumped up and down, trying to get a better look.

Chloe called out, but her voice was lost in the commotion. She pulled a woman back and shoved her way past a man, squeezing her body far too closely against his.

"I say!"

She ignored him and the other cries and shocked looks as she forced her way forward in a completely unladylike fashion. She pushed herself inside the innermost circle of people and emerged only feet from the hound. Its optical apertures were fully dilated, and its mouth opened and closed, exposing all of its teeth. It looked every inch the terrible monster.

The police were oblivious to her shouts, and the man with the cricket bat was climbing up the back of the cart. In a moment, he would be inside.

Chloe held her split skirt with one hand and leaped onto the side of the cart, wedging her feet into the bottom slats and clinging as best she could. As one, the crowd gave a startled cry and the officers shouted at her, waving her off. She ignored them.

The hound had turned to look at her, momentarily distracted from its escape attempts.

"There, there. It's going to be all right." She forced her voice into a calm tone she did not feel. She tore off her hat and tossed it away. Maybe without the hat, the hound could recognize her more easily. She wished that she had the head scarf she had worn that night, which seemed so long ago.

The hound paused and its ears swiveled. Its head cocked to one side and it closed its mouth.

"That's better," she said and leaned forward slightly.

It lunged for her. It came to the end of its rope in an instant, but managed to twist its head sideways and grab the hem of her skirt, which was protruding slightly under the bottommost slat. She hung on with one hand and with the other, tried to pull the cloth free. The hound shook its head, rending the cloth with a slow tearing sound. For an instant, she was amazed at its realistic canine behavior. But the next instant, she felt the piece of cloth tear free, followed by the thud of wood against cloth-covered metal.

The officer with the cricket bat stood over the hound, which was now bent down. Its eyes dilated, constricted and dilated again. The hound gave a low moan and lowered its head. The man raised the bat high.

"Stop it!" Chloe cried. A man from the crowd tried to pull her backwards off the cart, no doubt thinking he was helping her. She kicked at him and felt her foot connect with what she hoped was not his face. The motion threw her off balance and she grabbed onto the topmost slat hard to keep from tumbling head over heels into the cart. Her reticule swung crazily, and once she steadied herself, she pulled the cord over her head so the strap was diagonal and it was snug against her body.

"Finish it off!" cried a woman in the crowd.

"Kill the monster!"

"Inspector Lockton wanted it alive!" Chloe shouted in her loudest voice. She had no idea if it was true.

The man with the bat stopped at a command from another officer who had his hand up. The other constable looped a third rope over the hound's head and fastened it. The hound was lying on the floor of the cart and one of its ears hung at a wrong angle. Copper wires stretched from its head to the base of the ear which twitched now and then. The officer with the bat climbed out of the cart.

Chloe jumped down, hoping to follow them to the police station. It was the only place they could be taking the hound.

She caught a flash of blue from the corner of her eye.

"Just who I was looking for, Mrs. Sullivan," said Constable Bell. "I've been searching for you."

"It looks like you have found me. Now, I need to go to the police station immediately."

"That won't be a problem at all, as that is exactly where I am taking you."

The crowd had moved forward and the cart was pulling up in front of the police station.

"What do you mean? And where is Miss Haynes?"

"Miss Haynes went home on my orders. And I am placing you under arrest."

"What? What are you arresting me for? I have done nothing."

"Escaping for starters. Let me tell you something." He started to walk her toward the station. "Running makes you look awfully guilty. And I am under orders to arrest anyone from that house who tries to run, be it stable boy or the master himself." He was enjoying this far too much. But it got her closer to the hound, and that was not necessarily a bad thing.

"I wasn't running away from you. I had to take care of something. I want to talk to the inspector."

"The inspector isn't going to help you. And you'll be talking to the sergeant."

They waited to the side of the station doors as the officers pulled the hound from the cart, maneuvering him over the threshold. They pulled it down the hallway to the last room and Constable Bell followed with Chloe in tow.

"It's a lucky thing you are fond of that creature, as you'll be in the holding cell next door to it."

"You presume too much from too little information, Constable Bell. Aside from circumstantial evidence, there is nothing that proves me to be my husband's killer. I am innocent."

"I'll leave that to my superiors."

They entered the holding cell room to find the men trying to pull the hound into one of the cells. They were making little progress. The hound had regained its strength, or perhaps it had been faking injury, as it now struggled and thrashed. One man had a broom and was trying to push the creature through the door with it.

"Get the bat!" one of them called and another ran out the door.

"Wait!" Chloe ran forward. "I think I can help."

"You again! Get back. It's liable to kill you," said one constable. He looked at the place where part of her skirts had been ripped away. The ankle of her boot was exposed. He glanced away and then took another stab with the broom handle. "It tried to eat you."

"I think it may have been trying to pull me into the cart." She knew it was unlikely, but it was possible. Theoretically.

"What is going on in here?" said a man in the doorway.

"Sergeant," said Constable Bell. "I need to speak with you immediately."

"What we need to do immediately is to get this creature under control."

"But Sergeant, it's urgent."

"No, this is urgent."

Constable Bell scowled but said nothing.

"Please don't destroy it," said Chloe, touching the sergeant's arm. "I think I can turn it off. That will keep it intact. For scientific purposes."

The sergeant turned to her and studied her.

"You think you can control that thing?"

"I believe so."

The man with the cricket bat pushed past them and without hesitation, cracked the hound over the head. It groaned and staggered forward, its front legs collapsing under it, followed by its hind legs. Someone pushed it into the cell, where it tried to get up.

"Again!" shouted one of the constables. "Hit it!"

"No. Stop," the sergeant commanded.

He gave Chloe a sharp nod and she rushed forward. She dropped before the hound and rolled it onto its side. Its eye apertures were constricted and its ear hung by only a few wires. The remaining ear was at a wrong angle and twitched.

"Get back. We should hit it again. It could get up!" said one of the men.

"That's why I'm here," said Chloe, not taking her eyes from the hound as her hands slid over its chest and stomach. "It was beaten before, but then found renewed strength later. If I find the switch to cut its power, it won't be getting up again at all."

She didn't hear anything, but the sergeant must have given a gesture and the men stepped out of the cell. She was having no luck locating a switch on its chest or stomach, though she did find something odd. The cloth cover over the abdomen was a flat panel of fabric held closed by a fastening. That in itself was not so strange, but the fastening was a simple long dark bone button fitted through a narrow cloth loop. The threads at the edge of the cloth loop were loose, as if the button had been fastened and unfastened many times. She reached for it and the hound lifted its head and took a weak snap at her hand.

"Now none of that," she admonished. She undid the button and pulled open the cloth cover but found no switch, only a metal cover panel. She examined the seams of the hound's cloth covering for any indication of a switch. Could it be that Camille had created it without one?

She found a cover fastening where one leg joined the body and undid it. She found the other three and had part of the covering off the hound, leaving its belly and upper legs exposed.

"I'm going to need a tool kit," she said, an idea coming to her. "Even if I find a switch, I'm going to need to remove these panels and verify that the power rerouting couplings are intact, and then deactivate them. Also, the autonomous gear panel needs reworking. This thing has power reroutes that will allow it to heal itself, in a fashion. As you saw outside, it was beaten, but then it rerouted its power to allow it to fight once more."

It was all bluster with no meaning, but she counted on them not knowing it.

"Get her a tool kit," said a familiar voice. Inspector Lockton knelt on the other side of the hound.

"Just the man I was hoping to see," she said. "I have a little problem and I hope you can help me."

"If you mean your arrest, then no. I cannot help."

"But I am innocent. There's no evidence. This makes no sense."

He did not answer, but stood and stepped back.

She pulled most of the cloth covering off of the hound's body and moved around to be near its back so as to unfasten it and pull the cover off the head. She saw a puckering of fabric near the base of the neck, right where three seams met. She worked it with her finger. Once the cloth was pulled aside, she nodded in satisfaction.

"There's the switch," she said and flipped it. The hound stilled with a slow groan.

A constable set a toolbox near her and she dug around for the right size screwdriver and started working at the screws. She was certain that the hound would not rise again, but this was a good sight better than talking to someone from behind bars.

"Now, Inspector. What is this madness about an arrest?" she asked.

The sergeant ordered everyone out except Constable Bell and Inspector Lockton. He stepped forward but did not kneel down as Lockton had.

"It seems that there is a good amount of evidence against you, Mrs. Sullivan," said the sergeant. "There is simply too much for us not to hold you overnight, as we cannot risk you running. And of course, you will not be allowed to leave town tomorrow as planned, as the evidence against you is mounting."

"Mounting? What on earth do you mean?" she stopped working on the hound. She glanced over at the inspector, who looked pained but was trying to conceal it.

"Someone has come forward and told us about the loud rows you had with your husband. Also, about much of your unrestrained and, frankly, wild behavior. We understand that your husband wanted to keep two separate residences and that he was on the verge of contacting his solicitor to change the amount you would inherit upon his death. He would only be leaving you a modest sum."

"Those are filthy lies. Who said this?" But she was sure she already knew.

"I cannot say, but the person will testify under oath."

"Oh, I'm sure. You know this is wrong, don't you?" She turned to face Inspector Lockton. "You know it. Are they pressuring you for an arrest? Is that it?"

Lockton looked at a yellowed map of the moor pinned to the wall. She was sure that he was acting under orders from his superior, and it galled him.

"Why in the world would this mysterious individual be privy to this information when no one else is?" she said. "Why are you wasting time with invented domestic squabbles? Interview my maid, my husband's valet, anyone else in that house and this silliness will dissolve into the air."

"We have people on it now." The sergeant gave Inspector Lockton a look that sent him through the door, presumably to resume questioning the family. "In the meantime, we cannot risk you leaving town."

"Then send a guard home with me. I won't run."

"You already ran from one of our guards, so your word on that is, shall we say, questionable?" said the sergeant. "But for now, I need you to get that hound to a state where it cannot harm anyone again. I'll send someone in momentarily to keep watch."

She got back to work, removing the hound's chest cover panel. The sergeant left the room, and for an instant, she realized she was alone. The room had no windows, standard for a room that housed prisoners. And even if she escaped into the hall, the building would still be full of police officers. Besides, the hound was here, and she could see every single part of it. The prize was in her hands.

The interior of the hound was more complex and more beautiful than she had dared imagine. She understood most of the systems on sight, but some took further examination. She wished she had a notebook, or at the very least, a pad of paper in her reticule, but her heart was beating hard and she had the feeling that she would never forget what she saw. The design was elegant and complex, efficient with both space and energy while incorporating multiple complex modules and systems into interlocking larger systems.

The creature contained items that Chloe remembered from the schematics that Inspector Lockton had allowed her to see, but there was more. Oh, so much more. But for what purpose exactly was this extra processing unit? And why were there too many connection wires, and each marked with a different color ink, all leading from the hound's head?

She moved on to its abdomen and the panel that had been covered by the cloth with the dark bone button. She had not noticed it before in her search for a power switch, but this was very strange. The metal panel closure was too simple, just a hook pivoting on a screw into a small metal eye. There were scratches all around it, as if someone had fumbled with it over and over. She glanced at the hound's feet and then pried apart its toes experimentally. Once straightened, the toes were much longer and more nimble than they at first appeared. She turned back and opened the panel and removed the module behind the panel, setting it aside.

"There you are," she whispered, leaning down close to peer inside the hound.

The battery was marvelous, and now she really did

wish she had a notebook. The hound's battery fluid was low, which she could have guessed before opening it. The hound would never have succeeded in creating an alkaline solution for itself and then somehow getting it inside its body. At least she didn't think so.

The door opened and a thin young man came in. She recognized him from the front desk.

"Is everyone else gone?" she asked.

"Most of them went back on duty around town. After you finish getting that thing shut off, then you'll have to wait in the cell."

"I know."

"What's that there?" He pointed to the module that she had set aside in her excitement to see the battery.

"I'm not sure."

She opened it. Spools. There were two rows of brass spools. They all snapped into the larger module and she saw where the disconnected wires led from the spools into the main processing engine. And there was another part that led into what she had previously thought was an extraneous processing engine. She bent down close over the hound, not caring if her ample derriere stuck up in the air.

The extra wires, the eye apertures, the extra processing unit. She pulled open the hound's head and disassembled it with trembling hands.

"Oh God. This is—this is incredible."

"What is?"

She paused. "I'm going to prove that Dora Aynesworth is a murderer."

CHAPTER 43

"WELL, YOU'LL HAVE TO SPEAK with the sergeant about that in the morning."

"The morning?" Chloe pulled out her pocket watch. It was half past seven. How in the world had time flown so quickly? She must have been working on the hound for hours.

"I really must speak with the sergeant immediately, or at least Inspector Lockton. I can't wait for morning." By morning, Dora could be gone, or she could bring forward more accusations that would need to be disproven. The hounds were circling, but she would not let Dora win.

"Both the inspector and the sergeant will have gone home by now. It's just us and a few of the men on duty. Nothing to do until morning."

The young man sighed and leaned back in a chair next to the door. Her cell door was open, and Chloe studied the locking mechanism. She had enough sense to know that even if she had a hairpin somewhere in the bottom of her bag, she couldn't pick the lock.

But she had an idea. She worked fast, but with care, taking parts out of the hound and assembling them. She worked on her mechanism carefully, concealing the tiny thing behind the hound's body or under the edge of her skirt. The guard tipped his chair back against the wall and closed his eyes.

Half an hour later, Chloe put the last pieces of the

hound back together but left off the cloth cover. She had surreptitiously slipped all eight spools into her reticule, which now bulged. She hoped the guard would not notice.

In her palm was the small mechanism that was her only hope.

"Excuse me, but do you think I could get something to eat? I haven't had any supper at all."

The guard opened his eyes. "Oh, yes. I can get you something in a minute. I have to lock you in first though." He studied her with concern. Perhaps he was unused to dealing with upper class ladies or women of any sort. She did her best to look vulnerable and frightened, which in a way, she was. But the dark thing within her was calm and felt no such emotions.

"Can I take that thing out of there?" He came into the cell, looking at the hound as if it might still leap up at him.

"It won't turn back on. I made sure."

It had hurt her to cannibalize the hound's parts for her mechanism, but she was fairly sure she could reassemble it later. If there was a later.

The guard dragged the hound out of the cell while Chloe backed herself up against the receiving end of the cell door locking mechanism. She lost no time and stood with her hands behind her, working as fast as she dared. She blessed the extra pounds around her waist that helped conceal her hands.

"How long do you think I'll be in here?" she asked.

"No telling. But hopefully you'll be out in the morning." She could tell that he didn't believe it, but she needed to keep him talking.

"Do you really think so? Dora murdered my husband, and I need to talk to the inspector or the sergeant. Can't they be brought in?"

"No, mum. The sergeant specifically told me he would not be in until morning."

He stepped forward, keys in hand.

"Are your superiors pressing the police to make an arrest? Is that why you had to bring in Mr. Granger and me? So it looks like you are making progress on the murders?"

He appeared startled. "Now look here. This police force is a good one. They wouldn't accuse anyone without good reason."

"I'm sure," she said. "But all the same, I understand that there can be pressure exerted from the top. For example, I saw that Inspector Lockton wasn't happy with the development. He doesn't believe I am guilty."

"He seems to like you. I know he asked for your help with a piece of evidence they found. He maybe wishes you were innocent."

"I doubt he would be so unprofessional as to let his personal feelings get in the way of his duty."

"Maybe," he said. "Now, do you still want something to eat? I'll get one of the men out front to bring something."

He pulled the keys from his belt, but she still needed more time.

"Please," she said, changing tactic. "I'm too frightened to be locked up."

He paused, and she felt a moment of guilt as she saw pity in his face.

"I'm sorry, but I have to," he said.

A piece of the mechanism slipped under her fingers. She gave a little gasp, and barely managed to catch it. The young man misinterpreted the sound as fear.

"Don't worry, now. No one will harm you."

"I don't know," she said, letting her voice take on a tone of slight panic. "I—I have never been in a place like this, where common criminals have been kept."

The fumbled piece was in place, and she now needed to get one final pin through it to make it hold.

"Have you held murderers in this cell? Real killers? Like the Ripper?" She looked around the cell as if one such killer might be still there.

296

"No, no Ripper here. It's perfectly safe. Why don't you sit down now? It will be all right."

The last pin was in place. She lowered herself onto the bed and the cell door clanked closed. The guard left, and the dark part of her told her to stay calm so she did not make a mistake.

She slipped the reticule's strap across her body so it would be secure and got to work. The still voice inside her told her she had to twist the small mechanism slowly, very slowly, and at exactly the right angle so the pieces would not break off inside. Seconds ticked by, and she was almost sure she heard footsteps coming down the hall. Her focus did not waver.

The mechanism made a sharp snapping sound and she pulled the door. It did not move, but she was close. She worked at it again, this time hearing a satisfying clank. She eased the door open and slipped into the hall.

She did not stop to look, for even if someone had spied her, she would not have stopped. Lockton's office, said the dark part of her. The inspector was at the Aynesworth house and would not be there. She had just closed Lockton's office door behind her when she heard two voices in the hallway.

No time. She flung open the window and threw one leg out. She managed to get her split skirts through and was glad she was not wearing heavy petticoats or, heaven forbid, a bustle. She let herself out the rest of the way, and most of her body was hanging into the alleyway before her toes touched the ground.

A moment later, she was off running. She raced past stinking garbage bins and assorted alleyway detritus. She cut down a side alley, turned and ran until she reached the railway station.

Where was the blasted thing? The steamcycle was not where she had left it and she raced around the side of the station. Any moment now, police officers would be out looking for her, and she had to be out of town by then.

She saw pair of workers loading crates. "You there! Where is the steamcycle?"

They looked at her as if she were speaking in Swahili.

"The bicycle, with the motor. Like a motorcar?"

"Over there. We haven't crated it yet."

The steamcycle was to one side, behind a stack of boxes. She guided it out to an open space, silently apologizing to the engine, which she hoped had enough water inside to cool it. She lighted the burner and gave the flywheel a spin to set it in motion. The roar of the engine was beautiful.

She tore out of town, her hair flying behind her and her eyes squinting into the wind. She had left her goggles in the rear basket, but could put them on later. For now, she had one goal: the mine.

Once she got as close to the mine as the road allowed, she opened the basket, dumped all the spools from her reticule into her satchel and flung it over her shoulder. She then found the lantern, lit it and raced toward the entrance. Already, there would be officers en route to the Aynesworth house and the more there were, the harder it would be for her to accomplish her mission.

She had the feeling again of being watched, but did not pause. If the moor liked her so much, as Mad Maggie had said, then she could use some help about now. A crow cawed. It was perched at the top of the mine entrance.

The inside of the mine was muddy and wet. New hunks of earth were all over the ground. Parts of the roof had come loose, but Chloe did not pause. Once she was in the side tunnel, her boots were sucked ankle-deep into the mud. She slopped ahead.

The crate was in its place, though sunk a few inches into the mud. She held the lantern aloft. The spools were still there, and she gathered all four of them and shoved them into her satchel.

She now understood how the hound could see in the

darkness of the mine. Among other things, it had in its optical apertures a tiny light-emitting device that would probably be adequate to see in very dark places. She wondered why it had not used it at the stone circle. Then again, the light of the full moon might alone have been enough to illuminate the landscape.

But there had been something else in the hound's construction that had been far more critical. There were optical pathways that led to an image capturing and storage system. It was a sort of camera.

CHAPTER 44

SHE HAD TO ABANDON THE steamcycle far from the house lest the roar of the engine alert everyone to her arrival. She ran, not daring to use the main road for fear of being seen. It became cooler, as it had at the stone circle, and she felt the soft caress of the damp air on her skin.

Mad Maggie had said that things here on the moor did not change, while things in London did. And Chloe knew that with her modern machinery, she herself was a part of that change. But perhaps she had lost touch with something older and more primal. This place was wild and dangerous, and though some streets of London could be deadly as well, it was in a different way. There were strange places here, like the stone circle, the mines and bogs and there were large, empty places where a person could become lost. There were few places in London where one could be completely alone, and here, it wasn't any different. The moor was watching. She knew that now. But she didn't mind. She welcomed it.

She heard a snuffling sound, then a soft nicker. She froze and looked back along the road, expecting to see a constable on horseback, but no one was there. Up ahead, something moving was blocking the road. She crept closer, keeping to the dark and hidden places.

A herd of ponies was blocking the road. A sturdy little mare raised her head, her dark eyes meeting Chloe's. She tossed her gray mane and gave a soft whinny, baring her large, blocky teeth. Well, Mad Maggie had said that the moor liked her. She ran on.

No sooner had Chloe passed the ponies than she heard hoofbeats. Two constables on horseback were galloping toward the Aynesworth house, but they pulled up short at the ponies. As she ran, she heard them shouting at the animals to clear the road. Then she heard one of them yell something about bees. She didn't stay to listen.

She rounded the back of the house and slipped through the servants' entrance. After climbing the servants' staircase, she tore through the house toward her laboratory. The door was ajar. She entered and turned to lock the door, but there was no lock.

"Brrr?"

She lit the gaslight on her work table and found Ambrose's spool playback machine. She had just opened the case when the door opened. Chloe spun around to find Miss Haynes.

"I thought I heard something," Miss Haynes said. "Then I saw the light under the door."

One of the bookshelves that had held Ambrose's possessions had been emptied and covered with a dust cloth. Miss Haynes pulled off the cloth, threw it to the ground and kicked it to block the crack under the door. Chloe set up the spool playback machine on Ambrose's desk, facing it towards the wall beside the door. She emptied the spools from her satchel.

"We have to play these. One of them has what we want."

Chloe threaded the first spool in the machine and when she stepped back, Miss Haynes cranked the handle, making a ratcheting sound. The bulb glowed orange, burned gradually to white and then a grainy brown and white image appeared on the far wall. It was Camille, glowing with life, smiling and pointing to the flowers blooming in her greenhouse. She moved from plant to plant, turning toward the camera, pointing at each pot. Though there was no sound on the recording, Chloe knew she was describing each plant as one would for a child.

"This isn't it." She pulled the spool out, careful to avoid the hot bulb, and threaded a new one.

This one showed Camille in her laboratory, and Chloe recognized the hound's battery on the table in front of her. The hound must have had a second battery inside it while Camille recharged the original. Camille pointed to something inside the battery, and the image grew larger as the hound moved closer to see.

Chloe pulled that spool out also and was threading the next when the door crashed open.

"I told you I heard something," said Dora, standing in the doorway, a lamp in her hand. She strode in with a constable, Ian and Alexander. Where was the second constable Chloe had seen on the road?

"What is this?" said Ian, putting up a hand to shield his eyes from the light pointed at them.

"It's a projector. The spools are from the interior of the hound, and one of them shows Dora killing Camille Granger."

"This is madness," said Alexander, turning on a gaslight on a nearby table.

Chloe recognized the constable as the one who had used the cricket bat. He stepped forward.

"Mrs. Sullivan, I am placing you under arrest."

She backed away, and Miss Haynes, bless her soul, cranked the handle, saw that the next image was not what her mistress had described and threaded the next spool. Dora also saw the attempt and tore the next spool from the machine. She pulled the protruding film out in one long coil and took the glass cover from the top of her light. She then flung her lamp into the cold fireplace where it crashed into flames. The flames licked at a number of crumpled papers that Ambrose or Mr. Frick must have tossed in and the flames grew. Dora tossed the coil of film into the fire. It writhed and melted in on itself.

The officer grabbed Chloe's arm and she tried to yank free. "Ian!" she called. "You have to see what is on the spools. Don't let her destroy them!"

"Brrr?"

Miss Haynes had threaded the next spool and was cranking the handle when Dora shoved her aside and went to pull it out of the machine. Miss Haynes regained her balance and pushed down on Dora's hand, forcing her to press hard on the burning bulb. Dora howled a curse and after cradling her hand for a moment, struck Miss Haynes across the face, sending her staggering backward. She bumped the table and a spool fell to the floor and rolled away.

More people were in the room now, and the voices churned together into a cacophony of shouts.

"You have to let me play them!" Chloe pleaded with the constable, but his attention was on the other two women.

Miss Haynes went again for the spools, trying to gather the remaining ones into her arms to protect them, but Dora shoved her aside. The lady's maid lost her balance, caught her foot on the edge of the carpet and fell hard on her backside. The constable released Chloe for an instant, instinctively stepping toward Miss Haynes who, though resourceful and determined, still looked every inch the vulnerable female. Dora towered over Miss Haynes, and the constable insinuated himself between them.

Miss Haynes was getting up with the constable's help, so she must be all right, Chloe reasoned. Chloe ran back to the machine and grabbed the next spool.

Dora turned from the constable and tore the spool from Chloe's hand. Dora had the advantage of height, but Chloe had a good two stone on her and she threw her weight into Dora, pushing her down on the desk which quaked under their combined impact.

Chloe made a grab for the spool, but Dora elbowed her hard in the ribs. Dull pain spread through her side, but her whalebone corset took the brunt of the impact. Dora bucked and broke free. She made for the fireplace, ripping the film out of the spool as she went. Chloe tried to pull her back, but strong arms restrained her and Dora tossed the film into the flames.

The shouting was louder now, but Chloe did not heed the words being screamed back and forth. The dark thing within her was roaring. She had only one purpose.

Miss Haynes was back at the projector when Dora turned back. Chloe elbowed the person holding her and kicked with the heel of her boot. She heard a grunt and was free. Chloe caught a glimpse of blue serge, and knew where the second constable was.

"That's enough of that," growled Dora as she rushed forward and yanked Miss Haynes backward by the hair. The large constable pulled Dora away, dragging her backwards as Miss Haynes regained her composure and cranked the handle.

"Brrr?"

"Don't you touch my daughter!" shouted William at the constable as Dora cried out piteously.

Chloe let them argue. Dora was now screaming and Miss Haynes pulled the spool out of the projector as Chloe grabbed the next in line. A second scream joined Dora's, an unnatural sound, as high and unwavering as a train whistle.

Chloe knew what it was, but glanced up anyway. Giles must have been on top of the nearby bookshelf as he was now wrapped around Dora's head, yowling and clinging with all his might. Some of Dora's hair had fallen down over her shoulders in thin dark coils, but Chloe knew that even the generous amount left on top of her head would not protect her from the cat's claws. Ian was trying to pull the cat off, but Giles clawed and ripped again, tearing at her ears, face and neck. Chloe heard Robert yell her name.

Ian managed to pull the cat from his sister's head, but Giles thrashed so wildly that Ian was forced to release him. The cat pushed off of Ian and leapt onto the table, knocking over the lamp that Alexander had lit and sending it rolling off the desk. It hit the floor and shattered at the base of the window. A few agonizing seconds passed as smoke curled up from the carpet and then a flame blazed. The flame caught the curtains and climbed.

Robert stomped the carpet, and others were tearing the curtains down and stomping them. Chloe cranked the projector handle, but the mass of people running back and forth prevented her from seeing what was on the wall. Someone called for water, but the flames were already out.

Dora was beside Chloe in a moment, dragging the constable by the arm.

"Arrest her!" Dora's face was mottled and her hair was wild. Blood was beading up from the long thin cuts along her face and neck.

The constable hesitated.

"I know it was you," said Chloe. "And I know why you did it. Mr. Graves. The blackmail. And the pennyroyal tea."

She saw a flicker of something behind Dora's eyes. Then her face grew wild and her lips pulled back from her teeth. She gave a roar, guttural and terrible and launched herself at Chloe. Her momentum pushed both women against the wall. Chloe's world blurred and her ears roared as Dora struck her across the face again and again. Pain exploded from her nose, the side of her face and her mouth. Chloe got one hard strike at Dora and had just registered the metallic taste of blood when Dora was gone. The constable had her arms pulled behind her back. Aside from Dora's curses, the room had fallen silent, absolutely silent. Dora turned to look at something.

All Chloe heard was the blood pounding in her ears and the ratcheting sound of the projector. Miss Haynes was motionless with her eyes fixed on the far wall and the constable eventually turned as well.

Alexander was turning the handle. On the wall was the back of a dark-haired woman, kneeling over the prostrate form of a blonde woman who was motionless on the ground, a broken zoetrope on the ground nearby. The camera moved now and then, blurring and refocusing on the image, but there was no mistaking the dark-haired woman's arms as they rose and fell over and over, until they slowed and stopped. She heaved aside a rock that was light with dark smears. She rose and stood for a long time, looking at the dead woman at her feet.

CHAPTER 45

INSPECTOR LOCKTON LEANED BACK AGAINST the edge of Ambrose's desk and Chloe sat in her husband's chair, backed against the wall. Miss Haynes handed Chloe a cool rag, which she held to her split lip. The bleeding had mostly stopped, but there would be swelling and she was fairly sure a black eye was in her future. Her nose was bruised but unbroken, and had only bled a little.

"I'll say one thing for Dora, the woman can hit," Chloe mumbled through the rag.

"Three constables are escorting her to the station. She won't be able to harm you or anyone else again. Now, I need you to tell me everything." He had a notebook out, but no pencil. She doubted he would need one.

"Where do you want to start?" she asked.

"Why did Dora kill Camille Granger?"

"Blackmail. Camille was blackmailing her because Dora found herself with child thanks to Robert's tutor, Mr. Graves. Then, after Dora rid herself of the pregnancy, Camille decided to blackmail her. Dora killed her to end it."

"And how on earth did you learn this? What proof do you have?"

"During Camille's funeral, I took the liberty of exploring Camille's laboratory; looking for the hound's schematics. I stumbled across a little box filled with money—hidden money that she was saving up to escape her husband. I wondered where it had come from. How had she collected

HEATHER BLACKWOOD

so much money simply from selling a few items of jewelry?

"The hound is actually what provided the most important clue. It was hiding things in that little hole in the rocks near the bog. The hound seemed to like performing repetitive actions, and it copied its mistress. Camille would check the hiding place, where Dora would regularly leave money or various valuable items. So the hound did likewise, opening and closing the hole, leaving and removing coins and other detritus."

"So Dora was leaving items in the hiding hole as a blackmail payoff to Camille."

"Exactly. The hound was also trying to copy Camille's actions when she worked to recharge its battery. The cadmium and nickel battery required regular infusions of an alkaline solution. Because Camille was saving up her money to escape, she found a way to make her own solution using fen water and ashes. One night, I saw the hound scoop up ashes in its mouth, which only made sense after I remembered my visit to Camille's laboratory. I found a bottle of the fen water and ash solution in her laboratory and ph tested it. It had the same ph as potassium hydroxide which is used in the cadmium and nickel battery. She was making a homemade alkaline solution."

"As fascinating as I am sure that is, I need to know about the blackmail and the murder."

"Right, I'm getting there. Ambrose and I knew that the hound might be hiding, and we searched for it. A vital clue came when we saw the Hammond's shed. The hound had come looking for machine cleaning solvent. That's what led us to the mine, where they used the solvent to clean machinery. The solvent is also an alkaline, so Camille may have used it to try to make the solution for the battery.

"We found that the hound had another hiding place deep in the mine where it kept odds and ends in a crate. Included among the things it kept were data spools. See, when I took apart the hound earlier this evening, I discovered that it stored data on replaceable spools. Now, even an advanced mechanical like Giles only has a certain number of spools, and I would have to put them in and take them out. But Camille designed the hound so it could replace its own spools. The cloth cover on its abdomen had a simple bone button and the panel underneath had a simple hook closure. The hound could take its memory spools in and out itself. And it did.

"When I took it apart, I realized that the hound not only had a decision engine, but an extra processing engine connected to a series of wires from its head that seemed useless. It turns out that Camille gave it a way to generate a small amount of light, but more importantly, it had a camera. It was able to record images. That's why I had to escape from the cell. I needed to get all the spools, from the mine and from inside the hound, and play them. Camille had a playback machine in her laboratory, but Mr. Granger had probably destroyed it. Ambrose had a similar one, so I brought the spools here."

"We found the thing you built to keep the cell door from closing completely. Clever."

"Thank you. Now, after witnessing its mistress's murder, what did the hound do? It attacked a shop dummy dressed as a woman as well as a scarecrow wearing a skirt."

"You think it was imitating the murder?" asked Lockton.

"I'm not sure. The scarecrow had brown yarn for hair, but I'm not sure what the shop dummy looked like. Was it trying to avenge Camille or imitate Dora?"

"If I recall, the dummy had a black wig. I was called in to look at the shop window."

"Interesting ..." She paused, lost in thought before continuing. She supposed there was no way for her to ever know if the hound had acted in imitation or vengeance. "Ambrose and I also found the second part of the zoetrope in the mine, you recall. In the recording, Camille had the zoetrope near her hand. Dora must have brought it as a blackmail payment, and put it into the hiding hole. She waited until Camille took it, then bashed her over the head with a rock. The zoetrope breaks, and after Dora leaves, the hound took pieces to the hiding hole and its cave."

"So how do you figure that Dora was being blackmailed?"

"When we first arrived, Ambrose asked about the son of an old friend named Graves. The son was working here as Robert's tutor. We learned that he had left suddenly, supposedly because his mother had fallen ill. However, Ambrose wrote to the elder Graves and received a letter back. Guess who delivered the letter to us?"

"Dora?"

"Yes. Beatrice and Robert were there too, but Dora must have seen the return address. The letter revealed that the younger Graves was released because he and Dora had become too close. At least, the letter hinted at it. The tutor sounded heartbroken when he returned home, as if he and Dora had been very much in love. I spoke with Robert, and though he wouldn't confirm it, his manner suggested that Mr. Graves had, indeed, been released because of his relationship with Dora.

"Now, when we first arrived for our visit, Mr. Baxter, Dora's fiancé, came for supper. Baxter mentioned an illness that his men had suffered in the Klondike. Mrs. Malone said that Dora had suffered a similar illness last winter, which was right around the time Mr. Graves was ordered to leave. Ambrose was intrigued, as he usually is when an herb or plant is in some way unusual.

"Later on, Ambrose had mentioned over supper that he was meeting with Mr. Baxter to discuss a publishing and investment business that would mutually benefit them both. He also was still intrigued by the symptoms that the men had exhibited. See, they had the symptoms of pennyroyal, an herb used to rid a woman of pregnancy."

"But they were men."

"Yes. And I don't even know if they have pennyroyal

in the Americas. But the symptoms were similar enough for Mrs. Malone to mention it over supper. Dora must have started to see Ambrose putting together the puzzle. He knew that she had symptoms of pennyroyal use in December. And she suspected that he had learned from the letter that Graves had not left because of an ill mother.

"Then, when Ambrose said he was going to discuss things with Mr. Baxter, I think she panicked. When she saw the soup that Mrs. Block had always prepared for sick members of the household, she knew he would be eating it. She gathered some mushrooms, chopped them and added them. Thus she could rid herself of any risk to her upcoming marriage."

"Do you think Mr. Sullivan had figured out everything?"

Chloe shook her head. "I'm not sure. He said 'Graves' as he lay dying, but he also said other things. I don't think he put it all together, but he might have, given enough time. What I do know is that Dora must have thought he knew something. And I know that Josephine died for nothing."

The inspector nodded and paused for a moment out of respect. "How did you learn about the pennyroyal?"

"I saw that Mad Maggie had jars and jars of herbs in her kitchen. I know that many locals would come to her for remedies, especially people who couldn't afford a doctor. But I also knew that women have been coming to people like her for centuries to rid themselves of unwanted babes. So once I knew that Dora may have carried Graves's child, I asked Rebecca Hammond. She worked as an assistant to the three lady's maids in this house. She told me how she had to get tea, special medicinal tea, from Mad Maggie. She also mentioned that both Dora and her maid fell ill, and again, it was the symptoms of pennyroyal."

"Why would her maid become ill?"

"It is not unusual for a maid to finish up a pot of tea that her mistress left. If I understand herbal remedies properly, Dora would have had to drink as much of the pot as she could. If her maid did not know what kind of herb was in it, she may have decided to finish off the pot. So she had similar symptoms, but milder."

"And Miss Hammond told you this?" He pulled out a pencil and made a note.

"Yes, she also told me that Camille had come by to visit Dora that day. They were close, from what she said. Camille was brilliant, and if she knew that Dora and Mr. Graves were lovers, or even if she merely suspected it, she may have noticed the effects of the tea and deduced that Dora's goal was to lose the babe. Maybe she had even used such a concoction herself."

"Your opinion of Mrs. Granger seems to have fallen."

"She was a blackmailer as well as an adulterer."

"The letters from Alexander?"

"Yes."

"And you think Dora killed Camille so she wouldn't be blackmailed any longer?"

"I suspect that Camille asked for more money, threatening to reveal all to Mr. Baxter. Or perhaps Dora was simply tired of paying. You can question Dora yourself, but I would guess that something changed in the situation, something that drove Dora into desperate action. Camille pressing Dora for additional funds may well have been the catalyst."

"I will have our men look into it."

"I have a question. It seems that a number of the locals go to a stone circle to meet. They only eat bread and drink wine, but it seems so strange."

Inspector Lockton nodded. "I wondered about that as well, as soon as I learned about it. And there are other things that happen here too, things that outsiders like you and I naturally find strange. I have learned that the locals wink at those sorts of things. As long as everyone is at church on Sundays and no one causes any problems, no one seems to trouble themselves."

Giles leapt into her lap, and she stroked him. She thought about the herbs that Mad Maggie had given her for Ambrose. They couldn't have saved him even if he had taken them immediately. She would toss them out.

Mr. Lockton made a final note. "Are you are prepared to testify to all of this in a court of law?" he asked.

"Oh, yes."

Dora would hang or, if the authorities were reluctant to hang a woman, she would rot in a jail cell for the rest of her life. She would never wear her wedding dress or see La Tour Eiffel. Chloe doubted a jury would feel much pity for the woman after they heard of young Josephine's suffering, and her husband's lingering and painful death.

Her Ambrose. She saw him again at the riverside, touching the brim of his hat. Or across from her at the breakfast table, a book in one hand and his other gesturing as he debated some point with her, his eyes dancing in pleasure. She saw him laughing. Her vision blurred and she glanced up as Inspector Lockton offered her a handkerchief.

The dark thing within her was different now. It was cold, like black machine lubricant in winter, slow moving and nearly lifeless.

Her Ambrose was avenged. It would never be enough, not really. But the dark thing within her was satisfied.

CHAPTER 46

TEN WEEKS LATER, CHLOE RELAXED in front of her sitting room fire, her stocking-clad feet propped up in an unladylike fashion. Giles sat on the windowsill, watching the street traffic. A book was open in Chloe's lap, but she had not read a word. Night had fallen an hour before, but she had failed to turn on a light. She watched the flames move in their endless dance.

The house had been too empty when she had returned home. After the funeral, the staff had helped her sort through Ambrose's things, packing what she wanted to keep, sending off books and research notes to his colleagues and giving the rest to charity.

Mr. Frick had moved in with his spinster sister and they had purchased a pleasant townhouse. Chloe had made sure he had been given a handsome amount for retirement.

Miss Haynes opened the door. "I have a letter, mum. From Inspector Lockton."

"Do you? Please come in."

"My goodness, it's dark in here." Miss Haynes lit the lamp, sat and opened the letter. "Would you like me to read it?"

"Please."

"It says, Mrs. Sullivan. I hope this letter finds you well. All of the men in the office offer their condolences on the death of your husband and their apologies for your inconvenience at our station."

Chloe gave a laugh. "My inconvenience? I suppose I am fortunate they did not attempt to try me for avoiding arrest and escaping custody."

"They do owe you, mum."

Chloe did not take her eyes from the fire.

"Let's see," Miss Haynes continued. "He says that Dora's trial is impending, and her family has secured the services of a well-known barrister. There is sure to be a local media spectacle. He sends the date and the location of the trial in Exeter, as you are a key witness."

"So I am."

Miss Haynes continued reading. "Miss Aynesworth has told our officers that Mrs. Granger threatened to ruin her with lies. She admits to no pregnancy or relationship with Mr. Graves beyond a friendship. However, our questioning of the family and servants as well as the Graves family has given us reason to suspect that there may have indeed been a relationship."

Miss Haynes lowered the letter. "Do you think they will go after Mad Maggie for selling the tea? She could hang also."

"I don't know. I suppose they could. But something tells me that Mad Maggie wouldn't have lived this long if she didn't have a way to get out of such scrapes. Dora is not the first woman to come to her."

Miss Haynes paused, nodded and went on. "I know you are interested in the remains of the hound. On orders, we shipped it to a military facility in Liverpool, where mechanical specialists of Her Majesty's Royal Navy will examine it. I could not exact any promises that it would ever leave their possession in the future. I did however take the liberty of including a letter with the hound giving the address of one C. Sullivan who may be of assistance to them in understanding the thing's inner workings. They may write you."

"Kind of him," muttered Chloe.

"You've already made up drawings of the hound though. You don't need to see it again."

"I wouldn't mind seeing it again. But yes, I have enough information to build one, should I choose to."

"He also says that he wishes us well, hopes that Mr. Frick and I are both in good health, etcetera. He sent the address of his office in Exeter as well, should we wish to write him." She folded the paper and slipped it back into its envelope. "Are you all right, mum?"

"Hmm? Yes. I'm fine."

"Have you eaten? The babe needs nourishment."

Chloe sighed. She had not eaten, as she felt nauseated almost all the time. Her monthly courses were late, and she and Miss Haynes were now certain that she was with child. The thought made her unspeakably happy, though she was frightened also. Caring for a mechanical cat was one thing, a child was another.

"I'll take some toast and tea later," she said.

"You have not been in your laboratory much since we returned home."

"I don't have any projects currently."

"What about working on Giles? Or another type of mechanical?"

"I haven't had any ideas in a while." Since she had come home, she had felt too tired or sad to do much work.

"What about recreating the hound's moving image recorder? Don't you think that sort of thing might be useful somewhere?"

"Like where?"

"Oh, I don't know. For artists to study motion. Or to allow the police to record crimes. No, I suppose they'd have to know about a crime ahead of time for that. Oh, how about to record pictures of wild South American or African animals so naturalists here could study them without traveling?"

"For science?"

Chloe looked away from the fire and moved to the window. She stroked Giles. A street light cast a yellow glow over her street and a trap clattered past. Fog hung over the city, giving each street light a glowing halo. In the distance, behind the many buildings was the river, always moving, always constant.

"Or you could make something for the baby," said Miss Haynes. "Perhaps a toy."

That might be an interesting project. She knew it was not good for her to sit in the dark and mope. Ambrose's babe would never know his or her father, but the child would know her. She had to be the sort of mother that Ambrose's child deserved.

She could make a mechanical cat or dog, something like Giles, but without claws or teeth. Or perhaps she could make a set of birds that could sing in the nursery. They would sit on a tree, perhaps with a little squirrel that popped in and out of a hole. Ideas whirled through her mind, one after the other. The child would be born into a garden, not Ambrose's sort with real plants and animals, but one that she could create. It would be her gift to Ambrose and to their child.

"You know, Miss Haynes, that's not a bad thought." She turned and smiled. "Hand me a piece of paper. I have an idea."

THE END

AUTHOR'S NOTE

CPSIA information can be obtained at www.ICGtesting.com
Printed in the USA
LVOW07s1630170316

479616LV00001B/160/P